Patrick Gale

Little Bits of Baby

Flamingo
An Imprint of HarperCollins*Publishers*

Flamingo
An Imprint of HarperCollins*Publishers*
77–85 Fulham Palace Road,
Hammersmith, London w6 8jb

Flamingo ® is a registered trademark of
HarperCollins*Publishers* Limited

www.fireandwater.com

Published by Flamingo 1992
9 8 7 6 5 4

First published in Great Britain by
Chatto & Windus Ltd 1989

Copyright © Patrick Gale 1989

Patrick Gale asserts the moral right to be
identified as the author of this work

This novel is entirely a work of fiction.
The names, characters and incidents portrayed in it are
the work of the author's imagination. Any resemblance
to actual persons, living or dead, events or localities is
entirely coincidental.

Author photograph by Aidan Hicks

ISBN 0 586 09060 6

Typeset in Monotype Apollo by
Palimpsest Book Production Limited,
Polmont, Stirlingshire

Printed and bound in Great Britain by
Clays Ltd, St Ives plc

Dedicated, with love, to Jonathan and Celia

I would like to thank the Royal National Institute for the Blind for supplying me with so much helpful information. I trust they will not think it has been misused.

ACIS AND GALATEA:
   The flocks shall leave the mountains,
   The woods, the turtle dove,
   The nymphs forsake the fountains,
   Ere I forsake my love.

POLYPHEMUS:
   Anger! Fury! Rage! Despair!
   I cannot, cannot bear!

ACIS AND GALATEA:
   Not show'rs to larks so pleasing,
   Not sunshine to the bee,
   Not sleep to toil so easing,
   As these dear smiles to me.

POLYPHEMUS *(hurling boulder)*:
   Fly swift, thou massy ruin, fly!
   Die, presumptuous Acis, die!

Acis and Galatea
attrib: John Gay, Alexander Pope et al.

Prologue

As the brothers left the chapel, Luke lingered behind on the pretext of hanging some hassocks back on their hooks. Jonathan, the Abbot was listening to the end of the fugue someone was attempting on the organ. Luke considered that it would have been kinder of them all to have left so as to give the organist a chance to abandon the assault. All hassocks hung, he sat on the end of a pew where Jonathan would see him as he left. When the voluntary came to an abrupt close however, the Abbot rose and headed down the aisle towards the organ loft, presumably for a long, understanding chat. Luke ran short of patience, crossed his fingers and called after him,

'Jonathan?'

Jonathan turned on his heel, saw him and smiled.

'Luke. I didn't see you.'

'I was late in. I was down on the shore talking to the fishermen and I missed the bell. So I sat at the back.'

'Ah.' Jonathan waited, face attentive.

'Jonathan, I wondered.'

'Yes?'

'Whether I could try taking Robin outside. He's been here five years now and . . .'

'Is it so long already?'

'Yes. And I thought, if I could persuade him out to help me in the orchard, it might do him good.'

'Do you good, too.'

'I'm sorry?'

'You love him very much, don't you, Luke?'

'Well. We all do,' Luke said.

'Thank God someone does,' Jonathan continued, oblivious. 'The others all seem to have given up on him. Of course you can take him out. If he'll come. Has he been out before?'

'Never. Not since he arrived. He's so pale.'

'If he responds to anyone, it's only just that it should be you.'

'Thank you, Jonathan.'

'Not at all.'

The Abbot continued towards the organ loft. Luke hurried to his room, and pulled off his habit. His gardening clothes were on underneath. Like most of the regulations at Whelm, the dress rule was pragmatic. Habits were obligatory for all official and religious occasions but at all other times practically and comfort were the prime considerations. The heating system remained spartan so the warm traditional clothes were readily worn throughout the Winter, with an assortment of corduroy and jersey underneath.

Robin had lived in the same room for five years; a small white box. A fine view across the vegetable garden to the sea was some compensation for its cell-like proportions, but there might have been no window at all for all the pleasure Robin seemed to take in it. In the first year, when he was still having violent spells, he had smashed a picture and tried to cut his wrists with the glass, so they had taken the pictures away. Luke had stuck some Italian postcards around the mirror to relieve the gloom, but they had vanished so utterly without trace that Robin was assumed to have eaten them. More recently, Luke had sacrificed a favourite poster of *The Madonna of the Rocks*. This too was rejected, but Luke interpreted the care with which it was taken down, furled and left outside the door as a sign of improvement. Six months ago, Robin's mother had posted a small, white azalea. Luke had come in the next day to find Robin hunched over the plant, peering closely at its petals and softly humming, so he had followed hard on this breakthrough with a regularly restocked coffee jar of flowers, grasses and attractive leaves from the garden. He had also asked Robin's mother to send a sketch pad and watercolours but that had been expecting too much; after two or three nightmare daubs, the paintbox was left unopened.

Luke knocked and let himself in.

'Robin?' Robin was in his preferred position; on the floor below the window. 'Hello,' Luke continued. 'How did you sleep?' He sat cross-legged on the floor before him and touched the back of one of Robin's hands in greeting. Beneath his dark mop of hair, Robin's eyes stared, sightless at the floor. 'Look what I've brought you.' Slowly they travelled across his thigh, up his chest and focussed on Luke's own. Convinced that there was understanding in the gaze, Luke held out an apple on the palm of his hand. 'Look,' he said. 'Take it.' Painfully slow, Robin reached out and took the proffered fruit. It was grey-green with vivid pink stains. Luke had polished it carefully. There were still two leaves on the stalk. 'Smell it. It's fresh off the tree.' Slightly faster, Robin raised the apple to his nose and sniffed. Luke watched his chapped lips brush the skin. He smiled. 'Go on. Have a bite. It was still growing an hour ago.'

Robin kissed the glossy fruit for a few seconds more then twisted sharply up onto his knees and flung it through the window. As it arched out of sight in a small shower of broken glass, he let out a howl and crumpled over onto Luke's waiting shoulder.

'There, Robin. There. Quiet,' Luke said, rocking him gently and waiting for voices of concern on the path below.

1

'Jasper, *will* you be still!'

'It's OK, Ms Thackeray, we won't be ready for a while yet.'

'Jake?'

'Mmm?'

'Why's he calling Mummy "Thackeray" when we're called Browne?'

'Ssh.'

'It's my working name. Now Jasper do come and sit still. You'll make her cry.'

'She's called Perdita Margaux Browne.'

'I know.'

'Then don't call her "her". It's rude.'

'Jasper?'

'Yes?'

'*Sit.*'

Candida Thackeray had just come home to her house in Stockwell with her new baby, Perdita Browne, and was being photographed on a sofa with husband Jake and six-year-old Jasper. In fact she had come back, baby in arms, three days ago. For the sake of *Radio Times*, *Woman's Realm* and the *Daily Mail*, however, Candida had pulled back on her hospital-leaving coat and, when the time arrived, would dandle Perdita proudly on her knee with father and brother looking on, fresh welcome in their smiles. An empty overnight bag lay suggestively at their feet.

With a wilful glance at his mother, Jasper walked out of tableau briefly, to return with a painted wooden train. Having clambered back onto the sofa, he cradled this with an uncanny sense of his own appeal. Candida gave him a guarded smile.

'Good boy.'

With split-second timing, Jasper looked up into her eyes and beamed just as a photographer took an 'informal' shot.

'Great, Jasper,' shouted the photographer. 'And again.'

Jasper smiled again, the camera flashed two more times and Perdita awoke in bilious mood. Candida sighed and tidied her son's fine blond hair as Jake scooped up an armful of blankets and new daughter.

It was far too soon to tell if Perdita would be attractive. She was bald and, when roused, her small, creased face turned an alarming puce. Not prepossessing as yet, she at least had her complement of limbs and external organs and was all theirs.

'You're all ours,' Jake murmured to her. She bellowed in his ear and spat on his favourite shirt. He rubbed her back and told her to hush but she roared.

'Wants her milk bar,' said Candida.

'*I* want a Milky Bar,' said Jasper.

'They're bad for your teeth,' she told him, taking the baby.

'No. I mean I want a nipple. I want *your* nipple.'

'Ssh.'

'Nipple!'

Jake tickled his son deftly with one large hand, rendering him incomprehensible. A camera flashed as Jasper squirmed.

'I'll take her next door,' she murmured.

'Why not do it here?'

'Jake!'

'Well, you could. No one minds.'

'If your nipples looked like Bath buns . . .,' she began, rising.

'Nipple!' hooted Jasper. 'I'm coming too.'

'No. You stay here and amuse everyone. Won't be a second,' she added to the photographers over Perdita's yells.

Released from the sofa, Jasper jumped to the floor and began to chase his train, glancing up occasionally in the hope of catching a camera's eye. Jake followed his wife to the kitchen where she had quickly unbuttoned the top of her blouse and presented Perdita with a bloodshot nipple through a trap-door affair in her bra.

'I think it's too early for you to be going back to work,' he said.

'I've got to. I promised them I'd be back tomorrow so I shall be.'

'Well, call them. Trish can do it for a few more days, can't she?'

'No. Well. Hang on. Have you got a hanky?'

'Yes. Here.'

'Thanks.' Candida mopped Perdita's cheek with his handkerchief, then tucked it into her pocket. 'Yes, of course Trish could, but I can't stand getting up every morning seeing Jasper watching her do my job. It'll undermine his confidence in me.'

'Rubbish. He understands. I think he's far more excited about your production of a sister than watching you on the box.'

'Anyone can produce a baby.'

'I can't.'

'You lent your part.'

Jake leaned on the sink beside her stool, kissed his wife's ear and watched their greedy child with an element of envy.

'I did my best,' he said. 'She is rather fine.'

As Candida changed nipples, Perdita peered up, pig-eyed and breathless with gluttony.

'She's outstanding.'

Perdita belched then returned to her meal. Jake stroked his wife's cheek and grunted assent.

'We should get back soon,' he added.

'Samantha'll be back any minute. She can make them all coffee or tea or something. Jake, I've been thinking.'

'What?'

'I'd er . . . I'd like to have Perdy christened.'

'But you haven't been to church since I met you.'

'Yes, I have. Sometimes.'

'When?' He laughed, incredulous.

'Sometimes. Not with you.'

'But why christen her? You don't think it makes any difference?'

'Well . . . I . . .'

'And it'll make Jasper terribly jealous. We'd have to get him done too, which means finding twice the godparents. Unless they'd double up. Do you think they would?'

'No need. He doesn't want to be done. I asked him about it and he said "God's all crap, Mummy".'

'I knew that play-school was the right choice.'

'And I asked him if he'd mind my getting Perdy done and he said no just as long as a) Samantha was kept on to look after him as well as Perdy, b) that he could be allowed to stay up until eight occasionally and c) that I buy him a Cacharel jersey like Flora Cairns's.'

'Solves the birthday present problem. When is his birthday?'

Candida passed him Perdita while she buttoned her Bath buns away.

'Next month. I . . .' She broke off shyly.

'What?'

'I've already bought it.'

'Well. That's all settled then.'

'You're not cross?'

'Let's go in and get these pictures over with. I must be in by ten-thirty.'

'Jake?'

''Course I'm not cross.' He gave her a squeeze as he opened the kitchen door. 'I'd love a good Christian daughter.'

8

'Mummy!' Jasper ran from a conversation with a heavily stubbled photography assistant to hurl himself at Candida's thighs and walk backwards with his chin resting on her pelvis.

'Hello, Jasper,' she said and the four of them returned to the sofa. 'Sorry about that,' she called to the photographers. 'At least she'll be affable now. We're all yours.'

For a few minutes, Jake and his wife said nothing to each other as they were photographed, re-arranged, photographed, asked to brighten smiles, photographed, made to swop children and photographed again. Then, in a lull as she recovered her face from the onslaught of lights, he quietly asked,

'Have you got any candidates for her godparents?'

'As a matter of fact I have.'

'What for?' asked Jasper.

'Who?' asked Jake.

'And look out again if you wouldn't mind,' asked *Woman's Realm*.

'Your sis. I thought that would be nice. And then Dob,' said Candida, smiling outwards.

'Robin Maitland?'

'Who else? I think he'd be perfect.'

'He's got God I suppose but, Christ . . .' Jake looked away and ran a hand through his hair. 'Wouldn't that be a mite insensitive?'

'Who's Dob?' asked Jasper.

'An old friend of Jake's,' Candida told him.

'This way, please, Jasper. Once more.'

Jasper smiled perfunctorily for the *Daily Mail* then turned back.

'No, but who is he *really*?'

'Here's Samantha. Are you going to help her make coffee for everyone?'

'Oh. All right.'

Jasper slid off the sofa and made a passable show of joy at seeing his young nanny again, which quickly turned to genuine pleasure as she slung him onto her shoulders and piggy-backed him briskly to the kitchen, her arms stretched with shopping.

'And just a few of Ms Thackeray and Perdita alone now, please.'

Jake stood aside and stared nervously at Candida who beamed complacently as she held her daughter's nose close to her own.

Perdita was turning boss-eyed with exhaustion and began to whimper at the approaching lights.

'See you eight-thirtyish?' Candida asked from the corner of her mouth.

'Yup,' said Jake. 'Say goodbye to Jasper for me,' and he took up his briefcase, shook his car keys and left.

2

Robin was up an apple-tree. Through the crackling canopy of leaves he could see most of the tiny island's coastline and, in the distance, the thin anaemic scar of England. There was nothing else on Whelm besides the monastery and a cottage on the South shore where fishermen from the mainland sometimes slept.

A word or two about this place that absorbed eight of his precious years. The last Lord Whelm, a virgin mystic, had founded the order in the late 1800s and bequeathed it his island and house in perpetuity. Fundamentally Protestant in outlook, though still unrecognized by the established churches on the mainland, Whelm's peculiar marriage of discipline and informality was reflected in its relationship with a sister order on the nearby island of Corry. Ever since a childhood sweetheart and lifetime apostle of Lord Whelm's had risen to be Abbess there, the two orders had celebrated the harvest festival with a picnic. One year the nuns would cross to Whelm, the next, they would play host to the monks. Despite rich conjecture from the fishermen, free to pass from island to island all year, nothing untoward ever occurred. The ritual welcoming of one sex by another and the joint service which followed in a chapel filled with the sheen and rustle of the year's produce certainly bore more than a hint of fertility rite about them, but any such effect was undercut by the frank, housekeeperly exchange of the honey, mead and candles of Corry for the fruit, flour, and cider of Whelm.

Whelm possessed no television or radio set. There was one telephone, which rarely rung and was used even less, locked out of temptation's way in a box in the Abbot's study. There was a music room with an eclectic record collection and, while there was no control of reading matter beyond a proscribed passage of Scripture or divine writing for each day, most found that the library fulfilled their needs. Post, supplies, visitors and the Abbot's weekly newspaper were delivered by fishermen. Monks had two visiting days a year, novices four and Robin, as many as he cared for, (and he had cared for none). The air of pastoral isolation was furthered by the island's lying away from any major flight path or shipping route. Robin's emergence from a state of collapse to something approaching control, if not exactly mental health, was the passing from a nightmare without hours to a peace kept in motion only by the gentle nudging of a daily schedule of reading and tasks.

Luke, a novice and the nearest one could have to a friend in a place where every man was friendly, was working at the foot of the tree. They had a routine. Robin would pass him a small basket of apples in exchange for an empty one. As Robin filled the second, Luke would sort the first. The perfect apples he wrapped in squares of tissue paper and laid in smoke-blue moulded trays. The damaged ones he set in a larger basket for immediate pickling or bottling or, if they showed too many signs of life, for pressing into the brown juice that would make cider.

Robin liked being up the tree. The fragrant crumble of the bark against his hands and bare feet released draughts of childhood. He used to spend hours with a best friend up a beech tree in Clapham, wolfing handfuls of pilfered dried fruit and rehearsing the downfall of adults they secretly loved. He liked the weight of the new apples in his hand and the smell of seashore on the autumn wind when it came to rattle the leaves. He also liked Luke's company. Luke had the gift of knowing when to talk and when to listen. He listened a lot since he was an adept at leading questions; conversational pinpricks that released pent-up poison for his sympathy to wash away.

'I suppose,' Robin told him, arching up to a pair of apples that bobbed behind his head, 'I suppose that you're my nurse, really.'

'I'm your friend,' Luke corrected him.

'Well, yes. If you say so. But you're my nurse first and then you're my friend.'

'Hardly. I don't know the first thing about nursing. I trained as a structural engineer.'

'Apples for you.'

'Thanks. We can move trees in a second and I'll give you a turn on the ground.'

'No. I like it up here.'

'So do I. I had a childhood too.'

'All right. Damn!'

Robin dropped an apple.

'It's OK.'

Luke caught it and Robin carried on.

'But you do tell Jonathan everything I tell you, don't you?'

'I did to start with, to let him know how you were opening up, but not any more. Not for about five months.'

'Why not?'

'It's not his business any more.'

'Who said so?'

'He did.'

'So you were prepared to carry on reporting back?'

'Not really. I'd already started leaving things out; things I thought you were telling me as friend rather than nurse.'

'But he guessed and let you off the hook.'

'Yes. For a kind man, he's a perceptive one.'

'Mmm.'

There was a pause then Luke noticed that Robin had stopped picking.

'What's wrong?' he asked.

'Nothing.'

'You're not picking anything.'

'Nothing left to pick.'

'Then come down and we can change trees.'

'But it's nice up here. I can see Dorset.'

'That's uninspired. Why not a small cloud in the shape of a man's hand?'

'Very funny. Mind your head then, Elijah.'

'Do you want a hand?'

'No. Get out of the way or I'll kick you.'

Luke stood back and Robin half leaped, half tumbled from the tree. Robin had his hair tied back with a knotted handkerchief into a kind of pony-tail. As he swept the handkerchief off to wipe the sweat from his face and neck, he caught Luke watching him and his body in a slightly pathetic way he had. After Robin's summer in the garden Luke seemed slight and pale beside him. So Robin took the larger basket from him and they walked to the foot of the next tree.

'Well, up you go,' Luke said.

'No. It's your turn,' Robin told him.

'No. Go on.'

'No. You had a childhood too.'

He hesitated, grinning.

'You sure?' Luke checked.

'Go on.'

He swung himself onto the lower branch and half disappeared from view.

'I can see Dorset!' he shouted.

'Ssh.'

'What's the matter? We're allowed to talk.'

'But if you shout, old Snapdragon'll come out and put you on silence which would be very dull.'

Robin watched the wind send a handful of tissue paper

wheeling over the grass then thought to put a pebble in the box to stop any more from escaping. That was happening a lot then – a sort of delay between his eye and hand.

'Here.'

Luke handed him the first apples in exchange for the second basket.

'Thanks.' Robin started to wrap them. 'Luke?'

'Yes?'

'Why are you here?'

'Why do you want to know?'

'No. Tell me.'

'The nurse would tell you it's none of your business.'

'How about the friend?'

'He'd say erm and change the subject.'

'I mean, is it a God thing or a human thing?'

'I don't see how you can separate the two.'

'Don't give me that crap,' Robin pursued and felt himself scowl.

'Apples for you.'

'Thanks.'

'Well?' Luke held out his outstretched palm. 'Give me the other basket, then.'

'Not until you tell me.'

'Oh, *Robin*!'

'Go on.'

'My reasons are no different from anyone else's here, except Jonathan's perhaps. It's a human thing – running away from something till you find the strength to cope with it – and the God thing helps. Some of the time. Most of the time.'

'You don't mean God; you mean the peace helps, and the sea and the old house and having apples to pick and unworldly women to picnic with one day a year.'

'That is God, a part of Him, anyway.'

'That's a lie,' said Robin, quietly emphatic.

'Can we talk about this another time?'

'No.'

'Please, Robin?'

'Why?'

'Because I need to think,' he begged, 'and it's hard to think while dangling between earth and heaven like this.'

'But if it's the truth – if you *know* why you're here – it should be easy to say. The truth is what comes into your head first. We're born with truth; we learn how to lie.'

'*How to Succeed in Contemplative Society*. Rule One: Hold your tongue.'

'Coward. You always joke when you're afraid I'm winning.'

'Basket, please.'

Robin passed Luke the empty basket. He knew he was frowning from the way that Luke smiled at him from a faceful of leaves.

'I'll tell you another time,' Luke said. 'I promise. Better still, I'll show you.'

'I'll keep you to that.'

Robin sat and tossed three maggoty apples into the cider basket.

'Snapdragon's coming our way,' warned Luke. 'He's fairly trotting.'

'Damn. He's probably come to drag you off to Bible class.'

'That's not till this afternoon.'

Snapdragon, proper name Basil, was one of the middle-aged monks, his habit an ungainly contrast to the younger men's lither work-clothes, his complexion a testament to chair-bound decades. He puffed over the stile into the orchard and trundled towards them. His round, schoolboy's face shone with unwonted excitement.

'Here you both are,' he said. 'Luke, I'm afraid you'll have to manage on your own; there's someone on the telephone for Robin. They're calling from London.'

That was the first time Robin had truly run since he came there. Unless, that is, he ran in his madness. He could never be sure; Luke tried to spare him so much. Reaching the stile, he found an apple in his hand and hurled it into Luke's tree. Then he sprinted across the upper lawn to the terrace outside Jonathan's study. The Abbot had his back to the open windows and was talking into the telephone. Robin tapped on the glass and made him turn.

'Ah. Here he is. I'll hand you over,' Jonathan said as Robin climbed over the sill and crossed the room, rubbing his hands clean on his trousers. 'I'll be next door, Robin. Come and talk when you've finished.' He handed over the receiver and left the room.

Robin sat and stared down at it for a moment then lifted it to his ear and listened. There was quiet breathing then a woman's voice startled him by calling out,

'Hello?'

'Hello?'

'Dob, darling. It's your mother.'

'Hello! How are you?'

'Fine, darling. Fine. How are you?'

'Couldn't be better. Well, actually I could but . . .'

'Jonathan said he thought all was well. Did you get all my letters?'

'Yes. Did you expect me to answer them? I think perhaps I should have, but not a lot happens here.'

'Of course I didn't. I mean . . . Robin, I'm sorry to take you by surprise now, instead of writing.'

'No. It's great to hear your voice. It's only that . . .' He wondered coolly if he were going to crack up but found himself laughing. 'It's only that I haven't held a telephone in eight years and I'd rather forgotten what it's like and the one here's an ancient Bakelite thing. Weighs a ton.'

'Oh, darling. Well, the reason I'm calling . . .'

'Sorry. Yes. I'll shut up. This must be costing the earth. You should have waited till the evening.'

'Yes. No. The fact is I couldn't wait. Dob, it's rather extra-ordinary but I've just . . . I've just had Candida Thackeray on the phone.'

He waited for her to go on, then sensed she was waiting for him to make an exclamation of surprise.

'I thought she was Browne, now,' he said.

'Well, she is, but she's still calling herself Thackeray for work and things.'

'How was she?'

'She's fine,' said his mother, then snapped, 'Oh Robin, don't ask stupid questions!'

'Sorry.'

Her voice relaxed.

'She's just had a second child. I told you about the first one, didn't I, the little boy?'

'You must have done.'

'Yes, well, now it's a little girl, I mean, now there's a little girl, and Candida would like you to be its godfather. *They'd* like you to be . . .' Her voice trailed off. Again he waited. 'Robin? Are you there?'

'But she's not a Christian.'

'I don't think that's the point.'

'Oh.'

'I think she, rather I suppose *they* are trying to make their peace with you. It must have been an awful effort for them and, well, to be honest, I think it's only right that you should do it.'

'Do what?'

'Be godfather. You wouldn't have to come back for good, just for the service, but of course we'd love to have you home for as long as you'd like to stay. There's still your room and . . . Oh, Robin.'

Softly, his mother began to weep. He set the receiver down on the desk-top so that her grief was just a sort of insect-whisper, watched it a while, then held it back to his ear.

'Mum?'

'Yes?' She sniffed.

'Don't cry.'

'I can't bloody help it,' she snapped.

'I'll be home soon.'

'Oh, Dob. Oh. Oh. I'm *so* glad! Can I tell her "yes"?'

'What's the baby's name?'

'Perdita. Perdita Margaux Browne. I'm not sure if it's hyphenated.'

He clutched the receiver to his chest and laughed. He continued to laugh, throwing his head back and banging the receiver on the arm of the chair in an effort to stop. His mother called to him nervously from the earpiece and Jonathan knocked at the door and asked nervously if he wanted him to come in.

'No, no,' he called to them both. 'It's quite all right.' His laughter eased down into chuckles. He lifted the receiver again. 'Yes,' he said. 'Ring her up and tell her Brother Robin says yes.' Then he hung up.

3

Andrea Maitland sat at her study window, cradling the telephone in gentle hands, carelessly weeping. The long garden below her was filled with infants at play. She and her husband ran a kindergarten from their basement, so apart from two cherry trees and a towering beech, their garden grew nothing but swings and slides, a see-saw, a roundabout and a sandpit. Peter was out there now keeping a watchful eye on the speed of the swinging while the Señoritas Fernandez cleared the tables for lunch.

'For Christ's sake,' Andrea muttered, and exchanged the telephone for a clutch of tissues which she used to dry her cheeks and blow her nose. She had visited Whelm only once since her son's apparent decision to become a monk there. She caught the train and a boat on Whelm's annual Visitor's Day along with a crowd of tourists and other, happier relatives, but Robin had apparently not read her letters and, unaware of her visit, had gone off on a day's sailing trip. Discouraged from visiting after that, she had sent the occasional parcel when requested and had telephoned the Abbot once every five weeks. She kept her telephoning days marked in her diary and always rang at the same time. He first broke the news that her son was, as he quaintly put it, 'in Whelm's care', by letter.

'By all means telephone me,' he had written. 'I cannot guarantee that you will always be able to speak to Robin, indeed I would not advise it, but I am always at your disposal between noon and one.'

He would never tell her more than that Robin was 'well' or 'progressing', although he occasionally filled in comforting details such as that Robin was working in the garden today or that Robin had recently taken a long walk beside the sea. Brushing aside her enquiries concerning Whelm with the suggestion that she visit its female twin, Corry, and find out at first hand, he encouraged her to talk about herself. The conjunction of her worries and Jonathan's stern sympathy had therefore turned these calls into an occasion for counselling. Andrea had long disapproved of psychotherapy as timewasting and economically suspect. Several people she knew had been off and on costly couches since their mid-thirties and seen less return for their investment than a less expensive lover or some voluntary work might have afforded. Her talks with Jonathan were different. She was sure of this. They had never met – on her one visit to Whelm she had been led from the boat to Robin's empty little room by a prattling novice – and this lent their conversations the easy anonymity of the confessional. Unlike a priest, he offered no penitential solutions, but by voicing her worries she felt that she had passed them on and could leave her desk a lighter woman.

She reached for the telephone again, dialled and waited, staring at the scene below where the Señoritas Fernandez and Peter were now corralling the infants for lunch. The week's menu dangled from the board to her left.

Friday, she read, Hazelnut Cheddar Bake, Watercress Sauce, Chick-pea Salad, followed by Apple Crumble and Custard. She and Peter were vegetarians and so was their school. Principles aside, this was both vaguely chic and an economy respected by parents.

'Hello?' called a child's voice firmly.

'Is that Iras?'

'Yes. Who's that?'

'Andrea. How're you?'

'Fine. Except my cheek feels like a cushion. I've just been to the dentist. Still, I got the day off school, even if he did give me three fillings.'

'Oh dear. Is your pa in?'

'The dentist said I've got to go to a hygienist to learn how to brush properly,' Iras pursued. 'Yes, he is.'

'Could I speak to him?'

'Well, actually he's painting.'

'No I'm not,' said Faber, picking up another receiver.

'You were a minute ago.'

'Get off the line, Iras.'

'It's your friend, Andrea,' said Iras, getting off.

'Andrea. Hi.'

'Hello. You're sure you weren't painting?'

'I was, but I'm stopping for lunch. What's up? You don't sound right.'

'I've just been speaking to Robin.'

'How lovely. Was it lovely?'

'He's coming home.'

'Oh God. When?'

'Soon.'

'Come and talk this afternoon.'

'Can't. I've promised to take over from Peter downstairs and then he's dragging me to some nasty French film. Can I come tomorrow morning?'

'Of course. You can help me feed ducks. Come for a bite of lunch.'

'See you.'

'Bye.'

Faber was one of Andrea's young friends. Through their daily contact with young parents and through their stout refusal to grow up (e.g. change politics, accumulate wealth and stop sitting on the floor at parties), Peter and Andrea had lost touch with most of their generation and had a revised address book full of friends young enough to be their children. Faber lived with his adopted daughter on the other side of the common. He was a painter. His work was very challenging, certainly, but Andrea sometimes wondered how he and Iras survived quite so well.

Andrea left her study and followed nutritious smells to the basement. The children − there were twenty − were seated on dwarf chairs around five dwarf tables, wolfing their hazelnut cheddar bake while the Señoritas Fernandez, two satisfactorily bosomy creatures who came daily on a motorbike from Dulwich, clucked amongst them mopping up spillage, ruffling hair and topping up beakers of unfiltered apple juice. Peter, a lock of white hair tumbling over one eye, was crouching beside one table to correct a girl's murderous hold on her knife. He glanced up at Andrea, turned to his left to stop a boy from flicking his chickpeas, then came to her side.

'Have some,' he said. 'It's good.'

'I will in a sec,' said Andrea. '*Holá*,' she returned to Pilar Fernandez. 'Peter, I've just spoken with Robin.'

'Lord. How was he?'

'He's coming back to do their christening.'

'When?'

'He didn't say. Soon.'

'Oh, Andrea.' He squeezed her hand, caught her eye, then laughed. At that she laughed too, and he hugged her. 'That's marvellous,' he said and kissed her briefly.

'Ooh!' chorused several children.

'*Qué pasa?*' asked another, in perfect imitation of a Fernandez.

'Never you mind,' said Peter.

'Our son's coming home,' Andrea explained, accepting a plateful of food and perching on a stool between two tables. Trusting herself not to cry again, she carried on. 'He's been away for eight whole years.'

'Where's he been?' asked Jasper Browne, who told his parents everything.

'He's been living on an island.'

'Which island?' asked a little girl.

'Whelm. It's in the English Channel.'

'That's where all the holy people live,' Jasper told his neighbours. 'Her son's a holy person but he used to be friends with my father.'

'Eat up, Jasper, then we can all have some apple crumble.'

'Your wife hasn't finished hers yet,' Jasper observed.

'Oh, don't wait for me,' said Andrea quickly. 'I couldn't manage crumble too.'

'Well, it is rather fattening,' Jasper said, in his mother's voice.

'You finished yet, Cherub?' asked Paca Fernandez, swooping on Jasper's plate.

'No!' he fairly yelled and fell to eating again.

Andrea reminded herself who his parents were and smiled. Peter came back to her elbow. 'You off?' she asked.

'In a moment. I promised them another instalment of that story about the girl who makes friends with a dragon.'

'Right.'

'And Pilar's very kindly cleaned and chopped up some potatoes for printing with, if you've got the energy.'

'Great. Are you going to the gym?'

'Yes. But I'm looking in at the hospital first.'

'How is he?' Peter pulled a resigned face. 'Oh dear. How long has he got?'

'A month,' he suggested. 'Three weeks? Hard to tell. He might go overnight, but then they were saying that in the Summer.'

She touched his hand.

'Give him my love.'

'I will.' He paused and grinned. 'So Robin's coming home? How soon? Did he say?' he asked again.

'Soon. Just soon.'

Peter started to go.

'Bye, everyone.'

'Bye, Peter!' they shouted back, showering crumble.

'I'll see you at the cinema, then,' he muttered.

'Which?'

'That one behind the Greek restaurant you took me to in Soho.'

'Oh, darling, do we have to?'

'Good for us. Seven o'clock.'

She watched him go and thought of him and Robin building the treehouse when Robin was a boy. Then she remembered herself, shovelled in the last mouthful of chick-peas because they would do her good, and started a brave chat with the table to her right about what holy persons did.

4

Peter had started hospital visiting when one of his former colleagues fell gravely ill and died after two months in hospital. He only heard of the colleague's predicament towards the end of his illness, and was shocked on visiting him to realize that office chumminess had never revealed the sad fact that the man passed his private life in constant solitude. The bed had been surrounded by flowers and cards from workmates too busy to visit more than once, if at all, but none from family. He checked with the nurses and found that his only regular visitor had been a volunteer provided by the hospital. Shocked as much as inspired, he had enrolled as a volunteer too. So far Marcus was the only patient assigned to his care.

Peter stopped at the flower stall on his way into the hospital to choose a flower. The powerful drugs were affecting Marcus's sight and he found it easier to focus on a single bloom than try to distinguish the shapes and colours in a bunch. Peter was Marcus's only visitor. The nurses had confided that a man rang every few days to ask how he was but never left his name or came in person.

'I'm dying in splendid isolation,' Marcus had briefed him on their first meeting. 'But the whole farrago would be wasted without a Boswell to bear it witness and since you arrive knowing nothing about me but my Christian name, bed number and vanquishing condition, you'll make a rather fine one. For my part I know nothing of you but your Christian name and inexplicable charitable impulse so you must feel free to weave me all manner of lies about yourself.'

'Why ever should I want to do that?' Peter had asked.

'To divert my thoughts from pain and death? I assume that's why they've sent you. Are you married?'

'No,' said Peter. 'Yes.'

'Such a pity you forgot to take off the ring. That might have been a most rewarding falsehood.' Marcus had paused to look down mischievously at his own ringless hands. 'Or perhaps you slipped that on, just before coming here and this is a discerning double bluff and you a master deviant.' He looked Peter straight in the eye. 'Are you devious by nature?' Peter said he wasn't and smiled. 'Are you afraid of blood, tears or vomit?'

'We run a kindergarten.'

'You and . . . ? No. Don't tell me. Not yet. So. A kindergarten. Then we'll get along like a house on fire. Curious phrase that is. Washington Irving used it first, of course, not that that explains anything. Just gives you a door to lay the blame at. Get along like a house on fire. It seems to imply that the brightest new relationship will be swift, dangerous and end in the destruction of all material security.'

'It suits ours rather well, then.'

Their house had burned, but not so very swiftly. The volunteer co-ordinator had warned Peter that it might all be over in two months, but Marcus had carried on and on. He would grow worse, acquire rattles in his chest and an array of monitors at his bedside, lead his few spectators to the gates of Beyond, linger there teasingly to bid farewell, then come gliding back to Act One, Scene the First. On his more cynical days, Peter wondered whether it were not his visits that kept Marcus alive, so closely did his new friend's resurrections resemble the generous round of farewell appearances of an adored performer.

Peter stepped out of the lift into the carefully conditioned air of the ward. Months after his first visit, he still felt the clutch of death dread brought on by the smell of the place. No amount of lazar-house groaning could match that silent threnody of bedpan, antiseptic, hot-house bloom and sweated fear. During the last of Marcus's recitals at the doors of Beyond, Peter had sat up drinking machine-brewed cocoa with the night nurse and had asked her how she coped. She had sighed, rubbed an aching foot and said that she didn't, really, but that it helped keep her weight down.

The duty nurse was away from the reception desk so he presumed on familiarity and went directly to Marcus's room. He paused in the doorway. Marcus had plugged headphones into his new toy, a portable compact disc player, and so had not heard his approach. He lay staring away from the door to swaying treetops and a smoking chimney stack. Sweat shone in the exhausted folds of his cheeks and neck. The lavish score brought to life by the machine, seeped out from the edges of the headphones as a pattern of tinny whispers and clicks. The nurses were forever shutting windows with brisk explanations about airconditioning balance, but Marcus had Peter well trained. He moved straight from shutting the door to sliding back two panes of the double-glazing. The breeze he let in filled out a hated net curtain that was stuffed firmly to one side and gently swung a few Get Well cards that dangled from a washing-line affair at the bed's end.

'You're late, darling,' Marcus said, too loud for he was competing with his private orchestra.

'You're soaked,' said Peter. He ran the cold tap over a flannel for a few seconds, then wrang the cloth out and gently wiped it over Marcus's face, across his neck and up behind his ears. His fingers trailed across a thick scab.

'Bliss,' said Marcus and shut his eyes. Peter rinsed out the flannel once more and arranged it, folded, across Marcus's burning forehead. Then he pressed the stop button on Marcus's new toy (which he had been sent out to buy with a bursting wallet last week). 'Oy!' said Marcus.

'Talk to me,' replied Peter. 'Tell me stuff. What's new?'

'I'm dying.'

'I've heard that one before.'

'No, but really this time.'

'When did that scab come?'

'Days ago. But I got bored last night and picked it so it's probably disgusting now.'

'What were you listening to?'

'Such Nazi trash, but so glamorous.'

'What is?'

'*Ein Heldenleben.*'

'Sounds appropriate enough. I'm afraid I don't know it.'

'You don't *know* it?'

'You know how ignorant I am. I warned you when you sent me out to choose you that machine.'

'What?'

'Take those things off. You're shouting.'

Marcus took off the headphones and hung them on a hook by his bed. Peter was changing the water in Marcus's flower glass but watched him do this in the mirror, watched him twice miss the hook like a drunk.

'How are the eyes today?' he asked, setting the flower on the bedside table.

'For me? How sweet, and *such* a pretty colour!' Marcus exclaimed this over each day's flower. The repetition had passed from joke to ritual; the delight, though still sincere, had crystallized.

'Who brought in all those compact discs for you? I only got you five.'

'Miss Birch, my *ancilla constanta.*'

'Is she still in your pay, or does she work for love?'

'But of course I still pay her. She has a small empire to run in my absence.'

'What do you do?' Peter asked, smiling as he sat on the end of the bed.

'I told you. I'm an arms manufacturer. We sell death in all

its colourful variety. Our catalogue is found at the bedside of each world power.'

'No, but really.'

'You want God's own truth?'

'Please.'

'It's not half as exciting.'

'Still.'

'My mother inherited a small fortune in Argentine beef, which she expanded by supplying machinery to abattoirs and children's playgrounds. I never touch red meat and I never had much time for children so I branched out into optics.'

'Glasses?'

'And contact lenses and tubes that help people see around corners and down windpipes. Ironic really. Whenever they have to peer up or down my decaying insides, they do it with a load of vaseline and a machine that bears my name.'

There was a rap on the door and a nurse came in.

'Excuse me,' she said. 'Medication time.' She handed Marcus two tiny plastic pots, one with pills in, the other filled with water.

'Oh joy,' he said quietly and drained them both. Passing the pots back to the nurse, he followed her gaze to the open window and flapping curtain. 'My friend here has a problem with breathing second-hand air,' he told her, quietly. 'He apologizes for any inconvenience and promises to close it before he leaves.'

'Good,' she said and left the room.

'Well, now that I've told you the truth about my work, you can tell me the whole and nothing but about yours.'

'But I already have.'

'A kindergarten?'

'Yes.'

'But why? You have a brain, a wife, looks of a sort.'

'When we were first married I was a stockbroker.'

'Ah.'

'Why "ah"?'

'The finance houses are half-staffed with fantasists. They all want to do something else. Weren't you anaesthetized by the money?'

'Not really. There was never any time to enjoy it. We had a nice house, of course, and short, full holidays, but the quality of life is fairly minimal when all you want to do in your spare time is sleep.'

'So when did you leave and devote your expensive time to infants?'

'A little over seven years ago. Or is it eight now? Our son, Robin —'

'Oh Peter, I'm so sorry. How did he . . . ?'

'No, no. He didn't die; he went to live in a monastery. At Whelm.'

'Good lord! That God-forsaken place. Though, of course, it can't be God-forsaken. Not if it's a . . . Sorry. Go on. How often do you go and see him?'

'Never. Well, Andrea has once, but I couldn't face it. I prefer to remember him as he was. Andrea writes most of the letters, too. I think she rather wanted them to be her duty.'

'*Duty?*'

'Treat, then. She could go to see him there every six months, I think, but they prefer her to leave him alone and simply telephone. She talks to the man in charge. The Brother Superior, or whatever.'

'Abbot.'

'That's it. When Robin gave up everything and went there, Andrea went to pieces rather. He'd already left home, really, by going to university, but this seemed so much more final.'

'Like a death, in fact?' Marcus suggested.

'Yes.'

'Fascinating.'

'And suddenly it seemed wrong to be spending three quarters of my life away in an office full of people who weren't my friends and never would be, so I left work — although I still have the odd dabble in the market to make ends meet – and we set up the kindergarten. Andrea had been teaching in nursery school for years already and knew the ropes. It got off the ground in no time. It seems that having a husband-wife team was the chief attraction, paternal roles being the fashionable thing then.'

'Though of course it was you who had done the going to pieces rather than Andrea.'

'No. I . . .' Peter met Marcus's smile and capitulated. 'What makes you so sure?'

'Women strong enough to teach in nursery school for years don't crack up.'

'She was very upset.'

'But not half as upset as you.'

'You're the one that's getting volunteer counselling.'

'Did I ask for it?' Marcus held up withered hands. Peter laughed. 'It's only because patients without friends or family make them nervous, they find things tidier with visitors. Now. It's time for you to keep your assignation with your young gentleman friend and we haven't talked about me nearly enough. So. Business. I've been revising my will.'

'Why should that concern me?'

'No reason at all, my dear,' Marcus assured him, eyebrows raised. 'I won't be leaving you anything – the pleasure of my company in my last months will have been reward enough – but I want you to be my executor.'

'I'm touched, but shouldn't it be an old friend?'

'All my old friends are abroad and anyway they're all too decrepit and sentimental or just too plain dead to be of any use. You'd do very well. It won't involve much. I'm leaving everything to one or two people and besides, the capable Miss Birch will be handling all the money side of things, but you're such a charmer you can make the necessary phone calls. I'm getting bored of this filthy view and all this lying around so I intend to be dead within the next two months, which doesn't give you long to organize the concert.'

'What concert?'

'Listen, darling, and I'll explain. I have vaguely Quakerish longings in me and I've set my heart on scrapping the whole funeral bit and having a concert of music and readings instead. So much kinder to my *amour propre* than all that stuff about dust and worms. Miss Birch will give you a list of people to contact. The musicians will all be paid handsomely, so none of them will say no, and the readers, well, I'll organize the readers.'

'But, if it's not too indelicate of me, who'll be coming? I thought you had no friends or family.'

'Everyone gets friends and family once they're dead.'

'Where's it to be?'

'St Mary's, Battersea. I used to waste a lot of pleasant time painting in the graveyard there before I got involved in helping people look into stomachs, and the interior is so light-hearted. Does your wife, er, Angela . . .'

'Andrea.'

'Sorry, Andrea. Does your wife have a lisp?'

'No.'

'Does she read Donne?'

'Not habitually, but she'll have a copy somewhere. She read English before she trained as a teacher.'

'Then tell her she's got six weeks to learn the last sacred sonnet. Number six. I want her to read it on my special day.'

'But she doesn't know you.'

'Precisely. She won't cry or do anything silly. Now you must go or you'll be late for your assignation.' The nurse had come back in, a newspaper in her hand, and looked on approvingly as Peter closed the window once more. 'What's that? Another bloody prize crossword for me to finish for you?' Marcus asked her.

'Yes,' she said. 'Nice and stimulating for you.'

'And you collect the prize money. Has my anonymous admirer called again to ask after me?'

'Yes,' she sighed. 'I wish he'd leave his name. Better still, I wish he'd call in to see you.'

'No point. I know exactly how his mind works. He'll come in the end. Goodbye, Peter.'

'Goodbye.'

'Thank you for the flower. I can see it's white, but what exactly is it?'

'A rose,' Peter told him.

'Nice,' said the Nurse. 'Are you going to solve that last clue, then?'

'Fire away,' Marcus told her and rubbed his hands.

'"Virgil's through to Yugoslavia's first with interruption from tail-less doggy."'

'Perfidy,' said Marcus almost at once and grinned at them both. 'Such a sad waste,' he added.

5

Flawless in poison green, Jake's Vietnamese assistant handed him a file he had requested.

'Peter Maitland's in the lobby for you, Jake,' she said.

'Tell him I'll be right down, would you, Joy?'

'OK. I've booked everyone for the breakfast meeting tomorrow, except Saskia, who's got one with Kevin and Max and the people from Forbes.'

'Is she still on that account?'

'So it would seem.'

'Thanks. Have a good evening, Joy.'

'You too, Jake.'

Jake's desk, like his office, was large and uncluttered. In the course of his swift rise through the company's creative department, desks and work spaces had grown progressively so. Now he reigned over an expanse of highly polished royal blue glass and a chamber of eggshell grey. His telephone was svelte and wittily transparent and he commanded an oblique view across the opera house roof and the twittering spaces of Covent Garden. No family photographs spoiled the understated beauty of the desktop, but in the discreet triangular abstract to his left, the pink blob was said to represent his son, the blue his loving wife.

Once he had been paid to have ideas. How to convince the public in few words and one image that none but the cat food, instant coffee or parti-coloured toothpaste in question could help distinguish one customer from statistically similar neighbours. He had successfully conveyed sophistication in lavatory paper (largely by daring to call it just that), lured men into housework with black rubber gloves and a plump majority into voting into power the decade's least palatable party. Now he was expected to create less and to oversee more. He convened meetings at which others, younger and keener, brought forth outrageous plans for selling the unsellable and he had some say in whose offices were to be enlarged and whose desktops rendered less frantic. His income was more than he and Candida would ever find time to spend, even had she not been earning twice as much again.

Jake's briefcase was stainless steel with black rubber lining and handles. Candida had bought it for his thirtieth birthday. It held special compartments for his newspaper and car keys but he never used these as it made the case look too empty. Floor-to-ceiling Japanese sliding doors separated his office from the conference room where they would hold tomorrow's working breakfast. If both doors were slid far to one side they uncovered a small fridge and drinks cabinet, slid in the other direction, they revealed a hidden wardrobe. He took his lightweight overcoat and left the office. Joy had collected his squash kit from the cleaners in her lunch hour. He found the bag beneath her desk and slung it inside the briefcase on his way to the lift.

Jake had been playing secret squash games with Robin's father ever since Robin ran away to be a monk. They knew each other vaguely before that, of course; from the countless holiday evenings Robin and Jake had sat out at the Maitlands' kitchen table setting the world to rights. Peter would wander in apologetically in search of his crossword or reading glasses. Jake would give him a polite good evening and Robin would tease him gently and offer him a beer, but Peter rarely stayed and never for long. Jake had often been the Maitlands' guest, but he had avoided moments alone with the grown-ups. He used to lie awake in his room until

Robin came in to find him, then spend the day trailing in Robin's wake.

Then Jake and Candida. Well. Then It had happened and Robin had run away and they had all done Finals and Jake and Candida had got married. The news about Robin joining a monastery had filtered through. Jake forgot how exactly. They had all been slightly shocked at this apparent about-turn in Robin's principles, but their surprise was tempered with relief that he had not committed suicide as they had begun to fear, or run off with someone neither of them had met, as a kind of revenge. For some time after this, Jake had been meaning to pay a call on the Maitlands to make his peace, not least because locals were saying great things of the progressive kindergarten they had started and Candida was keen to send Jasper there when he was old enough, but Jake lacked courage. In the end it had been Candida, arguably in the more awkward position, who had broken the radio silence, driving over with cool impatience to the old Clapham house where she had spent so many childhood afternoons, and enrolling Jasper for the coming Autumn.

The squash games had been Peter's initiative. He had rung Jake at the office one day, out of the blue and suggested they meet for a talk. Flustered (he did not have an office to himself at that stage), Jake had suggested they have a drink together after work. Then Peter had pointed out that he no longer drank and made the counter-suggestion of a game of squash. Although he had opted out of the City, he retained the life membership he had taken out to a sports club along with the other stress sufferers.

'I don't play,' Jake protested.

'I'll teach you,' Peter replied. 'The club'll rent you a racquet until you're sure you want to carry on.'

Jake was fairly fit, but his jogging sessions were intermittent at best, and fell off with the onset of colder weather. He tended to clumsiness and had a horror of ridicule but as soon as he saw Peter waiting for him at the club doors, greying and with that familiar unfocussed look to him, he realized that this was as much an effort for the father as for the son's friend-as-was. They talked of nothing in particular while changing and, as soon as they were closeted in their court, talked only of the rules of the game. Peter was an adept teacher, Jake an attentive pupil and they managed to fit in a first match before their time was up. The changing-rooms were crowded when they had finished and the two men showered and dressed in shy silence.

'Want to go for a drink?' Jake asked as they left. 'An apple juice, or something?'

'Better not. I've got to get home. Do you want to play again next week?'

'Why not? I certainly need it,' Jake replied and made an exaggerated mime of panting, still feeling ill-at-ease. 'Same time?'

'Yes. Jake?'

'Yes?'

'This sounds a bit strange but I didn't tell Robin's mother I was meeting you and I'm not going to. Not yet, at least.'

His oddly distant way of referring to his wife took Jake back years.

'Would you rather I didn't tell Candida?'

'Heavens no. I mean, that's your affair. But I'd rather she didn't tell any . . . Actually yes, it would be easier if you didn't. Would you mind very much?'

'No.' Jake chuckled, strangely elated. 'After all, I'm sure there are things she doesn't tell me.'

'If you like,' Peter had offered, 'you could keep your kit in my locker. I hide my squash racquet here. Andrea thinks it's one of those games that give you heart attacks so I just pretend I'm going to a gym.'

'No, thanks. If she asks, I can just say I'm playing with someone from work.'

And they parted until the same time the next week. It was Jake's first deception of his wife. Although merely a trifling omission and nothing that he needed to cover up with complicated falsehoods, the accumulative deceit as, weekly, he deleted an hour from the account of his day, had come to weigh as heavily on his conscience as a full-blown love affair. (Not that he had pursued any such indulgence beyond the requirements of good manners.)

Seven years and some three hundred games later, Peter and he still pent up their meetings within the bare requirements of their sport, still held off from sharing so much as a carrot juice on leaving the club. They talked more though, not least because each was now considerably fitter and capable of panting more than half-sentences as he played. Curiously enough, the aggressions of the game did not prevent them from confessing their fears and weaknesses. Each now knew most, if not all there was to know about the other's marriage. The most important of their conversations however, dealt not with their women but with the son and friend whose absence had brought them such intimacy. Peter had admitted that he was partly to blame for Robin's inability to cope with life as the majority lived it. He had treated him too much as a son, he said, as someone who brought home school reports and prizes and made severe demands on a household budget; he had neglected to view him as an emergent adult. He confessed that the idea of having a child's respect had always frightened him out of getting too close to Robin.

Jake's birthday fell a few weeks after their first secret encounter. Peter had a parcel delivered to Jake's office. It was a squash racquet. The accompanying card was addressed 'to my almost-son', a phrase so weighted with need that Jake was tempted to cry off from their next appointment. He had an alarming four successive nights of most unsatisfactory sex with Candida, however, and Peter was the only person with whom such things could be discussed. He sent him a thank-you card (disguised with brown envelope and typing as some kind of bill) addressing him as 'my nearly-father' and their relationship became a sealed thing. He kept the racquet in the boot of his car; not hidden exactly, but undisclosed.

This was the first time that Peter had come to find Jake at his office. They had always met at the club. Seeing him here, sunk in one of the foyer's leather sofas beneath a shimmering *ficus benjamina*, pretending to read a magazine, Jake thought he now knew how a philandering husband must feel when his mistress comes out into the open to force his hand.

Peter fairly leaped up when he saw him approach. He laughed. Jake had never seen him this happy.

'What a surprise finding you here,' Jake said. 'Is everything OK?'

'Yes, yes. Fine. You look well. Are you well?'

'Couldn't be better. Well I could. I'm knackered.'

'Good.'

'Why?'

'Jake, I know it's not, well, not what we normally do but do you think we could skip squash for once and go for a drink?'

'Of course. There's a place next door. Come on.' He followed Peter through a revolving door and led him into the bar in the basement of the next building. He knew the management there so when he asked for the music to be turned down, it was. 'Are you sure everything's OK?' he asked Peter as they perched on their stools.

'Sure I'm sure, it's just that I've got some news for you that wouldn't wait.'

'What?' Jake asked, but Peter was talking to the barman.

'Yes,' he said peering closely at a cocktail menu. 'Could I have this vegetable pick-me-up thing only without the vodka?'

'Certainly, Sir,' said the barman. 'Usual for you, Jake?'

'Yup,' said Jake and turned back to Peter. 'So tell.'

'Andrea talked to Robin this morning.'

'How is he?'

'Fine. But he's coming home.'

'Christ!'

'Mmm.'

'I mean,' Jake went on, 'great. Great for you, I mean. Andrea must be thrilled.'

'She is,' said Peter. 'So am I.'

'Yes, and Candida will be glad to have got him as a godparent. He did agree to be one, didn't he?'

'Oh yes. No problems there, I think.'

'All the same.'

'Mmm. Quite.' They fell briefly silent, and to watching the barman whizz up a mixture of carrot, celery, tomato and ice in his blender.

'When's he coming back?' Jake asked finally.

'Soon. Any day now, I suppose. Maybe tomorrow. It hasn't really sunk in yet. Andrea only told me at lunchtime and I've spent the afternoon visiting Marcus.'

'How's he? I should have asked earlier.'

'Oh. Fine. That's to say, he's probably dying again and that's fine by him. He looks awful.'

'Poor old chap.'

'He's not that old actually. He must be about my age, well, maybe a few years older. He's aged so much these last few months, though; to look at him, you'd think he was my father.'

They drew themselves up slightly as the barman interrupted.

'One vegetable pick-me-up, no vodka.'

'Thank you,' said Peter.

'And one usual.'

'Great.' Jake's usual was a whisky sour made with bourbon. He raised his glass to Peter. 'Well,' he said. 'Cheers.'

'Yes,' said Peter, and drank.

'God!'

'What?'

'This is the first time I've ever had a drink with you outside of Clapham eight or nine years ago.'

'So it is.'

'It feels strange. As I was coming down in the lift – you'll think this is weird – but I suddenly thought it was rather like being accosted in the open by one's bit-on-the side. Not that you are; it's just how I felt.'

'Yes I am. In a way.'

'Can I tell Candida now?'

'Is that wise? I'd have thought she'd be rather hurt.'

'Not about all the rest, just the drink. After all, if Robin's coming back to be Perdita's godfather we'll all be meeting up soon anyway. It's the perfect moment to drop the cover. I'll say that you just rang up to tell me the good news and that we had a drink.'

'I suppose I should tell Andrea too. Which reminds me.'

'What of?'

'I'm meeting her at the cinema in half an hour.'

'Whereabouts? I can drop you off.'

'Thanks, but there's no need. I can walk, it's only Soho.'

'Ah. Peter?'

'Mmm?'

'Is he coming back for good? Does this mean that he's giving up Whelm?'

Peter stared at his nearly empty glass, sloshing the vegetable dregs from one side to another.

'I don't honestly know. Would you rather he didn't?' Jake met his gaze and gave his board meeting laugh; half cough, half throat-clearance. 'Mmm. Don't answer that,' said Peter and smiled. 'When's the christening?'

'Whichever Saturday we can all manage to be in the same place at the same time. If he's coming home straight away, probably the Saturday after this.'

'Right.' Peter paused then pulled a mock-innocent face. 'Are we invited?'

'Don't be silly,' Jake clapped him softly on the shoulder. 'Of course you are.' He chuckled.

'What's funny?'

'I was just thinking. We'll both have to be awfully careful to act as though we haven't met up in years.'

'It might take the girls in but Robin takes a lot of fooling,' said Peter.

'That had crossed my mind. Oh Christ.' Peter stood and took out his wallet. 'No. Don't,' Jake told him, waving a hand. 'I earn more than you.'

Peter held out a note, grinning.

'We're putting the fees up in the Spring.'

'Oh, well,' said Jake, making a playful show of snatching the note. Then he stood too and pushed Peter's hand away. 'No. Go on,' he said. 'Look on it as part-payment for my first squash lesson. Enjoy the film. What are you seeing?'

'*Le Financier Aveugle.*'

'Isn't that meant to be a bit grim?'

'Terribly.' They laughed and this time Peter clapped Jake on the shoulder. 'We'll speak,' he said, and left Jake alone with his whisky sour.

Jake gulped most of his drink and, for the first time since a brief flare-up when Candida first announced her christening plans, entertained thoughts of Robin. He remembered a gangling frame astride a speeding bicycle, one arm dangerously hampered by a clutch of library books. A broad grin and a wild cry of,

'No brakes!'

Unreadable blue eyes that sought his own too often for comfort. A bold tenor voice that wavered when reading aloud. Deafening Bach choral music dropped suddenly in volume for the same voice to say, 'Come in'. A huge, sunny room with a view onto a river, every surface collaged with open books, dust, forgotten biscuits, petals of dying flowers, candles tampered into sculpture and clothes thrown aside in mock despair. He remembered a mess of oranges on a lawn;

orange after orange diligently skinned until a whole peel could be removed to form an unbroken J. He remembered Candida laughing in a wild, infectious way she never did after she married him and felt a kind of expectation that had grown so long unfamiliar that it hurt him.

6

Watched by her attentive dog, Andrea stood and glared at her full-length reflection. A few months ago she had finally taken the hint her mother had been giving her Christmas after Christmas in the shape of panty-girdles for the filling figure. Peter had laughed when he first found a pair discarded in the top of the laundry basket. He called them her 'power pants'. She preferred not to speak of them at all. In an effort to be supportive, Peter had suggested they keep her mother's beige and cream ones for emergency rations, and go shopping in search of something in a sexier colour. Black or red or vivid purple.

'Look on them as an architect would,' he suggested. 'If you've got to have something that big, you might as well make a feature of it.'

Andrea shifted position slightly, with a critical frown, and regarded this new feature in her design. Her bottom never used to be large. It wasn't especially large now, but it had begun to relax slightly, like a neglected pear. She turned sideways on to the looking-glass and touched her breasts. She had always been proud of her breasts. Peter had always been proud of her breasts. Not too small, not too large, and firm as twin nectarines. They had begun to deflate. Looking at her silhouette now, Andrea thought she resembled some inflatable doll that swelled at her points of least resistance so that, on deflating her breasts with a cruel squeeze one could watch her buttocks swell and spread. She cupped each breast in a hand then, having raised them to their former level, let them flop. Her dog yawned, barked once then twisted around for a brief, ungainly washing of genitalia.

'Oh, all right, Brevity, I'm coming,' Andrea answered her and, turning away from her reflection, tugged back on a discreetly cantilevered bra and light summer dress. 'Who wants to see your mistress naked anyway?'

She fell onto her knees with a grunt and rooted in the dusty jumble under the bed for her walking shoes. Peter still remembered to undress her occasionally, but he no longer so much as blushed as he did so; even her bosom-weary gynaecologist Dr Jhabvala showed more excitement at her unpeeling. Finding a long-lost shoe-tree of Peter's, she tossed it to his side, then sat on the bed's edge to lace her suede brogues. She knew that they looked strange beneath a floral print but they were comfortable; now that the rot had set in with power pants and Brunel bras, she had decided to carry the look through.

Brevity frisked and danced a yard or two ahead as Andrea walked downstairs, picked up her cardigan and some stale bread and left the house. Then, clipped onto her fine leather plait of a lead, she trotted obediently to one side, pausing only once, politely to pee in the gutter. She was a Japanese spitz, a half-size version of the pomeranians painted with such uncharacteristic wit by Gainsborough, but larger and more robust than their papillon kin. Andrea hated small dogs but had bought her on impulse when Robin went away to Whelm. Brevity was eight; fifty-six in dog years. Dogs were banned on Whelm, which was a nature reserve, so Robin could never have seen her, even had Andrea braved a second visit. The wholly undoggy Peter had been won over in minutes. He lavished half-an-hour each evening on brushing Brevity's coat and taking her for a late night walk. He had dubbed her, 'The child of our menopause', meaning Andrea's.

Andrea walked up The Chase and onto the common. Faber

had said he would drag his daughter out on their tandem for some exercise and would meet Andrea by the duck pond, so she let Brevity off the lead and struck out in that direction, stale bread swinging in a bag at her side. She had first got to know Faber when he enrolled Iras in the kindergarten. The fashionable epithet, 'visually-disadvantaged' would have been a cruel euphemism applied to this little girl. Deprived by some genetic freak not only of sight but of eyes, Iras's American parents had put her up for adoption at birth and she had been nearly four when she found a home with Faber. There was nothing ugly about her disability since she still had eyelids and lashes, permanently closed over rounded bony shells where her eyes would have been. At worst, she resembled an animated sleep-walker. Faber had wanted Iras to have as normal an education as possible and Andrea had felt that it would be educative for the other children to have a disabled friend. The arrangement had thrived for a month or two – it was astonishing to see the games infants could invent that didn't involve sight – but it soon became clear that Iras was compensated for her blindness with a prodigiously fast brain. She was learning braille in outside lessons and was already leaving her contemporaries far behind in spelling, vocabulary and grammar. In the end her boredom became disruptive and Faber had been obliged to send her to a specialist school and an outside tutor.

'Andrea! Hey!' She looked round. Brevity was yapping recognition. There was no one in the playground but two little girls confiding at one end of the slide and an adult pair canoodling on the roundabout. 'Over here!' She turned and saw Faber racing towards her on his tandem and Brevity in hot pursuit. Andrea watched him swing a leg over, so that he slowed up standing on one pedal. She envied his grace. She smiled as he said, 'Hi,' and envied afresh his perfect dark brown skin. He made her feel pale and mottled.

'Where's Iras?' she asked.

'Home,' he said. 'Glued to that wretched computer. Mmm. Kiss you.' He kissed her cheek, she, the air.

'Is she still rewriting Genesis?'

'Oh no.' He laughed, wheeling his bike beside her as they walked. 'Much worse. I took Dot Halliwell on one side when I picked Iras up from her classes the other afternoon and said that she had got it into her head to rewrite the first books of the Bible from a woman's point of view and that I was concerned that this might be taking her away from her proper work.'

'What did Dot say?' Dot was Iras's tutor at the school for special children.

'Well she said that Iras was bang up to date with her maths exercises and so on − if anything, ahead of where she should be, as usual − but that she'd have a word with her about it.'

'And?'

'And the next thing I find is that Iras has been encouraged to "write something of her own".'

'Nothing wrong with that. Creative writing's a standard syllabus for any child.'

'Honey, Iras Washington isn't just any child. I mean, a sweet little story about a day at the zoo, or a poem or two, or My Worst Dream or something like that would be fine but my little girl's almost finished her first novel.'

'No! But that's wonderful. Isn't it?'

'Well of course it's wonderful. Iras W. is the wonder of Clapham Common South Side. But it's not normal. She's only twelve, for pity's sake. She should be out playing and instead she's shut away tapping at that machine hour upon hour. She's working harder than I am. She skipped school today to write.'

'They don't play at twelve, they sit together in corners and giggle about boys.'

'Well, even that would be fine, but she's way past boys. You know I can't work that computer much, and even if I could, you can bet she'd have put codes everywhere so that I couldn't snoop, but yesterday I had a good read over her shoulder when I went in to make her come and eat some lunch.' He stopped and turned to her. 'Andrea, my little girl has progressed into alien sex.'

'What?' she laughed. 'Little green men?'

'Precisely. Little green men. Together. Well, to be honest, she did start to explain that her little green men are actually hermaphrodite. She's got it all from some book on snails and earthworms so it's all slime and interchangeable slithering parts.'

'Sexy.'

'Oh, shut your mouth and give me some bread.'

'Here.'

They stood throwing bread pellets at the pondwater and were soon standing in a seething crowd of wing and darting beak. Andrea concentrated as usual on ignoring the queue-jumpers and throwing her bread to the less pushy birds, floating modestly in the background.

'Well?' Faber asked her.

'Well what?'

'When's he coming home?'

'Oh God. I'd forgotten. That's why we're meeting isn't it? Well all he said was soon, so I expect he'll turn up over the weekend.'

'You must be overjoyed.' He read her expression then added, '*N'est-ce pas*?'

'I'm frightened, Faber. He hasn't been home for eight years. People change in that amount of time. Last time he was here was his twenty-first. We offered to clear out of the house for the weekend to let him throw a party for all his friends but he insisted we stay and give a small dinner party, instead; just we three, my mother, Candida, of course, and Jake. It was all rather solemn and grown-up, with champagne, all the silver and I'd spent hours actually making puff pastry for a vast salmon *en croûte*. That was the May of their last summer term. Jake drove Candida and Robin back the next morning and four weeks later

I had Candida in tears on the phone. But I've told you all this.'

'Yes. Well, not really. Only bits. Come back for coffee.'

'I mustn't. You're working.'

'I'm not. I'm talking to you. Coffee?'

'Yes, please.' They set out over the grass towards Faber's studio.

'Were there any signs then? Of Candida's interest in Jake?'

'Oh yes. Robin didn't see, of course, and neither did Peter. I did. I suppose I should have said something. Robin would only have been cross with me. He was always being cross with me; it's one of the things I've missed.'

'Did he love her very much?'

'Oh, it wasn't Candida he loved.'

'No? But I thought she was his childhood friend and so on.'

'She was. But it was Jake that he loved. Poor Robin.' They were nearing the roadside. Andrea stooped to fasten Brevity back on her lead and felt tears well, stinging, in her eyes. Faber let his tandem drop on the turf and took her in his arms. She hugged him back, staring across his shoulder to incurious traffic churning by. 'I've been so strong. I've tried so hard,' she whimpered then realized the spectacle they were presenting. 'Come on,' she said, pushing him gently away. 'They must take us for a middle-aged woman parting tearfully from her young black stud; hardly flattering for either of us.' He laughed as she trumpeted into her handkerchief then stuffed it back up her sleeve. 'If only I were Irish. They love it when their sons turn into monks.'

'Only with them it's usually less of a surprise.'

'And as if Robin coming home in a habit and cowl weren't enough, I think Peter may have found a girlfriend some-where.'

'What in God's name gives you that idea?'

'Well, I don't really. But he's become terribly vain — obsessed with his age, spending hours in the gym keeping fit, that sort of thing – and he's suddenly trying awfully hard to make a show of interest in me by helping me buy new knickers and things, which my mother always said was deeply suspicious.'

'We won't talk about this until I get you home, Missy and give you a jug of coffee.'

'Strong and black?' She laughed, waiting for the familiar response.

'Like yo' man, honey chile, like yo' sweet hunk of man.'

7

Faber slung Andrea's mug into the dishwater and ate the one gingernut she had left in the packet. A slow thumping sound overhead reminded him of Iras's presence and that it was time to make something for her lunch. When she was concentrating deeply, or happy – the two being commonly simultaneous – she swung her feet hard against the sides of her desk. He walked out through the studio and up the stairs.

'Iras?'

'Yes?'

'Can I come in?'

'Yes.'

He pushed open the door to her room. It was only a baby's room, really. He had often asked her if she would like them to move to somewhere larger, or at least if she would let him buy her a sofa for her friends to sit on. This would have made it a kind of sitting-room for her, but she had always declined. He asked once if the smallness of the room made her feel safe. She had rubbed her wrists and given him one of her equivocal 'well's which they both understood should be taken as yeses. He stood in the doorway and watched her tapping at her word processor keyboard. In the old days, before the advent of this domineering machine, she would always raise a hand in the air, her left hand, stopping whatever she was doing until he had taken it in his and kissed its sticky palm. Now that his entrances were all but ignored, he contented himself with the occasional obstinate kiss on the crown of her head, where the mouse hair swirled in a perfect whorl. He kissed her there now.

'Has she gone?' she asked.

'The child speaks! I was beginning to forget.'

'Well?'

'She's gone. She sends her best wishes; she didn't like to disturb the young authoress.'

'She did well.'

'How's it coming?'

'Mmh.'

'Translation?' he asked, rubbing her narrow shoulders with two fingers of each hand.

'I mean just-so.'

'You're tense. Your shoulders feel like iron. Have you got a headache?'

'No.'

She was lying.

'Well, even if you haven't, it's time for a little parental control.'

'Oh, Faber!' she whined, 'I'm working.'

'You were working. Now it's time for a little exercise.'

'But . . .'

'Exercise. On the bike. Now.'

'Can't I do it after lunch?'

'Who said anything about lunch?'

'Isn't that why you came up?'

'Well, as a matter of fact it was. How do scrambled eggs sound?'

'They sound like what we had yesterday.'

'But I cook them so well. Now, come on. You can ride for ten minutes while I make lunch and then you can go back to your work this afternoon.'

'Oh, all right. But only if you put a record on for me. It makes it less boring.' She followed him out onto the landing where the exercise cycle stood. 'Put on that Nina record.'

'*My Baby Just Cares for Me?*'

'Yes but put on the album, not that short one.'

'OK.'

She clambered astride the machine. 'How far have I ridden this year?' she asked.

'Not far enough. We don't want you getting pasty and fat.'

'It wouldn't matter,' she claimed, starting slowly to pedal, 'I wouldn't have to see myself in the mirror.'

'True, but you'd feel yourself wobbling when you sat down and getting all hot and sweaty as you squeezed into clothes that didn't fit you anymore.'

'Eeurgh!'

'Quite. Now ride.'

'Put the record on.'

'Put the record on, please?'

'Put the record on, please.'

The needle was almost as old as the record player and the record was dusty and scratched from over-use. Nina Simone had to sing through an electric haze and compete with the oily hiss of the cogs on the exercise bike and the clunk of its constantly shifting handlebars. As Faber walked back through the studio to the kitchen and began to slice bread and crack eggs, he heard her groaning, 'My Baby Just Cares For Me'.

Iras's room was the only unillustrated part of the building. She quite understandably had no time for pictures, but hung her walls with last year's experiments in 'braille painting'. She occasionally spent her pocket money in a florist's on the Common. She chose on a basis of what smelled or merely felt good so would frequently return with an armful of plain foliage, ripped from someone's shrubbery as often as honestly bought.

The studio walls were crowded with Faber's huge, gaunt canvases; the unsold, piercing first drafts of portraits of generous friends, rich acquaintance, or interesting strangers. Most recently he had invited in a trio of female drunks. He had passed them every day for months where they sat by the Temperance drinking fountain, and without fail they hailed him,

'Wotcha blacky!'

'Is it true – you know – what they say about black guys' winkles?'

'Ere! Ain'tcha got lovely skin, then?'

'Ooh! Can I touch too?'

He would smile widely and there usually followed a brief exchange about the weather, the litter in the park or the fact that the Temperance fountain had dried up. One morning a few weeks ago they had complained in unison about the unbearable heat and he had asked them if, in return for a cold beer, a fiver each and a few hours in a big cool room, they would let him immortalize them in paint. He had quite forgotten inviting Andrea for lunch, so she was astonished to arrive, flowers in hand, to find him sketching and photographing the garrulous, unwashed threesome who were arranged on the dining-table. Mercifully it was not to be a nude study, not wholly. The sketches and photographs were now pinned at random on a broad piece of pinboard in a corner. The first three paintings taken from them hung on ropes from the central beams. The fourth had not progressed beyond the head and shoulders of the central figure; a lean, tallow-skinned woman called Winnie. She was throwing back her head to laugh, revealing her chicken neck and gold tooth.

The main wall, its base littered with a jumble of leaning canvases and empty frames, was ruled by Faber's favourite work to date: a huge charcoal drawing he had made for a portrait of the breakfast broadcaster Candida Thackeray with her baby son. He had known her sister-in-law at art college and this generous commission had come a few months after Candida's buying one of his sketches at the graduate show there. It was a marked contrast to her sharp, public image and caught a momentary expression almost of pain as she stared down at the baby in her grasp. Even had Andrea not told him first, he gathered from the newspapers that Ms Thackeray (alias Browne) had just been delivered of a bouncing baby girl. The hopes he entertained of a repeat commission were only faint; the Brownes were notoriously fashion-conscious and unlikely to repeat themselves.

Elsewhere there was not a vertical surface unillustrated. The walls of the kitchen cupboards, where some fathers might have stuck their daughter's adventures in poster paint or potato printing, were papered with newspaper cuttings interspersed with carefully selected postcards of morning-after gratitude or kitsch ones of holiday smugness. The bathroom walls were hung with a variety of mirrors and among the often unframed landscapes and still lifes on the galleried landing were plaster casts of Iras's left hand and left foot, made on her every birthday since her arrival and placed on a shelf within her grasp. Faber's bedroom was devoted to sleep and death. Mainly sleep. There was a painting he had made of Iras asleep on the grass with a book and a cushion. He had a collection of prints and paintings of sleeping figures (and occasionally dead ones) hung there, and a skull on his bedside table which served as a bookend. The latter had come away from its skeletal body when Iras had been allowed one cherry brandy too many last Christmas and tried her hand at a *danse macabre*. The headless remainder was now elegantly draped in black watered silk and arranged in a broken corner of the studio.

Iras suffered all this visual prejudice in good part, regarding it as a weakness of Faber's to be humoured and foreborne. Challenged, she made a brave show of being interested in the pictures for their smell (mirrors smelled different from windows, she said, and paintings from either), their feel, or the difference they made to each room's accoustic, but he could tell that she was only being kind.

Nina Simone sang 'Don't Smoke in Bed' and followed up with her peculiarly stately version of 'He's Got the Whole World in His Hands'. The scrambled eggs were ready too soon. Faber switched off the gas then buttered toast for Iras and spread margarine on Ryvita for himself.

'Iras!' he yelled at the ceiling. 'Lunch!' Then he reached for the telephone and dialled. 'Yes,' he said, when someone answered, 'I'd like Briar Ward please.'

'Putting you through,' said the receptionist.

'Hello, Briar Ward,' said a nurse.

'Hello. I'm ringing to ask after a friend there. Marcus Carling.

'Oh,' she said. 'It's you.'

'Yes.'

'You really ought to come in, you know, if you're a friend of his.'

'How is he?'

'Worse. Much worse. Visiting hours are nine to twelve-thirty then two-thirty until eight. Who shall I say called?'

Iras was coming downstairs, singing. Faber hung up and busied himself spooning the now rather flaky scrambled eggs onto two plates.

'He's got you and me sister, in his hands,' she sang. Her singing voice still had the softness she was trying to lose when she spoke. 'He's got you and me sister, in his hands. He's got you and me, sister, in his hands. He's got the whole world in his hands.'

'Ride far?' he asked, setting the plate before her.

'Yeah,' she said, reaching for where the pepper always was. She sang on. 'He's got the little bits of baby in his hands. He's got the little . . .'

'Itsy-bitsy.'

'What?'

'It's "itsy-bitsy baby"' he pointed out, sitting beside her and breaking his Ryvita. 'Not little bits of baby.'

'You're wrong,' she said, shaking her head and reaching for where the salt always was. 'Maybe in your version it's itsy-bitsy but the way Nina sings it, it comes out as "little bits". I prefer it that way anyway.'

'Why's that?'

'Well,' she set down her knife and fork and put her head on one side the way she always did when she explained a rudimentary truth to an idiotic world. 'If you listen carefully instead of singing along, you'll hear that she never says who "he" is.'

'Well, everyone knows it's about God.'

'I don't,' she said. 'I think it's about Death. It makes much more sense that way. Serene but menacing. And "little bits of baby" sounds harder and more frail. Itsy-bitsy's too cute.'

Faber told her to eat her scrambled egg before it got cold and they ate on in silence.

8

Robin had told her he would come home soon but he doubted that she expected him back this quickly. When he finished talking to her on the Abbot's ancient telephone, he had imagined he would need a few days to grow accustomed to the idea of leaving. Two or three.

It needn't be for long, he told himself, I can come straight back if I'm not ready.

He told the Abbot, who went on to say the same things.

'You needn't feel you have to stay away,' he said. 'You have nothing to prove by suffering. If you don't feel you can cope, if you're not ready for it, come straight back. Never mind the christening. I'm sure your friends would understand.'

But then the Abbot went straight into organizing a farewell supper for him, with a mead allowance and a honey-crusted ham and Robin saw that there was no need to hang around. He was ready. He would go tomorrow. He went back to the orchard to tell Luke and finish picking apples. After the first few questions, the news made Luke broody and they worked in silence. Robin knew he was there from sickness, not piety, but Luke's reaction and then the slightly hectic jollity of the farewell supper made it seem as though he had failed somewhere and they were kindly covering his failure with a show of celebration. He hated their mead and as always it made him long for sleep but he forced himself to stay awake for compline.

He had never been in all those years. He used to lie awake and hear the singing from his room but no one had ever told him to come and he had never felt interested enough to suggest it. But the end-of-term spirit had taken him, so he went. They were pleased and handed him a book with words in it.

It was a short, lyrical service; a sort of late-night spiritual insurance, full of lines about protecting us from the devil who prowls like a lion, or something. When they had to sing,

'Keep me as the apple of thine eye,' Robin glanced over at Luke, who was watching him carefully as ever, and he smiled. This was mean, he knew.

He said his goodbyes all round before going to bed then got up early and unseen to hitch a lift ashore with a fisherman. There was a red flag the monks hoisted by the cottage on the beach if they wanted someone to take them across, not unlike those orange signs that light up to read TAXI at night outside old mansion blocks. As luck would have it, Robin caught the post boat after about four minutes' wait. As it chugged him back to the mainland he leaned against some greasy fish crates and watched Whelm dwindle. The rule was that, before boarding a boat, one had to lower the red flag again and the fisherman had duly done this after dumping the post in the cottage for collection. As Robin watched, someone ran down to shore and hoisted it again.

'Someone being sent out to drag you back, I reckon,' his water-cabbie shouted from the wheelhouse. 'You done something you shouldn't? Eh?'

'No,' Robin told him.

'Not said your prayers, maybe.' He chuckled and crossed himself. It was hard to tell if he did this in mockery or superstition. 'Don't worry,' he went on. 'I'm not turning back this far out. He can just wait his turn.'

When he came to climb on the train to London, Robin scanned the thin crowd boarding with him but saw no familiar face.

He had almost no luggage – just the few things he had

first brought with him and a beeswax candle made by the sisters of Corry which the Abbot asked him to pass on to his mother. He had also handed over the small brown envelope in which he had sealed Robin's fistful of cash on his arrival. Eight years had dwindled its already paltry value, but Robin still had his chequebook, his wallet and his fountain pen, all three unused since his arrival. His mother had posted him four new chequecards in the course of his stay, which the Abbot had kindly intercepted and kept safe. The ticket clerk eyed Robin suspiciously as he now produced all four, gleaming new and still unsigned. Robin's signature had changed, with neglect, into a pale reflection of its former, italicized self but, with some effort, he managed to sign both card and cheque in roughly similar styles. He caught the clerk's stare and laughed in explanation.

'I've been away,' he said. 'Haven't needed any of them.' The sum demanded of him seemed vast but a tutting queue had formed and, in the wake of the display of cards, he thought it better not to query it. Parting with seemingly large sums for very little made him feel pleasantly like a tourist, giddy at the unreality of inflated foreign currency.

As he found a seat on the train he followed some long-hidden prompting and busied himself destroying the out-of-date chequecards. The difficulty of twisting the plastic to breaking point sent the recollection spilling into his mind of a bank account spectacularly overdrawn in student bravado. He realized that all this time his mother and father would have been fending off querulous demands from banks, bookshops, the college bursar and various ignorant acquaintance. They would have been cancelling subscriptions for him. They would have paid off his outstanding rent and had his things sent home (being, of course, too upset to drive over and pack them up for themselves, his absence being, as Luke put it, 'a kind of death'). For eight years they would have been maintaining the reduced, temporarily redundant mechanism of his now not so young existence and the thought of this saddened him. Robin's vacancy had been marked with a dry memorial; a mounting rustle of almost blank, unchanging bank statements, old boy magazines and invitations refused by proxy in his mother's disarmingly rounded hand.

As the train slid with unsettling speed away from the sea that had been, if not a home, then a refuge, he did his best to keep thoughts of his destination tamped down. Clinging from old superstition to his little cash, he had bought no newspaper, so he had to make do with reading the Bible. He had been in no state, on his arrival at Whelm, to dip into even the most featherweight fiction, but Luke claimed that he had read aloud to still him in his wilder moments. Once Robin was well enough to read again for himself, Luke had made the rather charming gesture of giving him the Bible that had been his principal sedative. It was a plain, elegant edition (Robin has it somewhere, still) and Luke had pressed various Whelm flowers between its pages for use as bookmarks (a typically nelly gesture, Robin thought, but sensitive nonetheless). For all the iniquities it had excused, the Bible was a surprisingly good read, a better companion in prison than Das Kapital, say, or what indigestible little he had ever managed of Proust or Mein Kampf.

'If only so much mystic crap had not accrued to it,' he had once told Luke, 'we might appreciate it for what it is; a cultural scrapbook, an anthology unsurpassed by anything the Greeks or Anglo-Saxons left us. Any novel maddens when picked up in the wrong mood, but there is something in the Bible for every shift of temper; history, ripping yarns, cool philosophizing, sex in plenty, love poetry, war poetry, even drug-influenced well-nigh psychedelic poetry.'

'And evidence of God's love,' Luke interrupted. He liked to chip in like that, Robin thought, spoiling things with his insidious sentiment.

This morning Robin read the Epistles. Most Bible-dabblers shied away from Saint Paul. They disliked his hectoring, house-keeperly tone and skipped on to the grander obscurities of Revelations. They missed a treat. Those endless strictures, homilies and transparent attempts at solicitude delivered by an insecure misogynist and bigot who believed himself to be part of God's senior management, were instructive in a way the author never intended and profoundly amusing.

At least, Robin tried to read but he was distracted time and again by the insistent presence of his fellow travellers. He gathered from the conversations around him that several end-of-season sales were to begin that morning and that this was the chief reason for most of them rising so early. There was a disturbing formality about their appearance that could not be explained as a mere display of provincial insecurity or by the need for early morning imbecility to be buttoned and pressed into sleepy decorum. For all the curiously open gabble of money and shop geography, the sharply dressed women and their few male companions might have been weekday commuters. While the women were no more than aggressively smart, most of the men in sight and those who boarded at later stations seemed to be cultivating an appearance older than their faces. A case in point was Robin's immediate neighbour who could not have left his twenties yet wore clothes and a manner more suited to a fifty-year-old. He had mimicked the old-young husbands of Fifties advertising with pompous shoes, sober tie, signet ring, brilliantine to make his short hair seem shorter and even a studiedly middle-aged frown which he wore to smack the crumples from his old man's newspaper or stride to the corridor to light his pipe.

Perhaps Robin had examined them all too blatantly for he soon felt their eyes on him. He tried again to hide in the Epistles but found that even new, unscrutinized arrivals glanced his way. Then he followed their sharp, incredulous glances and saw that the clothes he had come to consider a second skin were suddenly out of date; the cut of his trousers, his shirt collar, doubtless the handkerchief around his throat, suddenly belonged to an era. He shifted in his seat and shut his

Bible too loudly, sending a pressed violet to the floor, where he let it lie.

He had left in a time of New Romance and come back to one of hard lines, shoulder pads and grey discretion. He tried sitting with his face to the glass but already they had left real countryside behind. Graceful valleys were punctuated by supermarkets built to look like giant red barns. Plains bisected by motorways on which all the cars travelled in the same direction as the train, offered up Toytown housing developments, blank car parks and grey, reflective cubes. The train paused long enough at a platform for Robin to see a poster where a man in evening dress offered a half-naked blonde a solid gold apple. She was smiling at the camera, having a diamond-studded silver banana behind her back. Floating in the dark, doubtless expensively scented air above their heads, calm white lettering announced the arrival of a magazine called *Capital*.

Robin left his carriage, to the evident delight of the old-young pipe smoker, and passed the rest of the trip to Clapham Junction amid rolling beer cans and paper cups on the floor of the guard's van. He had a caged peacock for company and a large crate marked 'Hazardous Chemicals'. There was a trampled copy of yesterday's *Guardian* in one corner. He clawed it out of the dust and read about his new world.

Clapham, at least, had barely changed. Lavender Hill was still bright and smelly with traffic going nowhere loudly. The same tired grocers' and sticky-carpeted pubs remained. Now however there were wine bars and bistros every hundred yards. He counted twenty different estate agents between the junction and his home street. He stopped in a new boutique he judged to be suitably hard-faced, to write another outrageous cheque, this time for two bagfuls of black clothing. He changed inside a coin-operated public lavatory that filled its air with squirts of song and hostile perfume and promised to brush and flush its every surface on his departure, then gave his old things to a grey-skinned woman who appeared to live in a shopping trolley. She had the good grace to accept these colourful relics with an understanding smile. Robin smiled back, happy to find he was not the only one.

The Chase, scene of Robin's childhood, had always considered itself an oasis, a cut above its neighbours. It was twice as wide as any street in the district and few of its large houses had been split into flats. Long-established trees kept the rest of Clapham out of sight and long gardens ensured that, with the exception of Guy Fawkes night, residents sniffed only their own cooking and heard no one else's laughter. The common and the road to the Continent were within easy reach and a zealous residents' association with contacts on the council, held all plans for new building or for the reopening of an old meat pie factory permanently in the pending tray. The Chase swept up from the shabby anonymity of Wandsworth Road towards the oldest part of Clapham and the common. House prices and social pretensions climbed as the road did. Robin's family lived about three quarters of the way up.

At the last it was as if nothing had changed. There were the same battered estate cars, so practical for doing the school run, the same sleek cats, the same old roses, the same glimpses of overdecorated interiors; the same air of team effort. And the spare key to the back door was hidden behind the same loose brick in the garden wall.

9

Saturday being a holiday, Peter had been doing chores. He had been to 'Paw Relations (Canine Health and Beauty)' to pay the latest bill run up by Brevity, spent an hour trailing round a new jumbo supermarket tracking down the week's supplies in a space like a bank holiday airport and he had queued at the library to pay the fines on two lost books that had resurfaced yesterday under a sofa. Andrea was still out visiting her black friend, Faber, when Peter lurched in, laden, at the side door. She had taken Brevity with her – her chore for the day – but she had left a note.

'Darling,' it read, 'have walked over to Faber's for coff. Soup and bread and cheese for lunch, I thought, so no need to do anything. Sudden panic: there's no bedside light in Robin's room anymore because the one on your side of the bed bust the year before last when someone caught their ankle in the flex at our party, do you remember, and I replaced it with Robin's. Could you be sweet and brave and have a look in the loft for me? I know there are several up there somewhere that probably just need new plugs. Back by one-ish. A. xxx.'

Curiously, in a woman who read novels whose covers alone left him unsettled, who sat through the grisliest horror films and documentaries with a surgeon's composure, Andrea was afraid of the dark. By a quirk which they had never got around to altering, the roofspace had to be climbed into and half-crossed before one could switch on a light. Andrea had tried this a few times, when they had first moved in, but claimed that she became so disorientated in her fear, that there was a danger of her straying off the boarded area and tumbling through a ceiling. Ever an adept at conjuring up nightmare scenes, she would never argue a point of view when she could scare him into agreement. It was always he who ventured into the attic, to spare himself the image of her lying broken across a blood-spattered dressing-table in a cloud of plaster dust. She had controlled their son's upbringing with similar subtlety, painting visions of Robin and his first two-wheeler tossed aside by a speeding lorry, of Robin racked by dreams after watching television past eight o'clock, of Robin turned into a 'gun-junkie' by a syllabus with compulsory military training, of Robin trapped at the bottom of a slowly closing ice fissure on a school mountaineering trip. It wasn't that Peter had no imagination of his own, but it needed strong stimulation.

He stacked away the shopping and made his way upstairs. The other reason why Andrea preferred not to enter the loft was its lack of stairs. There was a hatch, its hinged lid darkly patterned with fingerprints, that could barely be reached from the top of a stepladder. There was a moment that Peter too found awful, as one hoisted oneself through the black hole above, when the ladder could easily be kicked aside leaving one stranded.

A hot noon sun had begun to heat the still, stale air up there. A pigeon was cooing on the other side of the tiles, dragging its wing feathers to attract attention and there was a splashing from the water tank. Keeping the hatch's square of light behind him he felt his way across to the light-switch that dangled free on its wire. With visits to the place so infrequent, it was wonderfully tidy and he was able to find four bedside lights in no time. Two were gutted of wire and one was a first generation Anglepoise, crippled by inexplicable loss of springs. The fourth was a Chianti bottle he remembered proudly converting at some date too distant to bear precise calculation, when they still drove to Europe without making any reservations and when Andrea was wearing things called, if memory served him right, Bolero slacks. He had even gone to the great trouble of drilling a hole through the bottle's bottom so as to give the flex a tidier exit. Peter blew some of the dust off the thing and went, sneezing, back to pull the lampshade off the least battered of the other lights.

Then he heard someone moving around downstairs. He glanced at his watch. It was too early for Andrea to be home. Besides, her passages through the house were virtually soundless. He set down the bottle-lamp and walked softly back to the hatch to listen. Someone was walking up the stairs from the hall. Peter heard the floor creak where it always did, outside the bathroom. Whoever it was went into the bathroom. Peter heard the rubberized clunk of the lavatory seat and was about to call out a greeting to his wife when he heard the sound of someone peeing. Even in their first outbreak of love, Andrea had never presumed so far as to leave the door open and even had she done so she would, to the best of his knowledge, have been incapable of aiming so directly into the water. Peter dithered on the brink of the hatch, torn between charging downstairs in a challenging fashion or pulling the ladder into the loft and quietly shutting the flap. But then he heard the intruder shut the bathroom door and start up the attic staircase at a trot, so he pulled his legs back – there was no time for the ladder – closed the flap and scurried for the light switch. Even if they took away the ladder, even if they locked him in, he didn't care.

He turned out the light and instinctively crouched. A dark, muffled voice said something. There was a pause then he heard footsteps on the ladder. The hatch-flap flew back with a bang, two hands grasped the rim and a strange bearded face came into view and said,

'Dad?'

Peter stared hard then stood to turn the light back on.

'Robin?' he asked. Then they both laughed and Robin climbed on up.

'Your hair's gone white,' Robin explained.

'You've grown a beard,' Peter told him. Robin came forward and they shook hands vigorously to hide their surprise. Peter held wide his arm to hug this son-turned-man but, more shy than moved, turned the gesture into a sweeping one to indicate the loft. 'I was up here to find a light for your room. My one got broken at a party — that was a year ago now — and your mother moved your one into our room. She said I should dig one out for you but I suppose, by rights, you should have your old one back. Oh look. Ha ha! Here's that terrible old one I made out of a Chianti bottle! I could use that one.' Robin was not listening. Peter babbled on. 'Actually, we weren't expecting you back quite so soon. I'd have come to pick you up in the car if I'd known. Get out at the junction, did you?'

'There's your old clarinet,' Robin said. Crouching, he pushed aside a pile of much-mended lilos and tugged a black clarinet case from under a bunch of magazines tied with string. 'What's it doing up here?'

'Well . . . I . . . After you . . .'

'You haven't given up?' Peter nodded. 'But why?' In its tone of slightly aggressive concern, he heard that, behind the beard, his son's voice was unchanged. He wished he had sold the clarinet, or hidden it better. It was a painful subject.

'Well. Yes. I suppose I have, really,' he confessed.

'But what about the orchestra? You used to enjoy it so much. You said it gave you something to look forward to in the office.'

'I didn't want to give it up, but they suddenly held a load of auditions and they found someone better than me, younger too. Not hard for them, really. So to make it less abrupt they said they were having to cut down on numbers to save expenses with hiring music and so forth. I didn't fail my audition but they'd obviously decided to replace me with the new chap as they demoted me to third clarinet.'

'Christ, that was mean!'

'There isn't often a call for a third clarinet, you see.' Robin, again not listening, had opened the box and was taking the pieces out, trying to remember how to slip them together.

'Go on,' he said. 'Play me something.'

'I couldn't possibly.'

'Yes, you could.'

'Careful. You're not doing that quite right. Don't force it. Here. Let me.' Peter took the instrument. Why was he doing this? The boy had barely arrived. The man had barely arrived and he was about to sit down and squawk at him from an old clarinet. Robin had always had the knack of making him look foolish in the kindest possible way. 'I've forgotten everything,' Peter went on.

'No, you haven't. You're putting it together perfectly. I'm sure it's like riding a bicycle. Play me that Mozart thing you used to do.'

'Which? The bit from the Quintet? It's far too long since I . . .'

'All right. *Peter and the Wolf*, then. Play me the cat's bit from that.'

'Well, pass me the reeds. No. In that little box down the side. That's it.' Peter picked over the reeds his son had passed him. 'They're all dried out and cracked,' he said.

'No excuses. Go on.'

He sighed and fastened one in. The instrument had a smell of locked-away spittle about it. It felt utterly familiar in his grasp, even though he had not touched it for over four years. After licking a few times at the reed to soften it he gave a few exploratory blows and a stab at a chromatic scale because he found a hazy memory that those used to make Robin smile. Sure enough, crouched on the floor against a tea-chest, like a ten-year-old in a beard from the dressing-up box, Robin was smiling. It *was* like riding a bicycle, even with such a dilapidated reed. Peter cleared his throat,

'The Cat,' he announced, 'from *Peter and the Wolf*.'

10

Andrea felt sick. She had been feeling sick anyway from eating several gingernuts too many but then Brevity had made things worse by falling prey to diarrhoea on the way home (a direct result of Faber having fed *her* gingernuts, too). Because Brevity had long hair, this involved a certain amount of wrinkle-nosed mopping up with a newspaper filched from a litter bin. Her dog had responded to this indignity by dragging all the way home, leaving Andrea to smirk her innocence at accusatory passers-by.

'I think she's trying to say "No",' chirped one.

'Ahh. Poor little thing!' sighed another.

She couldn't have felt less like eating lunch and thought of telling Peter that she had eaten something at Faber's. He had done the shopping then disappeared somewhere. She quickly liquidized some left-over vegetables in a jug of stock and set the resulting soup to heat on the stove. In a few brisk turns around the kitchen she found a loaf of suspiciously over-fragrant supermarket bread, a bagful of cheeses that needed finishing up, a dish of butter and a bowl of fruit. She stirred the boiling soup, slid it to a back burner to simmer then went in search of Peter, Brevity close behind.

In their days as a family of three, days when she had made more of an effort with her cooking (going to cookery classes on Tuesday evening; and tossing off soufflés or glamorous puddings without blinking), days when there were always

71

friends, relatives or children around for meals, she would stand in the hall and simply yell to announce a meal. Similarly, Peter or Robin would yell when a programme was about to start on television, when there was someone at the door or on the telephone for her or simply when they wanted to know where she was. Ever since Candida's tear-choked call to say that there had been a silly misunderstanding and that Robin had disappeared without trace, the yelling had stopped and the number of casual visitors had fallen off. Suddenly it seemed brutal to yell when there were only the two of them there, and each would spend minutes of every day in padding round the house in quiet search of the other.

The basement was wholly given over to the kindergarten and the Señoritas Fernandez's kitchen. Andrea toured the ground floor (effectively a first floor, it was so raised) looking into the dining-room, that doubled as Peter's study, and the drawing-room. No Peter; only, here and there, a dirty coffee cup or expired newspaper that she gathered on the move and returned to the kitchen. She was on her way to look in her study on the floor above when she heard him playing the clarinet in the loft.

He had been playing the clarinet when they first met. She was a soprano in the student choral society and at the dress rehearsal for a college performance of *The Dream of Gerontius*, found herself sitting right behind him. He had turned round and smiled at her, although they had never met, and asked if he might borrow the Hemingway she was clutching. She passed him the book, he read it during his rests, and then invited her for a coffee at the students' union when the rehearsal was over. He had given up the instrument for stockbroking until one of the firm's secretaries (a percussionist) dragged him to a successful audition for a City orchestra – one of those organizations battening upon the wealth of talent, and ready cash, languishing in the insurance and finance firms. After they lost Robin, Peter had given up again. The orchestra had let him stay on, although he was no longer a broker, but he claimed that he was fed up with having to explain that he had hung up his pinstripes to go footpainting with toddlers. It made him feel a freak, he said. Rather, the weekly contact with his old world made him feel a fool for not having started footpainting earlier. Andrea still belonged to a choral society (which happened to be rehearsing *The Dream of Gerontius* at the moment) but her husband's clarinet had been shut away in the loft.

Andrea continued her climb and stopped at the foot of the ladder into the roofspace. Brevity started barking. She had to pick her up to silence her.

'Peter?' she called. The music stopped. There was whispering then he called back,

'Coming,' and there were footsteps. 'Here. Can I pass you this?' he said and held out the clarinet through the hatch.

'I thought you'd given up,' she said, gingerly mounting the lower few steps of the ladder to reach it.

'So did I,' he said. 'And this?' He passed her down the instrument's case. The dust lay thickly on the once-black fabric, like a bluish fungal coating. 'Here I come,' Peter announced, and clambered down. His trousers were slipping down at the back. Andrea noted that it was now his turn to be taken shopping for underwear.

'Lunch is ready,' she said. 'I had a bite to eat with Faber, but I'll keep you company with an apple or something.'

'And here,' he continued, ignoring her, 'is a surprise for you.'

'Where?' she asked. 'Did you manage to find a bedside light for Dob?'

'Damn. I left it up there,' he said.

'OK,' said someone else. 'I've got it.'

A man started out of the hatch. He was all in black; black suede shoes, black jeans and a black cotton turtle-neck. He was thin – the jeans bagged slightly in the bottom – and he had a short, black beard. All manner of explanations suggested themselves.

'Hello, Mum,' he said and she recognized a grin and wrinkled eyes.

'I don't believe it,' she said. 'Kiss me.' She set Brevity down, who sniffed him suspiciously, and he stepped forward to kiss her. The beard tickled. He needed a bath.

'What in God's name is that?' he asked.

'That's Brevity,' said Peter, stroking the dog protectively.

'You're early,' Andrea said. 'We weren't expecting you so soon. Oh, Robin, nothing's ready! And that light!' She gestured at a terrible lamp Peter had once made from a Chianti bottle which she had only recently managed to banish. Well. Three years ago. 'Peter, we can't let him have that. Isn't there a . . . ?'

'I like it,' said Robin, touching her arm above the elbow. 'Honestly.'

'We must make your bed,' she went on, starting down the stairs. He was so thin. 'I haven't even hoovered in there.'

'I did it last week,' Peter piped up. 'Let's have some lunch first, anyway. What are we having?'

'Soup,' she told him. 'My God! I left it on the stove. Would you be a saint and rush down and turn it off for me? It's full of beans and things. They'll be burning on the bottom of the saucepan.'

'God,' said Peter and hurried past them. Them. There were three of them again. 'Have you looked round?' she asked, stopping at the next landing.

'No. I've barely got here. I came straight up to have a pee and then heard Dad tramping around under the eaves. You've had it painted.'

'Well, it was in a terrible state. The whites had all gone a sort of custardy colour.'

Robin pushed open his bedroom door.

'In here too,' he said.

'I thought you were a bit grown-up for that bright yellow now,' she said. They had painted his room pale blue. 'But I kept all your posters and things. They're on top of the chest of drawers. And look. We found you this lovely old mirror in a shop in Brixton. The gilt's a bit chipped but it's rather fun.'

'But I wasn't here, Mum,' he said, walking to look across at the treetops from his window. He murmured something to himself like, 'Beech tree still there.'

'But you hadn't got married or died or anything,' she replied and sat heavily on the edge of the bed. It was an extra long one they had bought for a sixteenth birthday surprise from a man in *Exchange and Mart*. 'And I couldn't stand having it all unchanged and waiting up here, with that yellow. Sunflower yellow had got so dated. I didn't want a time warp across the landing from us. It made me feel old. I'd see it every morning and remember the three of us sloshing it up.'

'Four of us. Candida helped.'

'So she did.'

'She wore dungarees and nothing else and you pretended to be shocked and Dad went all quiet.'

He tugged down the top half of the window then sat on the battered ottoman against the sill and regarded her with an alarming blankness.

'You're lovely and brown, Dob,' she said.

'All that gardening and sea air,' he told her. 'But please don't call me Dob anymore. I think it went out with Sunflower yellow.'

'Sorry. Robin.' She ran a finger through the dust on Peter's clarinet case, watching it furl into a tiny roll beneath her touch. 'You haven't become Brother something-or-other, have you?' she asked slowly.

'No,' he said and she recognized his grin again. 'I'm still just Robin. Do you like my beard?'

'I'm not sure,' she said. 'It makes you look rather like Jesus.'

'Is that a bad thing?' he asked, rising.

'I'm not sure. I like you in black, though. Very smart.'

'Thank you.'

He sat on the bed against the headboard, swung up his legs and bounced.

'Robin, darling?'

'Mmm?'

'I wish you'd written more. I wish you'd written at all.'

'Sorry,' he said. 'You weren't worried or anything?'

'Well a bit. Mainly I was hurt.'

'Sorry.'

'Don't apologize.'

'Why not?' He stood again and went to finger the frame of his new, old mirror. 'It was nice to get them. I couldn't always bear to read them, though. When you're so far away, so cut off . . . outside news gets to seem a bit . . . well.'

'I see.'

'No, you don't. Usually I get Luke to read them – he's a novice – he gives me a brief summary.'

'Oh.'

'Sometimes he cheats, though, and sneaks in a whole paragraph of your own writing. It's a kind of game.' He turned to face her and she decided that she did like the beard. He looked strangely like an Edwardian photograph of his grandfather, who was a priest. 'Why haven't you visited me, then?'

'Jonathan – the Abbot – said it was better if we didn't. I came once. Your father . . .'

'How do you know he's called Jonathan?' he cut in.

'He told me to call him that. We talk sometimes. On the phone. I came to see you once, on your open day. But you'd gone sailing.'

'You should have told me you were coming. I'd have stayed in for you and got someone to bake a cake.'

'I did. I wrote about it at least twice. It was awful. I sat in your room all morning then went to have communal lunch with all the other visitors and their friends and had to make polite chit-chat and try not to cry and then I went back to your room and waited some more. It was a very long sailing trip.'

'We went once around the Isle of Wight.'

'Do the monks often go sailing?'

'No. Only once every two years, when they cross to Corry
– more than that if there's an emergency and they have
to go home. I've got a special dispensation, more like an
honorary post.'

'Oh. That's nice. Do you really want that Chianti light
in here?'

'Yes.'

'It's ghastly.'

'I like it. Oh. And I forgot.'

'What?'

'This is for you.' He dug in his bag and pulled out a piece of
beeswax, still indented with tiny hexagons, wrapped around
a wick to form a simple candle. It smelt delicious.

'Lovely,' she said. 'Thank you, darling.'

'It's from your friend Jonathan.'

She started to pull at the clarinet in an attempt to take
it apart.

'I'd better put this away before someone sits on it,' she said
and heard herself sigh.

'No. Let me.' He half ran across the room and crouched at
her feet. She sat while he used her lap as a table on which to
dismantle the thing and put it away. She had a sharp burst
of memory.

He was eleven. He had almost finished building an intricate
plastic model of a human skeleton, bought with a postal
order sent for his birthday by some harassed godparent.
She had been sitting at the kitchen table flicking through
a magazine. She could even see its colours again: bright
yellows, electric plastic blues. A copy of *Honey* or, given
his age, probably *Good Housekeeping*. He walked solemnly
in, wearing shorts held up with a snake-belt, and handed
her the sinister 'educational' model.

'Hold it steady,' he commanded her. 'I've left the cranium
till last. *You* can put that on. It's not like a real cranium, of

course, because real craniums don't have a hook in them for hanging us up by. Now. Hold the rest of it. No. Like that.' She held the skeleton gently around its slithery ribs. He dug in his pocket for the tube of glue and smeared some around the open bowl of the skull then passed her the cranium. 'Go on,' he said. 'Put it on. No, silly. That way.' She held the cranium in place. 'That's it. Now. You've got to hold it for at least forty seconds.' Then they had exchanged broad smiles and he had wandered out into the garden leaving her with a headful of glue fumes and a handful of mortality.

When he had finished putting away the clarinet her lap was grey with dust. He tried to brush it off but, flustered, she pushed his hand away and stood. She became aware of a strong smell of burnt lentils and felt her hunger revive.

'Come on,' she said and they left his room to air. Down below Peter called out,

'Lunch, you two!' then coughed, embarrassed at the unfamiliarity of shouting.

11

On her way home from work, Candida asked the studio car to stop off at a florist's before they crossed the river. There were people coming to dinner and there was nothing in the garden but lavender, maggoty apples and a lot of tired foliage. She heaped the counter with lilies, birds of paradise and some elegant, sword-shaped leaves from a South American country where they executed children for sedition. On television this morning she had looked chic but humane while a revolutionary Catholic priest and his interpreter told her about this country's latest outrage, which was why the name on the box caught her eye as a florist filled a bucket with them. She also picked out an unusual large blue cactus and asked for it to be delivered to her secretary, Jason, who was turning thirty-two tomorrow. Then she paid with plastic, gave out a couple of autographs and sank with her dripping parcel into the back of the car.

Quite apart from the spectacular money (which, frankly, left her cold), the only compensations for starting her particular work at dawn were riding to and fro from her job in a studio car and being able to do so before the morning and evening rush hours. Even had her celebrity not proved a problem with the other parents, she preferred to keep meetings with Andrea and Peter Maitland to a minimum. While she was often far too tired to do much more than kiss Jasper and admire the latest *soi-disant* painting, she made a point of at least being in the house when his nanny brought him home. Candida found her nannies through Lady Canberra's, an agency that specialized in tireless, healthy Australian girls who replaced each other each year and so had no time to grow overly fond of child, husband or house. Her nannies never drove Candida's car, although it went unused during the day. Instead, she had bought them a customized jeep, safe for driving Jasper to kindergarten and parties, practical for carrying out the heavy shopping duties that fell to them in his absence. The agency insisted on a weekday off for its girls so, once a week, Jake would drop Jasper off and Candida would pick him up. At least, she would park her car across the road and he, well trained, would slip away discreetly and get in.

Samantha, Lady Canberra's latest, was peeling potatoes when Candida let herself in. She would soon have to be replaced; Jasper had twice unthinkingly referred to her as Mummy. Her straw-blonde hair was tied back in a pony-tail and she had on one of her unwise, short skirts. Seeing her mistress, she flushed pink behind her unkind freckles.

'Boy, am I glad to see you, Candy!' she exclaimed.

'And why's that, Sam?' Candida undid a button on her blouse and washed her hands at the sink.

'You're back just in time. Perdita's been guzzling all day and the last of your milk ran out an hour ago. Christ! Amazing flowers! Where'd you get them?'

'Is she awake now?'

'She's hollered herself to sleep but Jasper'll wake her in a sec with all his thumping.'

Jasper could indeed be heard crashing his pedal car around the playroom overhead.

'How was she with the bottle?'

'Hated it at first, but I did as the book suggested and squeezed a drop or two onto her tongue. Once she realized it was still your stuff and not something out of a can, there was no holding her. A couple of days and we can put her on to formula.'

'Goodee,' sighed Candida and went to inspect her mail. The envelopes were on the table beside the salmon, which Maison Rostand had dropped off as ordered. The fish lay under clingfilm on its returnable plate, poached, boned and with its skin replaced with alternating 'scales' of blanched arugula and radicchio. If Madame Rostand's promises had been fulfilled to the letter, its intestinal cavity was stuffed with a fluffy mousse of haddock and ricotta, coloured with flecks of tarragon and lemon zest. Maison Rostand was confidential to the point of invisibility. Each dish delivered to a household for the first time was accompanied by its easily memorized recipe, all ready for passing on to an enquiring guest. Candida paid the company a small retainer to keep her recipes unique and to buy the right to pass them off as her own in magazine articles. 'The hollandaise,' she murmured. 'They've forgotten the hollandaise.'

'It's in the fridge,' said Samantha. 'I'll slip it into the bainmarie before I put Jasper to bed.'

'Fabulous. What have you made us for pudding?'

'Two chocolate terrine. That's in the fridge too.'

'Good girl. You have been busy.'

The letters were more than Candida could face. She glanced at a couple of facetious postcards from abroad, peered inside a bank statement then, casting the rest aside, walked upstairs. She took off her shoes to free her hot, cramped toes, and tiptoed into Perdita's bedroom. Her baby was fast asleep, breathing heavily. Candida had spent the weekend trying to acclimatize herself to the indignity of a human milking-device and Perdita to the less-than-luxury of a rubber teat. The news that she had accepted the replacement so fast had come as a relief; Candida was a valuable commodity but the studio would not take kindly to a backstage nurse, not now that the baby had already been introduced to the nation and become stale news. As it was, she was having to hire a babysitter from Lady Canberra's to cover feeding times on Samantha's day off. She was tiptoeing out again when the playroom door was grappled open with a grunt and Jasper came pedalling to greet her.

'Mummee!' he shouted.

'Quiet,' said Candida, and gestured to the doorway behind her. 'She's asleep and Mummy's tired.'

'I'm tired too.'

'Are you, poppet?'

'Very. But Peter showed us how to make pasta pictures. Do you want to see?'

'Yes, please.'

'Oh. Well, I gave it to Rachel Highsmith because hers wasn't very good and she's always giving me kisses and things in the shrubbery . . .'

'Is she, by Jove?'

'Yes, so you can't see it but it was very good. At least, Rachel said so.'

'Do you want a kiss from me?'

'Yes.'

'Where?'

'Here.' He pointed to his cheek, turning his head to one side. 'And make sure you leave a red kissy-mark. Rachel can't do those.'

'All right.' She knelt on the carpet before him and planted a thick kiss where indicated. Still in the car, he trundled over to a full length mirror to inspect himself.

'Brilliant,' he said. Although the kiss mark was less red than *nymphe bronzée*, and he would have preferred one to match his car, he knew from a severe dressing-down she once gave him, that Mummy's lipsticks were fabulously superior to the redder ones Samantha let him play with.

'We've got people coming to dinner tonight, poppet, so you will be good about going to bed on time, won't you?'

'Yes.'

'Good boy.' Candida rose, stroked his hair and started towards her bedroom to choose what to wear.

'Mummy?'

'Yes?'

'There's a man peering up at the house from the play-ground.'

'Is there?'

'Yes. He was there when you came home, only you didn't see him. I did though, because I was watching, and he's been there for ages.'

'Never mind. I expect he's just another funny-man.'

'Like the one outside the station with all the plastic bags?'

'Yes. Now go and see if Samantha needs help in the kitchen, there's a good boy.'

Jasper abandoned his car and ran downstairs to his nanny while Candida carried on to her room.

The house was one of sixteen in an early Victorian square in Stockwell. The square was making up for its maiming at the hands of wartime bombs with an ostentatious flurry of self-improvement. A firm of builders and a pet decorator were forever being passed from recommending hand to hand within the residents' association. The Brownes' house was Jake's, bought when Candida was a rising researcher and he won the bulk of their daily bread. Stockwell would not have been Candida's first choice, or even her third, but she had come to appreciate its charms and had recently consoled herself by purchasing the bomb-site adjoining Jake's property. The square was too close to the council tower blocks for the playground in its centre to be a suitable haunt for Jasper and his friends; Candida proposed to extend her garden over the land she had bought to give them more room for a climbing-frame, a swing and, just possibly, a very basic swimming-pool. She had also applied for and won planning permission to build a garage with a staff flat on top. When the children were too old for nannies, she would redecorate the flat and bring her mother to live there as a babysitter. Or Jake's mother; whichever won the race for widowhood.

She shut herself in, rapidly stripped, draped her dress into the pile for Samantha to take to the dry cleaners, then walked in her knickers to the bathroom. She washed off all her make-up, cooling her face and arms with a cold flannel and dabs of scent, then pulled out the sort of clothes she would never parade for Candida-Thackeray-relaxes-at-home photographs. She tied her hair away from her face with a piece of rather stained white silk and slipped into an incredibly cheap but flattering tube of creamy cotton she had bought while shopping in dark glasses for Samantha's birthday. Then she remembered to peer out of the window to look for Jasper's 'funny-man'. Her first reaction was an involuntary, out-loud, 'Oh no!' her second was to dart behind the curtains where she could peer unspotted, her third was to replace half of the make-up she had just washed off.

There was no mistaking him, even with his beard and longer hair. She had not expected him to look so normal. She had not expected him so soon or so unannounced. Then she reflected that this was no longer the Middle Ages and monks would not be expected to swelter through hot weather in thick woollen habits. She also decided to be touched at her childhood friend's naïve assumption that she could be paid impromptu visits in mid-week and found in.

Why didn't he come and ring the doorbell? Perhaps he had missed her return home. (Impossible.) Perhaps he had merely come to spy out the lie of the Land of Marital Bliss; see where she and Jake had ended up. (An idyllic afternoon had been spent with him when they were thirteen, trailing their biology teacher for hours to see what precisely she did on her weekends.) She ought to ignore him. She ought to draw the curtains and take a couple of hours' rejuvenating sleep before changing for dinner. She flung the window up so hard that the sash weights clunked in their shafts.

'I don't believe it!' she shouted. 'It is you, isn't it?' He just smiled up and waved. It was him. He never shouted in public places. For once the playground was deserted. He was sitting on a swing, long legs stretched out before him. He had lost weight; it suited him. 'Will you come in or shall I come out?'

He stood, still smiling through his beard, which also suited him, short and Jacobean-looking. She assumed he was coming in. 'Be right down,' she called and pulled the window shut again. She stopped in the bedroom doorway, hurried back to dig in the back of her dressing-table drawer, and pulled out a thin silver crucifix on a hair-fine chain. She kissed it, thoughtlessly, and tied it round her neck, leaving it to dangle outside her dress. The bell rang. She heard Samantha shifting in the kitchen.

'I'll get it,' she shouted and ran downstairs.

She unlocked the front door with the unfamiliar sensation of a broad smile tugging her cheeks into craziness. He was taller than Jake. She had forgotten that. Eight years.

'Robin!' she sang.

'Hello, you,' he said. He stood there while she hurled herself at him. He was all in black, including fairly tight black jeans. Her hugging hands stroked his back and she found one falling briefly to his bum. He didn't feel like a monk. 'I came by to see where you lived,' he said. 'I saw you come home but thought I should give you time to unwind.'

'Thanks. You look wonderful.'

'Thanks.'

He said nothing of her appearance so she took his hand and led him into the sitting-room. There were still high wooden shutters in here, which they kept closed during the week as a security precaution. The shaded room was beautifully cool. Candida uncovered and opened the windows. Robin sat in an armchair in the dark. When she turned, he was smiling again.

'Why are you smiling?' she asked.

'Am I?'

'You know you are. What's so funny?' He laughed then smiled some more. 'What?' she asked, laughing too, but infuriated. He stopped smiling and reached in the pocket of his polo shirt.

'I've brought a present.'

'Oh, Robin!' she gushed, trying to see what he was holding.

'It's not for you, it's for my god-daughter.'

'Oh, how sweet. We were so glad when your Ma said you'd said yes.'

'Where on earth did you find that name?'

'What? Perdita Margaux Browne? Don't you like it?'

He laughed again. To himself. She reached up to tighten the cloth around her hair with a little tug.

'I brought her this,' he said, holding out a clenched fist. 'Hold out your hand.'

She smiled and did as he told her, shutting her eyes. Something hard and cold fell into her palm with a dry rattling. She opened her eyes. It was a tiny red coral necklace with a gold clasp shaped like a heart. She pressed the catch and laughed to see that the heart released another, thinner heart from its grip.

'That is what you give little girls, isn't it?' he asked. 'Coral to cut their teeth on?'

'Oh yes,' she said. 'Early days for teeth yet, I hope, but she'll look enchanting in it. She's getting the full works – godparents clutching candles to light her way and renouncing "the Devil and all his work".'

'And "all carnal desires of the flesh".'

'Yes. I'd forgotten that bit.' That strangely irritated her. Damn him. She laughed and went on, 'And we've got her great-great-grandmother's christening gown out of mothballs. It's about six feet long.'

She ran dry and he offered nothing. They sat in silence for a moment, staring with sudden candour into one another's sun-pinked face then he said,

'Aren't you going to welcome me back, then?'

and she said,

'Don't be silly. There's no need.'

He looked around the room, and stroked the underside of his beard; a mannerism developed behind her back.

'Nice house,' he said. 'Just what you always planned to end up in. Are you both fabulously rich now?'

'Fairly,' she dryly admitted, then stood and passed him back the necklace. 'Come and give Perdita her present.'

As they climbed the stairs, Robin paused to appraise the passing pictures and photographs, with his increasingly maddening smile. She heard Jasper shouting at Samantha in the garden. She glanced at her watch and guessed that he was refusing to come inside to eat his supper. She would have to get rid of Robin, soon. She had a dinner party to organize. The Director General and his depressingly well-read male consort were coming, as were a well-known, impossibly glamorous acting couple Jake was wooing towards a five-year instant coffee contract. The flowers were probably beginning to droop in the sink, she had her infallible spinach soufflés to begin and she had forgotten to tell Samantha to polish the silver. They would have to make do with a quick dust. Robin would have to go very soon.

He had stopped and was staring at the large portrait of her and baby Jasper that dominated the main landing. Jake had wanted it in the sitting-room but she had protested because it was rather too true to life and showed her all loose and puffy.

'Is that your other?' he asked.

'Yes. Jasper. He's out in the garden.'

'Mmm. We've already met.'

'Really? He never said.'

'Sons don't tell you everything.' Again that smile. 'Yes, he came out to the pavement and we had a little chat about what monks do. He told me how to make pasta pictures.'

'Sweet,' she said, distracted. He looked back at the painting.

'It's very good,' he said. 'Who did it?'

'It's a Faber Washington,' she told him, leading the way on to their bedroom. 'He's a friend of Jake's sister, Tessa. We snapped him up when he was just leaving the Slade. Of course, he's becoming terribly well-known now. I doubt we could afford another.'

'Of course you could,' he snorted. 'You're rich as Croesus. Now. Where's this baby?' He swung the necklace from a forefinger. She had forgotten the extraordinary length of his hands. They had once come near to blows when he beat her in a late-night Botticelli Hands Contest.

'In here,' she whispered, then carried on in her full voice. 'Don't know why I'm whispering because it's time she woke for a feed.' Actually she had no idea when Perdita should have her next feed, and was not altogether certain of the wisdom of waking her up, but she had felt a sudden urge to impress on him the authenticity of her motherhood.

He followed her into the nursery, having first darted in for a brazen peek at the room she shared with Jake and emerged with the inevitable smile. At what? The size of their bed? The fact that they each had a clock-radio? Her multi-gym? Did she care? Yes, oh dear, yes. Cooing without too much affectation – Perdita was a fairly pretty baby – she leaned into the antique Swedish cot and lifted out her sleep-heavy daughter.

'Hello, darling! Mmm? Yes! Ready for your tea are you?' They rubbed noses and she kissed the swirling crown of Perdita's sweaty hair. 'Look. It's your Godfather Robin,' she went on, pointing the baby to face the visitor. 'He's brought you a present.'

'Here,' Robin whispered, holding out the necklace, still on a long forefinger. Perdita blew a bubble, and her head wobbled. Robin smiled a quite different smile – the one Candida remembered – and laid the string of coral on a table.

'I'm afraid she's still a bit little to focus,' Candida told him. 'Want to hold her?'

He said nothing, but nodded and held out his arms. She passed the baby over and saw at once that he knew exactly how to hold one. Wondering where he had learnt and crossly waiting for her daughter to save the day by bawling herself puce, she stood back. Perdita lay quite still, bubbling slightly and turning her face in search of an absent bosom. Her heavy breathing seemed almost loud in the silent room. A police siren wailed by in the distance. Jasper yelled,

'No! I *hate* you!'

Smiling at this loyalty in her son, Candida turned her head for a brief check in the mirror. There she saw her childhood friend cradling her new baby, framed and distanced in reflection. All at once she sensed that the Dob of her childhood and youth had evaporated and with him her old comradely feelings towards him. This bearded stranger, who laughed at her, failed to be impressed and held her child so expertly, aroused quite another, less coherent emotion.

'Robin, I hate to sound rude, but I've an awful lot on my plate this evening. We've got people coming round and I haven't cooked a thing and I'm not even properly dressed.'

'That's all right,' he said. 'I was going anyway.'

'You must come back, though. We've so much to catch up on. Where are you staying?'

'Home.'

'Lovely. Can I say I'll ring you?'

'Say what you will,' he said and gave her the other smile – the new, uncomforting one.

She took back Perdita, whom he had lulled into a state of blissful trance, then saw him quickly to the door. With him safely on the pavement she went directly to the sitting-room where she sat, eased her dress off her shoulders and offered her daughter a nipple.

While Perdita sucked and slopped, Candida tried, as she always did when breastfeeding, to relax and think of cool white spaces. She succeeded for a few minutes but then Perdita stopped to draw breath. Candida looked down at her and felt herself blush hotly to the roots of her hair. The softly panting daughter's stare was condemning an idea that had barely formed in the mother's mind.

12

A week later Jake was walking the few hundred yards to their local church to greet the first arrivals. Candida was having problems fitting Perdita into the ancestral christening gown. Thrilled at the sudden revival in their children's respect for faith and tradition, and at the prospect of a party, both sets of in-laws had descended. All four grandparents had arrived early and had come to the house instead of waiting at the church, as directed. The grandmothers were cooing and meddling around the furious candidate for baptism. Their husbands, each a dangerous shade of red, took turns at pushing Jasper on his swing. Jake was meant to have brought these three with him but had slipped out of the kitchen door without a gardenwards glance.

The building was a Georgian one. At least, its shell was Georgian; the original insides had been burned down long ago by a discarded German bomb and rebuilt, with little eye for architectural sympathy, by a consortium of counsellors in the 1960s. Unversed, Candida and Jake had blithely assumed that any church would be free for a quick weekend baptism, and had set their hearts on somewhere rather finer than the St Thomas Community Centre, only to be made the ignominious offer, kindly meant, of a service shared with three other babies. The religious functions of Saint Thomas's were now contained in a small, glass-walled box draped with orange hessian curtains and furnished with matching plastic chairs.

The rest of the building housed a community hall and the local Citizens' Advice Bureau. A large noticeboard in the portico where Jake stood to wait flapped with details of weekly events held there: Gay Self-Defence (Women Tuesdays, Men Wednesdays); something called Aerobicise; bicycle maintenance classes; sitar appreciation classes; eurhythmics (introductory Thursdays, intermediary Friday) and Meditation Made Easy. The Woodcutter Folk (which Jasper wanted to join, apparently) took the place over on Saturday mornings. Across a poster for a concert by the Stockwell Glee Club someone had printed with a large rubber stamp in lurid green ink,

MAKE THE SWITCH!
DROP THE BITCH!
EAT THE RICH!

Jake tucked this out of sight behind an immensely comfortable Indian's invitation to join the way of truth.

The Maitlands were the first friends to arrive. He heard the full-chested banging of an old Volkswagen engine, looked up and saw their much-patched, first-generation dormobile rolling to a halt beneath the dusty lime trees. He had not laid eyes on Andrea since Robin's twenty-first birthday dinner, when she had tried to place him between two godparents and Robin had made a fuss and insisted he sit beside him. She had aged since then. She had let her hair begin to grey and had lost her firmness of outline, but she had still the kind of vigorous buoyancy that won children's trust and made the more youthful of her contemporaries seem faintly overdone. Peter looked hot in his suit beside her. Robin was not with them. Jake thought of their secret squash games.

The roles have reversed, he thought. Now I'm his bit on the side and this is his innocent wife.

'Hello, Jake,' said Andrea, taking his hand and drawing him closer. 'How lovely.' She kissed his cheek.

'Mrs Maitland. Mr Maitland,' said Jake. 'It's been so long.'

'Peter and Andrea, now, I think,' said Peter and winked.

'I see you've still got the old dormobile.'

'"Devon Caravette", please!' laughed Andrea. 'Yes. It's a collector's item, now. Some total strangers asked to buy it the other day. I was in a car park somewhere. They said they were surfers. They were very brown, so I suppose they might have been. Too funny really.'

'Is Robin not with you?' Jake asked them.

'Oh, of course. You poor thing. He's the reason we're here. You must be so worried,' she said. 'But don't be. He's only disappeared for a bit.'

'Disappeared?'

'Well,' Peter went on, 'not disappeared exactly. Just gone out. He's been doing this all week. We wake up and he's not there. Then he turns up halfway through the afternoon with a little bag from some museum or a bunch of flowers for Andrea and says he's been for a walk. Not to worry. He'll be here in time.'

'I made sure he had the address,' added Andrea. 'And he's bought himself one of those watches you don't have to wind.'

'Oh.'

'From a man with a suitcaseful in Leicester Square.'

'Ah.'

'Don't worry.'

'I won't, then.'

They stood between two pillars and stared briefly at the road.

'Lovely looking church,' said Andrea. 'I've passed it so many times and I've never thought to get out and look inside.'

'It's a bit of a disappointment, I'm afraid,' Jake told her. 'I think it was gutted by fire in the Blitz, or something.'

'Oh dear.' She brushed a hair from Peter's shoulder. 'Is Candida inside?'

'Actually, no. She was having a bit of trouble with Perdita's dress – one of those long, ancestral things – so she asked me to come on and usher you all in. In point of fact I haven't even seen the priest yet.'

'Nice and relaxed,' said Peter. 'That's the spirit.'

They stood a little longer, then Andrea said,

'Well, we'll go on in and have an exploring session.'

'OK,' said Jake. 'Our part is just inside on your left. You can't miss it. It's the bit with all the orange curtains and the concrete font.'

Andrea patted his forearm, smiled at him with Robin's smile and said,

'So good to see you looking so well, Jake.'

'Yes,' added Peter, following her. 'Fit as a fiddle as ever, I'd say,' and he winked again.

Jasper arrived next, buttoned at protest into a grey flannel suit with short trousers and a sky blue bow-tie. He had his grandfathers in tow, both looking the worse for wear and in need of a drink. Jake caught his father long enough to tell him that Jasper's teachers were inside. Sure enough the two older men emerged in a while on their own and pottered around the side of the building with furtive chuckles and a flash of silver hip-flask. His father could drink like a sponge but had an unfortunate tendency to lead weaker tipplers on. After a while the pair returned, greatly relaxed, and proceeded to chortle over the community centre notices, one by one, back on common ground for the first time since the occasion when one of them had been paying so handsomely for the wedding of the other's son.

Several cars arrived in quick succession. The first bore Jake's sister Tessa, who was to be a godmother, and her husband and toddler. They had given a lift to Tessa's painter friend, Faber and his daughter Iras. (Jake was frightened of blind people and found he couldn't look Iras Washington in the face, precisely because she was unable to return his gaze.) Then there was the priest. At last. He was a bouncy, overweight man in a collar and tie whom Jake had only spoken to by telephone. His tie was red leather, his crucifix a discreet gold lapel badge. He was late, he said, because none of the local shops stocked anything but birthday-cake candles. He did his well-meaning best to chuckle over the same things as the grandfathers then went inside to find candlesticks. The nanny, Samantha, came next with some Australian friends who had been helping her get things ready for the party. They were closely followed by Candida, a wailing Perdita in her arms and a grandmother guarding each flank. Jake told Candida that Robin had gone missing but she was already cross beyond caring.

'Give him ten, then come in and we'll start,' she said. 'After all, it's not vital we have him in the church. It's only a ceremony. He'll still be her godfather.'

Jake started to protest that it was precisely because of Robin that they were bothering to gather together so untypically in the sight of God at all, but she had gone in, leaving him to wait for Robin, and the grandmothers to marshal their husbands in before them.

When Robin did appear, in the ninth minute, it was on a double-decker. Jake failed to recognize him at first because of his beard. He only guessed it was Robin because, although he was in jeans and tee-shirt, he was accompanied by a young monk in a pale grey habit and sandals.

'Sorry we're late,' Robin called out when they were still yards away. 'Luke kept telling me we should take a taxi, but I knew there was a bus that came right past here so we just had to wait and see.'

'He was right, of course,' said the young monk. 'Was he always right when . . . when you knew him?'

'Yes,' said Jake. 'As I recall. Hello, Robin.'

'Hello,' said Robin. 'This is Brother Luke.'

'For heaven's sake!' laughed Luke and nudged him. 'Just Luke would be fine,' he told Jake with a smile. Jake shook his hand.

'Luke was sent by the Abbot to spy on me,' said Robin. 'We are horribly late, aren't we?'

'Yes.'

'Candida and Perdita already in there?'

'Very.'

Robin pulled a comic-apologetic face and took Luke's elbow.

'We'd better get in, then. See you afterwards?'

'Of course,' said Jake.

He lingered to check the guest list for anyone else who should have arrived, Candida had written 'P.O.' for 'Party Only' by all the remaining names, so he turned inside. Robin had acted as though their separation were a matter of hours not years. Jake was uncertain whether to be hurt or touched. He decided on reflection to be hurt.

13

It was the first time that Faber had set foot in a church for anything but a concert or an exhibition since the funeral of a close friend in America some years ago, just before he'd adopted Iras. His house was a church of sort, (the Elim Temple of the Pentecost, no less,) but it was deconsecrated and so didn't count. He was uncertain whether the St Thomas Community Centre should count either. The building had been cheaply divided up into office-like units. The chapel was little more than a four-square greenhouse. Orange hessian curtains were clearly intended to dampen the acoustics and to stop the room from becoming too hot, but were draped in the wrong places, so failed in either duty. The altar was a pine table and the font, tucked in one corner, could have come from a nearby garden centre. He was to gather from a conversation with the priest over lunch that the complete lack of ornament in the place was due to the council's original intention to use it as 'multi-denominational Church of the World'.

He spotted the Maitlands as soon as he entered. The obnoxious Jasper Browne was standing on the chair in front of them, telling what looked like a complicated story involving the picture he had just scribbled inside a hymn-book. Jasper raised the volume indignantly when Andrea turned away from his narration and saw Faber. She smiled and mouthed,

'Hello!'

Iras had insisted on coming out without her stick this

morning. Thrown by the sudden violent change in acoustic, she clutched his arm as they crossed the church. Jasper broke off his story to stare at her and seemed on the point of making some unintelligent enquiry. Luckily his Aunt Tessa had finished gently berating her father about something and was coming across to claim a kiss from her nephew.

'Jasper!' she said. 'What a grown-up suit!'

With an understanding smile at Andrea, she swooped on the child, kissing his brow and bore him away to say hello to his uncle. Briefly transformed by vanity, he submitted.

Andrea and Peter changed seats to make room for Faber and Iras.

'Ignorant little boy,' said Iras quietly, using 'boy' as a term of insult.

'Hello, Faber,' said Peter. He reached across to shake hands after which his wife kissed Faber's cheek. Sat between them, Iras kissed the air in mimicry and received a kiss in turn.

'That's a pretty dress, you've got on,' Andrea told her.

'Is it?' she said. 'Good. Is this going to take very long?'

'Not very,' Andrea promised.

'I thought you wanted to come,' said Faber.

'Well, I did. Quite. I've never been to a christening. What's it for?'

'Well,' said Peter, 'people who believe in the devil and think that babies need protecting from him ask friends of theirs to promise to fight the devil on the baby's behalf.'

Iras snorted.

'Is that all?' she asked.

'Well, no,' said Andrea, flicking through her old prayerbook, 'they promise other things.'

'What things?'

'Er . . . Let's see.' She found the appropriate page. 'Because the baby can't do the talking for herself they promise, in her name, to "renounce the devil and all his works, the vain pomp and glory of the world, with all covetous desires of the same, and the carnal desires of the flesh, so that they will not follow nor be led by them".'

'I see,' said Iras, cynical beyond her years. 'What then?'

'Then they reaffirm their belief in God and Christ and so on – they have to be confirmed Christians . . .'

'Is Robin a confirmed Christian?' Peter interrupted.

'Now that you mention it, we never had him done. He was christened, of course, but when the school asked if he wanted confirmation class he said no – don't you remember? But of course, he's a Christian now. I think.' A quick look of awful doubt spread across her face and she swept it aside with a smile and a brief sigh to Iras. 'What else?' she said. 'Well . . . That's it really. Except they promise on the baby's behalf to "keep God's holy will and commandments, and walk in the same all the days of their lives". Then the Priest splashes the baby's head and makes the sign of the cross on it with Holy water.'

'What's that?'

'Water that he's already made the sign of the cross over, I suppose. Water he's blessed.'

'Ah,' said Iras, and stifled a yawn.

'Then we go back to Perdita's house and have a party,' Faber told her.

'Can I drink wine there?'

'If you're extremely good, I might let you have a thimble-ful.'

'Good. Do you mind if I read a bit now?'

'Not at all.'

Faber smiled over her head at Andrea as, with the air of one who has wearied of amusing her juniors, she opened her braille edition of *Bleak House*, found her place and began to read.

'Where's Robin?' he asked her as the wailing of a baby announced the arrival of mother and child causing all heads but Iras's to turn in reflexive, smiling unison.

'Don't know,' muttered Andrea. 'Poor baby's *hideous*,' she whispered then went on, 'I think he's gone for a walk.'

'He'll be here soon,' Peter assured them half-heartedly, deep in a perusal of a copy of the parish notes.

'He's getting through so much pocket money,' she muttered. 'I wouldn't mind – he's looking for a job, after all – but he will keep giving it all away to people.'

'What people?' Faber asked.

'Anyone. People in cafés. Sad people. Beggars, mostly. All those pathetic girls with dirty babies you see around Trafalgar Square. That's why he's always late. He empties his pockets to a succession of hard-luck stories then has to walk home. Too sweet.'

'But a trifle irritating,' Peter added.

Andrea had paid several visits to the Elim Temple of the Pentecost since Robin's return, to sit at Faber's kitchen table and wail. It seemed that all the maternal concerns that she had kept in abeyance for the past eight years had returned on the same train as her son. She found herself worrying about the strength of his vocation, about where he was all day and whether he was eating enough, about whether she and Peter should not perhaps be more interfering, about the many ways in which Robin had changed and the many ways in which, alas, he had not. On his side of the studio, Faber would continue to paint and, growing increasingly dissatisfied with this man he had still to meet, assure her that Robin was nearly thirty and therefore old enough to look after himself. Yesterday she had come around in the evening, ostensibly to show off the blouse she had just bought for the baptism, but actually to moan. And Faber had made her cry. He told her that it was too late in the day to be worrying about Robin, that, if she really cared, she should have intervened eight years ago instead of blithely accepting that yes, her perfectly healthy, intelligent, atheist son had suddenly decided to join a strange monastic community unrecognized by the established churches. She had cried, he had given her a gin and had ended up letting her telephone Peter to say that Faber had asked her to stay for supper. Now Faber watched the priest lighting candles and considered that, having been such a good neighbour all week, it was meet and right that he find himself in a church at the end of it.

Candida was in place in the front row. Her mother and another woman of similar age and mould whom Faber assumed to be Jake's, sat beside her, alternately trying to hush Perdita's indignation and offering advice as to how the other could best do so. An enormous West Indian, whose suit gleamed in the sunlight and could barely contain him, had already run through the brief span of his devotional repertoire on the electric piano. He had played his version of *I Vow to Thee my Country* for the second time and was now starting on what sounded suspiciously like a Dusty Springfield number in a sort of devotional shawl. When a young monk came in accompanied by a skinny man with an Elizabethan beard, Iras had begun to hum along with the music rather too loudly. Faber's assumption that the young monk was Robin was confirmed by a ripple of interest through the scant congregation and by Andrea, who reached across Iras to tap Faber's leg and nod encouragingly in the new arrivals' direction.

They sat a row ahead, across the aisle. The bearded man muttered something to Robin and the two of them turned round smiling, to look at Andrea and Peter. The parents fell to whispering as soon as their son had turned to the front again. The bearded man didn't turn away. He had seen Faber and was staring. Faber stared back and was about to be offended when the spell was broken by Jake walking rapidly down the aisle between them to take his place by his wife. The bearded man glanced up at Jake then back to Faber, smiled at this invitation to conspiracy then faced the front. He had china-blue eyes, like a baby's. With the lower part of his face masked in beard, their blueness and their small wings of laughter lines were thrown into sharp relief.

At last the priest stood up.

'Hi,' he said. 'Perdita's mum has asked for *All Things Bright and Beautiful*. You'll find the words under number 45 in your copy of *Hymns for Now!*. I'm sure you all know the tune.'

'Finally,' said Iras rather too loudly, and they all stood and sang, while Perdita roared a descant.

14

Robin was late for the christening, naturally. Luke, of all people, had rung up the night before to say that he was in London for his father's funeral and was Robin all right. Robin said they should meet up and was he all right? So they fixed up to meet for breakfast in the National Gallery as Luke was in Holloway somewhere and Trafalgar Square was roughly a halfway point between his hotel and The Chase.

Luke was not especially all right. He had come away wearing his novice's habit as an approach-me-not armour. It turned out that his father had been in some kind of home for years. He was all that remained of Luke's family and had suffered from a condition that effectively turned him back into a baby. Luke's mum had been his nurse at first but she had later died of cancer and, there being no money, Luke had to sign papers for his father to go into state care. He told Robin all this over breakfast and Robin gave him a good talking to for not asking him along the day before as moral support. Luke said it was all very quick and a merciful release but Robin could tell he was buttoning his lip rather because he kept trying to change the subject, asking Robin questions about himself.

In the end Robin told him. They took a stroll around the weird John Martins of the Elysian Fields and the end of the world. Robin said that basically he was coping but that he was having a bad attack of the Rip Van Winkles. Luke had been away on Whelm for even longer than he had, Robin pointed out. Didn't he find everyone had changed in his absence? But Luke said that his nose had been in a book all the way to Holloway and that nursing homes and crematoria were fairly timeless places. So Robin took him away from the John Martin apocalypses and paradises and made him come for a walk outside. He made him look through a copy of the magazine called *Capital*. He made him look at the posters, at the things people were buying in the shops, and the things they were paying to see in the theatre. He showed him how all the cars were new and all the people's faces had closed up. But Luke was singularly unimpressed and just put an arm around Robin's shoulders (which raised some strange glances, not least for his being in his St Francis costume) and gave him a compassionate lecture on how there had always been greed and selfishness.

'I'm afraid you'll have to take it as a good sign,' he said. 'All this was here before but in those days you were too trusting and you didn't notice it. Now you've grown inside. You won't be betrayed again.'

'But I don't like being "grown inside",' Robin said, 'if this is what it's like. I think I'd rather be shut away, like you.'

'You can't just "rather be",' Luke told him. 'You've got to want to be, to have to be. Stay a little longer. You'll cope.'

'Jonathan said I could come back straight away,' Robin protested. 'He said I didn't have to prove anything to anybody.'

'But he doesn't know you like I do. Now that you've come back, you've got far too much to prove to be able to go and sit still in Whelm for long.'

'But I sat still there for years.'

'You didn't have much option,' Luke said.

He asked him when the christening was. That jogged Robin's memory (which hadn't been too strong since his return) and he realized he was already late for it. He told Luke he had to come too because he had every intention of making him see how dull and strange everyone had become and so convince him to take him back to Whelm. Robin's memory had kept a hold on its list of public reference libraries and good bus routes, for some no doubt metaphysical reason, so they hopped on a double-decker and went to watch Perdita being made over to Jesus.

Jake was waiting for him at the door. Robin had been slightly dreading this particular encounter. Luke had guessed this, typically. The bus pulled up right outside the Community Centre so Luke had time to see Jake standing there, to touch the back of Robin's hand and say,

'I'm here.' Sweet of him, but useless, of course.

Jake looked a little worn away, but then this was eight years, a career, a wife and two children beyond when Robin had seen him last. Jake's hair was still all there and still curly. His face still bore a built-in apology. He still held his hands behind his back rather than put them in his pockets. He had lost, however, the immeasurable ingredient that had made his simple attractiveness an invitation to folly. Robin's heart was sinking as they left the bus and he was all prepared to greet Jake with school-reunion sobriety to mask the awkwardness of having suffered a kind of death on his account. Then he met Jake's eyes and felt this drastic, invisible alteration. He remembered that on their last, briefest encounter he had tossed Jake's incalculably valuable final year essays into Jake's full, hot bath, so he smiled instead, and deepened the apology on Jake's face by introducing him to Luke with no explanation.

'I'm glad you made it, Dob,' Jake said, having shaken both their hands.

'We're unforgivably late,' Robin told him.

'Well, yes,' Jake replied, with a twitch of a smile, and gestured for them to hurry in. Luke threw Robin a quick, accusatory glance as they paused in the aisle, a centre of attention. Robin pointed crossly to two empty chairs and they sat down.

Robin looked around him. His parents were there. His mother was looking anxious and slightly reproachful, as she had been ever since Robin's return. It had been something of a surprise to learn that she had been in regular communication with the Abbot; Robin had not realized that Whelm's rule of honesty could be bent to allow the withholding of information from members of its community. Taking her lack of curiosity to mean that she had already been told all there was to know about his condition in the past few years, Robin told her nothing. It had come as a shock to find her beloved garden paved over and turned into a playground. He was touched to think that this revolution in their lives had been a direct result of his 'almost-death', but now that he was back the arrangement felt strained, as though his unlooked-for presence were throwing some delicate domestic equation out of true. The appalling, yappy Brevity was as much a son-replacement as the kindergarten and Robin felt bound to regard the dog with the chilly politeness of a resurrected first wife for her successor.

Altogether charming, however, was the change in Dad. His last-ditch bid for eccentricity, throwing in his job at Warburg and Orff for a life of multi-cultural fairy tales and potato-printing, disarmed his son. Dad still wore spiritual pin-stripes, but he had proved himself human and slightly mad, which left Robin to draw the sentimental conclusion that he had been short-changing his father all his life. Determined to compensate in some way, he had begun a one-man campaign to get him back into an orchestra, even if only a local one. Every evening, after supper, he had forced him to sit down with his clarinet and practise. At first Dad had acted all embarrassed, treating it like a party-game humiliation, then he had tried to make feeble excuses about helping to wash the dishes or catching up with some television serial, then quite suddenly he had begun to practise without Robin's bullying him. He was keen again. Mum still sang with her choir, after all and Robin decided that Dad envied her this.

There was a girl beside his parents in the chapel, a twelve or thirteen-year-old, who seemed to be fast asleep. And beside her sat a man. He was black, about thirty and with an expression that could only be described as luminous. His skin was smooth, his nose perfectly Roman and he had a strong-willed, inviolate air like a piece of living propaganda for some difficult but beneficial philosophy. Robin could not stand the unreality of him so he tried to make him smile. He beamed at him without success at first but then, once they had mumbled through *All Things Bright and Beautiful* and the godparents were gathered around the font, Perdita roared so loudly that the priest had to shout the bit about 'grant that carnal affections may die in her' to make himself heard. The service actually broke down for a moment. The congregation turned briefly into an audience and laughed out loud. Candida didn't laugh, she was too busy trying to stifle the baby, and neither did Jake, who'd been in a satisfactory sulk throughout. But Robin laughed and he caught the black man's eye again and made him smile back.

15

'Jasper, *will* you stop whining!' begged Candida. 'And let go of my skirt.'

Jasper persisted in hanging on. The skirt was made of a delicate cotton and his hot little hands were crushing two fistfuls of it. Judging by the quantity of egg mousse around his mouth, they were probably staining it too. Candida's mother, able once more to appear at the same functions as Candida's father, now that the stepmother was thoroughly out of the way, had never been so welcome.

'Need a hand, darling?' she offered.

'Oh, Ma. Could you?'

'Come along, Jasper, poppet. Come and see your uncle's smart new car,' she wheedled.

'Don't want to,' Jasper told the skirt. 'Seen it. Ugly and . . . and very boring.' The little tableau was beginning to attract an amused audience. First Perdita had played up, and now the ex-baby. Candida was close to cracking point.

'Ma?' she asked, dangerously.

Ma stooped and took her grandson firmly by the armpits.

'Lovely car,' she assured him, 'lovely *German* car!', and bore him off.

'At last!' Candida clapped her hands together and laughed for the benefit of her onlookers. 'Somebody give a mother a drink.' Samantha was passing with two full glasses for somebody. Candida took one.

'Oy!' the nanny complained without thinking.

'Thanks, Sam,' said Candida and went on a tour of her party.

Faced with the ghastly prospect of the St Thomas Community Centre, she and Jake had decided to invite only nearest and necessary to the service and to summon the rest straight to the house a little later. This also neatly saved neglected candidates for godparenthood the pain of seeing who had been chosen over them. There were about fifty guests in all: family, a clutch of good friends and then a crowd of broadcasting and advertising colleagues. The buffet laid out in the kitchen had been laid waste by the hungry and the disaffected. Candida came in to find something among the ruins to blot up her alcohol and surprised some children highly amused at something awful they were doing with a beef bone and some strawberries. She left them to it, drained as she was of grown-up rage, and grateful that at least they were occupied and in one easily washable place. She paused in the hall to sign a stranger's plaster cast then carried on to the conservatory and the garden where most of the guests were surrendering to champagne and autumn sun.

Her mother and father were burying their post-divorce differences in the conservatory swing seat, at least, her mother was burying their differences and her father seemed beyond either protest or withdrawal. She looked for Robin and found Jake instead. His cheeks were flushed in a way she would once have found sweet.

'Hello, wife,' he said and kissed her cheek.

'Hi,' she said. 'Have you seen Robin?'

'He's sitting on the hammock with Faber Washington.'

'*Still?*'

'Yes. I've scarcely managed to get a word in. He looks well.'

'Doesn't he. Shame about the beard, it ages him so.' She shifted so as to see the two men draped across opposite sides of the hammock as though it were a Victorian love-seat. Robin was laughing aloud at something, Faber Washington looking less certain. Andrea Maitland was watching her son too, from a deckchair on the terrace. She turned, saw that Candida had seen her watching and smiled benevolence. Candida smirked and, feeling caught out, looked back to Jake. He had been poached by Peter Maitland, however, and drawn into some argument with one of the better-looking men among her researchers.

Candida rose from the momentary vexation to her duties as a hostess. She snatched a passing, fullish bottle with a proprietorial grin and topped up a few glasses on her way to Andrea.

'There you are,' she said, emptying it into Andrea's glass. 'The luck of the bottle.'

'Oh, no more children, please!' Andrea begged.

'Is that what it means?'

'Usually. Unless you're not married, in which case I think it's meant to mean you'll be married within the year. Like catching a bride's bouquet.'

'Was one child enough for you?'

'I think so,' Andrea said. Candida noticed that she wasn't touching her glass and wished she had saved the champagne for herself. 'They need so very much and every new child means a halving of whatever you have to give. Not that it isn't perfectly lovely about Perdita . . .' she added hastily and drank some champagne after all. Fast.

'Mmm.' Candida said. 'I've had enough of my two for the moment.'

'Oh dear,' said Andrea and gave an unfocussed smile at the crowd beside them to fill the pause. 'She did cry rather hard, poor thing,' she added.

'Certainly did,' Candida agreed. 'She's asleep now and if she wakes before six, her grannies are *welcome* to her, bulging nappy and all. Whose is that?' She pointed at the blind girl, sitting in a corner of the garden on her own and reading in such sinister oblivion to the chatter around her.

'Iras Washington. Faber's daughter.'

'Is it really? I didn't recognize her. Of course, I haven't seen her since Faber did the painting of me and Jasper; she was tiny then.'

'That must have been when she was still coming to the kindergarten.'

'Oh. She didn't go to a . . . a *special* school?'

'Not then. Faber and I agreed that it was best for her to be with sighted children. But she had to go in the end, not because of her disadvantage, just because she was so very brilliant.'

'Tell me more.'

'Well, her brain is exceptional. She was learning to read with her braille tutor long before any sighted children of her age. I think it's because she couldn't fiddle around with pots of paint like the rest of them, she just jumped the picture stage and went straight to words.'

'So keen to communicate?'

'Exactly. But it hasn't stopped there. The special schools teach them how to use computers now. I think the machines are basically word processors but the keyboard and print-out are in braille. Naturally, once they've learnt to tap away on a braille board you just have to plug them onto a traditional printer and, hey presto, communication. The thing is, little Iras has developed a flair for fiction.'

'Sweet little stories?' Candida picked a hair off her dress.

'Far from it. Faber says she's nearly finished her first full length novel and that it's most alarmingly grown-up.'

'How exciting!'

'The trouble is that it's cutting her off,' Andrea went on with a wave of her hand. 'As he says, it's all very well for a writer of twenty-five to shut herself away in a garret, but at twelve she's hardly in a position to know if she's doing the right thing.'

'Fascinating,' said Candida, with only half her mind because Robin had stood up. 'Andrea are you sure you've had enough to eat and everything?'

'Perfectly, thanks. It's all so delicious. And, well, I'm so glad you asked Robin.' She laid a cool hand on the back of Candida's own. 'You were such friends for so long. It was time to start talking again.'

Candida hugged her briefly because it seemed the easiest thing to do.

'Yes,' she said. 'Thanks.' She extricated herself, and saw the rather pretty young monk, hovering to talk to Andrea. 'Now,' she said, 'I must go and be good.' She stood, shaking out her skirt. 'But do keep in touch, now, won't you?'

'Of course,' said Andrea and noticed the monk with a tipsily vague smile.

Robin was standing alone because Faber had just left his side to talk to his peculiar daughter. Candida crossed the lawn towards him but was beaten to her goal by Jasper who came charging across from the summer house.

'It's you again,' he said.

'Yes,' admitted Jasper, twining short fingers in the hammock strings. 'So. If we've just been to church and if you're a holy man, why aren't you dressed like the one over there?'

'If you're a little boy, why aren't you dressed like that one on the climbing-frame?'

'No,' said Jasper, wriggling. 'That's not fair. I'm not that little, anyway.'

'True,' said Robin. 'You're fairly fat, really.'

'Mummy!' the child objected, turning to Candida for support.

'Run along, darling,' she told him.

'I'm talking to the holy man,' he said. 'I've nearly finished.'

'Jasper?' she warned.

'So, what makes you think I'm a holy man?' Robin asked him.

'You come from a holy man's island. And Daddy said you were, I think, and Andrea, your mother.'

'Well, not all holy men look alike.'

'But. Oh. OK,' Jasper replied, then saw the other little boy move to the swing and sprinted off to defend his property.

Robin turned to Candida.

'Hello,' he said. 'Irritating son you've got.'

'I thought you and Faber Washington would never get out of the hammock. Nobody liked to interrupt you.' She felt herself leer. 'We were beginning to think it was true love.'

'Could well be,' he said quietly.

'Your mum was just telling me about his daughter's gifts,' she told him, ignoring this.

'Does he have a daughter?'

'Yes. Adopted. Didn't he tell you?'

'Funny. No. He didn't. We were talking about gods and baptisms and things. She's a lovely baby,' he added, with a kind smile.

'No, she's not. She's vile.'

'Well. She was fairly vile today, and no one's baby looks especially appealing to start with.'

'Perdita Margaux Browne is hideous,' she heard herself say.

'Who did think of that absurd name for her?'

'Joint effort. I'd wanted a Perdita ever since doing Florizel in *A Winter's Tale* in school, and Jake's mother's a Margaux.'

'Is she, now?' He looked across at the conservatory where Margaux Browne was now spreading herself for a talk with his own mother. 'Yes. She looks like a Margaux.' He stopped to pick a white rosebud which he tugged through a buttonhole of his black cotton jacket. 'Candida, could I see that portrait again, the Faber Washington, now that I've met him?'

'Of course. Come on. Shall I get the man himself to explain it to you?'

'No,' he said, 'It doesn't need explaining.' He put an arm around her shoulder. 'Let's just go. Can we walk round and go in by the front door to miss all the people?'

Still with his arm around her and with her daring to place her own around his waist, they half-circled the house.

'This feels too good,' she thought. 'Why am I doing this?'

'Thank you for coming today, Dob,' she said.

'Thank you for asking me. But I'm not Dob anymore, you know.'

'Sorry. Robin, then. Why not Dob? I liked Dob.'

'Why not Candy?'

'I've become a media star. I haven't been Candy since I was a researcher on *Coffee Morning*. Samantha calls me Candy, but she's Australian. I call her Sam to get my own back.'

'Who's Samantha?'

'The nanny.'

Robin stopped on the landing and turned to her.

'You have a *nanny*?'

'And a cleaning lady on weekdays.' She chuckled. 'Isn't it awful?'

He carried on towards the painting.

'It's worse,' he muttered. 'Christ, it's clever!' he added, almost at once.

'What?' she asked, then saw that he meant the painting and shut up.

It was a clever painting, catching the loving absorption of the scene even while rendering it with a certain coldness. She remembered distinctly the two mornings she had given up for preliminary sketches and photographs. Faber Washington had made housecalls in those days, like a doctor. In those days she had been as close as she ever came to abandoning all attempts at a career in order to sit back, have babies and woo Jake's bosses; she had seemed so bad at work, so good at having babies. The old rocking-chair she sat on to nurse Jasper for the sittings had been disastrously restored last year. She realized too late that its principle charm had lain in the bad repair of its rushwork seat; in replacing this, she had wrecked the chair and remorse had forced her to remove it to the nursery.

'Of course, it doesn't look much like you,' Robin said.

'It looked like me then.'

'Were you really that shape?'

'I'd just had Jasper.' She came to stand beside him. 'It's funny, but because I see it every morning and every night, I don't really look at it any more. The only thing that I really notice now is how desperately dated those clumpy yellow sandals look.'

'I helped you buy those.'

'That's right,' she laughed. 'From that hippy couple in the market.'

'I bought some too, green ones.'

'They had soles made from old car tyres. So comfortable. I lived in them.'

'Candy lived in them.'

'Mmm.' She paused. 'Dob?'

'Robin.'

'Robin?'

'Yes?'

'Are you going back to Whelm very soon?'

'Probably tonight.'

'Oh. What a shame. I thought that perhaps . . .'

'Hell!' He started downstairs at a run. She followed him.

'What's wrong?' she called. Jake was in the hall, waving some friends of his off; mystery squash partners probably.

'What's the rush?' he asked Robin, laughing. 'Have we turned out so very unspiritual?'

'Have you seen Luke?' Robin asked, not laughing.

'Who's Luke?' asked Candida, coming down beside them.

'Dob's friend from Whelm,' Jake told her. 'We had a good talk. He trained as an engineer before he . . . And he actually knows Lurking Kimberley – you know, that village where you saw the cottage you wanted to buy?'

'Is he still here?' Robin almost shouted.

'We're not to call him Dob anymore,' said Candida in an undertone. People were coming in to find discarded jackets and bags.

'No, he isn't,' Jake went on. 'He went about ten minutes

ago, said he had a train to catch, but he left a note for you on the table there.'

'Where?'

'Over there.' Jake pointed.

Robin raced to the table, snatched up the note, swore and ran out of the open front door.

'Something up?' asked Candida's father, drifting out of the sunshine by the same route.

'Nothing at all, Julian,' Jake told him. 'One for the road?'

Candida walked out onto the porch and watched Robin run halfway round the square then give up and walk back, red and panting, into the garden. Faber Washington was standing just inside the side gate and they fell into another conversation and drifted out of sight. She picked up the note he had dropped in his hurry.

'You'll cope, Robin,' it said, then 'Talk to Iras Washington sometime. Blessings. Luke.'

She folded it several times, neatly, but on her way round the side of the house let it fall.

16

On one, sometimes two nights of the week, Andrea made her way from Clapham to a public hall in the City for choir practice. Since the traffic was always slow at that time, she would take the bus there rather than the dormobile. She enjoyed the opportunity this gave her to do nothing more strenuous than stare out of the window or read without shame one of the horror or crime paperbacks she bought for the purpose; something with a suggestion of violence on the cover.

For all its bluff, amateur atmosphere, the choir was a much-praised and busy one. Attached to a major orchestra, it made something in the region of three records, two short tours and ten London appearances each year. The choir master was a professional, employed by the orchestra, but the singers were representatives of every world save the musical one. There was a high-court judge among the basses, a star of the tenor ranks was an Irish plasterer and one of the sopranos was a kind of orderly in the London Zoo monkey house. The group's heterogeneity meant that it functioned like a masonic lodge; all manner of useful contacts could be made through friendly introductions, then cherished over the mid-rehearsal visit to the pub. When Peter was still a broker with Warburg and Orff, Andrea had often gleaned him helpful snatches of office gossip from judicious barside eavesdropping on two colleagues of his, a *basso profundo* director and a grim, comparatively young soprano called Melissa Something-Andrews who wore a grey velvet hairband and was one of the firm's legal advisors. Elsewhere in the choir there were lawyers to consult, town planners, dentists, typists, architects, linguists, a women-only plumber, a mechanic who spoke fluent Dutch, three estate agents and a second-hand car dealer. A travel agent contralto regularly fixed members up with cut-price flights and an extremely pretty manicurist, who always kept a seat for her, seemed to have taken up singing simply for the thriving trade she ran in the half-hour before each rehearsal. There was even a priest among the baritones, said to be available for exorcisms and informal confessions.

Andrea had joined as the last of her thirties were vanishing. Robin was a fairly grown-up teenager then, spending hours up in his room, working or deep in discussion with Candida. It was a time when many of Andrea's contemporaries and their husbands were going through the same awkward patch – unneeded by children, frightened of admitting that either might be slightly bored with the other and anxious not to submit an ageing relationship too soon to the test of a return to life *à deux*. Apart from the obvious, and far from certain solution of taking in lodgers, one or the other's widowed mother or a large, demanding pet, the awkwardness seemed most frequently neutralized by the adoption of time-honoured pastimes. With their back-to-school associations, hobbies (from embroidery to matchstick cathedrals) and evening classes (in anything but Psychology for Beginners) laid the perfect foundation for the mock-virginity of late middle-age. The Maitland family's garden had never been more than a long lawn with contented weeds and a few bushy roses around the edges so Andrea coaxed herself into taking up a trowel and for a while had tried to interest herself in bringing it up to neighbourhood scratch. Gardening only took over precious, inoffensive weekends, however, leaving bare the awful stretch of weekday evenings: frantically conversational suppers, from which Robin escaped as soon as possible, followed by four long hours of television, reading or – most dreaded of prospects, – each other.

It wasn't that she was ever bored with Peter, not really, but as they were left increasingly alone together, she had sensed him growing bored with her. The gradual erosion of her few slender mysteries had been worrying enough during courtship – letting him discover what, if anything, she did with her spare time, what she ate, how often she washed her hair – but the destruction after marriage of almost all barriers save, in her case, the bathroom door, had been cause for major alarm. The idea of a weekly musical vacation from each other came to her from a bad historical novel she had borrowed from the library, just for a change, in which a young wife in Edwardian Middlesborough joined a madrigal society. The wife hoped that by gently arousing her husband's jealous curiosity then restoring him her company after two hours' deprivation, she could refresh her charms. Andrea's charms for Peter lay as much, she was sure, in such perilously temporal areas as her bosom as in the quality of her mind. Determined not to spread herself too thin, she auditioned for the choir and was accepted.

She finished the Middlesborough saga some weeks later, alarmed to find, too late, that the woman's husband used her choral absences for hot dalliance with his step-sister and that she found true love and a second marriage with a dashing organist from Gwent.

For some time Peter had been toying with the idea of reviving his clarinet-playing. When he announced that he, too, had been for an audition and would be playing with an amateur orchestra one night a week, she was mildly upset. Not only did his rehearsals happen on a night when she would be free, thus confirming her fears about his boredom, but it emerged that his percussion-playing secretary had suggested the audition, a complicity that smacked too much of Middlesborough. She could express nothing but delight, of course. It was only fair.

On her night out (or nights out when the season was a demanding one), she took care to leave him her love in the shape of a meal complete with full serving instructions. She was ashamed to admit that, percussive secretary notwithstanding, she soon came to enjoy the nights when he was with the orchestra and it was her turn to be on her own. Robin would be there for supper (briefly as ever, but it gave them a chance to talk in a way that they never could in Peter's presence) then she would lie on the sofa and make long phone calls around the family or watch a film or go to bed early and write letters there. Peter had expressed disappointment at being deprived of her company two evenings a week, but she suspected that this was no more than a handsome gesture and that he had as good a time on his own as she did – perhaps some whisky (this was before he gave up) and a radio play. He maintained that radio plays were far superior to anything television could offer, but could never listen to them with her around because she couldn't focus her attention properly and would interrupt them with idle chat and amusing things she had forgotten to tell him over supper.

When Robin left for university (which was effectively when he left home, so small were the spans of holiday he spent in Clapham) Andrea had let herself be drawn into a deeper involvement with the choir. She took time off from the nursery school in Barnes where she then worked, and went on singing tours of Denmark, Israel and Holland, not enjoying herself greatly, because she missed Peter, but writing him long, amused letters and assuming that such extended leave from her presence would be a treat for him. When the choir librarian took time off to have a baby, Andrea stood in for her then accepted the post full-time when her predecessor miscarried and defected to sing for the BBC. Not content with the considerable task of ordering, numbering, distributing and recovering music, Andrea stood for election soon after this and was voted Alto Representative. This was a sort of Head Girl post. Any alto unable to attend a rehearsal had to call her in advance to apologize, she had to organize lift rotas for altos stranded in the suburbs, take headcounts, issue disciplinary warnings to absentees, sell choir pencils to those who had forgotten to bring one, welcome new girls and acquaint them with the vagaries of the dress and attendance codes.

When Robin ran away to become a monk and his childhood friend (to whom Andrea had shown such kindness, having her to stay for the entire summer holiday of her parents' divorce) married Jake Browne, Peter had gone to pieces. At first he took a week's holiday and, convinced that Robin had been brainwashed by some right-wing cult, had set about trying to get Abbot Jonathan to release him then, when that failed, trying to alert the police and press. Eventually, once Andrea was in communication with the Abbot, Peter accepted that Whelm was a bona fide religious community but the thought that his only child had rejected them both and the life for which they had so carefully nurtured him broke some inner support of his and he crumpled before Andrea's eyes. He didn't throw in his job and he wasn't sacked; it was a compassionate in-between with an early pension. He gave up the orchestra soon after that, or was tactfully eased out of it. The idea of starting a kindergarten of her own had always been at the back of her mind and she had never got over her relief at the way he had seized on her suggestion and used it to climb out of his collapse.

The visits to Marcus's hospital bedside and trips to the gym were now Peter's only regular outings from the house without his wife so, more than ever, Andrea clung to the choir as his important respite from her. She knew that he had no time in his life for fitting in any but the most self-effacing mistress. Inflamed by magazine articles, despite her intelligent scepticism, she nevertheless made half-jokes to Faber about her suspicions in the superstitious hope that these would defuse the risk.

The evening was cloudy-hot and humid and, with thin windows twenty feet off the floor and impossible to open, the practice hall was almost entirely unventilated. To make matters worse, a nervous fug lingered from an exam held in there that afternoon. Andrea had arrived early, as usual, and helped the Honorary Secretary set out chairs. He was a bossily efficient administrator with a military bearing she suspected of being bogus. He had never been particularly amiable towards Andrea but tonight it seemed that no courtesy would suffice.

'I say, you look well!' he said, and 'Easy now. We don't want to strain that graceful back of yours,' and then, 'I'll do the rest with young Tompkins, here. It's so frightfully stuffy in here tonight. You sit down there and get on with your bookery.'

So, perturbed but grateful, she sat at her table by the swing doors, reading some more of *Blood Will Out*, and occasionally signed out copies of *The Dream of Gerontius* to those who had missed its first rehearsal last week. The heat had made people pink and short-tempered so it was possible that she was mistaken in detecting a strangeness in the manner of the altos she greeted. The pianist arrived, deep in chortling conversation with the choirmaster, and the rehearsal began. The piece being a choral society standard, most of the singers knew it well and by halftime they had covered Gerontius's dreamed death and run once, erratically, through the devils' chorus. The men could leave early, it was announced, because the second half would be devoted to the women-only angelical sections.

'However,' the Honorary Secretary continued, 'an EGM has been called for.'

'What's an EGM?' Andrea's neighbour asked her.

'Extraordinary General Meeting,' Andrea told her.

'Presumably none of you gentlemen wants to come back from the pub just for that, so would anyone object if we held it now?' said the Honorary Secretary. 'Shouldn't take too long.' He looked around. There were questioning looks, not least from Andrea, but no objections. 'Right,' he said and cleared his throat. 'I declare this extraordinary general meeting open. Mrs President?'

The President, a soprano with an imposing manner and silver coiffure to match, rose to take the floor.

'Very briefly,' she said, 'I've been asked to call an election for the post of Alto Rep. It seems that Andrea Maitland, who has served us well and long, has a challenger in the person of Maeve Mckechnie.'

Andrea froze. She knew who Maeve Mckechnie was, of course, having welcomed her into the choir, but they had never spoken since then. Maeve Mckechnie went to a different, younger pub in the rehearsal interval and always sat in the back row, while Andrea sat at the front. Maeve Mckechnie had a close-knit circle of sharp-faced City-worker friends.

'Now, if you ladies could both stand up briefly in case anyone doesn't know which you are . . .' Andrea stood and heard a giggle somewhere behind her, presumably where Maeve Mckechnie was standing. 'Lovely,' the President went on. Andrea's cheeks were burning. This had never happened before; voice rep elections were only called on the announcement of a rep's death or voluntary retirement. She could sense the awkwardness around her. 'Right. You can both sit down, now.' Andrea sat. The tenors and basses were muttering, some even chuckling in embarrassed disbelief at this palace revolution. She could meet no one's eye but fixed her stare on the President's clipboard. 'Now, those voting for the present Alto Rep, Andrea Maitland, please raise a hand,' the President asked. Andrea felt hands rise close by, but the President's counting didn't take long. 'Thank you. And now, those voting for the new candidate, Maeve Mckechnie?' She began to count then said, 'Only *one* hand,' which raised a giggle. 'Thank you. Now, any abstainers.' There were several abstainers, kindly embarrassed at so public a taking-of-sides. 'There,' said the President with a satisfied smile, totting up figures on her clipboard. Her nickname, doubtless known to and enjoyed by her, was HRH. 'Now Andrea, do we have any absentees today?'

'Oh. Erm. Yes,' said Andrea, and felt for her diary. Her cheeks burned as she turned to the day's entry. 'Five,' she said.

'Would you like us to wait and find out their votes?'

'I don't think so. Unless you think they would . . .'

'Actually, it wouldn't make much difference,' the President warned her.

'Well, no, then,' Andrea conceded.

'In that case,' the President raised her voice and took a few paces back so as to be more in the centre of the choir's horseshoe, 'I announce that Maeve Mckechnie has been elected as new Alto Representative with thirty votes against Andrea Maitland's ten. There were five absentees and ten abstainers.'

Damn the abstainers, thought Andrea.

As was customary the choir clapped. Maeve Mckechnie's supporters cheered. The President begged for silence.

'And would we just show our appreciation for all Andrea's hard work. She will, of course, be continuing as choir librarian.' She turned on Andrea with a gracious smile. '*Thank* you, Andrea.' Several people were already halfway across the room to the pub but they paused to clap again.

'Is there any further business?' asked the President, hushing the chatter and stopping would-be drinkers in their tracks. Nobody offered further business. 'Very well then. Honorary Secretary, ladies and gentlemen, I declare this extraordinary general meeting over.'

There was a rush for the pub. Several people, including the President, came to shake Andrea's hand or pat her back with condoling murmurs. The Honorary Secretary, doubtless feeling that he had already done his bit by being charming before the event, disappeared without a word. Andrea sat on in the swirl of light Autumn cardigans and tangled chairs.

'Coming for a Guinness, old girl?'

She looked up. It was Victor, the used-car dealer. He had taken a long-standing shine to her and was forever standing her drinks. Or perhaps she merely aroused his compassion.

'Be with you in a sec, Victor,' she said. 'You go on.'

The hall was almost empty. A few of the women never went to the pubs but brought thermoses of coffee and boxes of homemade nibbles which they passed round amongst themselves in a corner. The pianist had already returned from the local hamburger bar with his customary milkshake. A few men were poring noisily over newspapers or displaying records they had brought in to lend to friends. Andrea picked up her bag, left her music on her seat and left. She walked past the pub, however, and the place where Maeve Mckechnie would be celebrating her victory, and stood at the bus stop for the journey home. There was no sign of a bus so, not wanting to be found waiting there when the singers emerged from their drinking, she damned the expense and hailed a taxi.

17

Peter was alone at the kitchen table trying to solve even half the crossword that Marcus had been filling out so effortlessly that afternoon. He had long ago abandoned the honourable method. Andrea's dog-eared 'backstairs' dictionary lay close to hand and he was riffling through Roget's Thesaurus in search of an elusive synonym for seduction that seemed to be spelt S blank blank blank P blank R Y. If he didn't find it soon he would be forced to go upstairs, burrow in the jumble of mending heaps, neglected embroidery and hoarded magazines under the sofa to find the Scrabble set; a three-dimensional alphabet often jogged his memory. It wasn't cheating, not as much as Roget's Thesaurus, even if it felt like it whenever Andrea caught him pushing and rearranging the little letters.

There was a newly familiar thunder on the stairs overhead – Robin coming down. Brevity was yapping at his heels. At first her jealousy at his return had sent her into a bleak decline. She had refused her food for days and spent hours on end unreachably beneath a tallboy in Andrea and Peter's bedroom. Now that it was understood that his visit would be a longish one, she had changed tactics and taken to trailing him adoringly through the house, all the more excited for his scorn. Robin stopped in the doorway and, bending, turned to face her.

'Go away,' he pronounced. 'I *hate* you.'

Brevity sneezed then rolled on her back and waved her legs at him. He snorted disgust and turned back to his father. He was transformed. He had been to a barber to have his hair cut and beard tidied. Peter felt he couldn't say anything, but his son had looked none too clean since his return and on some days had been downright smelly. Now he shone as though he had been scrubbed, and had brought a scent of sandalwood to the room. The black clothes, it would seem, had finally found their way to the laundry basket. Robin had dug out an old dark blue suit that was a hand-me-down from his paternal grandfather and a white collarless shirt that was spotless, if unironed. With a flash of red braces, he slung himself into a chair across the table from Peter.

'Aren't I smart?' he said with a knowing grin.

'Well,' Peter ventured, 'It is an improvement.'

'What are you stuck on?'

'I'm not stuck, exactly.'

'What's the clue?'

'"Blonde goddess is heard to lay foundations for naughtiness after success at rugby football." I've got S blank blank blank P-blank-R-Y.'

Robin frowned, looking suddenly like Andrea in a stage beard, and gently took the newspaper. He tapped the pencil across the squares as he counted letters in his head.

'Well,' he said, 'The S and P are wrong, for a start; it's "Husses" not "Skates" and "Torrid" not . . . What's that word, with the P?'

'Er. Oh. "Spires".'

'Spires?'

'Yes.'

'Where did you get *that* from?'

'Not sure.'

'Anyway,' Robin spared him, rubbing out the wrong letters and filling in three new words, 'it's "Torrid" in there which means we can put in "Harlotry" in six across.'

'Ah!' said Peter, as though he saw, but his curiosity got the better of him. 'Why?'

'"Blonde goddess is heard" — that's "harlo" which sounds like Harlow, as in Jean,' Robin explained. '"To lay foundations" that means harlo comes first. "After success at rugby football" that means you put "try" after "harlo" and the whole thing makes a word for naughtiness. Well. Not really, but if you look it up in the thesaurus they'll probably give it as a synonym.'

'Thanks.'

'Not at all.'

'Want to do any more?'

'No. It's all yours, but twelve down's an anagram.'

'Oh,' said Peter, taking the crossword back. 'If you say so. Are you going out?'

'Yes. I'm out for supper.'

'Where? Not that you have to tell me, or anything.'

'Faber's asked me.' Robin smiled at his father's delicacy. 'Faber Washington.'

'Oh. Your mother didn't mention it.'

'Why should she? I haven't told her.'

'But Faber's her best friend. Well. One of them.'

'Is he? He never said.'

'She's been going round to him for cups of coffee and stuff almost every day since you . . . while you were away. However unlikely it might seem.'

Robin stood and slouched, hand in pocket, to the dresser where he picked up an apple and bit into it.

'When does she get back from choir practice?' he asked, through his mouthful.

'Lateish. She does insist on taking the bus so she can read. About ten-thirty, usually.'

'You'll be OK then?'

'What an extraordinary thing to ask! Of course I'll be OK.' Peter laughed. 'Do I look as if I wouldn't?' The question was rhetorical but when Robin merely chuckled in reply, it felt less so. 'I was planning on having a session on the clarinet when I got fed up with this,' Peter continued.

'When are you going to find another orchestra to join?'

'I'm not all that sure I could face it.'

'Well, a wind band, then.'

'But I'm always so tired in the evenings.'

'No, you're not.'

'After hours of toddlers? I'm knackered. And anyway, I'm not back to that level yet.'

'Yes, you are. I heard you playing yesterday. It was fine.'

'I've forgotten half the fingerings. They come automatically on pieces I already know, but if someone gave me something to sight-read, I'd probably squawk like a beginner.' This was a lie; his technique was coming back more rapidly each day. 'Do you want a drink of something? Keep me company in my alcohol-free lager?'

'No. I must get going. See you.'

'I'll leave the chain off the back door so you can get in again. You know what a locker-up your mother is,' Peter said. The last words came out in a near-shout as Robin was already outside and closing the door between them.

Peter took another of the powerless beers from the fridge, flicked off the cap with an opener and gulped from the bottle. This, the eating of an unaccompanied pork pie (bought after a walk with Brevity, in a local pub that wasn't *their* local) and the devotion of an entire evening to the day's crossword were things peculiar to Andrea's choir nights, along with radio plays and long, mid-evening baths. None of these activities was especially hateful to Andrea or cherished by Peter but, initiated as consolation for his evenings without her, they had come to assume all the intimate witchery of sin. He returned to the table and was delighted to find that the three words inserted by Robin had made the crossword suddenly much easier. He entered 'Steerage', 'Trug' and 'Edict' before the bottle was finished. He took another from the fridge, opened it, threw Brevity a Doggy Roll to stop her feeling left out, filled in 'Corpse' and felt very pleased with himself.

There were rapid footsteps on the gravel. Brevity gave her single friends-and-family bark, knowing it was Andrea before the door had opened. Peter had no time to snatch a glass for his beer.

'Whatever's the matter?' she asked then pointed and laughed, 'Your face!'

'You were back quickly,' he said. Brevity was snuffling and turning circles. Andrea gave her a quick pat so that she could stop.

'I know,' she said, 'I took a taxi.'

'Good grief!'

'Just what I thought.'

'But you'd have been early even in the bus. What happened?'

'I've run away,' she said and sat on his lap. She sat carefully, as though worrying about the unusual move. She was still light; he couldn't imagine why she fussed so about her weight. She kissed his forehead. She was wearing a scent he hadn't smelled before. He liked the way it mingled with the faint, gingery tang she gave off whenever she had run or was hot. He chuckled, holding her round the waist.

'What? You've skipped the second half?'

'More than that,' she said proudly, 'I've skipped for good.'

'But why?'

'I wanted to be with you!'

'No, but really?'

'It was horrid, actually. There was a sort of uprising and they voted me out of carrying on as voice rep and suddenly I thought, Well if that's the game you're at, then I don't want to play any longer. I just jumped in a cab instead of going to the pub with the rest. I was in a panic at first, but then that sort of taxi comfort spread through me and I sat back and was all relieved and free. Oh, Pete, I'm so glad to have left! All those silly opinionated men and lone, lost females. Are you very horrified at having me back?'

'What do you think?' he asked her. 'Look at me. I was going to spend the evening drinking beers and doing the crossword.'

'Sounds lovely.'

'Not two nights a week, every week,' he said and kissed her. She kept her lips together, giving him a soft peck.

'It dawned on me on the way home,' she said, pulling back and arranging herself differently on his lap, 'that most of the people there were there for some painful reason. They're bored, frustrated, lonely, things like that. Of course they love music, and they may even tell themselves that that's why they go there – I know I did – but deep down they go for sad reasons.'

'Kiss me properly,' he said. 'You hardly ever kiss me properly nowadays.'

'I . . . oh,' she said and he pulled her against him, slipping his tongue between her parting lips. Her mouth always felt deliciously fresh inside, as though she had been eating snow. Still kissing, he slid her more firmly onto him, with her skirt up. They bumped the table and the beer bottle fell to the floor. It didn't smash but Andrea pulled back, startled and made housekeeping noises. The ginger in her scent made him tug her down into another kiss. Then she slid round and leant her back against his shoulder, staring up at the ceiling as he slid a hand round inside her blouse to cup one of her breasts. The nipple was rigid beneath his touch and he gently teased it with a fingertip, moved to see how hotly she blushed. There was a quiet, slapping sound from somewhere in the room.

'Brevity's drinking your low-alcohol lager,' she said.

'I know,' he told her. 'Don't you dare clear it up.'

'All right. I won't,' she promised and settled more heavily against him with a sigh.

'And don't you dare change your mind and go back to that choir next week,' he went on.

'I promise,' she said, and he remembered the leaflet he had seen in the reference library about auditions for a new amateur wind ensemble; remembered, and let it fall.

'Where's Dob?' she asked.

'Out for the whole evening,' he said.

'Where?'

'Faber Washington's.'

'Faber? But I . . .'

'. . . Why don't we go upstairs and change?' he cut in. She gave a dirty chuckle at this dusted-down code phrase from early marriage.

'Yes,' she said. 'Why ever not?'

'Then I'll call a cab and we'll go to *Les Pavoines* and drink a bottle of Bollinger and eat all the favourite things we never get to eat at home because the other one hates them.'

'A true celebration,' she sighed. 'But let's go upstairs and change first.'

18

He lived, they lived, in a converted chapel off the South side of the common, a long, totally symmetrical red-brick building with high windows, not unlike a Victorian schoolhouse. There was a small space at the front. One would hesitate to call it a garden; it was nothing but box hedge and dustbin. A sign, neatly painted in electric blue paint on yellow, announced,

This is no longer
the Elim Temple of the Pentecost
but a PRIVATE HOUSE.

There was a small ship's bell dangling from the lintel so Robin rang it once and waited.

He had tried to see Faber on the evening of the christening – Luke having abandoned him for the security of Whelm – but Faber said it was impossible. Robin rang the next day and suggested a film, but he found some excuse. Robin left him in peace for a while then asked if he'd like to come round to The Chase for supper but again Faber had an excuse. He was very kind about it; they laughed and chatted about nothing in particular, Robin asked him to supper and he said,

'That would be lovely, Robin, but I've got a meeting with Iras's tutor.' He said it without a moment's hesitation, so Robin knew it was a lie. The other excuses had been about Iras too. Then, the morning after that, Robin had a brainwave. He simply rang him up, very business-like, soon after breakfast, and spoke to his answering machine.

'I'm coming round for supper this evening,' he said. 'Eight o'clock.'

So here he was.

He stood there for a while with lorries crashing by in the road behind him and sparrows chattering crossly in the dirty hedge. Then a little, sliding panel shot sideways in the door and a girl's voice asked,

'Who is it?'

'It's Robin,' he said. 'I've come for supper.'

'Oh,' she said. 'You. Hang on.'

The panel slid shut again and the door opened. She stood to one side to let him in. She had on a pair of dark-blue cotton dungarees over a white tee shirt. She was wearing black lace-up plimsolls like the ones he remembered wearing for gym classes at school.

'Well? Come inside,' she said and he realized that he had been staring. He came in and she shut the door with a bang behind him. 'You're a bit early.'

'I told him eight.'

'Well he's not ready, anyway. He's dressing,' she went on. 'Please sit down.' He sat on one end of a large sofa.

'I suppose it helps to know where people are in a room,' he said.

'Fairly,' she replied, 'although I can usually tell that from the way sound bounces off them. You were feeling nervous, though, and sitting down seems to make people more relaxed. I often make people nervous. Faber says it's because I don't remember to smile enough. Dot – that's my tutor – Dot says that too. She says that people smile when they're nervous as well as when they're happy, which is why smiles make nervous people feel at home. Would you like a drink?'

'Well . . .'

'He had a glass of cold wine upstairs earlier, so there's probably an open bottle in the fridge.'

'Yes, please.'

She disappeared through a door behind him. The chapel had been converted simply. The main space was stripped of pews, except for a couple which had been left on either side of a long dining table, their hymn book shelves stuffed, as was every available surface, with newspapers, much-read paperbacks and paint-stained pieces of cloth. The original stairs ran up to the gallery on which two rooms had been built, leaving a landing the width of the building. Below the gallery were two more doors. Iras emerged from one of them, clutching a glass of white wine.

'The kitchen used to be where they arranged flowers and made tea,' she said, holding out his drink until he took it from her. She had not spilled a drop. 'And the bathroom's next door, where the priest used to dress up.'

'The vestry.'

'That's right,' she said. 'Don't worry. I'm going out with my best friend Peggy in a minute and I'll leave you alone.'

'I'm not worrying,' Robin said. 'How long have you been blind?' She sat on the other end of the sofa as one who has been told to keep a visitor amused.

'I'm not blind,' she corrected him, 'And I'm not visually disadvantaged, either. I'm just an eyeless person. Blind also means "Lacking in intellectual, moral or spiritual perception", which I'm not.'

'Sorry.'

'Would you like some music?'

'Yes.'

'Good. I'd put it on myself, but my hand always shakes and that scratches the record. The player's over there. My favourite album's on it at the moment.'

'Fine,' he said and went to put on the record. He noticed each in the pile of albums scattered by the machine had a small piece of punctured paper stuck to the sleeve. 'Nina Simone?' he checked.

'Yes,' she said. 'Put it on the third track. I want to test your hearing.'

Wondering why it was taking Faber so long to dress, Robin set the record playing as she asked and went back to the sofa. It was 'He's Got the Whole World in His Hands'. Robin had been made to join in performances of it at primary school, where it was sung in a jolly cotton-picker sort of way with much hand-clapping and a tambourine or two. Nina Simone sang it slowly, with only steady piano chords for accompaniment; a kind of solemn march. Robin felt he was hearing it for the first time.

He's got the whole world in his hands.
He's got the whole wide world in his hands.
He's got the whole world in his hands.
He's got the whole world in his hands.
He's got the fishes of the sea in his hands.
He's got the birds of the air in his hands.
He's got the fishes of the sea in his hands.
He's got the whole world in his hands.
He's got the gambling man in his hands.
He's got the sailing man in his hands.
He's got the gambling man in his hands.
He's got the whole world in his hands.
He's got the little bits of baby in his hands.
He's got the little bits of baby in his hands.
He's got the little bits of baby in his hands.
He's got the whole world in his hands.
He's got everybody here in his hands.
He's got you and me, brother, in his hands.
He's got everybody here in his hands.
He's got the whole world in his hands.

They sat through it in silence then Iras turned to him in the way that she had obviously been taught in some 'natural behaviour' class.

'What would you say it was about?' she asked, her pale, sleepwalker's face sharp with curiosity.

'Well, I was always taught to think it was about God. That's what most people think. They sing it in church, sometimes. In some churches.'

'Yes, but what do *you* think?'

'Well, I would have said it was about God, too, but now I'm not so sure.'

'It's about death,' she said. 'Sung like that it is, anyway. It makes much more sense. Shall we hear it again?'

'If you like. Yes. But what about Faber?'

'I told you. He's dressing. Go on. Put it on again.'

So Robin put it on again and she fetched him another glass of wine. While Nina sang, he looked at the big canvasses that were dangling from the beams overhead, broad examinations of human decay in the form of three barely-gendered down-and-outs. In the most finished, one stared at her/his empty bottle, stared at herself by the second, while the third bared a withered breast and grinned broadly out at the room. Robin wondered how much Iras knew about Faber's work.

This time she turned to him at the end of the song and asked,

'Now, think carefully and tell me what Death has in his hands in between the gambling man and everybody here.'

He thought a moment, running through the words in his head.

'The baby,' he told her. 'The little bits of baby.'

She crowed with triumph just as a door opened on the gallery and Faber appeared.

'Two against one!' she shouted, throwing her head back to face the sound of the door.

'Robin,' said Faber. 'Good evening. Has Iras got you something to drink? Good. Iras?'

'Robin says it's "Little bits of Baby" too,' she said still strangely triumphant. She turned towards Robin again, 'Faber said it was "Itsy-bitsy" . . .'

'Iras?' he repeated, more firmly.

'Yes?'

'Are you ready to go out? Peggy'll be here any minute.'

'I know,' she said. 'I'm ready.'

'You haven't brushed your hair.'

'I have.'

'Please, Iras? For me.'

She sighed crossly and started up the stairs but stopped at the sound of laughter outside. Someone rang the bell and Iras turned and ran to the front door. Robin was to learn that she only moved this fast at home, where she knew things. She opened the door and called over her shoulder,

'Don't wait up.'

'Hang on. I want to say hello to Peggy's mum,' said Faber, crossing the room, but she had already shut the door. Faber hurried to the bathroom and threw up the window there. The panes had been replaced with mirror, making the room rather dark. He leaned out in a sudden blare of traffic and pavement sunshine. Robin saw his bare feet. 'Dodie!' He called out, waving. She seemed to be on the other side of the road. 'No. Don't come over. The traffic. When'll you be dropping her off? . . . Great. Bye.' He pulled the mirrors down again, cutting the noise and turned back to the room. 'Drink,' he said. 'I've lost my glass. Yours all right?'

'Fine,' said Robin.

Faber wasn't meeting Robin's eye properly and seemed to seize this opportunity to go and bustle in the kitchen.

'That child,' he said. Sitting at last on a sofa several feet away from Robin's. He had opened another bottle. His glass was red.

'She's hardly a child,' Robin said.

'You noticed, huh?' His voice had an air of culture to it, like a newscaster's, but he softened the effect with an occasional Americanism. 'Would you like music?' he asked.

'Yes.' He started to stand. 'No,' Robin said, standing first. 'Let me. You talk. What would you like.'

'You choose. Anything but Nina Goddamned Simone. She's been playing that to death.'

'You could always try swopping the labels round to confuse her fingers.'

'That's not funny,' he said, deadly serious, then chuckled. Then he laughed. 'Yes, it is,' he conceded. 'How long had you been here?'

'Since eight. I forgot to be late, I'm afraid.' Robin picked through the pile. The collection was eclectic to the point of formlessness. Or perhaps there was a pattern? Gregorian chant rubbed shoulders with Stan Getz. Beatrice Lillie read Edward Lear poems on one record, Dinah Washington sang the blues on the next. He left the pile and looked in the shelf, hoping to find something neglected. Bartok. The *Cantata Profana*.

'Where did she tell you I was?' Faber had swung his legs up onto the sofa beside him. Their long thinness showed through the linen.

'Changing,' said Robin, coming back to his wine and sofa. 'You took long enough doing it.'

'I was asleep. I'd still be up there and she'd have gone out with Peggy and left you just sitting there, if she hadn't put that bloody record on again.'

'I'd have taken myself on an explore and found you.' Faber caught his eye, albeit briefly, but his laugh was nervous.

'She has no shame, you see. Embarrassment is such a visual complaint. What are we listening to?' he asked, looking away again.

'*Cantata Profana*.'

'Is it mine?'

'It was on your shelf.'

'Mmm,' he said, sipping wine. 'Someone must have lent it me.'

'Don't you like it?' Robin asked.

'Yes, I do,' he said. 'What are they singing about?'

'Do you really want to know?'

'Yes.'

'It's about a man with lots of sons. He complains that he doesn't want them to have the same dull life that he's had.

Then they all go for a romp in the forest without him. When they don't come back he takes a gun and goes out to look for them. He finds . . . Do you really want to hear this?'

'Yes,' he laughed. 'Go on. I'm hooked.'

'Well. He goes out to find them but comes across a big crowd of fine young stags instead. Naturally, being a ravenous Slav, he raises the gun to shoot them but they tell him, "Stop! It's us. Your sons." Well, then he tries to persuade them to come home and stop messing around but they refuse and say they've found a better way of life than his and want to stay in the forest for ever and ever. I think that's it. More or less. Can I have some more wine?'

'Yes. Give me your glass.'

'It's OK.' Robin wanted to see the kitchen. The walls were covered with postcards, cuttings, recipes, letters and the occasional bill. He brought the bottle back with him and set it on the floor between their sofas. The fugue was hotting up. 'I like that,' he said, pointing the bottle to the canvas where the tramp was smilingly revealing a battered dug. 'Very much.'

'It's weird,' said Faber, 'I think someone must have lent it me or left it behind or something. Some people are very bossy about bringing their own music to parties.'

'No, I meant the painting.' Faber turned, met Robin's gaze again and smiled. 'Oh that! Do you really? I think your mother found it faintly repulsive. It isn't really finished.'

'Yes, it is.'

'If you say so.'

Robin stood and went to sit on the end of Faber's sofa.

'Faber, why are you so nervous?' he asked him.

'I'm not. It's just . . . Jesus!' Faber threw up a hand, spilled a drop of wine and busied himself mopping up the splash with a spotless handkerchief.

'You forgot to put your shoes on.'

'I never wear shoes in the house.'

'What's wrong? Tell me.'

He chuckled and took a gulp of wine.

'Robin,' he confessed. 'Look. I like you and everything. I like you a lot, but.' He looked at the ceiling for inspiration then blurted, 'I'm not a Christian, you see. Not at all.'

'You're not?'

'No. I'm not even agnostic.' He looked at Robin as though this explained everything. Robin looked at him waiting for him to go on, because it didn't.

'Sorry,' Robin said at last. 'I don't quite see. If it makes you any happier, I'm not a Christian either, though I was a bit Buddhist, once, and these things leave deep roots even after you give them up, so I can't really say I'm atheist.'

'But . . .' Faber looked thunderstruck.

'You look thunderstruck,' Robin said. 'Has someone been telling you stories?'

'You're a monk,' he replied.

'No,' Robin corrected him. 'I'm a mental patient. Was. I think I'm better now. As better as anyone ever gets.'

'Andrea said that you were a monk. They both assumed . . . Haven't you told them anything?'

'Of course I have, but no one seems to want to listen, so I've rather given up.'

Robin laid a hand on his knee. Faber stared at it wide-eyed, like a man chancing on a well-fed spider in a cake-tin. He jumped up, knocking it aside, chuckling nervously again and sounding American.

'Jesus!' he said. 'Andrea always thought . . . and that bitch, Candida Thackeray. Even she told me in passing that . . . And look at me. You're sitting here waiting to be fed and I haven't made a thing. I wasn't asleep. I gave Iras strict instructions to say that I'd had to go to the other side of London and not to let you in.'

'Like a Jehovah's Witness.'

'Quite.'

'But you still arranged for her to go out.'

'What? No. Not at all,' Faber gabbled. 'I mean. She was

going out anyway. And there's simply nothing to eat. Look, there's quite a good Italian place about a hundred yards down the road. I feel so awful about this. Let's go there and you can let me treat you.'

'No.'

'Why not?'

'Because I want us to go to bed.'

'*What?* Oh, my God. Well. Yes. So do I but.'

'Faber.' Robin stood, offering him his glass, which he took abstractedly and drained. 'Faber, you're losing control. I'm not that exciting.'

'No. But I mean, yes.'

'Faber?'

'Mmm?'

'Ssh.'

'But can't we, I mean, shouldn't we wait a little?' Faber asked, wildly. 'There's so much I want to tell you. Ask you. Everything.'

'Bed,' said Robin. 'Then talk.'

'Oh, God,' said Faber, 'the sheets.'

'The sheets are fine.'

'I spilled a whole glass of wine on them earlier.'

'We can spill some more.'

'Iras.'

'She won't be back for hours.'

'No,' he admitted, taking Robin's hand, but still failing to catch his eye. 'She won't.'

'Can I open another bottle?'

'Sometimes,' he said, staring down at Robin's palm as he wound it round with fingers, 'when she's gone to Peggy's for the evening, she stays the night there.'

19

'Peggy, hello it's Faber, Iras's Dad.'

'Hello. We're writing a play.'

'That's nice. Is your mother there?'

'Hang on.' There was a loud clunk as Peggy dropped the receiver and went to find Dodie.

Faber disliked change. However sweet, Robin's head, dozing heavily in his lap, threatened a violent upheaval. Darkness had finally fallen and the orange streetlamp outside the open window threw a fiery wash across them. Faber admired the hellish *pietà* they made in the bedroom mirror then looked back at Robin. He ran a hand softly across his cheek. Robin gave a shut-eyed smile, raised a sleepy hand, caught him firmly by the wrist and began to chew a finger. Peggy's mother came to the phone.

'Faber, hello. Is something wrong?'

'Oh no, Dodie. Everything's fine it's just that, well, I've suddenly realized that this dinner party I've taken my friend to in Camden isn't going to end for hours – we're all drinking like fish and they still seem to be cooking.'

'North London,' Dodie sighed, nostalgically.

'Exactly.'

'And you'd like us to hang on to Iras for the night?'

'Could you?'

There were loud childish cheers in the background.

'Popular decision,' said Dodie grimly. 'They've been

writing a radio play and now they'll have time to perform it too.'

'Please, Dodie,' he begged, pulling his fingers free and giving Robin's hair a playful cuff. 'I'll paint all your babies one by one.'

'Done.'

'Better still, I'll paint you.'

'God forbid. Bye Faber. When's her first class tomorrow? Shall I take her in with Peggy?'

'She's got the morning off. We're going to the dentist to have her new braces fitted.'

'I'll get Oz to drop her off at your place, then, on his way to work.'

'Bless you. Bye.'

'See you.'

As Faber leaned across the bed to set the receiver back on the telephone, Robin reached up to pull him back into a horizontal. The receiver lay exposed, whining and ignored while Robin kissed him then rolled astride him and kissed him more. Despite himself Faber kissed him back, then came up for air and managed to say,

'Stop!'

'Why?' said Robin and kissed him.

'My cheeks are sore.' He tipped Robin back onto the mattress and tugged a fat pillow between them. 'And yours.'

'Are they? They don't feel it.' Robin put a hand to his jaw with a look of boyish concern. 'Are they very red?'

'When did you trim the beard?'

'This afternoon.'

'And your hair! You've cut it all off.'

'Do you mind? It was getting such a bore to wash.'

'No. I like this.' Faber ran a hand over the bristled nape of Robin's neck. 'Jailhouse chic. But the beard's still a bit godly.'

'Let's shave it off then.'

'Are you sure? Don't you like it?'

'Not much. I could shave it off now.'

'Later,' said Faber. 'But this I *really* like.'

He ran his hand over Robin's nape again. In reply, Robin ran his tongue across Faber's wrist. Faber sucked in his breath and began to pull the other's head towards him then pushed him back. 'Explain yourself,' he said. 'I want your story.'

'I'm hungry. Is there really nothing to eat here?'

'Talk first, eat later.'

'Are you sure?' Robin asked. 'It's quite long. Longer than *Cantata Profana.*'

'Quite sure.'

Robin pulled away, sat up, plumped out his pillows, then lay back against them, watching Faber watching him.

'I gather you see my mother often enough. How much has she told you?' he asked.

'Well,' said Faber, discomforted and vaguely resentful at Andrea's arrival in the bed between them. 'She told me a bit about Jake. And she said that you and Candida Thackeray were best friends.'

'We were. I've known her for years, through our grand-mothers, funnily enough. They were bosom pals − they went on butterfly-hunting expeditions together, propped one another up in widowhood, that sort of thing − and when I was about five I was dumped at Granny's for a bit and Candida and *her* granny came on a visit. We were both loners, really, but we sort of clicked and spent hours shut in our rooms or up trees together. We were always up trees. There was a tree house in the garden at The Chase and Granny had an ancient mulberry and a victoria plum you could climb into − she used to send us out there with nothing on so we wouldn't stain our clothes with the juice. I think she was a bit of a 'thirties nudist too − she was a Fabian and things − wanted to keep our inhibitions down. Candida used to swear she found an old photo of the two grannies at a naked picnic in their youth but I never saw it. Anyway, we ended up at the same day school in London and then, after her parents split up − I suppose we were about eleven – she spent whole summers staying with us because she couldn't stand her stepmother.'

'What was she like then?'

'The same, physically. Ash-blonde hair, perfect skin, long, intelligent face, sexy voice. Candida was born twenty-seven, born to have a public.'

'You know she's been top of one of those lists for the last three years?'

'Woman men would most like to marry?'

'No. The woman most desirable as a mistress. Did everyone think she was your girlfriend?'

'*I* thought she was my girlfriend. We did everything together.'

'Everything?'

'Nearly. We kissed a lot and went to lots of French films over in Notting Hill. We spent hours together. Then she told me that I didn't find women attractive, not sufficiently. I asked her what she meant and she dragged me off to Soho to other cinemas to prove her point.'

'And did she?'

'No. Porn always made me laugh so we had to leave. I didn't believe her, not really. I just took it as her typically devious way of saying that she wanted us to be just friends. She didn't run off with anyone else, and neither did I. They were a fairly grim bunch at school so we used each other as camouflage and let people think what they liked. Then we went to university, of course . . .'

'Of course.'

'Are you laughing at me?'

'No.'

'We went to university and met Jake. Or rather, he met us. He trailed after us everywhere. Lectures, library, mealtimes – we couldn't shake him off. We were rather silly and exclusive, you see. Eventually he was terribly brave and actually asked us round to his room for lunch. It was awfully touching. He'd blown most of his grant cheque. There was champagne, caviare, smoked salmon and strawberries. Everything. And we'd never really spoken. He'd just sat near us and listened in and occasionally volunteered a comment or two. Of course he didn't have a sense of humour and he was totally obsessed about having gone to a grammar school and having a father who'd made his money in showroom dummies − both of which we told him couldn't matter less − but he was horribly attractive.'

'Was he?'

'Oh, not physically. I mean, he was good-looking but not half as stunning as some people. No, the main thing was − this is fairly horrible − the main thing was his devotion and complete lack of self-esteem. We were vain and exclusive and he was devoted and rich (rich by our standards, anyway, probably not by his now) so we let him into our little club of two.'

Robin broke off to kiss Faber. Faber kissed him back then sensed that he was trying to slip past the subject and firmly pushed him away.

'What happened next?' he asked.

'I want something to eat.' Robin bit softly at Faber's shoulder.

'Tell me,' Faber insisted.

'Candida found herself a boyfriend. Not just anyone, of course, but the current college sex symbol. You won't have heard of him. William Warner. He was one of the ones that burned out − like me. He was a rowing hero who somehow happened not to be hearty but a sensitive, intelligent soul who was heavily involved in some campaign for the release of literary dissidents in Central America. Suddenly Candida was spending days on end in his rooms, professing a new interest in radical politics but getting so much sex she could hardly write a cheque, much less hold an intelligent conversation. Naturally that left Jake and I alone together.'

'And?'

'And I brought him home to stay and he took me to stay

with his parents and we took rucksacks and a tent and spent a summer touring Greece.'

'And?'

'And nothing. You don't seem to understand, we were very naïve. In fact I . . .'

'What?' Faber felt himself smile.

'I've only lost my virginity this evening.'

Faber wondered how he should react.

'No wonder you're ravenous,' he said. 'My God! What'll it be? Beans on toast? A bacon sandwich? There's really nothing very edible in the house.'

'A bacon sandwich would be lovely.' Robin made as if to get up.

'You stay right there,' said Faber, pressing him back against the pillows. 'I'll bring it up.' He headed down to the kitchen, jokily muttering, 'Poor ravished thing,' caught his own eye in a mirror and beamed.

20

OK, Joy. Tell him to come on up,' said Jake.

He set down the telephone and lost two minutes to blind panic. He had been meaning to ask Robin out for lunch ever since the christening, he honestly had, and Candida kept nagging him about when they should invite him over for dinner to meet some old friends, but Jake had been frantically busy. And too plain cowardly. Now Robin had turned up out of the blue, claiming that they had an appointment and, to save face, Jake told his assistant that this was true but that he had forgotten to enter it into his desk diary.

'In you go!' Joy chirped and ushered Robin into Jake's office.

'Very smart,' said Robin, looking around him. 'Very smart indeed. This all yours? Like the picture, what's it meant to be?'

'The blue blob's Candida and the pink blob's meant to be Jasper.'

'*Candida Albicans*.'

'What?'

'You remember. It's the proper medical name for thrush. It used to make us laugh.'

'Oh yes.' Jake chuckled obediently.

'It is good to see you on your own,' said Robin, grasping Jake's hand and shaking it vigorously between both of his. 'Hope you don't mind my barging in but I thought that perhaps you were feeling nervous about it all and I should just force your hand. Were you?'

'Feeling nervous? No.'

'Good. Can you make lunch?'

'Of course.'

'Sure?'

'Don't be stupid. Of course I can.'

'That girl thrust this glass into my hand.'

'It's a new mineral water we're launching. It's quite good. Not too bubbly.'

'Got anything stronger?'

'Not really. Let's go out.' Jake held open the door, waiting for Robin to stop admiring the view. 'Come on,' he said. 'Joy, I'm just going for a bite of lunch with Robin here. If Saskia needs me, tell her I'll be back by three.'

'OK, Boss,' said Joy.

'No. Make that two-thirty.'

'Does he pay you well?' Robin asked her, leaning on her desk.

'Can't complain,' she told him and laughed, throwing her hair out of her eyes.

'I haven't had lunch with him in over eight years,' Robin told her confidentially.

'What a lot he'll have to tell you,' she said.

'Come along,' said Jake, holding open the lift door.

Robin admired the interior of the lift in much the same, slyly ironical way he'd admired the view.

'I like your lift, Jake. Is this malachite real?'

'Yup.'

'Good lord.' They stopped at the next floor to let in some typists, giggly from too much coffee and too little sleep. One of them stared at Robin with frank admiration but he didn't notice, being too busy smiling at Jake. 'That's a strange name for her to have – Joy,' he said suddenly. 'Not very Chinese.'

'She's Vietnamese. Her sister's called Pamela, which is

stranger still.' The lift stopped again and they walked out into the atrium. 'Where shall we eat?' Jake said.

'You choose. London's moved on and left me behind.'

They went to a French-Vietnamese restaurant in Joy's honour and, Jake realized, because none of his professional contacts ate there anymore.

'How's Candida?' Robin asked as they sat down.

'Fine. Tired but fine.'

'And my bouncing god-daughter?'

'Rosy-cheeked and filthy-tempered.'

'Good. Cheers, Jake.'

'Cheers.'

Candida had talked about Robin in her sleep for seven nights running. She would mutter his name then prattle on incomprehensibly, stopping from time to time to let out little moans of need. She would wake in a bad mood, taking care to wake Jake too, although he had two hours' sleep to go, and would blame her crossness on Perdita. This morning she had claimed that the baby woke her three times between midnight and dawn. Jake had appeared to accept this lie although he had lain awake all that while and had given Perdita her bottle each time she asked for it, without Candida waking once from her troubled dreams.

'So tell me about this wonderful job of yours,' Robin asked, having gleefully ordered the most rarefied items on the menu because Jake was paying. 'How long have you been there?'

'Six years. Nearly seven. Do you remember? I'd already made contact with them through that time I spent there during our last Christmas vac.'

'That's right. You were researching a thesis.'

'Essay.'

'It was longer than an essay. I remember. It said very clever things on marketing the Conservatives; rather frightening.'

'Anyway, I sent them a copy of it when I applied – they hadn't advertised, you see – and the pushiness seemed to appeal to them. They took me on unconditionally.'

'What as?'

'Nothing much, but they let me sit in a corner having ideas which they then made lots of money out of. Did you see that toothpaste advert that ran all year a while back? The one with the little girl in a space station?'

'We don't have telly on Whelm.'

'Oh no. Of course not. Anyway, that was one of mine. Then I realized that they needed me so I threw my weight around and made them give me a decent salary and a desk of my own and so on – I was in a sort of corridor to start with.'

'Poor thing.'

'And now I'm called Creative Director and I don't do very much at all. I suppose I've sold out really.'

'Oh, I wouldn't say that.'

'Yes, I have. I mean, when I went there as a student it was very much a case of spying on the enemy camp. And then they started paying me – well, you know how I never had a bean to spare – so that rather numbed me. Also I felt I was at least being creative. I'd think how you used to go into raptures about ads for carpet cleaner and public service announcements to stop children getting run over and that would make me feel less grotty. Everyone else was being properly creative, you see.'

'Not making any money out of it, you mean?'

'Not exactly. I mean, Diana and Toby were acting, Roger buried himself in Cornwall and wrote things, Clem left banking and took herself off to art school . . .'

'But advertising's very creative . . .'

'In a way. But it's still dubious. I mean, my team were so creative with the Tories that we got them back in. Twice. And then the Tories went and cut back all the government grants to the properly creative people.'

'There's no point being moral about it. Creativity's got nothing to do with morality. And besides, you must be fearfully rich now.' Robin chuckled and began to lay waste the first of his valuable *hors d'oeuvres*. 'You can't deny it,' he said with his mouth full. 'Not now that I've seen the house.

And dear Candy must be worth a bomb, by now. I thought she was just a continuity girl, I hadn't realized she was a star!

'Don't buck the system,' he went on. 'It works so beautifully. Now that you're stinking rich and feeling guilty about it, you can both start paying your poor contemporaries to be creative for you, like paying an architect to build a chantry round your grave then paying in perpetuity for nuns to save your soul in it.'

'You're playing devil's advocate, naturally.'

'No, I'm not.' Robin sipped his wine then laughed at Jake outright. 'Well, there's no need to look so upset.'

'But you're the one with ideals. You're the one who's turned his back on all this. You should be coming amongst us snorting disapproval.'

'Why on earth? I can appreciate comfort and achievement like the next man.'

'You've just spent eight years in a monastery! Now you *are* playing devil's advocate.'

'Just a little.'

Jake relaxed.

'How's your sea bass?' he asked.

'Delicious. Piquant and perfect. You're hardly eating a thing. Here. Try some of this.' Robin slipped him a piece of fish wrapped in crisped seaweed. 'Of course it isn't really seaweed – they just call it that – it's actually sea spinach or something. They dry it and shove it through a shredder. What's wrong? Aren't you hungry?'

'Not very. We had people round again last night – third time this week.'

'Lord. Oh well. Cheers.' Jake's guest drank to him then munched on unabashed. Jake toyed with a piece of duck. 'Of course,' Robin declared, 'when you expect me to come along and disapprove of how you've sold out, what you're actually saying is that you want me to attack you for having run off and married Candida when you were meant to settle down with me.'

Jake felt his face burn.

'That's hardly fair,' he said.

'Or proper,' said Robin, apparently still intent on his food. 'Sorry. Tell me about Jasper. Does he give his parents hell?'

As the conversation was swung away from this emotional precipice as violently as it had been launched towards it, Jake felt relief, also a lingering disappointment. Since first taking the initiative so dramatically eight years ago he had been assiduously learning to do so with more aplomb. In his first year of marriage he had enrolled himself on an expensive course in Gloucestershire to learn assertion techniques and, in equal secrecy, had returned for remedial weekends every year since. Now that he was back in Robin's company Jake's training evaporated and he doubted that he could possibly have withstood a thorough raking-over of the past. Once again Robin was taking the lead acting as though he were always right, and once again, damn him, he was. Maddening though this might be, Jake had quite forgotten how pleasurable his old passivity was. He sat back, drank more than his regulation two glasses, regained his appetite and let himself be entertained.

When Robin had to leave the table briefly Jake caught himself picking at the label of their second bottle and thinking, What a waste. What a sad, sad waste.

Robin came back, bringing with him a faint whiff of soap.

'I've suddenly noticed!' Jake exclaimed.

'What?'

'Your beard and hair. You must think me terribly rude for not saying anything. I honestly hadn't noticed.'

'Better, isn't it?'

'Much. You look like you again. The beard made you look like a cross prophet.'

The waiter took away their collection of little dishes and asked if they would like anything else. Robin successfully persuaded Jake to order a mango ('They slice them up so prettily,' he said, 'Look. Like two golden hedgehogs.') then said that no, he would have just a small, black coffee.

'You always did that to me,' Jake said.

'Did what?' Robin asked, clean-shaven innocence itself.

'Egg me on into ordering a pudding then have nothing yourself – make me feel like a greedy child.'

'Well, quick,' he was all concern now. 'Call him back and tell him you don't want it after all. He won't mind.'

'But I do want it,' Jake protested. 'Besides, you know I'd never have the courage to cancel it. Here it is anyway,' he added.

'There. You see?' said Robin as the golden hedgehogs were set down between them. 'Isn't it perfect?' He smiled at the waiter who nervously returned the gesture and left them alone again. Robin waited until Jake had taken his first mouthful of mango, which was quite delicious, of course, then grinned. 'Just wanted to see I still could,' he confessed and blew lightly on his coffee.

'I saw you got on very well with Faber Washington at Perdita's christening,' said Jake to show he was not quite unmanned.

'You noticed. He's enchanting. Have you known him long?'

'I don't know him at all, in fact. He's much more my sis's friend – you know they were at the Slade together?'

'Yes. I think Candida told me first.'

'And of course Candida knows him slightly from when she sat for him when Jasper was little. You saw the painting?'

'Oh yes. Wonderful. If you're meant to be buying some work by young artists for your company collection you should get some of his.'

'He wasn't cheap several years ago. God knows what his stuff costs now.'

'Quite. Just the sort of thing your colleagues would appreciate, I imagine.'

'Mmm,' said Jake and pushed aside the wreckage of the mango. 'Where did he go to school?'

'Why do you ask?'

'Just wondered. He sounds so educated.'

'For a black person or for a painter?'

'Neither.' Jake refused to be baited. 'For some reason I thought he was American. The surname, I suppose.'

'He went to Barrowcester.'

'Really?'

'It's quite a sad story. You know what those do-gooding cathedral cities are like. Faber's little town in Africa happened to be in Barrowcester's adopted overseas diocese. A group of Barrowers thought it would be rather noble of them to club together and "educate" an African. They got the bishop of Faber's diocese to seek out a candidate from a suitably poor and amenable background and were sent young Faber. He came from a big family and his parents were thrilled to get rid of him and give him a future in one fell swoop. He was brought up in Barrowcester, spending holidays with anyone who'd have him (far beyond the adoption committee's means to fly him home all the time, of course) and by the time they'd finished with him he'd lost contact with his family and felt about as African as Elgar.'

'Has he never gone back?'

'I don't think so.'

'And what about the girl?'

'Iras?'

'I suppose he adopted her to return the favour, as it were.'

'Yes, only he was rescuing her from state care rather than uprooting her from her family. You know she's a prodigy?'

'Really?'

'That was as much a reason for her not being adopted as her blindness.'

Jake felt his concentration sag. He watched the rapid movements of Robin's mouth and felt very far away. He sat mutely through Robin's recitation of how sinister Iras Washington was talking perfect English at three, reading braille at six and using a braille-converted typewriter at seven. He heard without listening how she had now mastered braille-adapted word processing and had nearly finished her first novel. The waiter brought back Jake's credit card and at last Robin ran dry. Jake watched him smiling to himself and playing with the pastel-printed papers that had wrapped their *amaretti*. Robin took one in his beautiful fingers, formed it into a kind of parachute then lit one of its corners in the candle flame and rested the burning paper in the ashtray. The small fire flared, died down then, just as the paper turned black, sent the parachute flying over their heads on a small mushroom cloud. Robin watched it enchanted, then let his eyes drop back to Jake's.

'You're terribly happy, aren't you, Robin?'

For the first time that day, Robin answered him without irony.

'Utterly,' he said, and his smile was sweet-natured, and winesaddened.

'This is Faber Washington, isn't it?'

Robin lent across the table, urgency in his face, his hands fingering the air for right words.

'Jake, it's never . . . I mean, this has never, well. I think I might be losing my mind.'

'But that's wonderful,' said Jake.

'No, it's absurd. Calf-love's grotesque at this age. I know I've only just met him but he's so very . . . Oh, I don't know, just so . . . I can't stop thinking about it. It's a kind of madness. I'm not a well man.'

'You'll get over it,' Jake told him, standing. He had to get out. 'God! Robin, what's the time?'

'Coming up to three. Why?'

'I'm late. I must rush. Look, you'll be around for some time, won't you? You're not going back to Whelm straight away?'

Robin stood too.

'I'm not sure I'm going back at all.'

'Really?'

'Well, I can't very well. Not now. I think it's better for me to stay and face things here. For a while.'

'Robin, I must go.' Jake held out a hand.

'Lovely lunch. Thank you.' Robin clasped his hand and, before he realized it, Jake found he was being pecked on the cheek.

He drifted back to the office through the Covent Garden crowds like a drunk, which, on reflection, he was. Slightly.

'It hurts,' he thought. 'This really hurts.'

He lurched up the fire stairs in an effort to sober up. Joy looked up from her desk.

'Bad boy,' she said. 'You told me two-thirty.'

'Sorry, Joy.'

'The men from Genisan are here early.'

'Toothbrushes. I thought that was tomorrow.'

'I've put them in the boardroom with a jug of coffee and a smile.'

'Where's Saskia? I thought she was seeing them first.'

'She's still tied up at Cicero and Morse. I already paged her. She'll get over as soon as she can.'

'Joy. Keep them amused. I've got to make a call. I'll be two secs.'

'OK. And while I remember, Candida just rang. She says she's got to work late and as it's your nanny's day off, could you pick up Jasper from kindergarten. She says there's no rush. They'll hang on to him until you come.'

'Perfect,' he muttered. 'Thanks a lot, Joy.'

'Bad boy,' Joy sighed, slipping back into the boardroom.

He shut himself in his office, checked his watch, then dialled a number from memory. He kept a hand over the mouthpiece in case the wrong person answered. They didn't.

'Hello?'

'Peter. Hi. It's Jake.'

'Jake! What a lovely surprise!' Peter's tone was oddly hearty. 'What can I do you for?'

'Well, I was wondering if you'd like a game of squash tonight. An extra one. I need a bit of punishing.'

'Oh, Jake, I'd love to but I promised Andrea I'd cook tonight.'

'Ah.'

'Any other time would be fine, but . . .'

'That's OK, Peter. Actually, I won't keep you. I'm in a bit of a rush.'

'Fine. Speak to you soon, Jake.'

Like son, like father, Jake thought. He walked to the window and glared down at some pigeons that were bedding down sordidly on the ledge below. On his way to the door he stopped to pick up his dictating machine. Pressing a red button, he held it close to his mouth. 'Memo to Accounts re: Art Fund,' he confided. 'Request authorization to release moneys for purchase of work by Faber Washington, that's F-A-B-E-R and Washington as in White House. You'd better look out his agent for me, Joy – I suppose he has one – and get some figures together, as I'm not sure what he's worth now. Ring round a few galleries too. We'll want to buy quite a lot, four or five.'

21

Andrea was in the sitting-room teaching Jasper Browne how to play Hangman. Brevity was taking up all his small lap. He was not an especially bright boy so Andrea had let him hang her several times in succession. Normally he made up for his dimness with confidence which, in its turn, could be a problem when his jollity quashed the responses of brighter, more timid children. In the last few days however, both she and Peter had noticed him change. Twice today she had come across him sitting on his own in a corner, watching and trying to pass unseen. As a rule, if there was any delay in his being collected at the end of the afternoon, he ranted and sulked but today he accepted the prolonged absence of nanny or either parent with dull, almost unfeeling equanimity.

'So what have I got left?' she asked. 'Oh no! Only one go and then you can fill in my left leg and I'm dead! Help!' He laughed but not properly; only to placate her. 'Let's see; F-blank-T-blank. Shall I make a guess?'

'All right,' he said, quietly.

'Umm. OK,' she enthused. 'Fate!'

'Wrong,' said Jasper.

'Oh, dear. Well, fill in the other leg then. That's right. Kill me off. You've won again. Now, what was your word?'

Breathing heavily with concentration, he filled in the remaining two letters.

'Oh. Jasper, dear, you don't spell photo that way.'

'I do,' he said.

'Well, it's wrong, I'm afraid. The proper way to spell it is with P H at the beginning instead of the F. It's not a real word, really. It's short for photograph, but that's a bit harder to spell.'

'Oh.'

'Shall we call it a draw and do something else?'

'All right.'

He sat there staring at the pieces of paper they had covered with letters and executed pin-persons. She glanced at her watch.

'Well, look at the time!' she said. 'Mummy *is* late. You must be hungry. Shall we go to Peter's and my kitchen and see what we can find?'

'All right.'

'Would you like a piggyback?'

'No, thanks.'

He set Brevity gently on the sofa beside him then trailed Andrea to the kitchen and sat on a stool while she made him a sandwich.

'Can I have a banana in it?' he asked.

'What, banana as well as cheese?'

'I like it.'

'OK,' she said, eager to get through on any level.

'Thank you,' he said as she set it before him. There was a rattling of keys in the lock and Robin let himself in at the back door.

'Hello,' he said, rushing across the room. 'Can't stop. Got to have a bath. Love you lots.' And he thundered up the stairs, chased by the adoring Brevity. Jasper had suddenly perked up.

'That's your son,' he said.

'That's right,' said Andrea.

'He's a holy man,' he went on.

'Sort of,' she said. 'He's very special to me.'

'We've got lots of photos of him at home. Lots and lots.'

'Have you?'

'Yes. Mummy was looking at them all the other day. She had them all over her bedroom floor. She keeps them in a shoebox.'

'You eat your sandwich,' she said, dying to know more and wishing she were not so scrupulous. 'Mummy'll be here soon.' Once he had his mouth full she went on. 'She's got lots of photos of Robin because they were best friends when they were little. Your mummy used to come and stay here. You know the tree house at the bottom of the garden?' Jasper nodded, munching. 'Well, she used to climb up and sit there for hours and hours. She and Robin would take a bag of apples and a pocketful of sultanas each and then climb up there and pretend it was where they lived.'

Now, I mustn't cry, she thought. I've got Robin home again and Peter loves me again. I'm a very happy person.

'It kept them happy for ages,' she added out loud.

The doorbell rang. Andrea jumped up.

'That's probably Mummy now. You stay there and finish your glass of milk and I'll go and see.' She hurried into the hall. Robin's bath was filling loudly upstairs. She heard him cross the landing and shut the bathroom door. To have the now celebrated, elegant Candida Thackeray waiting until well into the cocktail hour to pick up her child from school made Andrea suddenly aware of her unfashionable, motherly dress and harassed hair. She stopped to check herself in the mirror then thought, 'Mud on her knees. Sultanas in her pocket. What the hell?' and opened the front door. 'Jake! How lovely!'

'Didn't Candida tell you I was coming?'

'No. She didn't tell me anything. Jasper said it was nanny's day off so naturally I assumed that Candida would . . . Come in, come in. Robin's just come home but he's already in the bath, I'm afraid. Rushing out somewhere, I think. Come to the kitchen. I've just given Jasper a cheese sandwich. Cheese and banana, actually – is that all right?'

'Sweet of you. That's his favourite. We've got an extra

nanny, you see, to cover Perdita's feeds on Sam's days off and so on but it turns out she can't drive and the agency hadn't anyone else to spare. Stupid of us to be so dependent on them, really. I am sorry Candida didn't ring. You must be wanting to get on with things . . .'

'Nonsense. It's been lovely having him to chat to. We played Hangman, didn't we Jasper?'

'Yes,' said Jasper.

'And Peter's still visiting at the hospital so, er . . .'

'Well, we must be off and leave you in peace,' said Jake.

'No. Stay for a drink. Do.' She touched his arm. 'It's such fun to have you here again. Please?'

'You're quite sure?'

'Quite. What would you like? Wine? Lager?' Andrea peered in the fridge. 'Gin?'

'Lager, please.'

'I'm afraid it's low-alcohol stuff.'

'That's fine.'

She poured Jake a low-alcohol lager, awarded herself a gin and French and led father and son back to the sitting-room.

'Have you got any photos?' Jasper asked her.

'Several books of them.'

'Have you got some of Mummy and the holy man?'

'Of course, dear, but his name's Robin. There are even some of your daddy. You see that shelf there? The bottom one? Well, all those big books have photographs in. Let's see. Yes. Try the navy blue one. That's it. Take them over to the table so you can look at them comfortably – it's a bit big to hold on your lap.'

'Thank you,' said Jasper and hauled the book onto a writing-table by the window where he sat and pored over his parents' mysterious past. Andrea turned back to Jake and smiled.

'It seems so long ago, now,' she said.

'No seems about it,' said Jake. 'It was. I had lunch with Robin today. Did he tell you?'

'No. He's only just come back.'

'Oh yes. You said. Sorry.' Andrea noticed that Jake had still not found the ability to sit back on a sofa and relax. She half expected him to call her Mrs Maitland. 'It was rather strange,' he said. 'He just turned up out of the blue.'

'Oh dear,' she said. 'I hope he didn't disturb your work.'

'No. It was good to see him properly. We didn't really get a chance to talk at the christening.'

'Mmm.' She sipped her delicious drink, which she had made rather strong, and wished she were drinking it alone with Peter. She wished Peter would hurry up and come back. 'We're so thrilled to have him back.'

'I bet. I gather he may be staying back for good.'

'We hope so. He seems to have missed London terribly. He's out all day, nearly, walking around, taking favourite buses, talking to strangers in cafés – same old Robin.'

'You don't find him changed?'

'Do you?'

'Yes,' Jake frowned. He was still fairly good-looking, she decided, but only because she knew how he used to look and laid her memories over the thickening neck and now indelible frown. 'He's changed all right. He's the same Robin but now he's more so. Everything's slightly exaggerated, imbalanced almost. Sorry, that's an awful thing to say, especially when you're so pleased to have him home again.'

'No, of course not.' She took an icy sip, knowing exactly what he meant, and stared across at Jasper for a moment. The child was either fascinated by the photographs or extremely sly. She turned back to Jake. 'You know,' she said quickly, 'No one's ever really told me what happened, why he ran away.'

'But surely Candida did. I thought.'

'Not really. She was so hysterical when she called us up. All she said was that he had disappeared and that "it was all a stupid misunderstanding" and then we hardly saw her after that. Not until after your marriage, of course.'

'I wrote a letter.'

'Yes. To Peter. I remember. It was sweet of you but it didn't explain much.' She dropped her voice. 'Dob was very in love with you, wasn't he?'

'No. Not exactly. He hadn't told me. It was stupid of me not to notice I suppose, but he hadn't told me and when he finally did I panicked. I wasn't the last one to see him, though. Candida was.'

'Yes. I know. But surely, when you heard he'd turned up at Whelm you must have been surprised. You knew him so well. He'd never shown any interest in God before?'

'He was reading theology.'

'Well, I know that, but that didn't make him Christian. He was far more interested in Eastern things. If we'd had a telegram from an ashram, *that* would have been understandable, but Whelm of all places . . . Peter went half-mad, you know. He was convinced they were holding him against his will. It almost broke him.'

'He's coming up the steps now,' Jake said.

They both coughed; ridiculously, she thought, like adulterers in a bedroom farce. The front door opened and shut.

Peter called out,

'Hello?'

Andrea called back, 'Hi! In here,' and Jake stood up.

'We really must be off,' he told her. 'Your supper . . .'

'No,' she said.

Peter came in saying,

'Hello, darling,' then, 'Hello, Jasper. Still here? And Jake! What a lovely surprise.'

'I came to pick up Jasper,' Jake explained. 'It's Samantha's day off and there's normally a supply nanny to cover her but the supply . . .' He saw Andrea was smiling at him. 'Well, anyway, there was a mix-up and Candida was kept on late by some emergency. Can't think what it was. She's normally home by two-thirty or three.'

'Oh, well,' said Peter, who had been rather too obviously not listening, grinning as he was at Andrea.

'How was Marcus?' she asked him, receiving his welcome kiss.

'Bad,' he muttered. 'It's nearly over.'

'Poor thing,' she said.

'Can I get you another drink, Jake,' asked Peter, taking Jake's glass. 'Another lager, was it?'

'Actually, I really must be off. Candida may be home and worrying about Jasper. It's long past his bedtime. Thanks so much, Mrs Maitland . . . I mean, Andrea.'

She laughed. They all did.

'It's having Robin back here,' Jake muttered. 'Feels so strange.'

'We'll give him your love,' she replied, thoughtlessly.

'Sorry about the squash,' Peter told him. 'Any other time. Oh. Sorry.'

'What squash?' asked Andrea, sleepily, feeling the drink reach her knees as she stood in farewell. 'Come along, Jasper. Time to go home. Did you like the photos?'

'Yes,' he said. 'Very much. Bye.'

'Bye.'

He ran out into the hall after the men. She heard the front door open again amid muttered manly goodbyes. She went to sit where the child had sat and began to look at the photographs. Robin and Candida grinning from their treehouse. Another one with Candida in a cowboy hat and Robin in a dress Andrea had once been made to wear as a bridesmaid. She turned some pages and found a terrible, wet camping trip to Suffolk. A much younger Peter grinning up at the camera while frying bacon in a field amid strings of wet clothes. Andrea, unbelievably twee in a sou'wester, glaring from the shelter of a church porch. Candida and Robin curled up under the same blanket in the back of the dormobile, then brand-new, boxes of groceries looming behind them and Candida's irritating penny-whistle discarded in merciful sleep.

There was a clinking of ice cubes on glass and Peter came back. He had poured himself a grapefruit juice.

'I should have told you,' he said. 'It was so silly.'

'What was?' She had no idea what he was talking about.

'The squash. I've been playing secret squash games with Jake every week since, oh, well for ages. Years.'

'But that's lovely,' she said. She laughed. 'Why on earth didn't you tell me?'

'To be honest, I can't remember. It seemed vital at the time that neither you nor Candida should know. I think . . . I think it was because I still missed Dob so much and Jake was a last kind of link to him. What was curious was that he obviously felt enormously guilty over something and seemed to regard the weekly contact with me as some kind of penance.' He was standing by her and stroking her hair. 'Do you mind very much?'

She thought a moment.

'No,' she said, meaning 'I'm not sure,' and she looked up at him, 'but I'm glad you told me.' He sat on the window seat beside her.

'Darling,' he said and they kissed. He looked at the photographs with her for a while. He said nothing but she could hear the slight snort he always made when he smiled.

'Peter?'

'Yes.'

'Don't think me stupid, but your visits to Marcus are real, aren't they?'

'Of course!' he laughed.

'And the squash games with Jake are the only other thing you do away . . . away from me?'

'Yes,' he said. 'And I won't be doing those much now.'

She understood what he meant and kissed him back to show she did.

'Funny,' she said. 'When Robin used to bring him home for weekends and things I thought he was so nice – rather serious and loyal and things – and now he's faintly pathetic.'

'Mmm,' said Peter. 'Even dull.' He kissed her.

'Before you cook me supper,' she said.

'Mmm?'

'Shall we go upstairs and change a little?'

'Mmm.'

Groping one another, half-crippled with desire, they made their way towards their bedroom. She had forgotten that Robin was home however and, giggling with nerves, they had to hide in her study until he left the house. Robin called her name twice before hurrying out.

22

'No. Poor Venetia couldn't make it, they've sent her on location again already. Such a shame. Good for her, though. I'll just see how things are next door.'

Candida left her guests alone in the twilit conservatory. She took a quick look in the dining-room – Samantha's place settings tended towards the erratic – then moved quickly to the kitchen. Madame Rostand's latest delivery, *noisettes d'agneau fourrés en croûte* was already in the oven, which was risky as some guests, including Jake, had yet to arrive. Candida stirred the mint sabayon nervously, having made it herself, then took little bowls of chilled soup from the fridge and arranged them on a tray. She had made the soup herself, too. The deceptive simplicity of carrot blended with coriander and a hint of jerusalem artichoke was an appeal to Robin's new asceticism. The evening would finish with one of Samantha's remarkably good summer puddings.

The front door opened and shut.

'Jake?' she hissed.

He came in looking tired, crumpled, less than adorable.

'Sorry,' he said.

'I said seven-thirty,' she reminded him.

'And I said sorry.'

'It doesn't matter. Venetia's cancelled and Robin and Faber are late. Heini too.'

'I don't know why you had to ask those two.'

'I'd like Gilda to meet Faber and Robin's my oldest friend,' she said. 'And yours.'

'But I took him out for lunch only the other day.'

'Well, I wasn't there, was I?'

He slumped to a chair and watched her being fast.

'And they're so in love,' he complained.

'So?'

'Calf love's disgusting at our age.'

She stopped in mid-action to check his suit.

'Are you going to wear that?' she asked.

'Well, I . . . Who else is here?'

'Never mind,' she said. 'There's no time.'

The doorbell rang.

'That'll be them.'

'It could be Heini.'

'It'll be them. You go. I'll finish this.'

Jake went to let in young love. Candida feverishly scattered chopped coriander across the soup bowls then ran after him. Robin and Faber were both in white. Entirely in white.

'Faber. Robin,' she noted.

'We're very, very late, aren't we,' Robin told Jake smugly. 'I never used to have the self-control.' His hair was neat and his beard had gone. Faber's influence, she decided.

'You look lovely,' said Faber, holding her fingertips and admiring her admirable dress.

'Is that white stuff muslin?' asked Robin, moving in beside him.

'Yes,' she said, holding out some of the fabric and looking down at it, 'And the silver's just sort of splashed on with a brush. The dry cleaners will have a fit. And look at you two, all in white. I could eat you both.'

Faber chuckled, Robin licked his lips and Jake, embarrassed, led them to meet the others. Candida went upstairs to find Jasper. Samantha had just finished getting him ready for bed.

'Perdy-M's out for the count,' she told her mistress.

'Thank God,' said Candida then held out her hand to her son. 'Come along darling,' she said. 'Come and say goodnight to everyone.'

'No,' said Jasper.

'I'll read you a story,' Samantha suggested.

'All right.'

Candida took his hot newly-washed hand in hers and led him downstairs. Heads turned as they reached the top of the few steps into the conservatory and the geranium air was full of warm greetings and affected surprise.

'We've just come to say goodnight,' said Candida.

'You off already?' asked Robin.

'It's the holy man,' said Jasper, pleased. 'Do I have to go to bed?'

'Yes, darling. Say goodnight.'

Jasper looked around at his parents' guests.

'Bye,' he said and was passed back to Samantha who was waiting behind in the candle-lit shadows.

'Not too long a story,' Candida told her. 'He's running rather late. Now,' she went on, turning back, 'Has everybody met?'

'Er. I don't think I have.' Tanned and tiny, Uncle Heini was grinning at her from a capacious reclining-chair.

'Heini!' she bent to kiss him. 'I didn't see you arrive.'

'I came in through the garden,' he chuckled, 'Your roses smell so beautiful.' He turned to the others to explain. 'They're always at their best on their way out,' he told them. 'Like old men.'

'Now everyone, this is Heinrich Liebermann.'

'Heini, please,' he said.

'Heini, then. A dear friend of my grandmother's. He's normally unget-atable in the Aegean, so we're honoured. Heini this is Gilda, my friend from work.'

'Oh, I remember you,' Robin told her.

'And this is Steve, Gilda's . . . Gilda's friend.'

'Hi,' said Steve.

'*Ja*,' said Heini.

'Jake you know, of course, and this is Faber Washington.'

'Now why do I know *your* name?'

'You probably saw the painting on the landing,' said Faber quickly, and turned away.

'Of course.'

'And this is Robin, my childhood friend.'

'Her granny brought you to tea once at my granny's,' said Robin. Heini looked puzzled. 'At Charmouth,' Robin added. 'You had very baggy shorts on and a panama and you insisted on getting the old motor-mower going to do the lawn.'

Heini turned to Candida for confirmation.

'But this is not that little boy . . . Irma's grandson?'

'Yes,' she nodded, 'Robin Maitland.'

'Ah so, the *holy* man!' Heini exclaimed and roared with laughter. 'He sits by me, *ja*?'

'Yup. OK, Uncle Heini,' said Jake, standing. 'Darling, do you need a hand?'

'No, it's all ready. Come in, everyone, and sit.'

They followed her, Gilda chatting busily to Faber, who she had suddenly recognized as someone everyone would soon be dying to know. Steve, lost, was feigning interest in geraniums. Jake rescued him, took him in earnest, and started telling him the story of a lemon-scented plant that was a cutting of a cutting once picked off by Uncle Heini for Candida's grandmother from a parent plant at Buckingham Palace. Steve thought this was meant to be a joke and the story got quite out of hand.

'Now. Sit wherever you like,' Candida told them, 'No bossy set places, except that I go here as it's nearest the door and Jake goes there because he understands the awkward legs.'

'And Uncle Heinrich and I are going to sit together.'

When Candida returned with another bottle of wine for Jake to pour and her tray of carrot soup, she was pleased to see that she would have Robin and Faber on either side of her. Faber was still trapped by Gilda, Jake and Steve were busy boring

one another, so she enjoyed her soup and hung on the edge
of Robin's conversation with her ancient godfather.

'So you became a monk?' said Heini.

'Not exactly,' Robin told him.

'But you spent eight years in a monastery?'

'Precisely.'

'He's been living on Whelm, Heini,' Candida offered. 'You
know? The little island?'

'On Whelm, but not *of* it,' said Robin.

'And you find England much changed?' Heini asked, dab-
bing some soup off his chin.

'It's as though I've been asleep for a century,' said Robin.
'Delicious soup, Candy. Nice and simple.'

'Thank you, Dob.'

'*Ja. Sehr gut.*'

'Thank you, Uncle Heini.'

'Perhaps I'm being paranoid,' said Robin, 'but it's like some
old science fiction film; the people I thought I knew have been
replaced by near perfect replicas who pretend that nothing has
changed.'

'But now they all have the razor mouths and little mean
eyes of sharks, *ja*?'

'You noticed too! So I'm not paranoid?'

'Why you think I move to a tiny island on the Aegean? So,
it's too hot and my skin is like brown paper but,' Heini smiled
seraphically, 'no sharks. They don't even holiday there, it's
too cheap for them. Nothing but dolphins.'

'Have I got a mouth like a shark, Dob?' she asked.

'Robin.'

'Sorry. Robin. Have I?'

'Well . . .' Robin smiled cruelly at her. 'Not exactly, but
you've grown a shark's skin.'

'They can flay a man just by brushing past him,' added
Heini.

'I'm not sure I like that,' she said.

'You couldn't help it, *Liebchen*. You had to survive.'

'And how wonderfully you did it,' said Robin. 'My old Candy, mud on her knees and sultanas in her pockets, now a mother of two, household name and national sex symbol.'

'Candida,' she corrected him, but he had turned back to Heini.

'It's not just friends,' he said. 'Strangers have changed too. The streets are full of sharp young men with unkind faces and the girls . . . I went into a pub I used to like, over in Chelsea, and found myself in a sea of them, all blonde and about seventeen and it was all, oh, horrible, sex-and-money. No. Not even sex, it was just money and sex with money. Everything's gone hard and shiny and fast. Like that dreadful new magazine.'

'*Capital*,' prompted Gilda.

'Jake's doing the promotion for that,' said Candida.

'No soul,' Faber put in. Then he caught Heini's eye and seemed to dive back into his talk with Gilda.

'Has it changed or have I just got old overnight?'

'Oh, it's changed,' said Candida, feeling obscurely riled. 'We've all changed, but I think it's for the better. Now people do instead of sit around and think. I hated all that passive communing. You'll change too. If you stick it out. Could I have everyone's bowls?' She took the table's bowls and went to fetch the *noisettes d'agneau* while Jake poured wine.

Samantha was sitting in the kitchen watching a personal finance programme on the small television. She took the bowls from Candida and loaded them into the dishwasher. As directed, she had already arranged pretty circles of cucumber, mint and thin-sliced new potato on seven plates.

'Want me to serve up, Candy?'

'Yes, please, Sam,' Candida told her. 'You could take it through for me. I'm just going up to have a look at Perdita.'

'Right you are.'

Perdita was sound asleep. Candida looked at her long and hard before stroking her scant hair. Then she went to her bathroom, locked the door and took some small pills supplied her on a regular basis by a studio technician to whom she had once confessed stage fright. She sat on the edge of the bath waiting for them to take effect. She began to feel her blood hum through her and was suddenly as acutely aware of her posture and the arrangement of her limbs as if she had been watching her beauty on a studio monitor.

'You want him so much,' she whispered and she could feel the breath hissing between her lips as they formed the words. 'You want him but he's Faber's now. Look at me.' She looked in the mirror. 'You are attractive, you are unavailable and, Candida, you are calm.' She stood, shook out her dress and stuck out her tongue. The coating on the pills had stained it blue. She scrubbed at it briefly with a toothbrush then let herself out and went back to join the party. 'Sleeping like a lamb,' she told Faber. 'Now tell me all about your Iras. Is it true she's actually writing a novel?'

She tried hard. She even did well. She gave Faber all her attention and drew out Gilda on her divorce. Once Samantha's summer pudding had arrived, she even swopped places with Jake and drew out Steve on the subject of his Hong Kong youth, which was really quite interesting. She was constantly aware of her childhood friend, however. His voice rose warmly above Faber's baritone and Heini's childish fluting and occasionally someone would call out to her, making her look across the table and see his teasing eyes on her reply. When at last she steered them into the drawing-room she could suffer it no longer. When Jake offered to fetch coffee she said,

'No, you sit there, darling, you've had far too hard a day,' which raised a laugh. 'Dob can help me,' she said, 'now that he's one of the disapproving unemployed.'

'Robin,' he said.

'Dob!' she insisted. 'We may have changed, but you haven't.' This raised another, less certain laugh.

He followed her to the kitchen.

'Delicious grub,' he said. 'You are clever – career and *haute cuisine* too.'

'Well, Samantha made the pudding.'

'The soup was best.'

'Did you really think so?'

'Yes.'

'Good.'

'You didn't need any help doing this at all. Did you?' He gestured to the tray where Samantha had already laid out coffee cups, saucers, sugar and milk before retiring, with a thriller, to bed. 'Your slave had done it all already.'

'We pay her a very tidy sum. But no, I just wanted to talk to you away from all the chatter.'

'Oh, good.' He pulled himself up onto a work surface, popped some coffee sugar in his mouth, and sat up there, looking expectant. She filled the cafetière with boiling water then went to stand before him.

'I just,' she said, looking down and tapping softly at his kneecaps with her knuckles, 'I just wanted to say how happy I am about you and Faber. I think it's a match made in Heaven.'

He stopped playing, stopped teasing, drew her between his thighs and kissed her once on the forehead.

'Thank you,' he said. 'That's very, very sweet.'

'I am attractive,' she thought, feeling his hands on her shoulders and smelling him faintly through his loose white shirt. 'I am unavailable and I am utterly calm. And this hurts.' She pulled back and took one of his hands in hers. It was heavy with wine. 'Welcome back,' she said and kissed the back of it gently. 'Robin. Dob died, didn't he?'

'Eight years ago,' he said. As she lifted the tray he jumped down. 'Let me,' he muttered and took the cafetière from her to lighten her load.

'Ah, caffeine,' said Steve as they came into the drawing-room. 'Just what the doctor ordered.'

'It's decaffeinated I'm afraid, Steve.'

'That's all right,' said Steve, crestfallen.

'Faber and Heini are upstairs looking at the picture,' said Jake.

'I'll get them,' said Robin.

'No.' Candida was at the door before him. 'Let me.' She gave him a discreet smile and he gave way.

Heini and Faber were standing on the landing before Faber's painting, the old man dwarfed by the younger. Each stared upwards and they seemed not to hear her approach.

'I think it's time you talked to our mutual friend,' Heini said.

'I don't see what business it is of yours.'

'I hadn't seen him or you for several years until today but, as I say,' Heini went on, unruffled, 'our friendship is mutual. He's very ill. He wants to see you.'

'Did he say so?'

'Not in so many words. But I understood . . .'

'You don't understand anything!' Faber rebuked him and turned away to see Candida waiting at the head of the stairs.

'Ssh,' she whispered. 'You'll wake Jasper.'

'A lovely painting, *Liebchen*. A truly lovely painting,' said Heini. 'So much family feeling.'

He remained looking up at the canvas but Faber strode past Candida and down the stairs. Minutes later, as she and Heini stood watching her sleeping baby, she heard the sounds of young love leaving.

23

As Saturdays brought a rush of visitors, the Friends of the Hospital flower-stall had already closed for lack of stock. Peter scoured the local supermarkets and found a lurid bucketful of plastic-wrapped bouquets. He chose the least offensive, a thin clutch of freesia with a frond of unlikely fern, in the hope that at least it might still have some scent to it. Riding up to Marcus's ward in the lift, he tore off the plastic wrapping, chose a deep yellow bloom that had scarcely opened, and offered the rest of the bunch to the one person in the lift whose hands were empty.

'Here,' he told him, 'I only need the one.' The man looked at him with deep suspicion but accepted the flowers and was gingerly sniffing them when he left the lift.

Marcus's body had been taken over by machinery. He had a drip feeding his arm on one side and a tube, emerging from under his sheet on the other, was draining something from him into a bag on the floor. He was wired to a beige machine on wheels that clicked and hummed, and since Peter's last visit he had suffered the pain and indignity of having a pipe thrust down his throat by way of his nose.

A small, neat woman with short, falsely-chestnut hair and a plain silk blouse was sitting near to the drainage bag. She had found herself a table and had improvised an office. She had a portable telephone there, three sharp pencils, pens red and black, a desk diary and seven or eight thick, navy-blue files. As Peter knocked and came in, she was talking on the telephone.

'No, I said via Hawaii and then onto Oslo . . . That is correct . . . I beg your pardon? . . . Yes, the moneys will be with Messrs Schwab for collection on production of suitable proof of identity.' She looked up, bowed to Peter as though their acquaintance were a long one, and said, 'I shall need written confirmation by the eighteenth . . . Good . . . *Hvala. Nazvat cu kasnije . . . Da. Zbogrom.*' She set the telephone down and stood with a smile. 'You must be Peter. I'm afraid we don't know your last name.' She shook his hand. 'Dorothy Birch.'

'It's Peter Maitland. You must be Marcus's "*ancilla constanta*".'

'Quite so.' She gathered up a pen and two files. 'I'll leave you alone with him.'

'Oh, please. Don't let me disturb you.'

'Not at all, not at all,' she said. 'I need to stretch my legs. I've been sitting for hours. He's much worse,' she went on, in a stage whisper. 'That's why I've set up camp in here. I'll be on the fire escape if you need me. It's so very airless in here – the nurses will insist on keeping the windows shut.'

As soon as she had shut the door, Peter weighed down the pages of her diary with the telephone then opened a window wide.

'Hello, Marcus,' he said and kissed Marcus's forehead. 'It's Peter.' He changed the flower water, threw out an already browning pink rose and set the new freesia in its place. 'Marcus?' He watched the old man's slow breathing and listened through nine bleeps of the monitor. 'Smell this,' he said. He took the freesia from its vase, wiping off the water drops with his sleeve, then held it immediately under Marcus's nose.

At first there was no reaction, just the fluttering of a petal in Marcus's breath, then the old nose wrinkled and took a sniff. It was a long sniff, alarmingly loud. It reminded Peter of the early morning yoga he had just persuaded Andrea to abandon, which in turn reminded him that he had led his wife to bed as soon as the last child was collected yesterday and had stayed there with her until making them a fried breakfast towards three in the morning. The nose breathed out again with a slight rattle and Marcus sighed,

'Such a cheap, totally disarming smell.'

'Hello, Marcus.'

Marcus's eyes remained shut.

'Like those awesomely clean waitresses upstairs in Fortnums,' he went on. 'The sort that wear their hair up and scrub the backs of their necks till they glow. Lily of the valley.'

'Freesia.'

'Well, I'm sure they're related.'

Peter set the freesia back in its vase.

'I thought you were meant to be much worse,' he told him.

'I am, but not that much. I keep my eyes closed to stop Miss Birch from asking my advice. She's perfectly capable of running the entire concern on her own, but now that I'm on the way out, the extraordinary creature feels she must consult me in my every waking moment on everything from a deal in Budapest to her new choice of paperclip. What colour's the freesia?' He opened his eyes but they had filled with a milky glue. Peter tried to bathe it away for him but then Marcus found the sudden brilliance too much and raised his hands as blinkers.

'Marcus, I'm sorry I didn't come to see you last night.'

'Perfectly all right, darling,' said Marcus. 'Your time's your own.'

'I know, but I said I'd come and I didn't. So, I'm sorry. It was just that Andrea . . .'

'Is she learning that Donne piece for my funeral do?'

'Yes. At least, I've told her to and she's got the book out.'

'Not long to go.'

'Nonsense.'

'What about her anyway? Is she ill?'

'No. Far from it. It's just that, well, ever since Robin's come home, we've started . . . Well. You don't want to hear this.'

'Yes, I do.'

'Well, it's childish but we seem to have started a second honeymoon.'

'You mean you're going at it hammer and tongs?'

'Yes,' Peter laughed. 'I suppose we are.'

'Splendid,' said Marcus and Peter knew he was quite uninterested. 'That reminds me,' Marcus went on. Peter waited.

'Yes?' he asked after a moment or two.

Marcus said nothing. His hands had been slipping down and his eyes had closed again. His breathing was slower and Peter was aware once more of the chirrups and clicks of the beige machine. A junior nurse knocked, came in, mouthed 'excuse me' to Peter and took a reading off the machine. She marked this on the graph at the foot of the bed. Then she slipped a thermometer into Marcus's placid mouth and took his pulse. Smiling once more at Peter, she filled in pulse and temperature on the graph and left the room.

'Marcus?' asked Peter, touching the old man's hand. Sweat glistened in the old runnels of his brow. Peter ran cold water over Marcus's face flannel, wrang it out and washed the sweat away. Marcus's head sank deeper into his pillows. As Peter was rinsing out the flannel at the sink, Marcus spoke again.

'There's a man. He rings up every so often to find out how I am. We used to live together. I gave him a great deal of time and money and rather too much love. The love proved highly problematical and he's been avoiding me ever since. But I blame myself and I wish him well. His details are in an envelope in the drawer by my bed. If he hasn't been here before I go, I want you to ring him. I don't want him finding out from the nurses, that would be too hard. You'll have to contact him about the funeral arrangements in any case.'

'Marcus, of course I will.'

'Promise.'

'I promise.' Peter touched the hand again and squeezed it but Marcus drew it away.

'You'd better let Miss Birch get back to her telephoning,' he said.

24

'That's right,' called Andrea. 'All the chairs and tables against the walls. Gently, Flora. Gently. There. Now. All spread out and find a space. Make sure you can stretch your arms out without touching anyone. *Gently*, Flora! Now. When I start the music playing, you're all going to become seeds. Apple seeds in the cold earth, tight and small and blind. OK? Quiet now. Flora? Thank you.'

She took the record from its battered sleeve. The swan's movement from *Carnival des Animaux*, an old favourite much used for everything from butterflies dying in autumn to goldfishes circling bowls and even, in the days before yoga, her own stretch-and-tone exercises. She set it playing. Much scuffling followed and a thunder of knees on floor. She turned to face the class who had curled up like so many Muslims at prayer. The exception to the startling unanimity was Flora Cairns, ever the individualist, who lay on her side in a toppled lotus posture.

'Now,' Andrea announced, 'I'm a cloud full of rain and as I walk among you I'll make a rain noise. When you hear that near you you'll know it's time to wake up and start growing.' Andrea took a tambourine and walked barefoot amongst the seeds, gently rattling it. 'Here come the raindrops,' she said, 'falling like tears on your hard, little cases.' Seeds jerked awake. 'It comes down through the soil to wake you. You swell. You stretch. That's it, Rupert. Slowly, Flora. Slowly.

Now you push out a shoot to find the sun. That's the way. Gently push. And let a leaf open on it to feel the warmth. Mmm. Delicious, isn't it, Tom? Now another shoot. Slowly stretching. And another leaf. Now the shoot swells into a little bush. Here's some more rain,' – she shook the tambourine – 'to get you growing.'

Peter came in at the back and stood watching her. She smiled across. He winked back. 'Now you grow a little more. That's right, Joshua. Sit up. That's right. Little saplings now. Grow some more. Up into the sun. Now you can feel. Now you can see. Big branches growing. Wind in your leaves. Come on, let's hear it.' Several children hissed, then more. Soon the room was alive with spitty whooshing sounds. 'Not a storm,' said Andrea, 'Just a breeze.' The wind obeyed her. 'Now, touch branches here and there. You've turned into a forest of apple-trees. An orchard, I mean.' Jasper Browne giggled. 'And keep stretching. Tiptoes now. More rain for you.' She rattled the tambourine. 'And now, let's see you grow an apple each.' Palms curled into fist fruit. Andrea picked one. 'Delicious,' she said, munching air. 'Well grown, Emma!'

The swan finished and Andrea hurried over to switch off the record-player just as the next movement began.

'Now,' she announced. 'You're all relaxed and ready for story-time with Peter.'

Several children cheered and there was a scramble for their story pillows and once again gentle thunder as they dropped to the floor. Peter picked his way through the bodies and sat on a table at the front.

'Faber's upstairs,' he told her, smiling.

'Now?'

'He dropped in on the off-chance. I'll read for twenty minutes if you like.'

'Bless you,' she said.

'Today's story is a very sad one about a little mermaid,' Peter told the class as she left the room. 'It's by Hans Christian

Andersen. Who can remember what else he wrote? Anyone? Joshua, you tell us.'

'*The Snow Queen*,' said Joshua.

Andrea mounted the stairs in growing shame. She had been neglecting her friend. Ever since the evening when she walked out of the choir, she had thought only of Peter, and Peter, it seemed, only of her. The pair of them had rediscovered the heady selfishness of fresh love, setting aside every spare moment for one another. Not even setting aside, for that made it sound too premeditated and they had no choice. Whenever they weren't in the kindergarten (and even there they found it impossible not to touch each other at every opportunity) they were in bed. Or on the sofa, twice on the bathroom floor and even, this morning, in the kindergarten storeroom where Pilar Fernandez had surprised them just in time. They hardly saw Dob − sorry Robin − who only seemed to come home to bathe, change or sleep, if that. Peter had actually forgotten to visit poor Marcus the other day and Andrea, she realized now, had not so much as thought of Faber since the christening.

'Faber, hello. I'm sorry,' she said and hugged him. He kissed her cheek.

'Why sorry?' he said.

'Well . . .' She stood back and sat in an armchair, feeling immediately that her new rapacity must somehow show − hot pink blotches on her neck and chest or tender toothmarks on her inside leg. 'Coffee?'

'No,' he held up a mug. 'I've got some. You're glowing,' he went on. She sent Brevity to her basket because she had a tendency to make Faber sneeze.

'We've just been being apple-trees,' she said. 'Hot work.'

'No,' he laughed, 'I mean, you look happy. Sorry. I mustn't keep you.'

'No. It's OK. Peter's reading to them. We've got twenty minutes or so.'

'Where's Robin?'

'Out. He's always out. I think he muttered something about a film.'

'*Le Financier Aveugle?*'

'That's right. I told him it was dreary.'

'He hasn't told you where he's been all the time?'

'No.' She grinned. 'The thing is, I know it's awful but, Peter and I have . . .'

'Andrea, he's been with me.'

'Really?'

'We're having an affair. Or does that sound too temporary? We're in love. Extremely in love.'

Andrea felt laughter welling up in her throat, jumped up and hugged him. Then she fell back onto the sofa, tugging him down beside her. His relief was palpable.

'You don't mind?'

'Why ever should I? I'm just thrilled it's you and not another broken reed like Jake.'

'Bless you for that.' He hugged her and they laughed.

'Can't you stop him from going back?' she asked.

'He won't.'

'But hasn't he sworn or anything?'

'That's just it, Andrea. He isn't a monk.'

'Well, I guessed that much. He's in training though, as some sort of novice, I think.'

'No. He isn't anything.'

'But he spent eight years there.'

'He was very sick.'

'Sick?'

She turned to him for confirmation. Faber took her hands in his.

'They were nursing him. The business with Jake drove him to some sort of collapse.'

'No.' She held his hands and stared away, following the patterns of the rug beneath their feet. 'He never said. No one told us. God, I feel so awful!' She turned to Faber again. 'Has he told you what actually happened back then?'

'Yes,' Faber sighed. 'It's more ambiguous than you thought. Apparently Robin had said nothing and it was Jake who made the first advance, which Robin duly rebuffed. The next evening Robin called round and Jake told him that he and Candida had been to bed and decided to get married.'

'Poor Dob. Poor, poor Dob!'

'He already knew someone with connections at Whelm — one of his theology tutors or something like that. I didn't quite grasp it. And he took himself off there.'

'So he . . . fell ill after he'd got to Whelm?'

'I think so.'

'You're so calm,' she said, suddenly maddened.

'How do you mean?'

'Christ!' She rounded on him, regretting her emotion but unable to choke it now she had begun. 'You don't seem to realize what you've just told me. Faber, I hadn't seen my boy for eight years. *Eight years.* You're not passing on gossip, you're telling me my son has gone mad and been locked away.' Embarrassed she turned aside and banged a cushion back into shape as he apologized.

'I'm sorry, hon, but you must see. I only met him a matter of days ago. The feelings he's stirred in me are strong — so strong but they make everything before seem flat and unreal. Unimportant, even. You do see that, don't you? But I'm sorry. I should have told you more slowly. Maybe I should have made *him* tell you. I didn't think. I didn't realize.'

Andrea stood and walked to the garden window, tugging on her fingers.

'Does he blame us very much?' she asked.

'Why you?'

'Well, we should have known. We should have interfered, got him away, found him proper help, medical help.'

'Why?'

'We're his parents.'

'The monks cured him.'

'Are you sure?'

'I didn't know him before but he seems wonderful to me.'

She hurried back to the sofa and sat beside him.

'Sorry, Faber. That was tactless of me.'

'Don't be such a berk.' He hugged her and she held him tight against her, trying to laugh. He spoke hesitantly over her shoulder. 'Do you find him very changed, then?'

She pulled back and tidied her skirt briefly.

'Yes,' she said. 'At least, he seems so but maybe we're the ones who've changed and he's just stood still. It's a good change, though. He's calmer inside. It's rather scary, as though he wasn't trying any more. He used to be so competitive; always trying to make people listen. Poor Dob. Poor Robin. We didn't know.'

Faber touched her hands again.

'I'm so glad it's you,' she said. 'You'll look after him.'

'Andrea, the two of us have scarcely met.'

'But you'll look after him. I know. What about Iras?'

'Cool as ever.' He sighed. 'That frightens me slightly. I think she's punishing me.'

'How so?'

'She does all her talking to him rather than to me.'

'But that's just the novelty of it. You've been there for ages, he's new.'

'But I don't really know how she feels. I don't want to hurt her.'

'Oh, come on, Faber! Since when could any child talk honestly to their parents about sex?'

'Iras used to. When we were still speaking.'

'But not *you* and sex. That was Outer Space sex or sex in books.'

'Suppose so.'

They sat there a while, holding hands. She remembered about her and Peter and prepared to tell Faber then felt a doubt and let the words subside. There was a childish cough from below.

'I must get back downstairs,' said Andrea. 'Let's meet soon. What are you doing at the weekend?'

'Well . . .'

'You must ask Robin. Of course you must.' She lent some brightness to her voice. 'How strange and well-arranged it all is.'

'What is?'

'Getting you for a son-in-law, of all people, and dear Iras for a grandchild.'

'Andrea, I told you, we've barely met. Give us a few weeks' courtship at least.'

She smiled.

'Listen to me,' she said and stood. 'I must go.' He made as if to rise. 'No,' she said. 'Stay and finish your strong-and-black. Help yourself to records and books.'

He grinned at her and clicked his tongue reprovingly. She smiled and shut the drawing-room door between them.

'And everywhere she went,' Peter's voice rose up the basement stairwell, 'she felt a pain as of knives in her little feet and still she smiled and tried to please her prince and still she wept with frustration that she could not speak.'

He glanced up at her as she came in at the back of the room but continued the morbid tale. Enthralled, the children sat and lay around him. No small head turned at her entry.

She moved quietly to let herself into the kindergarten kitchen to see how the Señoritas Fernandez were coping. They had finished the washing-up and were packing food away into the fridge as she came in.

'*Holá*,' said Paca.

'Hi,' said Andrea.

She must have been betrayed by some expression on her face because at once their own crumpled in sympathy and they came to support her, stroking, tutting, sighing as over a mildly injured child.

My son is not a monk, she thought. My son is mad. Was. I mean was.

Wrapped around in fat, capable arms, pink nylon overall and the scents of cooking, she dissolved in tears of appalled gratitude.

25

As in all the most hackneyed television series, the death had come suddenly and been dramatically curt. Peter had driven to the hospital straight after school as usual. Some lilies had arrived in the Friends' Flower Shop and he splashed out on one because he thought Marcus might appreciate its honeyed smell.

His friend was beyond sniffing flowers when Peter arrived on the ward, being plunged in deep, drug-induced sleep. Peter went through the motions, as he had for the last three days. He opened the window, he exchanged yesterday's flower for today's and he bathed Marcus's brow. Then he sat at the bedside for maybe twenty minutes, holding a dried old hand in his. He was about to leave when Marcus started to cry out. His moan was so even it was almost song; only the sudden fierce grip of his hand told Peter otherwise. Afraid to leave the room, Peter rang frantically on the emergency bell push and soon was unable to see Marcus for the activity of two nurses and a masked doctor who arrived and set about doing something with pipes and a syringe.

Marcus's 'song' rose in pitch and volume until Peter was tempted to laugh. It made him think of a clever short film he had once seen called 'Dog's Eye View' in which the viewer came suddenly face to face with a vast, yelling baby as seen by an inquisitive poodle.

'More This,' said the doctor. 'More That. Give him thirty mils.'

'No use,' said one nurse.

'Pulse is getting weaker,' said the other. Then they turned to leave and the nurse whom Peter recognized as the one who liked Marcus to finish her crossword patted his shoulder and said kindly,

'We'll leave him in your capable hands.'

The lament was dying down, stilled by an injection, and soon Peter's hand was held less tightly. He freed himself to fetch the cloth again and lowered it onto Marcus's forehead. Marcus sighed, made a noise midway between cough and snigger then stopped. There was no light to stop flashing or heart monitor to go dead – the machinery had all been unplugged yesterday – but Peter knew Marcus was dead from his absolute stillness and a sense of sudden solitude.

Peter tidied the sheets, brushed Marcus's wet hair off his face then took an envelope from where Marcus had said it would be and left the room.

The nurse at the reception desk looked at him with sympathy. Don't, he thought. I'll cry and then you'll be sorry.

'Has anyone called or visited him?' he asked.

'You mean Mr Mystery? No. It's all over, then?'

'Yes,' he said. 'All over.'

'Are you going off straight away?' she asked. 'Don't want a nice cup of something?'

'No. I'm not off just yet. I need to call someone. Please?'

'Yes?'

'Please don't move him or anything yet. There's someone coming who'll want to see him first.'

26

'Do that again,' Robin told him. Faber did it again. 'And here,' Robin begged. He did it there. 'And please, here.' Pleased, he did it there. It was almost too much and Robin didn't want it all to finish. Not yet. This was his new treat and, having heard *ad nauseam* how it lost its thrill through over-indulgence, he wanted to make it last. 'Stop!' he said. 'Please stop.' And he kissed Faber to make it stop. Faber kissed him back.

'Why?' Faber asked, flushed. 'Don't you like it?'

'On the contrary,' Robin said, 'It's quite extraordinary. Lie down.' Faber lay beside him, his head on Robin's armpit. His hair smelled faintly of coconut oil. They had recently run wild in a shop specializing in soaps, shampoos and essential oils and as a result were pampered to softness all over. They smelled rich, woody and edible. Faber had washed Robin's hair with a walnut extract, which he said gave its colour depth. Then he had combed enough oil through his own to make it shine and fall into short ringlets. Robin ran his hand through it to release more good smell. He opened his mouth to speak.

'Ssh,' Faber said and laid a finger on Robin's lips. Robin kissed it.

'Do I talk very much?' he asked.

'You do rather.'

'I'm sorry.'

'Don't be.'

'It's only because you make me so secure.'

'Liar.'

'You do.'

'I know that,' Faber admitted, 'but you were a talker long before you met me.'

'Oh, talk. Talk is talk but with you to talk to I tell the truth. Always.'

'All the more reason to hold your tongue and weigh your words.'

'But I'm happy,' Robin insisted. 'And when I'm happy I talk.'

'I noticed.'

'You'll miss me when I'm gone.'

'Don't say things like that,' said Faber. Robin felt him tense, so he knew he meant it.

'Well, you talk then,' Robin said. 'Tell me how you got your gold tooth.'

Faber touched his cheek.

'I just got it,' he said, offhand.

'You don't "just get" gold teeth,' Robin pursued. 'How did you lose the real one? Did it rot? You never eat sweets.'

'It was a fight. I got in a fight and someone punched the tooth out.'

'My god! Who were you fighting? A jealous lover? Or was it that poor Ellen Mae you told me about?'

'No, it wasn't that poor Ellen Mae,' Faber scoffed. 'If you must know,' he muttered, 'it was my father. He was sorry straight away, of course, and he paid for the gold one.'

'Let me see.'

'No.'

'Open your mouth, Faber.' Faber grinned then opened his mouth. Robin slipped his forefinger in and rubbed it against the tooth. 'I thought you never saw your father after your eleventh birthday,' he said. 'This is a grown-up tooth.' Faber bit his finger hard. 'Ow! Bastard! Yes. All right!' Robin begged. 'I believe you. No more tooth-talk. Promise.' Faber loosened his bite. Robin pulled his finger out and nursed it briefly in his own mouth. 'So,' he went on, talking with his mouth full, 'where were you when I got here?'

'I'm sorry. Did you wait long?'

'Half an hour. Maybe more. I opened a can of creamed corn. It's very good if you stir in an egg and throw the whole lot into a really hot frying pan.'

'Is that what the smell is?'

'I can only smell your wonderful hair.'

'I was visiting your mother. I felt guilty about her. Before you came back we used to see each other, or talk at least, almost every day, and since then I've neglected her.' He tapped Robin's chin. 'Cruelly.'

'How did you find her?'

'Well, you've obviously done her a power of good.'

'You think so? I've hardly seen her either.'

'She was glowing. I told her about us.'

'And?'

'Robin, you are a monster of insensitivity, you know.'

'Why?'

'She had no idea why you spent so long at Whelm.'

'She could have asked.'

'People don't ask that sort of thing.'

'Well, I thought the Abbot would have told her. They talked enough on the phone. Poor Ma,' Robin added but he knew he failed to convince.

'Promise you'll find time to talk to her.'

'I promise. Now, do it again.'

'Where?'

'Here.' Faber did it again. There. 'Where does one *learn* things like that? They're far too sophisticated to come naturally.'

'Let's pretend I read it in an unsuitable novel and leave it at that.' Robin threw him off and sat on his stomach.

'But I want to know everything,' he told him. 'All your dark, variegated past.'

'Such a glutton for suffering,' Faber said. 'We've barely met. You can't be needing to feel jealous already.'

'Tell me,' Robin said and tried to do it to him. Faber winced then yelped so Robin knew he had it wrong. 'Was it a he or a she?' he pursued.

'One day,' Faber said, 'when you're bored with my body and tired of my mind, I'll entertain you with my past.'

His words were flippant but he was frowning with an irritation he'd only shown once before, when Robin had pressed him for details of his adoption by the citizens of Barrowcester. Robin fell silent therefore and let him change the subject. The lust had drained out of them completely. Robin was finding that too much talking *in media res* had that effect; he thought that perhaps it had something to do with the oxygen intake.

'How did you spend your day?' Faber asked. 'I didn't expect you back so soon. I thought you were going to see that Swiss film.'

'I'd meant to but then I started job-hunting.'

'But why?'

'That's what the woman in the Job Shop asked me. I wanted to have a go at being a laundry assistant or working in a chocolate shop – they had vacancies for both of those (can't you see me in those little cotton gloves they wear in that place in Bond Street?) but she got quite cross. I had to write down where I'd been to school and so on, what exams I'd passed or failed and what experience I'd had. Well, first of all she was highly suspicious that I wasn't on the dole. She wanted to know if I had private means. I told her that no I was just confused and that seemed to bring out her motherly instinct. I was far too well qualified to be a chocolate-shop assistant, she told me, and much too clever – I'd be bored. I asked her how she knew. "It stands to reason," she said. "But I want to sell chocolates," I told her. I didn't, but it was fast becoming a matter of principle. "With your brain, then," she said, "you must go to a bank, borrow the money and start your own chocolate business." And when I said that that sounded rather frightening and permanent all the motherliness evaporated. She said that my reaction proved her worst suspicions correct. I was clearly a parasite and timewaster, she said and told me that if I was truly keen for gainful employment I would find something more high powered in a sits vac column.'

'So you want a job?'

'Not much, but since I went away to be mad it seems to have become obligatory. Anyway I'm going to need a job soon. I couldn't possibly live off you. And living off pocket money is out of the question – Maitland *père* is too careful to give me just enough to keep me amused but not enough to make me satisfied. What can I do, Faber?'

'What do you want to do?'

'I told you, nothing. I want to be, to think, to go for walks, take bus rides, observe.'

'Become a novelist.'

'I can't write.'

'So? Have you tried?'

'No. But I can't. Anyway, novelists work hard nowadays, they've been given shark-faces like everyone else. I've read some interviews with them. There's one in *Capital* today.'

'How about money? Does money interest you?'

'Earning it?'

'Partly that but mainly how it's made, how it reproduces, the sex life of the pound. Surely your father could use his old contacts to get you into the City?'

'Would you still love me if I worked in the City?'

'Only if you left it for my sake so we could set up a kindergarten.' Guilt made them giggle.

The phone rang. Robin reached towards it, being the closest.

'No,' said Faber. Robin stopped and they lay with it jangling beside them. The shrilling stopped. Robin turned back to Faber, who kissed him but then the phone started up again as though whoever it was were checking that he hadn't misdialled.

'Sorry,' Robin said, 'I can't stand it.'

'Pull out the plug,' Faber suggested but it was too late and Robin had answered.

'Hello?' he said.

'Robin?'

'Dad?'

'Sorry. I must have dialled home without thinking.'

'No, you didn't. Did you want to talk to Faber?'

'Er . . . Oh. Well, yes I did.'

'Passing you over,' Robin said. 'It's Dad,' he told Faber.

'Hello?' said Faber. 'Peter. How are you? . . . Good . . . What? What . . . When?' Robin had started doing it to Faber again but Faber shoved him away quite hard then grasped his wrist as he concentrated on whatever Dad was telling him. Robin sat up and watched. Faber's eyes had narrowed slightly with fear and he was breathing fast. He hung up.

'What is it?' Robin asked.

'Someone's ill. Very ill. An old friend.' He let go of Robin's wrist, jumped up and started tugging on clothes. 'I've got to go. I'll just fix up Iras.'

'I'll pick her up,' Robin offered.

'No, honestly. She's happy going to Dodie's,' Faber promised him. 'But, look, stay as long as you like. Stay till I get back. I should be home in a couple of hours but I'll call from the hospital if I'm going to be later.'

'OK.'

Robin dressed too, feeling in the way for the first time since setting foot on Faber's territory. While Faber made rapid calls to Iras's special school and to Dodie, Robin walked slowly downstairs. Faber had given him a set of keys days ago but suddenly he felt uncomfortable about remaining alone in the building. Faber clattered down the stairs, swore because he had forgotten his wallet, clattered up to find it, clattered down again, kissed Robin and ran out. He slammed the door and

Robin noticed, as if for the first time, the pride of place he had given to a wonderful charcoal sketch for the portrait of Candida and her first-born. He followed the gentle curve of her supporting arm beneath the baby and the answering outline of her proffered breast. Then he felt an attack coming on.

He called his mind's trouble madness not illness, because it had neither cause nor rational treatment. At its centre was a terrible void, an area of which he either knew or recalled nothing. Around the void was a kind of trumpet mouth of depression and uncontrol and around that were tendrils of disorder that reached into his conscious mind. He saw nothing untoward, no black serpents coiling through brickwork, no putrescent eruptions of the floor; the attacks came through his ears. Even the slightest sounds, no, *particularly* the slightest sounds, such as the rustle of his shirt sleeve, the breath leaving his nose or a fly at a distant window, became charged with hostility. He had had these attacks often as a child, in isolation and with no ill after-effects. His mother called them his 'feelings' and so tidied them away along with bad dreams and his dislike of the space under the bath. She thought they were growing pains and he didn't like to alarm her. She was easily alarmed.

Robin's 'feelings' made reading impossible, for the most harmless words – elderflower, toothbrush, looking-glass – were vocalized in his head to mock him. Occasionally he tried to interrupt the sounds, beating them down with the sound of his voice, but his voice no longer sounded like his own. On Whelm, Luke, instructed by the Abbot, had followed a similar course to that proscribed for men convinced they are possessed by evil spirits. He would seek to calm Robin with music, unambiguous poetry or simple words of love; either his own or Christ's.

Robin forced himself to the record-player. He couldn't choose a record of his own as this would have involved too many words and too much rustling. Inevitably, since no one had played anything since Iras's exercise session last night,

the record on the turntable was Nina Simone's. He jumped
the tone arm to the third track.

'He's got the whole world in his hands,
He's got the whole wide world in his hands . . .'

Robin crouched with his back safely to the wall and met Nina's
gaze from the record sleeve. Suddenly he could see what Iras
meant, but he saw more than her. Nina was telling him that
God and Death were the same.

27

Candida's day had tried her sorely. One of her breakfast guests had been run down by a lorry the night before. Ordinarily she could have filled his untimely vacancy with an obituary hastily cobbled together from 'Death Row', the video and clippings archive kept for the purpose, but he had been only a minor unrecorded playwright. Out to publicize his latest glum offering, he had found a slot on the show solely by virtue of his former relation to one of the producers. The only self-publicists consistently available to appear at dawn after seven hours' notice were politicians, so Candida had found herself saddled with a spontaneous debate on the free market which lost half her usual audience and over-ran disastrously. The more antagonistic of the two MPs, a man she used to admire, kept interrupting her summary with, 'Ah-ha! You see? That bears out my point *exactly*!' which meant that the all-important weather bulletin spilled over in turn into a crass but equally important location report from outside a royal labour ward. Her autocue had gone awry no less than three times after that. The pathetic excuse for this being that the usual operator had also enjoyed some involvement with the deceased playwright and had only learnt the sad news when Candida announced it on air. The newsprint summarist had gaily passed her a tabloid where an unrecognizably hideous photograph of her in her puppy-fat teens had been printed with the caption 'GUESS WHO??!!' This less than perfect morning had been rounded off by a dressing-down from the studio boss on the subject of tumbling viewing figures which he somehow related to her dress sense. He had snapped his fingers at her most offensively and told her to 'run along and fix her hair or something'.

Candida's coiffure had admittedly gone slightly to seed since Robin's return. She had paid an amount even she found painful to have it 'fixed' on the way home, and was regarding the treacherous result in her bathroom mirror when Jasper ran in.

'Mummy, Mummy!'

'I've told you before *not* to come racing in here when the door's shut, without knocking,' she snapped. 'My bathroom is *not* a playground.'

'Sorry,' he whimpered, now seeming lost for words.

'Well? What is it?' she demanded.

'It's Andrea Maitland but she doesn't have the Holy Man with her.'

By the time Candida had tried on and rejected a headscarf and come down to greet her, Andrea had already rung the bell and been let as far as the hall by Samantha.

'What is it about this family,' Candida wondered, 'that they think they can just turn up and find me both in and available? Still, the parents once told me they regarded me as one of their own,' she reminded herself, 'and now I regard their son with an affection more than sisterly.'

'Andrea!' she exclaimed. 'Sorry to keep you waiting.' She made as if to kiss the older woman's cheek but Andrea was already starting forward to the sitting-room.

'Not at all,' she said briskly, her face unusually frosty. 'Sorry to turn up out of the blue. I'm afraid we have to talk. Shall we go in here?'

She was already in there. Candida waited, trying to huff and puff a little, but all her will seemed to have gone the way of her hair. She followed and sat across the room from her visitor.

'Has something awful happened?' she asked.

'Not recently,' said Andrea, 'But, yes.'

'Tell me.'

'You stole Dob's lover. Jake and Robin were in love and you jealously worked on Jake's weak nature to steal him.'

Candida gasped.

'I hardly think this is the . . . Really, Andrea, it was so long ago.' She found a trace of indignation which enabled her to stand.

'Sit down,' Andrea told her. 'I haven't finished.'

Candida sat.

'We all thought Robin ran away afterwards to be a monk,' Andrea said. 'I've just discovered that these last eight years he's been having a complete mental breakdown, entirely due to your envious meddling.'

'But . . . Poor Dob. I had no idea.'

'Of course you didn't.'

'Is he better? I mean, he *seems* better. He must be as he wouldn't be out. Home, I mean.'

Andrea was staring at her in disbelief.

'Is that honestly *all* you can think to say? Don't you feel any remorse?'

'Oh, for Christ's sake, Andrea,' she shouted, jumping up. 'What do you think? I loved Dob. He was my childhood friend. Of course I feel bad. I feel awful. So will Jake when he hears. But you've misunderstood.'

'Well, you'd better put me right.'

'I hardly think it's your business.'

'Of course it's my bloody business. You've broken my son. Thanks to you I lost him, we lost him, for eight whole years. And now he's changed. You must have noticed.'

'He's just older. We're all older.'

'It's more than that.'

'Look, Perdita needs her feed and Jake'll be home soon.'

'They can keep a little.' Andrea rubbed a hard hand across her forehead. Her wedding ring left a brief white line there.

She changed her tone. 'Look, please Candida. Tell me. Tell me everything. You never have.'

Candida watched Jasper helping Samantha take clothes off the line. She turned back to Andrea and sat down. 'It's all so long ago,' she complained.

'Please.'

'They weren't lovers,' Candida muttered. 'None of us were. Of course Dob had an almighty crush on Jake but he never did anything about it. I know. I was there. I even urged him on. He was convinced that if he said anything, Jake would run a mile. I mean, Jake knew about the crush, but Dob made a joke of it as though it were all a pose. Eventually Jake proposed to me and I turned him down. The next thing I knew, Robin turned up in my house and attacked me.'

'Physically?'

Candida hesitated.

'No. He threw a lot of things around. He shouted. He wept. He was obviously drunk and that was the last we saw of him. I rang you the next day. You remember.'

'I remember.'

'Where did you hear this story about them being lovers?'

'Dob told me but I exaggerated. They weren't lovers, not yet, but Jake had made, well, proposals to Robin and Robin says he panicked and pretended to be revolted. The next evening Jake was being mortified and apologetic, saying "Never mind, I've been to bed with Candida a couple of times and I see now it was all just confusion. It was her I wanted and we're going to get married."'

Candida froze.

'At least,' Andrea qualified, 'that was the gist of it.'

'My God,' spat Candida. 'The little jerk. The *bastard*.'

There was a sound of high performance engine and crushed gravel from beside the house. 'That's him,' Candida muttered, half oblivious of Andrea now. Andrea jumped up.

'I must go,' she said. 'Oh. Oh dear.' She wavered, then darted forward and patted Candida's shoulder. 'I didn't realize and now I've gone and stirred things up. Candida, I didn't mean . . . I only wanted the truth. Oh dear.'

Andrea fled through the house. Candida heard her greetings fluttered at Jake in the porch and her trotting shoes on the pavement a few seconds later. There was the unmistakable thunder of a Volkswagen starting up then peace except for Jasper going for some sparrows with a plastic machine gun. Finally Jake popped his head around the door, said a chirpy hello and vanished.

'Jake?'

He came back.

'Yup? Hey! I like the hair-do.'

'Andrea Maitland's just been here.'

'Yes. We met on the steps. Any trouble with Jasper?'

'No. Nothing like that.'

He came in and flopped noisily onto the sofa beside her, clearly not listening.

'You bastard!' she hissed.

Stung, he laughed.

'What? What have I done now?'

She lashed out, not to slap but to punch him hard, on the jaw. It hurt her more than she'd expected but she followed through with another punch, this time to his shoulder. Taken by surprise he had fallen off the sofa. She stood and kicked his shin fiercely. Twice. After an initial yelp he took the blows quietly, merely sucking in air through his teeth. She stood back and stared at him as he clambered onto the sofa, rubbing his leg.

'Jasper's outside the window,' he muttered and touched his jaw.

'I don't fucking care,' she said. 'Think back, Jake. Think back eight long eventful happy years to a certain evening just before our finals.'

'Yes?' he frowned.

'You told Robin we'd had sex. You told him we were going to get married. You little shit!' She kicked his shin again.

He struck back this time, setting the sole of his shoe firmly against her thigh and shoving so that she toppled back and sat down hard, striking her coccyx on a wooden chair arm as she went down.

'Cunt!' he shouted and hurled several large books at her in quick succession. He was making a strange coughing noise as he did so and she realized that he was crying. Jake never cried. Ever. They never fought. She sat up, rubbing her back and watched. He stopped throwing things and blew his nose.

'You fancied him,' she said. 'You tried to get him into bed only he didn't want you.'

He stood and walked out. She heard him calling softly for Jasper in the garden, turned and saw him hugging the child to him. Milky white, Jasper stared over his father's shoulder towards the window where she watched. There was a knock at the door.

'Yes?'

It was Samantha.

'Sorry to butt in like, Candy, but Perdy-M's crying fit to bust. Shall I give her another bottle or . . .'

'I'll feed her,' said Candida, striding out past her, 'And don't call me Candy. Ever.'

Perdita was roaring. Her fists wrenched at the cot sheet as she sucked in tiny lungfuls of air and with each fresh bellow her alarming shade of scarlet intensified. Strings of spit webbed her toothless mouth and her eyes had sunk into veined wrinkles of fury. Candida kneeled on the carpet, rested her head on her arms and watched her daughter's miniature despair.

28

Faber spent all the cash in his wallet taking a taxi to the hospital. If Peter offered him a ride home he would feel duty-bound to refuse it; he would need the punishment of the walk home. Although he had telephoned the ward several times almost without thinking, he found he had repeated its name over and over in his head on the journey so that it was now quite meaningless. There was a large crowd waiting for the lift so he threw himself up the emergency stairs.

'I've come to see Marcus Carling,' he panted at the Briar Ward reception desk.

'Ah, yes. If you follow the corridor,' he was told, 'it's the last room on the right.'

He expected a ward or at least a bed, with Marcus in a net of drips and monitor wires. In their stead he found a pink, bedless room with a spider plant, a view, a kettle, Peter and a box of teabags.

'Where is he?' he asked.

'Faber.' Peter stood. 'I'm afraid it's too late. I said not to rush on the phone.'

'Where is he?'

'I'll show you.'

Peter opened the door, then held another open across the corridor. Faber walked across and heard the door shut behind him.

The window faced the street and the noise of traffic from

below was a surprise after the cushioned quiet elsewhere. He stopped at the foot of the bed.

I haven't laid eyes on you for ten whole years, he thought.

The man before him looked old enough to be his grandfather. Faber saw thin white hair, loose skin and liver spots; a bag of chicken bones with ostrich legs. He pulled up a chair and sat close to the corpse.

Why don't I feel anything? he wondered. This is a grand reunion.

He took one of the hands and pressed it to his lips then, clawlike, hard against his cheek. Feeling came now, sliding into the back of his throat and up behind his eyes. Faber wept briefly and without tears. The cruel wrenching at his lungs and face made his nose run. He had no handkerchief and someone had cleared the bedside table. He had to use the sheet. As he blew, the linen twitched off Marcus's shoulders and revealed an emaciated torso and a recent surgical scar like a long zip pattern branded on with a sizzling iron. Disgusted, Faber finished blowing his nose and pulled the sheet right up over Marcus's head. He stood, hesitated, then pulled back the sheet to kiss the old man once on the lips. Then he went to find Peter.

'Cup of tea?' Peter offered. 'It's all they've got.'

'Thanks.'

Faber accepted the mug then sat heavily on one of the grey plastic armchairs. It sighed beneath him as it subsided.

'How did you know to ring me?' he asked.

'Marcus told me. At least, he left a note for me to open if no one had been to see him before the er . . . end. I found your name and number. It was a bit of a shock.'

'What? Finding my name on the note?'

'Well. That was, of course, but I was thinking more of Robin answering your phone, actually.'

'Oh, that. You haven't talked with Andrea since this afternoon, then?'

'Not really. She seemed a bit down after you'd gone. What had you told her?'

'About Robin and me.'

'Oh. That he was coming round?'

'That he and I are lovers.'

'Oh. Oh God, *sorry*,' Peter spluttered. 'You must think me so stupid. I hadn't . . . Oh.'

'Look,' Faber raised a hand. 'Could we talk about that some other time? I'm not really . . .'

'Oh yes. Of course. Sorry.'

Each sipped his tea.

'Miss Birch,' said Peter suddenly.

'Who's she?'

'His assistant. I clean forgot to ring her.' Peter stood. 'Back in a sec.'

Alone, Faber poured his tea into a small corner sink and rinsed out the mug. He walked to the window and stood with his forehead pressing against the cool glass.

'God,' he whispered. 'God, God, God.'

The bad day he had been expecting for so many months was incalculably worse than he had imagined, chiefly because he was finding it so hard to react. He was still Faber, father of Iras, painter of pictures. He was still falling in love with Robin. In the core of his being he was the happy man he had been this morning and yet, from the moment he had heard Peter on the phone saying 'It's Marcus' he had known he was now a briefly tragic figure; one to be pitied, cosseted, given cushions and stiff drinks. It was this prospect of sympathy more than the stark vision of Marcus Carling, recently ill, now deceased, that caused the sadness which he could already feel spreading down from his surface thoughts like so much ink in water. I must talk now, he thought, now while I'm in this room. As soon as I step outside, I become a bereaved person.

He heard Peter come back in. He heard a chair subside. He turned and found himself sitting on the floor where he could relax.

'I'm sorry I snapped just now,' he said.

'Don't be,' said Peter. 'I feel such a fool.'

'I need to talk,' Faber went on. 'Ask me things. Ask anything you like. Or don't like.'

'How long have you known him?'

'Just since the baptism.'

'I meant Marcus.'

'Needing to, they laughed out of all proportion.

'Years and years,' said Faber at last. 'I can't think of the date. Longer than I've known you and Andrea.'

'And when did you split up?'

'I haven't . . . hadn't seen him. Just now was the first time I'd seen him for ten years.'

'And you'd been together long before then?'

Faber grinned, despite the heaviness that was seeping through him.

'Er, Peter . . . I think you've crossed wires again.'

'I don't quite see.'

'Marcus was my father. My adoptive father. How well did *you* know him, for Chrissakes?'

'Oh, me? I've only known him since he fell ill. I was sent to him by the hospital because . . . He had no visitors.'

'Well,' Faber smiled wryly. 'I'm glad I was instrumental in a beautiful friendship.' Peter looked hurt.

'I have to go on. I don't care,' Faber thought.

'He was an Old Barrowcesterian,' he told Peter. 'A group of them clubbed together to adopt and educate a poor African from their overseas diocese and I was the "little Piccaninny", bright enough and oh so photogenic. So I was uprooted from the family and sent to the heart of provincial England. To a fourteenth century school with its own goddamn language.' He sighed with the effort of saying so much so fast. Peter paused, digesting facts.

'Andrea never told me,' he said, at last.

'I never told Andrea. She's never asked and it's not the sort of thing I talk about. That's why I'm telling you now.'

'Go on.'

'Marcus and the others would take it in turns to have me to stay for holidays but the other two got married, and their wives disapproved or their own children made trouble so Marcus took me on completely.'

'What about your family?'

'Marcus became my family. We got on. I adored him. He loved educating me. He took me on wildly exciting trips. He took me to Florence, to Rome, to Venice, to Athens, to Cairo, to Madrid. Then he suggested I go on to the Slade. Great idea I thought, as I was keen on painting already and I wanted to stay at home in London with Marcus. But he never even paid my first term's bill.'

'Why not?'

'I left home. He tried. He . . . Well, he thought the time had come for him to be more to me than family and I couldn't cope.'

'Why not?'

'He was my fucking father, that's why not.'

'Sorry.'

'So we didn't meet for ten years. I got myself a scholarship and hid from him all the time I was at the Slade. He was a creature of habit so it was easy enough. I lived in bits of London he never went to, with people he wouldn't like, then, as soon as that was done, I ran away to America. Lots of painting, lots of uncomplicated sex and no "family".'

'Where you found Iras.'

'Where I found Iras.'

'You didn't need to hide, you know. He was in America all that time. He ran away too.'

'Where in America exactly?'

'He lived in San Francisco.'

'Like father, like son.'

'He went to the opera a lot.'

'I bet that wasn't his only entertainment. Jesus! He might have started picking me up in a bar.'

'Surely he would have recognized you.'

'Of course he'd have fucking recognized me!' Faber snapped, incredulous. 'I was joking, you jerk. Sorry.' He snatched some tissues and blew his nose. He continued more quietly. 'Why am I telling you all this?'

'You seem to want to.'

'Sorry, Peter. Yes. I "seem to want to".'

A nurse laughed loudly in the corridor. There was a lull. Peter stood.

'More tea?' he asked with all the nervous deference of an aide at a grand masters' tournament.

'No, thanks.' Faber watched him make himself another cup of tea. 'So, tell me truthfully,' he asked him. 'Since we're in the sort of place where we can be frank. How do you feel about Robin?'

Peter frowned then turned back to the kettle to speak.

'Generally, you mean?'

'Yes.'

'Guilty.'

'Why? What could you do?'

Peter abandoned his tea and paced.

'I could have been around more,' he said. 'And had more influence, not been so bloody non-committal. Confronted him, even.'

'You think that would have stopped him going to Whelm?'

'I think it might have stopped him being homosexual.'

The scientific term dangled in the anaesthetic air between them. Challenged, Faber spoke up after a moment's thought.

'I had no idea you felt that way,' he said.

'You did ask for the truth,' said Peter as though by way of apology.

An orderly opened the door abruptly, apologized and tiptoed away again.

'I think we've sat here long enough,' Peter said.

'Quite. There might be a queue of the newly-bereaved waiting to use the place.'

They paused at the door to Marcus's room.

'Hang on,' said Faber.

'Of course,' Peter agreed. 'I'll wait for you by the lift.'

He walked on down the corridor, which was busy now with the arrival of the evening meal-trolley.

Faber opened the door. The bed was empty. Stripped. The chain of Get Well cards had been removed too.

There's tact, he mused.

The room was hot and airless. He tugged back the sliding panels of the window to let anything left of Marcus out into the night. This would be one of the rare nights when he dreamt of Africa. He stared briefly at the orange-lit view then went to join Peter at the lift.

'I think these are yours, now,' Peter said, holding out an overnight bag gaudy with international flight labels.

'I don't want them, whatever they are.'

'Take them,' Peter told him, pressing the handle into Faber's hand. 'They're Marcus's.'

Offered a lift back to Clapham, Faber refused. On Battersea Bridge he stopped to open the bag and found, amongst carefully folded clothes, a portable compact disc player, head-phones and numerous discs. He moved on into the light from an off-licence window in Battersea then stopped again to read the titles. It took him a few moments to see how the machine worked, then he walked the few miles home listening to his father's favourite music.

29

Andrea was pacing her study with a dog-eared paperback swinging in her hand.

'Why swell'st thou then?' she asked in rhythm with her pacing. 'One short sleep past we . . . We . . .' She paused to cheat then thrust the book back at her side. 'One short sleep past we wake eternally, And death shall go . . . Death shall . . .' She stopped, glanced at the page a second then tossed the book aside and left the room.

When she came home, hot and frightened from her disastrous call on Candida, she had found that Peter was still not back from visiting Marcus. She had made a hasty, pulse-heavy supper, which was drying out now on top of the oven. She had helped herself to a couple of drinks, which she quite often did when he was not there, since it seemed unfair to drink much in his presence. She had rung Faber to tell him what she had done but there was no reply. She had tried ringing one of her older friends, a woman with whom she used to be close, but had lost courage and hung up when her husband answered. Driven by nerves, she had washed an indignant Brevity with insecticidal shampoo and conditioner. Newly bathed, Brevity was always wildly excited. While she danced from room to room, yapping and shaking dry her now absurdly fluffy pelt, her mistress went on to attack the master bedroom with hoover, dusters and lavendered beeswax. Her dressing table glowed and their shoes lay in rows of tidy pairs under either side of the cleanly sheeted bed. She wanted to change Robin's sheets too, which surely needed it by now, but his door was still firmly locked. He always locked it and rarely answered her knocking so she could never be sure if he was in or out. She left his room in peace, then came across her copy of Donne's poems and was sidetracked into carrying out Peter's rather beautiful request that she learn one. Brevity had calmed down and was now trying to make a nest in the bundle of dirty sheets Andrea had dropped on the landing.

'Shoo!' Andrea shouted. 'Shoo, you silly thing!'

She picked up the bundle and carried it down to the kitchen, hugging it close.

Supper had not been thrilling to start with, and now it was ruined. She shoved the saucepan under a running tap. The brownish stew mixture sizzled a second then was swamped. She dug around in the freezer, burning her fingers on the ice as she looked for something else. Peter came in at the back door.

'Hi, darling,' she began, 'Where have you . . . ?' then stopped, seeing that something was wrong. 'What is it?'

'Marcus,' he said.

She hurried to meet him and held him close, his face against her neck.

'Strange,' she murmured, rocking him slightly. 'I was just learning it.'

Peter pulled away from her and walked upstairs. She followed him to their room where they lay fully clothed in a smell of soap and clean sheets. He held her closely from behind. When she woke, cold in darkness, hours later, she found that their sleep had been like death and neither had moved.

30

Candida was lying in wait. She had fed Perdita then taken her car and driven it fast to the South side of Clapham Common. Still with no particular plan in mind, she had walked to Faber's front door and peered in through the window. There was music playing and she slid out of sight when she saw Robin crouching on the floor in a corner. She edged around the window and peered in again. He seemed to be in some sort of trance. Perhaps Faber had given him dope; most artists were hopelessly outdated and still smoked things. There was no sign of Faber. She watched until the music stopped and Robin suddenly stood up and began turning off lights. She hurried back to her car and waited, breathless, for what seemed like ten minutes.

At last he was leaving the studio. Through a gap in the threadbare hedge she saw him shut and lock the door. He came out onto the pavement and began to walk away from her. She started the engine and cruised forward until she was just behind him then she pressed a button that caused the kerbside window to wind down.

'Psst!'

He walked on. Those long, long hands thrust deep in his trouser pockets.

'Psst!'

Now he turned. He frowned then saw who it was.

'Candy!'

'Dobbin! You want a ride?' She had drawn alongside and he was already opening the door. Fool.

'I wasn't really going anywhere,' he said, 'But sitting inside was driving me mad so I thought I'd kill time by walking. Let's just drive. Where were you off to?'

'I came to look for you,' she said, glancing in the mirror then pulling out into the evening traffic. On hurrying back to the car she had dabbed on some scent but her hand had shaken with excitement and the car's interior reeked richly of the stuff.

'What a bit of luck,' he said. 'Nice car.'

'Do you like it?' She smiled, pleased.

'Very. Where did you get it?'

'Hamburg. Our fifth anniversary.'

'Sexy. Can I have a go?'

'What? Drive it?'

'Yes.'

'Why ever not? Hang on.'

She pulled over, opened her door and walked round to his side while he climbed carefully over the gearstick. Without thinking, she had taken out the ignition keys. 'Here,' she said, handing them over before fastening her seat-belt. 'Are you insured or anything?'

He started the engine and pulled them gently out from the kerb.

'Not really,' he said 'But it's all right. If a policeman stops us, you're a star. Let's just drive round and round the common.'

'If you like.'

She let him drive her three times around the common then she made him stop and change places once more.

'Oh. Do I have to?'

'Yes.'

He relinquished the driving seat, walked round to the other side and, before long, she was kidnapping him.

'Where are we going?' he asked.

'I'm not sure,' she answered. 'South and fast.'

He didn't seem to mind at first, lying back on the soft leather and playing with the radio, then some way beyond Blackheath he grew restless.

'Faber'll be back soon,' he said.

'I thought you said he was out for the evening,' she replied, pressing her accelerator foot gently towards the horizontal.

'I did. He was. But he should be back by now.'

She pulled off into a sort of lay-by picnic area with some trees. They were alone there. The only light came from a distant street lamp and the headlamps of rapidly passing cars. She flicked off the radio and drew a breath.

'Dob.'

'Robin.'

'Robin, listen. I made a mistake.'

'How do you mean?'

'Kiss me?'

'*What*?'

'Kiss me.'

'All right.' He kissed her, softly but on the cheek, then sat back. 'Can we go home now?'

'Properly,' she said. 'Damn you.'

'No.'

'Please.'

'No!'

She hated him for his chuckle. She turned aside and pretended to cry a little.

'Robin, this is so degrading but I want you so much,' she muttered.

'Don't cry,' he said. 'Please don't cry.' He patted her shoulder and she found she wasn't pretending anymore. 'You know I like you very much. We're childhood friends, remember? Oldest friends.'

She spun round and slapped him savagely on the cheek. A car flew by just at that moment so she saw the surprise in his eyes.

'Don't,' he said.

'Which?' she asked slapping him again. 'Cry or hit you?' She slapped him a third time, much harder. He raised his hands to push her away but she grabbed his wrists and found herself the stronger. He was fresh out of hospital after all. 'Kiss me,' she said, 'Hold me.'

'Candida.' His voice was maddeningly calm. 'I really don't want to.'

Again there was that mockery in his voice. With a snort of pure frustration she let go of his wrists, put the palm of her hand in his face and shoved his head hard against the window. He cried out, so, clutching his hair to pull him forward, she did it again. He said nothing this time. She had knocked him out.

'Hell,' she said, bluntly and lowered his head onto her lap. His eyes were shut. She had drawn blood. She felt its wetness on her hand then realized that it was her own where he had bitten her. With her other hand she reached to the back of his head and found only a swelling bruise. Quickly she undid some buttons on his shirt and slipped her hand inside to find his heart. Only when she felt it pump beneath her touch did she see the appalling pleasure of her action and pulled her hand away, almost ripping the shirt in her haste. She heaved him back onto his seat then pulled a lever to make it recline like a dentist's chair. She saw he had not fastened his seat-belt and did it for him. Then she started the engine again, waited for a gap in the traffic and executed a swift U-turn towards London.

Just over eight years ago he had broken into her bathroom while she was taking a bath. Summer term or no, it was bitterly cold and wet. She had been revising solidly for six hours and was trying to soak away the stiffness in her neck and spine and to deaden the painful chill the library draughts had brought to her feet. The electric fire was plugged in and waiting on an old bentwood chair. When she got out she would crouch before it to dry her hair. The two other girls who rented the canal cottage with her were away for the weekend. She had locked the bathroom door nonetheless; a compulsive action, making the relaxation more complete. When she heard him shouting her name downstairs she realized he must have climbed in through the garden window with a broken catch.

'Up here,' she shouted.

'Where?'

'Bathroom.'

She heard him thump up the tiny stairs and along the corridor. 'I've got to see you.'

'I'll be out in a second.'

'I've got to see you now. Let me in.'

'I can't. I'm in the bath.'

At the first terrible thud as he ran against the door she had heard herself give a pathetically inadequate shriek of 'Don't!' but the wood was old and damp, like most of the house, and he had burst in on the second.

Nakedness was common between them – they often shared a bed for companionship – but she still clutched up a towel, frightened at his uncharacteristic violence.

'You've stolen him,' he shouted. 'Bitch!'

'What? No! I didn't. Look. Don't be silly.' She stood, wrapping the towel about her, cross because she hadn't washed her hair yet. 'What's he been telling you?'

'You've stolen him. He was mine. You knew it. I *loved* him, Candida. I still do.'

The most frightening thing had been his tears. They had known each other for over a decade and she had never seen him cry. His weeping was womanly, wild, without shame. It was with a lung-defying moan, like a child in a tantrum, that he seized the electric fire and threw it at the bathwater. Then everything happened at farcical speed. She screamed and jumped. Her leg struck the airborne fire and knocked it back onto the floor, out of danger's way. Then, still shuddering with grief, he ran forward, snatched the fire up and jumped into the bathwater with it.

There was a thick cloud of steam and a smell like burning

dust. Robin had fallen silent in an instant. She had darted on the flex and, with no thought to her own safety, tugged the plug from the wall. Furling her towel about her hands, she pulled him from the bath, letting him flop on the bathroom floor. Only then, seeing him lie there, soaked and white as death, had she panicked and run in a dressing-gown to the cottage next door where there was a telephone. An ambulance was called, with the police who seemed to feel they should come too. Dressed by the time they arrived, Candida was forced to greet them in deepest embarrassment. After making the emergency call she had sprinted back to the bathroom to find a small flood, a bad smell and no Robin. A search was put out, without success, and rather than leave it to the police, she had elected to call the Maitlands with the strange bad news.

She had half hoped, on calling them, that it would turn out that he had run away home to Clapham. He might, she dared hope, even answer the phone and laugh at her. It was only when he hadn't and when, weeks later, a postcard from his parents let her know that Robin was safe and well and living in an island monastery, that she had accepted Jake's persistent requests that she take him to bed and accept his hand in marriage. When Robin had burst into her bathroom she had been innocent of his charges except, perhaps, in her failure to inform him of Jake's recent, embarrassing overtures. In marrying their mutual friend, however, she knew she was assuming a share of blame.

By the time she pulled up outside Faber's studio, Robin was snoring heavily.

'Robin?' she said, trying to wake him. 'Dob? We're there. We're home.' He mumbled, and stirred slightly. She left him to wake up and went to find Faber. There were lights on but the artist took a long time to come to the door. He was obviously surprised to see her.

'Candida!'

'Faber, hello. It's Robin.'

'What's happened?' He was galvanized by concern. It made her sick.

'Nothing. He's all right. I've got him in the car. I picked him up to give him a lift and, well, we had to stop suddenly and he hadn't done up his seat-belt properly and he hit his head.'

'Jesus!'

'No, honestly . . .' she touched his arm and they hurried out to the car. 'He was knocked out for a bit and . . .' she tugged on his sleeve to slow him for a moment, 'and I'm afraid it may have brought on a sort of funny turn. He went very strange and panicky, as though I was attacking him.' He looked at her questioningly. 'Andrea's told me all about Whelm,' she explained. 'Poor Dob.'

'I'll put him to bed,' Faber said. They stood by the car a moment, watching Robin who had fallen fast asleep again. 'You're not meant to let concussion patients sleep at first,' Faber went on, 'but if he's snoring I don't think he can be sleeping heavily. Do you mind giving me a hand?'

'Of course not.'

Between them they walked Robin into the house and laid him on a sofa. Candida suspected he was wide awake and enjoying himself immensely. Faber covered him with a sky-blue blanket up to his chin, then the two of them stood and watched him a moment.

'Where's Iras?' she asked.

'At a friend's. I should be going round to fetch her.'

'Shall I stay with him while you go?' she offered.

'Oh. Could you?'

'Of course.' She touched his arm.

'That would be sweet.' He stopped and rubbed his forehead. 'What am I saying?'

'Faber? Are you OK?'

'Yes. Not really. I'm just a bit tired. I'm talking nonsense. I've already rung Dodie's and they're hanging onto Iras for the night. Sorry, Candida.'

'Don't worry.' She pecked his cheek. 'I must go,' she said.

He barely registered her touch. Infected with the same, oddly suspended state, she found herself sitting down instead of leaving. Just as she had re-run through her mind the images of Robin's terrifying disappearance, so she now saw herself kicking Jake again and again. He was staring up at her. 'Cunt!'

'Faber, there wasn't a crash,' she said. 'I didn't have to stop suddenly. I hit him and somehow I knocked him out. I lost control. I'm awfully sorry. I'm a stupid coward and I'm sorry. It's these pills you see.'

'What?' He had looked up suddenly.

'Er . . . My doctor gives me pills for a sort of, well, for a hormone problem and they make my temper short if I take too many.' He said nothing. He had already turned back to Robin. 'Faber, are you all right?'

Robin snored softly.

'Mmm?' asked Faber. 'Oh. Not really.'

'Well . . .'

He came to himself with a jerk.

'No. I'm fine. I'm just tired.' Again he rubbed his head. 'Of course you hit him. I knew that.' He looked back at Robin briefly and chuckled.

'How?'

'Bump's on the back of his head, not the front.'

'Oh.'

'He must have pushed you pretty far. I know how maddening he can be. He doesn't know his own strength. He can be very cruel.'

'Faber? I love him *so* much!'

'I know. We all do.'

'I don't want him to hate me.'

'Don't be a fool.' He smiled kindly. 'You're his oldest friend, his childhood friend.'

'Yes,' she said.

'You must go.'

'Yes,' she said, staring at the floor. 'Yes,' she said again more briskly, and hurried away to what might be left of her family.

31

'It's no good if you look,' Iras told him.

'How can you tell I'm looking?' asked Robin, amazed because he had been.

'Because of the delay. I can tell you're trying to count the bumps with your eyes. Eyes always make people slower. It's bad enough that you vocalize when you read printed text.'

'How can you tell I do *that*?'

'Same way. Speed. You turn the pages so slowly I can tell you're reading aloud in your brain.'

'I might just be enjoying it, or not concentrating hard. Reading doesn't have to be a race.'

'No. But it's much more exciting if you can read nearer the speed you think.'

'Impossible.'

She tapped the page between them. She nearly smiled. Iras often nearly smiled when talking to him now; he began to see that, in the depressed currency of her physical communications, a near-smile was valuable.

'Next word,' she said. 'And don't look.'

'I'm not. I'm staring at you.'

'Try shutting your eyes. There are fewer distractions that way.'

Robin shut his eyes. He had been trying so long that his fingertip was beginning to itch. Iras had said he must use that sensitivity, push through it and soon he could tell what letter he was reading without having to slide his finger back and forth. Or cheat.

'C', he said 'and one dot is A so it's Ca. Cat sat on the mat?'

'No. Much easier.'

'Two dots vertically.'

'Think.'

'I'm thinking. Got it. Cab!'

'Finally.'

'Iras, this is too hard.'

'It's the simplest primer there is. It's uncontracted.'

'What?'

'Uncontracted. Grade one. Grade one and a half is simply contracted.'

'What happens then?'

'It speeds up. You leave out letters, as many as you can before the meaning gets muddled. So B on its own is but. M on its own is more but with dot five before it becomes mother and if you add dots four five and six it turns into many.'

'How do you ever learn it?'

'You have to. You would soon enough if you lost your sight. People need books. Proper people.'

'That's monstrous. You can't judge people on their literacy. It's too external.'

'Yes, you can. Anyway, as I was saying, after simple contraction it gets harder still.'

'More grades?'

'Quite. Grade two is moderately contracted and grade three is highly contracted.'

'What does that involve?'

'Getting quicker still. Immediate becomes imm, blind becomes bl, beyond becomes bey.'

'What's deceive?'

'Dcv.'

'But that takes away all the beauty of it!'

'What's beauty? If it's the look of the thing you can

hardly blame the sightless for not having much time for it.'

'I mean the sound.'

'You can still read aloud or vocalize in your head. It just means that you can skip out all the unnecessary letters. Think how many letters in English are unpronounced or unnecessary. Most of them are just historical.'

'But that's nice. People like historical.'

'It's hard work if you do all your reading by hand. Braille still has poetry. There's a special sign to show when you're leaving prose and moving into verse.'

'Like a gear change.'

'Exactly. Like when Andrea puts on her poetry voice. Punctuation comes alive too. From what I can gather, most sighted people don't really understand punctuation and they certainly don't see much beauty in it, but when you read it with your fingers a punctuation sign has an equal importance to the letters on either side of it. It gets dramatic.'

They were sitting on either side of Faber's old dining-table. Faber was away at his father's funeral but had asked Robin to stay at home with Iras. Iras had been keen to go too, never having been to a funeral. When Robin explained what happened at one, however, she lost interest, saying that it sounded remarkably like a christening without a party.

'All that clumsy poetry and primitive symbolism,' she scoffed.

'Some people find it helps,' Robin assured her. 'People in pain especially. Faber's in quite a lot of pain at the moment.'

'Yes, but he doesn't need poetry. He's got us. And his painting. He's been painting a lot. Is it any good?'

'Which?'

'His latest?'

'It's of us.'

'That makes a change.'

'Come round and we'll have a look.'

'You mean you'll have a look.'

Iras left her seat and followed him to the far end of the table where Faber's easel stood in the sunlight.

'Sorry. I'm learning.'

'Gradually. So?'

Robin had stopped in front of the canvas and took her shoulders to guide her in front of him.

'Give me your reading finger,' he said. She held up a hand with forefinger extended. Gently he grasped the finger and drew it around the rough edge of the square before them. 'This is the canvas he's been painting it on,' he told her.

'Big, isn't it? He's always moaning about the price of paint.'

'But the bigger the painting, the more money he can ask for it.'

'Strange,' she murmured. 'Like paying more for *Great Expectations* just because it's longer than *Lolita*.'

'Have you read *Lolita* already?'

'Last year. I wouldn't let Faber watch it on television unless he promised to buy me a copy. I'd heard all the fuss.'

'Which did you prefer?'

'Well, *Great Expectations* is far more subversive.'

'Iras Washington. You'll go far.'

'Yes, but show me the rest of the painting.'

Robin took her finger again. 'This is the table we're sitting at.' He drew her finger through the air, tracing Faber's design just above the glistening surface of the thickly laid paint. It was a beautiful painting, with the deep slate blue of Iras's dungarees and the red of Robin's shirt. There was no direct source of light in the scene, but the sunshine from elsewhere was bouncing up from the pages of braille onto their faces. 'And that's the book on your side and this,' he continued to trace with her finger, 'is you teaching me to read braille and this, over here, is me trying to learn and failing dismally.'

'You weren't that bad,' she conceded. 'Not for your first day. You've such a lot to unlearn before you can get much further.'

'Do you honestly think so? Shall I persevere?'

'We could pass notes behind Faber's back.'

'I think he understands more of it than you think.'

'Not much.'

'Well, he tries. He knows a lot about blind history.'

'But any fool can learn that, it's so short. Here, I'll show you.' He followed her to her room. She felt along a very full bookcase.

'It's here somewhere,' she said. 'Ah. Here we are. My first exercise book from my "special school". They try very hard at making us proud of blind culture. Our first homework was to learn this list.' She ran her finger down a brailled sheet pinned inside the front cover. 'Homer,' she said, 'Tiresias (well, he hardly counts), Phineus, (who?), Didymus of Alexandria 4 A.D., theologian and teacher, Nicholas Saunderson 1682 to 1739, Yorkshireman, Lucasian Professor of Mathematics at Cambridge, John Metcalfe 1717 to 1810, English road engineer and bridge builder, Thomas Blacklock 1721 to 1791, Scotch poet and minister, (ha!), François Huber, Swiss naturalist and bee specialist and last, but not least . . . Oh. Sorry. The paper's all squashed here. Yes. Maria Theresia von Paradis 1759 to 1824, Viennese singer and pianist and Marianne Kirchgessner, the glass harmonica virtuoso who inspired works from Mozart and Haydn.'

'What about Monsieur Braille and Helen Keller?'

'Oh, they're not culture. They're God.'

'Ah. Is this your novel?' She had left the word processor switched on, its screen full of a dense paragraph.

'Yes. But you don't want to see that.' She reached to clear the screen.

'Can't I?'

'It's not very good.'

'Well, it's better than anything I could do. You don't seem to realize that I'm washed up compared to you. I have no degree, eight years missing where my career should be and no outstanding abilities. I couldn't write a novel if I tried.'

'You can read them,' she suggested.

'Yes, but alas one doesn't get paid to do that.'

'Critics do.'

'Not much. Change the subject, there's a dear. Tell me how this machine works for you. I can see the braille keys but how can you read what you've written?'

It was treachery but, as they chattered, he started reading her novel. He found himself plunged into a weird scene in which the heroine flew somewhere on someone's back (an alien of some kind) and had to keep them afloat in a dangerous mist by improvising poetry. The language was not advanced, but not childish either. Iras's age only showed in the strong influences of her recent reading, chiefly Dickens, which emerged as an occasional archness or clumsy formality. Carried away, he started tapping keys in an effort to see another page.

'Hey! Stop!' she shouted, seizing his arms. 'What did you just do?'

'Sorry. I was trying to see another page.'

'Did you type anything new in?'

'Er. Yes. A few letters. Nothing much.'

She reached round him to find the delete key.

'Here,' she said. 'Tap this once or twice until all the new letters have gone.'

He did so.

'Right,' he said.

'Now,' she felt the keyboard again, 'This is the relay key. Press this once to tidy it all up.'

He touched the key and a kind of ripple ran through the paragraph, tucking in stray letters and filling unwanted gaps.

'Done.'

'What did you think of what you read?' she asked.

'Iras, you've probably heard this already, but it's very, very good. You have to finish it.'

'Oh, I already have.'

'When?'

'Days ago.'

'But why didn't you say? We must celebrate. Faber will be so pleased.'

'I didn't think it was a good time to tell him.'

'No. Honestly. It would give him something else to think about.'

'Well. Perhaps. Hang on.' She pushed him gently to make him move from the seat so that she could sit at the keyboard. Expertly she tapped a few times. The screen cleared, offered her a list from which she chose a chapter simply by counting the number of times she tapped a key then a new chapter appeared. 'Now,' she muttered to herself, 'it was at the end.' She pressed a key and the pages rushed by to stop at the end of the chapter. 'Since I've taught you braille you can teach me something.'

'What?'

'I didn't ask Faber because he gets so embarrassed but, well, you're less grown-up than he is so I think you won't mind.'

'What?' Robin laughed.

'This is the only bit I haven't done because I haven't got the right information and I want to get my facts right. You'll have to fill me in.'

'Fire away.'

'Well, I need to know what you two get up to in bed.'

'Oh.'

'You're not going to get all coy?'

'Of course not. Er. We touch.'

'Where?'

'Everywhere.'

'I need scientific names. This is a scene between two Minervans, you see – that's the planet the girl gets taken to – and they're all the same sex, you see, rather like worms, only much more attractive but they only bother to make love in a physical way when one of them knows they're going to die soon and I need to know what they'd do.'

When Faber returned, drained, from Marcus's funeral he would find Iras thrilled at having finished her novel, with a little help, and Robin thrilled at having finally decided what it was he wanted to do with his life.

32

In the days when Marcus used to take summer afternoons off to sketch the view of Chelsea from its riverside graveyard, Saint Mary's, Battersea had nestled in a long line of great flour warehouses, gin distilleries, mysterious factories, and unloading places alive with cats and smells of exotic rot. Then the church had been a lone eighteenth century feature amid a mass of looming red brick, watched over by the council estate tower blocks. Today it still looked as though it had been shipped over from some quaint New England parish but only the riverside brown bread factory held out against a tide of dubiously prettifying alteration. Dozens of toytown houses had taken the place of the wharves and warehouses. Each had its spotless, new Georgian fanlight, Victorian streetlamp, patch of expensive grass and set of Dutch gables. They seemed to press as close to the church and riverside as was seemly or possible and their proximity had infected the older building with their counterfeit elegance.

'Good lord!' Andrea exclaimed as they left the car, less at the houses, whose style was common enough across the city to have become the unremarkable signature of a decade, than at the crowds. A line of taxis and cars stretched almost to where they had left the Volkswagen. People were being set down at the graveyard gate or were spilling out earlier and making for the already crowded pavement. 'I thought you said he didn't have any friends.'

'He was so precisely spoken,' Peter said. 'I expect he would have called this lot acquaintance.'

'Where did Faber place announcements?'

'I told him to put them in all the big papers. He put one in the *Herald Tribune* too.'

They walked on, bemused. Around them old friends greeted one another in German, Italian, French and unfamiliar, Eastern-sounding tongues. The average age looked like sixty-five and everyone was in black. Andrea was wearing grey, 'Because it suits me and after all I never met the man.'

Peter had donned an old City suit, rather loose in the waist after eight years without boardroom lunches.

When finally they were on pillowy grass and in sight of the river, they saw Faber standing in the portico. He waved and came towards them smiling.

'At last some familiar faces!' he said.

'Who are all these people?' Peter asked him.

'Perhaps we double-booked?' suggested Andrea.

'I've no idea,' sighed Faber, kissing her then shaking Peter's hand. 'I've been standing there for nearly half an hour saying hello to people but none of them have the faintest idea who I am so it's fairly pointless. Besides, they're all having such a fabulous time. Listen!' It was true. The air was full of gaiety and release, as though the service were already over. 'I was convinced it was going to be just we three and maybe Candida's godfather.'

'Which is he?'

'There he is. Uncle Heini!'

'My dear boy!' A dapper old man in a well-cut suit black as night turned from another conversation and came towards them, beaming. He shook Faber's hand and patted his shoulder. 'I'm so very sorry,' he said, still smiling but saddening his voice a little.

'Heini, these are dear friends. Andrea Maitland, Heinrich Liebermann.'

'How do you do?'

'*Enchanté.*'

Uncle Heini all but kissed Andrea's hand.

'And this is Andrea's husband, Peter.'

'*Ja*, so it was you who visited dear Marcus all this time. We all owe you so much.' His pronounciation turned Marcus into something rich and rare, something from Ancient Rome. Embarrassed, Peter shrugged.

'He left me the richer,' he told him and yet again Andrea wondered what he and the dying man had talked about all this time. Whenever she had asked him, Peter told her, 'Nothing, really.'

'Heini, you must tell me,' Faber urged. 'Who are all these people?'

'Oh,' Heini dismissed them with a scornful raising of eyebrows and a wave of a hand, 'Acquaintance. Marcus had very few friends left alive, but he had an enormous acquaintance.'

'But this is so embarrassing,' Faber said. 'Shouldn't I be providing them all with food and drink or something? Some of them seem to have come miles.'

'St Johns Wood,' Heini snorted. 'Have they said hello to you?'

'Not really.'

'Then you needn't worry.'

The four of them had reached the church's elegant West end.

'Shall we see you inside?' asked Andrea.

'Oh no. I think I might as well come in with you now,' Faber said.

'But what about Marcus?' asked Heini. 'Shouldn't you be walking in with him?'

'He's already in his place,' Faber said with a smile. 'I'd have felt such an idiot walking up the aisle all on my own behind a load of bearers so I got them to come early and put him up at the front before anyone else got here. You can hardly find him for flowers. Come and see.'

234

He turned inside and they followed him, Andrea taking Peter's arm and Heini bringing up the rear. Peter saw with relief that the musicians were already in place and playing. Marcus had left him a letter in Miss Birch's care. It gave him strict instructions concerning the paying of musicians and some nurse together with advice concerning the handling of meddlesome priests.

The coffin was quite buried in flowers as were the trestles that supported it. Flowers dangled from the pulpit and someone, an anonymous donor, Faber muttered, had paid for green garlands to be draped around the length of the horseshoe gallery. The smell was delicious – rosemary, bay and late honeysuckle. The pews were already filled to bursting and the gallery creaked under an unaccustomed burden but the front pew had been left respectfully empty. It was clear to Andrea as they walked up the aisle, that no one there was quite sure exactly who the chief mourners would turn out to be. Not being in mourning herself, she felt no harm in enjoying the sense of attention on her as the one woman in the quartet that now took the principal places. She saw Peter bow to a tidy-looking creature on the other side. In answer to Andrea's questioning glance he whispered, 'Miss Birch,' which left her none the wiser. She reached into her bag for the piece of paper on which she had typed out her Donne poem. It was all so exciting, like being in a school play or local pageant. Peter had told her that he really had very little idea what was going to happen. All he knew was that the form of the service would probably be 'free' and that she was to go into the pulpit and read the poem 'after the song'. Faber sat on her right, beside the aisle, as seemed proper, although he was to play no active part in the proceedings. She reached across to pat his arm. He smiled slightly but continued to stare at the heap of flowers on the coffin.

The music, something for string quartet, came to an end and a priest appeared in front of Marcus's coffin. He had a boyish face, although he must have been in his forties, and black hair so well-combed it looked almost false. He was not in robes, but he had a dark suit on and a shiny dog collar. Silence fell at once and they all stood.

'Erm,' said the priest, 'hello. We are here to mark the passing of our friend Marcus Carling. I confess I met Marcus only once, when his assistant Miss Birch asked if I would visit him in hospital. He was charming but business-like. He wanted my assurance that I would be prepared to be here in my legal capacity as priest rather than my spiritual one as Christian and I gave it him willingly. He struck me as a man of profound belief, if only in the importance of living fully and with grace. I can see from the wonderful number of you who have turned up this morning that he was popular and will be missed. I'm sure Marcus would not mind if I said that I trust, from the number of you here, that he will live on in your hearts. As requested, I shall refrain from blessing his departed soul but I see no reason for not saying bless *you*, all of you, for coming.' He smiled in benediction. 'Please sit,' he said. Everyone sat and he walked to one side and sat too.

A nurse now climbed into the pulpit. She was pretty but looked hot and rather cross at having to be there.

'Hello,' she said quietly.

'Speak up,' some woman called in a thick accent.

'Sorry,' muttered the nurse then continued more loudly. 'Hello. I'm staff nurse Rosie Walsh. I nursed Marcus on and off throughout his long illness and was nursing him for his last three weeks. I can't say he was an easy patient, there's no reason why anyone that ill should make life easy for anyone, but we got on. He teased me, I teased him and he used to finish my crossword for me.'

'*Ses mots croisées*,' a man behind Andrea explained firmly to his neighbour.

'Towards the end he made me confirm that this time it was nearly over – there had been a lot of false alarms, you see – and then he made me promise that, when he died, I'd come along here and stand up and read you all a letter from him.

I've not read it yet myself, I've only just been handed it, so you'll have to forgive me if I don't read it very well.'

'*Ah, c'est chouette comme idée!*' exclaimed the Frenchman's female neighbour and was silenced.

The nurse tore open an envelope and drew out a single sheet of paper. She looked up at the congregation, then down again.

'"Greetings from beyond the grave!"' she read and coughed. '"Thank you, whoever and however many you are, for bothering to come to what, after all, is a fairly spiritless occasion. Doubtless you would have been indignant had I summoned you all to a hired 'function room' in some stuffy hotel and the English climate scarcely allows us to forgather in a field or park. I would have preferred the latter, for its lack of ambiguity, but this church will have to do. Blake came here, and his views were fairly unorthodox, so the precedent is honourable.

"I am, as you will have gathered, dead. This had been a bastard of a disease and any release from it, however undignified, will have been merciful. I have no hopes of a heaven and no fears of a hell so please don't insult my intelligence and waste your energies wishing me in either. If it's any comfort to you, however, I do have a profound sense that all is not over. When alive I was far too aware of the fact for it all just to stop at the flick of a switch. I shall continue as influence, as spirit, as memory, or something. This is not just the fear of death speaking. Death has become as companionable to me in the last few years as a plump fireside cat and no more awe-inspiring. If nothing else, I shall live on as my hard cash."' (Here several people chuckled.)

'"I would willingly leave my body to science, but what's left of it would be precious little use to anyone. Tombstones are a hypocritical expense and a burden to those who come after. I have accordingly arranged to be cremated in privacy. No friends, no family; just the priest the law in its infinite wisdom requires. You shan't have to climb any hills to watch the scattering of my ashes since I have no great love for any particular piece of England and every hope of finding my way anonymously onto some municipal flower-bed.

"Just before you leave, you will be read a poem. I don't hold with all the theology behind it, and I don't believe its author did either, but I do believe in its defiance. John Donne would no more have been an easy patient than I was. Yours sincerely, Marcus Carling".'

The nurse looked up for these last words then folded the paper away somewhere and left the pulpit. She walked away down the aisle, her sensible shoes making muffled thumps all the way to the swing door by which she left. Someone was crying. Someone up in the gallery. Faber blew his nose heavily but otherwise seemed fine. His composure did not last, however. The next mystery item was a rather breathy performance of Britten's setting of Yeats's *Salley Gardens* by a small boy in school uniform. The melody and bittersweet words were touching enough even without the poignant contrast between the boy's youth and the poem's world-weariness. Faber pulled out a handkerchief and had to blow rather more. His tears were infectious, even though Andrea had never even met Marcus, and she had to breathe deeply to keep herself under control.

'Stage-fright,' she reminded herself. 'Bank balances. Haemorrhoids. Evening classes.'

The song finished, causing a few people to clap. Peter tapped her arm to show it was time to stand up, which she already knew. She lost her nerve at the last moment and took the typed sheet of poetry with her. Faber stood with a sniff to let her out. She passed within inches of the coffin and climbed into the pulpit. Suddenly the sun was full in her eyes and she knew she had the poem by heart. Without bothering to glance down she rested her hands on the rail before her and faced the crowd of expectant strangers.

'"Death be not proud,"' she told them and paused to muster a smile of triumph.

33

The children were going home.

'Lots of egg-boxes? Wonderful!' said Andrea, taking an armful of cardboard from a collecting mother. 'Oh, and a squeezy bottle too! What fun.' She tossed the useful offerings into the domestic junk-heap corner known as the Quarry. 'I'm afraid they'll be back with you in another form in no time. Tabitha's getting so creative. Ah, hello Mrs Tang.' She looked round wildly for the little Chinese girl who had only started that week. 'Louise? Anyone see Louise? Ah. There you are, dear. Your mum's here.' She turned back to Mrs Tang and whispered, 'She's so bright!' with a smile.

The weather had suddenly changed gear. Autumn had stopped being golden and had turned wet. From now until the Spring there would be small Wellington boots to be retrieved and dufflecoats to be found. Something about bright winter clothes brought out envy in children, Andrea found, and much grabbing and weeping at going-home time.

'Josie, don't cry dear. This is your mac. This pretty pink one. Very pretty. Much nicer really. Give Rupert back his Barbour.' She grinned at Josie's mother who was taking far too long getting her out of the room. Peter came running in from seeing the twins to their car.

'Robert's panda,' he muttered. 'Have you seen it?'

'In the kitchen,' she told him. 'Drying over the stove. He got soup all over it. Ah. There we are, Tony. See? Daddy's come for you today. Hang on. Don't forget your lovely spaceship you made. There we are. Careful, the glue's not quite dry. Oh dear. Well, leave it here and I'll fix it for you to take home tomorrow. All right? Bye bye.'

Peter ran out of the room again, clutching a still wet panda. She heard him explaining the mishap to the twins' mother and realized that the last child had gone. Bliss. She yawned, stretching, then set about pushing chairs and tables to the wall ready for the Señoritas Fernandez to do their mopping in the morning. Lentil soup seemed to have got everywhere, as had the hundreds-and-thousands Flora Cairns had been using to make a glue picture. She had set the children to making a new alphabet this morning, one letter each with a picture of something that began with it. She took down the old one from over the blackboard and began to pin the new one up in its place. She had reached F with its carnivorous-looking bluebottle when Peter came back in.

'Have you seen Jasper, darling?' he asked.

'He went home with that Australian nanny of theirs, didn't he?' she said, pinning up Flora's G for girl and Jasper's subversive H for Halo.

'Er. No. I don't think he can have done.' He coughed. She turned round on her stool and saw that Candida was with him.

'Hello,' said Candida, who for Candida looked awful.

'Candida, what a lovely surprise. I didn't see you were there.' Andrea climbed down. 'Samantha not well?'

'She's fine but she had to go home to Melbourne suddenly,' said Candida, 'and the agency still haven't found anyone.'

'What a bore for you,' said Peter airily. 'I'll go and look for him outside. He must be on the swing or something.'

The two women waited tensely for him to walk into the playground.

'Candida, I'm so sorry about what happened the other day.'

'Don't be. Honestly.' Candida's words were relaxed enough

but her manner was distinctly off-balance. 'It was right of you to tell me. I was glad. Is Robin here?'

'I don't think so. He's usually round at Faber's nowadays. I think it's only a matter of time before he moves in officially and we have to buy them things from a list at Peter Jones.' Andrea looked at the gaudy alphabet pictures in her hand then set them on a table. 'I can't think where Jasper can be hiding if he's not out there. I'm so sorry. This is rather awful, isn't it?' None of her charges had disappeared like this before. They enjoyed themselves too much to run away and she never entrusted them to strangers without a warning phone call or letter from the parents.

'Can I go and see?'

'Well, Peter doesn't seem to be having much luck. I doubt whether . . .'

'No. Robin.'

'Oh. But I said he's not here.'

'You're not sure, though?'

'No.'

'I haven't seen his room for such ages.'

'All right.'

Bemused, Andrea followed this tired, elegant creature through her own house. Candida hadn't set foot in the upstairs area since coming to arrange for Jasper to start at the kindergarten and, before then, since Robin's twenty-first.

'I like your new colours,' she said, peering into rooms as they went. 'And the white on the stairs is much better. It makes it all feel sunnier.'

She doesn't realize that we're on the verge of a panic about her son, thought Andrea. God help us when she does.

Candida quickened her pace as they reached the next flight of stairs and was almost running up them by the time they approached Robin's door. Andrea couldn't keep up. Candida knocked on the door then tried the handle. Andrea was about to tell her that he always locked it nowadays when the door opened. She walked in close behind the younger woman; after weeks of exclusion, her curiosity was almost as strong.

'Oh,' Candida exclaimed. 'Something's changed. What have you done?'

'I got rid of that dreadful old yellow paint. "Tolstoy Sunflower" it was called, or "Van Gogh" or something. The two of you chose it together, don't you remember? It was the last word then.'

'Oh yes.' Candida laughed. 'And that mirror's new. But it's nice. And he's still got all the same old books.' Candida ran a finger along the spines. *Tales of Ancient Greece, Our Island Story . . .'*

'His grandmother gave him those.'

'The pictures used to make him laugh. So camp, especially Perseus. And there's that funny medal he won.'

'For essay writing.'

'I used to spend hours up here with him.' Candida flopped down on the old ottoman beneath the window. 'He'd lie on the bed and I'd curl up here and we'd talk ourselves hoarse.'

'What did you talk about?' Andrea asked, standing at the end of the bed, tense.

'Everything. God. Politics. My parents' divorce and why you two were still happy and together. Exams. Books. It all seemed terribly important at the time. And when it was hot we'd run down to the kitchen, grab something to eat and climb up to the treehouse. Is it still there?'

'Oh yes.'

'Let's see.' Candida twisted as she sat, searched the view for a moment then leapt up. 'Jasper!' she shouted and ran downstairs. Andrea went to the window just long enough to see that Jasper was up in the old, now rather rotten treehouse and that Peter was looking up at him waving his arms then she too hurried panting down.

'No. Don't try to climb down,' Peter shouted up. 'Don't move. Stay and talk to your mum while I get a ladder.'

'We haven't got a ladder long enough,' Andrea said.

'Yes, we have,' said Peter.

'The Thurstons borrowed it to take to Sussex to fix their gutters. Jane said sorry they'd forgotten it but they'd bring it back next time.'

'Get him down,' said Candida. 'He should never have been allowed up there in the first place.'

'You were that age when you first went up,' Andrea reminded her. 'Nearly.'

'I'm sure I wasn't.'

'Yes, you were.'

'Well, that was then. It was different.'

'Peter, no!' Andrea's hand went to her mouth. Peter had thrown off his cardigan, rolled up his sleeves and was shinning up the tree. 'I'll find a ladder somewhere. We can call the firemen.'

'Don't move, Jasper,' Candida shouted. 'Peter's coming. Stay in the corner.'

'It's OK,' Peter puffed. 'Not that hard, actually.'

Andrea and Candida and several people in neighbouring windows froze to watch him climb. The magnificent jays that nested a few yards away swooped close by him in a flash of blue and grey. Andrea pictured him tumbling through snapping branches and cracking his skull on the brick path beneath. She had never felt this fear when Robin used to clamber up there. Children were so much more flexible; foolishly, one always felt they would bounce. With his shock of white hair Peter looked suddenly like someone's mad grandfather who had taken to the woods. As he reached the treehouse and began to disappear up through the trapdoor in its floor Jasper suddenly clambered out of the window and onto the roof. The whole structure seemed to sway, or perhaps it was just the wind in the trees. Candida bit a knuckle. Someone in the garden next door gave a little shriek.

'No, Jasper. Go back!' Andrea shouted, furious. The brat

was trying to kill her husband. Peter's hand appeared in the window reaching for Jasper's hand. Jasper was visibly weeping and retreating. Peter started to climb out of the window after him. 'Peter don't!' called Andrea. Suddenly two firemen, black and silver in full uniform, ran into the garden from the side of the house. They were carrying a ladder. Not stopping to ask which sensible neighbour had thought to call them, she only said, 'Quick. Please, quick.'

Both Peter and Jasper saw the firemen and stopped whatever they were doing. Jasper relaxed at the sight of their uniform (a milkman or nurse would have had the same effect), and allowed himself to be slung over a shoulder and carried down. Peter waited until they were at the bottom then clambered down unassisted.

Candida held out her arms to her son but, free of the firemen's charm, he began whimpering and ran past her to cling to Andrea's legs.

'What's all this?' joked Andrea gently. She prised off his hands and handed him bodily over to his mother who put him firmly on the ground and made him hold her hand.

'Thank the firemen and Peter,' she told him stiffly, but Jasper broke loose and sprinted round the side of the house. Helpless, Candida followed. One of the firemen had just recognized her.

'Hey,' he said, 'Wasn't that . . . ?'

'Yes,' said Andrea, dropping Peter's hand which, unconsciously, she had seized as soon as he was down and safe. 'Her nanny's just gone back to Melbourne.'

'Will you have a cup of tea or something?' Peter offered.

'Can't stop,' said the other. 'They've got cat trouble over at number 51.'

'Well, thanks so much,' Andrea said and she stood with Peter to watch them go. 'What happened?' she asked him when they were alone. 'Jasper was being so strange.'

'He wouldn't come down,' he said. 'He only ran up there

when he saw her arrive and then she came out and he wouldn't come down.'

'I love you so much, Peter.'

'I love you back.'

'Really?'

34

'Jake, hi. Come on in.'

'Hello, Faber.'

Normally dressed so sloppily, Faber was all in Sunday-best black. Jake reflected that drop-dead chic was strangely indistinguishable from mourning.

'Come in. Come in.' Faber waved Jake past him. 'I'm afraid we're in chaos but you didn't come to buy the house.'

'No.' Jake laughed. 'You on your own?'

'Yes. Peace and quiet. Robin's taken Iras straight from school to a concert somewhere. Can I get you a drink? I'm afraid we've drunk all the wine but there's lots of beer. Here. Give me your wet coat.'

'Beer would be lovely.' Jake looked around him, letting Faber lift his coat from his shoulders. The rain had drenched it in the short sprint from car to door. He had not seen Faber's studio home since coming there to collect Candida's portrait several years ago. In those days it was still unconverted. 'It's changed here,' he called after Faber who was finding beer in the kitchen. The gallery had been a kind of junk yard of canvasses, old frames, packing-cases and chipped mirrors. There had been a mattress draped in tangled bedding in one corner and no apparent sign of a bathroom. But then, in those days, Jake reflected, he and Candida had been living in a rented flat where passing trains shook the bathwater.

'So,' said Faber, coming from the kitchen and handing him

a chilly glass of bitter. The first gulp hurt Jake's stomach. He had eaten nothing since breakfast but a quail's egg sandwich. 'You want to buy another painting.'

'Not just one. Several,' said Jake, 'only it's not me who's buying them – I wish it was. It's for the firm's collection. Just because Candida and I have made a few lucky buys in the past, they seem to think I'm an expert. I've become their sort of unofficial buyer.'

'Lucky you.'

'Yes, quite. Shopping with someone else's money.'

Faber gestured for Jake to sit on a sofa.

'Please,' he said.

Jake sat down beside a headless skeleton that was already reclining. Then he rose to pull something out from underneath him. It was a jersey Robin had borrowed from him eight years ago, a fisherman's jersey, speckled black and white. He sat down again abruptly.

'Have you hurt your leg?' Faber asked.

Jake tried to laugh it off.

'Stupid collision on the squash court,' he said. 'Playing doubles.' He rubbed his bruises through his trousers and felt shame. Candida's kicks the other evening had drawn blood.

Faber was dragging a large canvas across the room to lean against an easel. Jake was appalled. Faber tugged out three slightly smaller ones and ranged them around the large one like a grotesque altarpiece. Jake was appalled still further. The largest and two of the others showed wretched tramps, barely female, sitting massively on a table top. Jake recognized the table as the one where Faber had evidently eaten lunch earlier. Another painting was a nude study of a chubby youth with a grin and flaming red hair.

'He works in the butcher's,' Faber explained, pointing to the still bloody cleaver in the youth's hand.

'Stunning,' said Jake and hurt his stomach with more beer. Was this the onset of an ulcer?

'And then there are these,' said Faber, lifting six canvasses one by one from a corner, placing them in a line along the other side of the room so that Jake had to stand to see them. 'I did these in the Spring over at Tooting Lido. Do you ever go there? No, I don't suppose you do.'

'Where? Tooting? No. I'm afraid we don't. Candida wants to build a pool of our own. I don't think the neighbours will approve much, though.'

Seeing that Faber had finished arranging the paintings, Jake subsided and examined them respectfully. He saw three more women and three men, all of them overweight, over fifty or both. Lit by warm spring sunshine, they were pictured in detail one could almost touch. Each male painting had a brightly-coloured changing-room door as its backdrop while the women were painted against various views of an aeration fountain in swimming-pool blue. Two of the women (and one old man) wore rubber bathing-caps, while the third and oldest of them stood with her hands combing out her hair into a damp white mane. Her bathing-cap discarded at her feet, she looked utterly mad.

Jake was aghast. 'Incredible,' he said. Faber had walked around to look at them too. He showed mercy enough not to ask whether or not Jake liked them. 'Which are your favourites?'

'Oh,' said Faber, 'I'm always most interested in what I'm working on at the moment. By the time it's finished, something else has usually started bubbling up. Projects often overlap. I'll be at the photograph and sketch stage for one before another is all painted out.'

'Do you often use photographs?'

'Nearly always, yes. The lido set were photos. So was Henry.'

'Henry?'

'The butcher's apprentice. He didn't have much time.'

'Ah,' said Jake and looked back at Henry who smiled lewdly back at him and wobbled his cleaver suggestively. This was much harder than Jake had at first imagined. 'And are they all for sale?' he asked.

'All except Henry. An interested party from the Burden Friday gallery has already reserved him. God knows where they'll manage to hang him.' Faber laughed.

Relieved that this was permissible, Jake laughed too. He wandered over to the easel, trying not to limp.

'Can I see the work-in-progress?' he asked. 'The latest favourite?'

'Please do.'

Jake looked at the near-finished painting of Iras and Robin and was strangely moved to anger.

'What are they doing?' he asked quietly.

'She's teaching Robin to read braille. He's coming on quite well. Better than I ever did. I had to give up because shutting my eyes for long makes me too nervous.'

Jake finished his beer. Faber promptly removed his glass to fill it again. Jake looked on. One of Robin's hands was gently fingering the page before him, the other was reaching out towards Iras across the sunny table-top as though she could somehow hand him understanding the way she might pass the pepper.

'What would you ask for this one?' Jake asked.

'Not for sale,' Faber called from the fridge. 'If you're talking about the one I think you are.'

'What have they gone to hear?' Jake went on after a moment.

'Bartok, I think,' said Faber, coming back and giving Jake a second beer.

'Thanks,' Jake muttered.

'And Beethoven and then there was Britten to start with. Or Bax, perhaps. Robin was joking about how the only thing which seemed to hold the programme together was the names beginning with B.'

Jake walked back to the Lido Group, where he stood and drank some beer.

'I want you to sell me the whole lot, excluding Henry, of course,' he said at last and named a figure that would have the company accountants demanding an explanation. Faber seemed surprised. Perhaps he was not doing as well as Candida pretended.

'Well,' he laughed, 'that's very generous of you but, as I say, Robin and Iras aren't for sale.'

'You must realize,' said Jake, 'how our buying all your extant available work for the collection will raise its market value. My secretary's already talked to your agent and to several galleries so I know we'd be the first to make such a confident gesture.'

'Wonderfully confident,' said Faber.

'If you're not convinced, we can let you have a breakdown of how the artists we've bought have taken off. Not that you need to take off much further . . .' he added.

'Wonderfully confident,' Faber repeated, setting down his drink and ruffling his hair in what Jake hoped was indecision, 'almost foolhardy, and I know you'd be buying more than the firm told you to, which would be sweet of you, but as I say this one isn't for sale.' Jake waited. 'This is family,' Faber stressed.

'You'll go off it when the next idea starts "bubbling up",' Jake suggested.

'No, I won't. This one's finished and I still love it.'

'No, it's not.'

'It is. I left it on the easel to enjoy.'

Jake raised his bid by a quarter, making rapid calculations and trying to visualize his latest bank statement.

'No,' laughed Faber, weakly adding, 'I said it's not for sale.'

Jake raised his bid by another quarter. Faber gasped and flopped down on the sofa.

'Why?' he asked. 'After all that's happened?'

Jake repeated the bid. He was buying with his own money now.

'You can always do more,' he said. 'You could do that one again standing on your head.'

Faber scoffed, unable to meet Jake's eye.

'Please,' said Jake, more a command than a request.

Faber continued to sit. Unable to protest with words now he merely shook his head slowly. Jake sat at the dining-table and wrote the cheque for his share of the purchase. At the soft rasp of it tearing from the stub Faber sat up.

'Just don't take it right away, OK?' he said.

'OK,' said Jake. 'We'll ring you about packing and transport next week.' He left the cheque on the gnarled, crumb-scattered wood where the filthy women had crouched. He found his coat himself.

35

Robin knew it was his own fault, for snooping. He still scarcely knew Faber. He was fast becoming familiar with every memorable inch of Faber's body but something in him, the Bluebeard's wife he supposed, had to know more. Marcus Carling's death started it, suddenly filling their temple with memories and reminders of Faber's past of which Robin, naturally, had been quite unaware. Faber only told him the minimum; he told him everything, that is, but only the facts. Overnight a corpse had moved in to share the marriage bed and now Robin's dreams were troubled. Marcus's funeral seemed to have laid a painful ghost and since then Faber had been cheerful as ever but from time to time as they embraced Robin felt him look over his shoulder at the past. So, Robin had taken to snooping. He found several lovingly annotated photograph albums and snatched compulsive painful minutes with Faber's sunlit memories, scouring the pages for proof of handsome intimacies before his own, and finding all too many.

'Who was Jack?' he would ask. 'Tell me about Fabrizio. Who exactly was this Ellen Mae?'

Blithely, Faber would tell him, though just the facts; location of holidays, approximate lengths of affairs. He neither hinted at the relative depths of his emotional involvement in these emotional excursions nor sought to distinguish sunny fling from tortured passion, and this seeming failure to take his past seriously, increased Robin's discomfort.

Last week is now your past as well, Robin felt like telling him, and the week before that, and you spent them both with me.

This morning lust had woken him early but he couldn't rouse Faber.

'You just need to pee,' Faber told him. 'It happens to everyone. Go and pee then come back to sleep. It's only six-thirty.'

But Robin didn't need to pee and he couldn't bear lying there watching Faber sleep without him, so he got up and went snooping. He found a recent letter from Ellen Mae, who Faber had said meant so little. Ellen Mae seemed to think she meant quite a lot. She wrote to Faber from darkest California. Ten pages – twenty sides – of wild, angry writing about how, ever since he'd gone, she coudn't seem to stop having babies without taking to the bottle. She complained that she gave so much of herself and Faber never sent her more in return than two-phrase postcards which she dismissed as 'sentimental *haiku*'.

Then Robin found a cheque, dated yesterday, worth an awe-inspiring sum and signed Jake Browne. It was from an unusual London bank and reminded him of the time when Jake was the rich grammar school friend who bought endless treats for him and Candida and drove them anywhere they liked in his fast car.

'What's this?' he asked, tossing it onto the bed.

'Nothing,' said Faber. 'Come back to bed.'

'Why is Jake Browne writing you obscenely large cheques?'

Faber groaned and rolled over to push his face into the pillow. He muttered something like 'Later.'

'Now!' Robin said and tugged hard on his shoulder. Faber slapped his hand away and turned round.

'He's bought a whole load of paintings for his firm's art collection. Now can I go to sleep?'

'No. Why didn't you tell me last night?'

'You two came back late and I was busy getting Iras off to bed. I forgot.'

'You don't forget a sum like this.'

'That's only the deposit,' Faber muttered, rubbing his eyes and frowning. 'Try timesing it by six.'

'*What?*'

'Or maybe seven. I haven't really worked it out.'

'Which did he buy?'

'The lot.'

'I thought Henry was sold already.'

'The lot except Henry.'

'And the one of me and Iras.'

'No. He bought that. He bought that especially. I told him it wasn't for sale.'

'But you love that one. I love that one. It's ours. Why did you sell it?'

'How often does someone offer you seven cheques like that for something you can do without shaving or putting on a suit and tie?'

'Faber, that's disgusting.' Robin sat on his pillows beside him. 'From him, of all people. I'm going to tear this up.'

Faber grabbed Robin's wrist with one hand and snatched the cheque with the other.

'Don't you bloody dare!' he said.

'But you don't need money,' Robin told him. 'No one does. Not that much. What would you spend it on?'

For a moment Faber stared at him as though Robin were out of his mind then he jumped up, pulled his dressing-gown around him and headed out onto the landing.

'I'll show you,' he said.

Downstairs he tugged open the top drawer of his desk and took out a handful of papers and letters. Robin had never seen him so angry before.

'Electricity,' Faber said. 'Gas. Telephone. Water. Rates. And here, look, my mortgage book. Look at the size of the monthly payments. Iras's school fees. Her clothes. My clothes. Our food – we're feeding for three now, don't forget. Bus passes. Tube passes. Bike repairs. Bottles of wine when people ask us out.

Bottles of wine and more food when we have to ask them back. Cheque stubs. Just look at them. Have you any idea at all what it costs to "simply be", as you so quaintly put it? To ride on buses all day, eat in cafés, visit galleries and go to the cinema? Look at this notebook. I keep a record of the household accounts here. Look how much it was there. OK? Now look how much it was there, after two weeks of you.'

'But . . . look, I can give you money. I'm always offering and you always say no because I don't work.'

'It's your father's money. It's not yours to give. Besides, you need every penny for your fucking bus journeys across London and back.'

'But . . .'

'And what would you give your blessed beggars if I docked your pocket-money?'

'Well . . .'

'And then there's Iras. Iras never used to cost me anything. Two or three months after the adoption papers came through I got a letter from some solicitors saying that they acted for her parents. They were busy, wealthy people, the solicitor said, who could not have given Iras the time she so obviously needed, poor thing. They knew they were not meant to contact me in person and that Iras should never meet them but now that she had found a home they were keen to support her anonymously. I was given no option. Every month money piled into a special bank account in Iras's name. When I found this place and took on the mortgage the solicitor seemed to know all about it and, before I'd been here a week, the payments into Iras's account doubled "to cover her share of board and lodging". Well, I wasn't going to complain. She was their flesh-and-blood daughter, and if they felt guilty for abandoning her and wanted to pay her way that was fine. If I wasn't having to worry about milk bills it would be that much easier to give her a happy home.'

'So what's the problem? Faber, why are you so upset?'

'This is the problem. Here. Look.' He held out a bank

statement. 'Her special account. Look. The payments ground to a halt just here. Right after when I met you. No help with the mortgage, no help for her school fees. Have you any idea how much that place costs? She's not just any blind kid, she's a hyper-intelligent blind kid which means paying for a hyper-intelligent tutor who can keep up with her. And as if that wasn't enough, there's you deciding that you want to be trained to teach in blind school.'

'I told you. I can get a grant. Maybe.'

'But you still need money. It doesn't cover everything. Grants, if you're lucky enough to get them, cover less and less.'

'Never mind that now.'

'I *do* mind. It's important. It's your future.'

'Well, never mind it *now*. What about these payments? Didn't you try her parents' solicitors?'

'Of course I did. I rang them straight up and asked what the hell was going on. Had the parents died, I said, and if so, why hadn't I been informed? They had not died, the solicitors said, but they were unable to disclose any further information.'

Just then Iras left her room in her nightdress and came yawning downstairs.

'Hi, honey,' said Faber. 'Did we wake you?'

'I'd been up for ages,' she lied. 'Morning, Robin.'

'Morning, Iras.'

She shut the bathroom door and soon they heard taps being turned on.

'What about Marcus?' asked Robin.

'What about him?'

'Well, surely . . . Now that he's died. I mean, he was your father.'

'Marcus was in hospital for nearly a year. Or maybe more than that. He was certainly ill for longer. I hadn't seen him for years before that and I didn't visit him once after he fell sick. Hardly the action of the faithful son who gets remembered in wills. He won't have left me a sou. He's wasted quite enough on me already.' Faber paused. 'Damn!' he snapped.

'What is it?'

'Look.' He pointed to the tears that were already springing from his eyes.

36

Jake and Candida were making love at three in the morning and he, for one, was astonished. He had been woken by Perdita. He went to feed her and had a brief chat with Tanya, the super-efficient new nanny who had woken too and fairly raced him to the feeding bottle. When he sunk back into bed Candida, wide awake, had reached out for him.

He had always enjoyed mid-sleep sex. He liked the way it uncoiled seamlessly from the sleep on either side of it, free of social or domestic preliminaries. The darkness was somehow darker and, to be honest, one's partner somehow less one's partner. Candida, however, had taken to forbidding sex in the middle of any but Friday or Saturday nights because her working days began at dawn. The cameras, she claimed, highlit a wrinkle for every minute of sleep lost.

'Your alarm goes off in two hours,' he reminded her.

'I don't care,' she whispered. 'Come on. Come over here.'

Her invitation was all the more astonishing for the fact that they had been barely speaking since she beat him up. He was sure that she was as appalled as he at the violence that she had summoned up between them and knew that its shadow could only be exorcized with discussion. Guilt at her accusations however, kept him silent. In the days that followed, the days hideously full of long-planned social engagements that bounced them grinning back to each other's side, he behaved towards her with all the polite mortification of one who has made a regrettable pass.

His bulk purchase of Faber Washington paintings had begun as a kind of expiation between him and Robin, and for that reason he had said nothing of his plans to Candida. Nevertheless, he had no sooner seen the new painting, the one of Robin and the blind girl, than he felt his motives expand to include his wife as well. As he made his increasingly wild offers for it and made the decision to buy it with his own money rather than the firm's, the gaudy canvas took on an irrational, totemic value. He felt that, the more it cost him, the more he could save of his marriage.

Peter and Jake had played squash that afternoon. Peter had heard about the firm's generosity to Faber and queried Jake's motivation. The game had ground to a halt as, watched by the curious few through the perspex rear wall, Jake opened his heart.

'It was almost as though Faber had been blackmailing me,' he said. 'He knew how badly I'd want that painting once I'd seen it. He knew I'd pay any price. It could almost have been an incriminating photograph or a clutch of love letters.'

Peter had apologized afterwards and said that it would have to be their last game.

'Andrea was all right about it at first, but she's gone and left the choir and I think she's being a bit funny about things. You know?'

Jake knew this was untrue, but he was not greatly surprised. Since Robin's return, their games had come to seem slightly redundant for him too. Sending Peter away burdened by so full a confession of guilt brought a satisfactory full stop to the proceedings. Secretly, wanting to spare Peter's feelings, Jake had recently taken out a membership at a club with slightly more cachet and a more convenient address. An attractive colleague, younger and fitter than Peter, seemed keen to discuss a strained marriage and Jake had already challenged him to a match there.

Candida's orgasms were usually minor miracles of vocal restraint. Tonight however, as she wrapped her legs across the small of his back to control his rhythm, he almost told her not to wake the baby. Then, as she was retreating into her separate ecstasies beneath him, an image crossed his mind which wasn't hers and he too had trouble keeping quiet. He was quite used to fantasies about other people intruding between them – it was an experience they shared and she had dimissed it as 'only natural' – but this particular, spectacularly effective fantasy, was socially inept to say the least. In the first years of their marriage she would, charmingly, use her last, panting breaths, to sigh that she loved him. As time took its cynical effect this was trimmed to a brief, if loving moan or an eloquent little sob of 'Oh, Jake!' Tonight, with the perfect timing of an actress in some tired marital farce, she sighed, 'Oh, Dob!'

A silence, fat with estimation, fell between them as he rolled to one side. She chuckled shortly then, as she rolled over into her precious, pre-dawn sleep, muttered, 'Well that makes two of us.'

From then until shortly before her alarm went off, as he lay staring through the darkness to her side of the bed, he could almost believe she had read his mind.

37

Peter and Andrea took it in turns to stop work after lunch once a week in order to bring the kindergarten accounts up to date, place orders with various suppliers of wholefood, paint, coloured paper and so forth. The idea was also to finish all the administrative work in time to have a couple of hours of precious free time before going downstairs to help the other see the children off with their parents. Andrea had just finished ordering a week's supply of salad ingredients and a sack of baking potatoes and was on her way to brave an end-of-season sale when she found Robin slouching at the kitchen table. He had more or less moved into Faber's studio now and Andrea was embarrassed at their mutual failure to talk about something so important. They never talked about anything important, come to that; Robin never stayed in the same room long enough. Now he seemed unusually deflated. She pulled out a chair and sat across the table from him.

'Hello,' she said. He hummed by way of reply. 'How are things?' she asked him.

'Things are fine,' he said, looking at his hands.

'Are you, by any chance, a bit bored?'

'I am a bit,' he confessed. 'I've seen everything I want to see, Iras is at school and Faber's working.'

'Oh.'

'Why aren't you?'

'It's my afternoon off. I was just going into Chelsea. Do you want to come too?'

'No thanks.'

'You could always go down and join Peter.'

'Could I?' He brightened.

'Of course. He's getting them to build things with cardboard and glue. He can always do with a bit of help.'

'I will then. Thanks, Mum.'

He rose briskly and went downstairs.

Why did I do that? she wondered. He was good with children – better than Peter, in fact, who could be a mite patronizing with them. Peter had mentioned Robin's interest in teaching the blind. A friend of theirs, one of the old ones no longer greatly seen, was the principal at a specialist teacher-training college in Kent. Andrea had not told Robin this, uncertain whether he would welcome helpful interference.

She let herself out of the back door and was heading down the Chase when a taxi slowed beside her and a woman's voice called her name from its window. Andrea stopped and turned, raising her umbrella. It was the tidy woman with the dyed hair who she had seen at the funeral. Peter had told her the name but she had forgotten it. The woman, tidy as ever, all in grey today, asked the taxi-driver to wait and came to join Andrea on the pavement.

'I nearly missed you,' she said. 'You don't know me, although I have met your husband. I'm Dorothy Birch. I was Marcus Carling's assistant.'

'How do you do?'

They shook hands. Miss Birch clicked open her slender briefcase and took out a small brown envelope.

'Marcus asked that this be given you after the funeral but I lost you in the crowd. I'd have come sooner but things have been fairly demanding, as you might imagine.'

'Of course,' said Andrea.

'I'm afraid he did make a stipulation about it. I told him it was hardly fair since, after all, the two of you were complete strangers and your agreeing to read that poem was a great favour. Still, he was adamant so all I can do is pass it on and leave it to your discretion.'

'I see. What was the stipulation?'

'Well,' said Miss Birch handing her the envelope, 'he asked that you spend it entirely on pleasure.' She fluttered her eyes slightly as she said this word, giving Andrea a glimpse of another Dorothy Birch, bold and sensation-seeking.

'Goodness,' said Andrea. 'I'll do my best. What fun! Thank you.' She looked at the unassuming envelope then raised it in a half-wave as the taxi took Miss Birch away into the Clapham drizzle.

Andrea had put the funeral from her mind easily, unattached as it was to the fibres of her ordinary life. Learning and reciting the poem had been fun, however. She could still remember it, word for word, and caught herself performing it in the bath or in the steam of the stove. She had resolved to learn more poetry, on the basis that it was good private entertainment and probably an early defence against senility. Being paid for her slim performance was an unlooked-for bonus. She paused in the shelter of an overhanging chestnut tree and tore the top of the envelope. It would be a mere financial gesture, she supposed, enough to buy a book, perhaps, or a record. She could buy a book of poetry. When she saw the sum involved her first reaction was to make sure that the cheque was hers and not that of some legatee given her by mistake. Her name was clearly printed on the first line. A neighbour trotted by, complaining of the weather. Startled into circumspection, Andrea took out her purse and stuffed the cheque behind the notes there.

Peter had received nothing and he was surely far more worthy of Marcus Carling's gratitude. The idea was probably that she should think of something that would be a treat for Peter as well as her. She looked at the lid of thick cloud that hung on the dreary vista at the bottom of the street and knew that she had to buy them a holiday somewhere. Somewhere hot. There was a travel agent on the Wandsworth Road which specialized in trips to the Caribbean. She hurried there and stood outside looking, as she had often done when waiting for a bus, at the visions of palm trees, white sands and adorable black children in its window. Martinique. Trinidad. St Lucia. Guadeloupe. The Grenadines. They could go for Christmas. She envisaged them lying on chairs in the shallow surf, glutted with fruit-flesh and glistening with monoi oil.

She sat herself before a sleek young West Indian in electric-blue mohair.

'I want to go to the Caribbean,' she told her.

'Don't we all, lovey,' said the woman and her colleague, unseen behind a filing cabinet, gave a short shriek of laughter. 'How soon did you want to go?'

'Let's see. Well, over Christmas.'

'December twenty?'

Andrea looked at the woman's calendar.

'It would have to be the twenty-first,' she said. 'Any two weeks between then and January the seventh.'

'And where were you wanting to go?'

'Martinique or the Grenadines.'

'*All* of them?'

'I don't know. You tell me?'

The woman laughed kindly.

'Let's start with Martinique. Is it just you?'

'No. Me and my husband.'

'OK. Two to Martinique.' She opened a file and began flicking pages.

'Second class.'

'Economy class. Mmm. Well, there's a flight leaving on the twenty-second, coming back on the fifth.'

'That's a bit late. We start work again on the seventh and we'll need to get things ready. Couldn't we come back earlier?'

'They're all booked, unless you just went for a week.'

A week in the Caribbean was better than none at all.

'OK. A week.'

'Have you got somewhere to stay?'

'No.'

'Well, we could arrange that. Let's see. Right. Here we are,' she found a chart in the file she was flicking through and ran a long red nail down a list of entries. 'One week, staying at the Hotel Fort de France – that's central, lovey, very nice – double room, breakfast and the economy flight there and back.'

'Sounds perfect. How much would that be?'

The woman named a price nearly twice the value of the cheque in Andrea's purse. Andrea hid her shock, nodded her head and hummed as though thinking it over. 'I'll have to ask my husband first,' she said.

'Don't be too long over it,' the woman said. 'This close to Christmas, the places go fast.'

'I'll get back to you straight away,' Andrea said, then rose and left, feeling a stupid fraud.

She slid the cheque into an envelope especially provided then fed it into a machine in the wall of their bank. The machine's mouth shut after it with an accusatory clunk.

'Idiot,' it said. 'Dreamer.'

She flagged down a bus and rode it into Chelsea to fight with the bargain hunters.

38

When Peter was alone with the children he liked to fantasize that they were all his by a harem of women as varied as the small people around him. He had never shared this with Andrea. It was after all only a fantasy and not a plan. When Robin walked in he spoiled it all, reminding Peter that his true son was old enough to make him a grandfather. Peter went on from cynically considering that at least Robin had spared him grandfatherhood, to depressing himself with wondering how many of the noisily industrious infants around him had similar surprises in store for their parents.

Jasper Browne, whose behaviour became increasingly nervous with every passing day, greeted Robin with enthusiastic shouts of, 'The Holy Man!' so when Robin asked if he could help, Peter sent him in Jasper's direction. The two of them were now hard at work on what seemed to be a cathedral of egg-boxes and cardboard tubes.

'And what's this?' Peter asked as he went the rounds.

'We're building Willum,' said Jasper proudly.

'Whelm,' said Robin who was deeply involved in their creation.

'Whelm,' repeated Jasper.

'Keep up the good work,' Peter chuckled and patted Robin on the shoulder. Robin didn't look up but continued to scowl with the effort of stapling tubes together, sideways on, to make a bell tower. They had started work with glue, like everyone else, but Robin had grown impatient (as had Jasper) and as a grown-up he had been allowed to borrow a stapler. Peter carried the other stapler with him as he walked, stooping occasionally to help fix some aeroplane wing or catfish's whisker too heavy for glue to hold alone.

'Do you want some music while you work?' he asked, when he had seen to everyone.

'Yes, please,' they chorused, except Robin, who had fixed on the tower and was glueing on gutters made from plastic straws.

Peter put on a Duke Ellington record which always went down well then walked around with little paint trays and brushes, setting down four colours and a brush by each child. Robin seized on Jasper's paints as soon as they arrived and proceeded to paint Whelm sunflower-yellow. Peter had just shown Rupert and Robert how to make brown when he heard Jasper shout, 'Windows. Let's do windows!'

He looked up just in time to see Jasper make a darting movement with a brush which made a hole where the west window would have been.

'Stupid little git,' Robin snapped and brought a palette tray full of paint hard down on the child's head. Jasper promptly shrieked. The other children froze in horror then, as Robin stamped from the room and slammed an upstairs door, began to point and laugh.

Peter ran to the stairs and shouted for Andrea. The Fernandez sisters emerged from the kitchen to see what the laughter was about, saw Jasper, who by now was wailing, and bore him upstairs to the bathroom for a shampoo. Red, yellow, blue and black ran in alarming swathes across his hair and onto his shoulders. Blessing Andrea for having insisted they invest in full length 'activity smocks,' Peter gave up searching for either wife or son and ran back to the room. The laughter died and they all looked up to him for a cue.

'Silly Robin getting cross like that,' he said.

'Yes. Silly,' said Flora Cairns and the rest began to agree.

'Come on, then, let's finish their church for them. Who's going to help me rebuild Willum?' Everyone shouted at once. 'Right,' Peter stilled them. 'We need stained glass windows. How many? One, two, three, four. Four down each side and a big one at each end. Do you all know what they look like? Mmm? Yes? Right. Here's a bit of paper each.' He hurried round the circle doling out paper. 'Now if each of you decorates a piece of paper, all over one side, then we can cut them up into stained glass window shapes and finish Willum by the time Jasper gets clean again. You don't have to do pictures – just colour splotches will do, as long as they join up. That's right, Flora. Keep it dry, Louise, or it won't cut properly. That's it.'

While the children were frantically absorbed in finishing the church Peter watched his son in the garden. After the escapade with Jasper the other afternoon, he had borrowed a ladder and brought the treehouse down from the tree. It had slid down from its moorings with horrible ease and stood now in a corner, a pile of rotten planks with three-and-a-bit walls rising out of them, capped by half a roof. Peter turned up the Duke Ellington and encouraged children to sing along. Robin balanced himself against the wall on his hands and demolished the rest of the wooden house with kick after brutal kick.

39

'Stop here. No. Here. Right here!' Candida shouted at the driver. 'That's right. I'll be about ten minutes, maybe a little more.'

'It's a double yellow line,' the driver told her.

'Well, drive around a bit. Drive round the Common a few times. Get yourself a cup of tea or something.' She was excited and had no time to think about parking tickets. This was studio work. The studio would pay. She left the driver to amuse himself, snatched up her bag and crossed the road to the curious place where Faber had chosen to make his home.

She wore her crucifix outside today, enjoying the ill-disguised sensation it caused amongst the make-up team who were used to her decoration being less discreet. They were notorious sellers of gossip; it was more than likely that one of the Sunday tabloids would carry a close-up of the unusual piece of jewellery with a dramatic story of Candida's spiritual rebirth.

She had rung Faber several times since the embarrassing episode with Robin and had given up speaking to his answering machine after the third attempt. He had returned none of her calls so she had opted for the surprise tactic. He opened the door wide and seemed satisfactorily surprised to see her.

'Candida! Come in.'

'Faber, you haven't returned any of my calls. Are you OK?'

'Erm.'

'The thing is,' she pushed on, not wanting to hear, 'I've got some thrilling news about Iras's novel.'

'Oh?'

'Is she here?'

'No. She's at school. But she's finished it, if that's what you were going to ask.'

'Fabulous! Faber, it's so exciting.'

'What is?'

'How'd you like Iras to go on television?'

'What? Well . . .' he chuckled. 'I'm not sure.'

'You'd come too, of course.'

'In that case . . .' he smiled.

'The thing is . . . Faber, you might be cross with me.'

She did her winsome best, sitting down so she could look up at him from her best angle.

'What have you done?' he asked. He was playing the game and she didn't trust him.

'Well, I know a couple of editors fairly well, Brian Delaney at Pharos and Rhoda Fairing at Termagant – I know Rhoda from that maternity book I did a few years ago.'

'I remember.' Faber sat on a chair arm and watched her.

'And I mentioned to them, just in passing, that I knew of an extraordinary girl who was blind but was writing a novel. Faber, it's wonderful, they both got so excited. They both love the idea!'

'But they haven't even read it. I haven't read it. It may not be any good – think how embarrassing that would be. I think Robin read some, mind you; he was fairly stunned.'

'You see? And he's a good judge. Of course it's good. No one's expecting her to be Charlotte Bronte at her age, but they'll still be amazed at what she's achieved and from what Andrea was saying the other day . . .'

'When did you talk to Andrea?'

'Oh. At the christening party. She told me about the spaceman sex.'

'God! That. What will people think?'

'Oh Faber. Don't be so suburban. Let me see a copy.'

'But there isn't one. Not yet.'

'There must be.'

'It's all inside that machine of hers she guards so jealously.'

'Let's see.'

'Well, I'm not sure we should.'

'Oh, come on. I know how to work them.'

'All right.'

He led the way up to her room. She relaxed. She had steamrollered him.

'Stunning,' she said, looking at the weirdly blank space about her. 'Now, look. She's left it on. All we have to do is find out which disc the novel's stored on.' The keyboard had been braille-converted but she bore with its tickling and typed from memory. 'Third time lucky,' she exclaimed after two tries. Iras had typed in a title page. '"*Touch*: a novel by Iras Washington". Great name. I can just see it.'

'The book's or hers?'

'Both. Now, to make a copy.'

'We haven't got time. It prints out very slowly,' he told her. 'Someone's dropping her back from school soon.'

'I thought of that,' she said, digging in her bag. '*Et voilà.*' She presented the disc she'd stolen from work, pushed it into the second disc drive and set the machine to copy the old disc onto the new. 'Lovely, lovely technology,' she said.

'How did you know what kind of machine she had?'

'I got her to tell me at the christening.'

'You sly bitch.'

'Faber, really!'

'What next?'

'I get off copies to Rhoda and Brian, set a little auction going, and by the time Iras is on the air she'll have a publisher. At twelve she'll have what some people are still praying for at forty-eight.'

'Would they pay much?'

'Lots.'

'But you must get a cut; an agent's percentage.'

'We can find her an agent later. Let's say I'm doing this for love.'

'But Candida . . .'

She held up a hand to silence him and smiled.

'Either Brian or Rhoda will be greatly beholden to me — that can be my percentage.'

'I can hardly believe this. But it might not be any good.'

'I told you. That doesn't matter.' The ship's bell rang outside. 'I must go,' Candida said, snatching back her disc from the machine, picking up her bag and re-arranging things as she found them.

'No. Hang on. I still want you to explain. It's probably just Cancer Research or someone.'

He hurried downstairs. Candida followed slowly behind. Faber opened the door to an older woman, elegant though plain, who introduced herself as Dorothy Birch.

'I'm acting as a sort of go-between for the solicitors as well as Marcus's factotum,' she told him as they shook hands. 'He was forever complaining about the "coldness of the Law". As you probably gathered, he had to use solicitors a great deal in his life. The least we could do was conform with his wishes that we keep them out of sight after his death.'

'Do sit down,' said Faber.

'No, thanks,' she said, eyeing the skeleton briefly. 'This letter explains it all. Very straightforward. The gist of it is that you and Iras are his principal legatees.'

'Iras?'

'That is your daughter's name?'

'Yes.'

'Well then.' Faber was looking at her in disbelief. 'There was some mix-up with the payments recently,' she confided. 'In fact I think it's only fair to tell you that he was withholding them on purpose in the hope that it might bring you back to him before the end. As I say, it's all explained in the letter. I'm afraid that the business matters have been off-loaded onto my feeble shoulders for the meanwhile so we'll be seeing each other at regular intervals for me to make my reports and to talk about your shareholdings and so on.' She looked around at the room, wrinkling her nose slightly. 'This is your usual address?'

'Oh yes.'

'Good. Then I can contact you here. Do get in touch if there's anything you don't understand.'

'Fine.'

'Goodbye.'

'Goodbye.'

They shook hands and just as she was leaving, Miss Birch caught sight of Candida waiting in the shadow on the staircase.

'Oh!' She made a little hoot of delighted bewilderment. 'It is you, isn't it?'

'Yes,' said Candida, coming forward. 'It's me.'

'I watch you every morning,' said Miss Birch, letting tumble her businesslike poise. 'I wouldn't miss it for the world.' She realized she might be intruding on something. 'Oh, so sorry. So very sorry,' she muttered and hurried out. They heard her call for a taxi outside. Candida caught Faber's eye and laughed. He laughed back. They laughed almost fiercely.

'God,' said Candida, 'Faber, I'm so sorry. I had no idea anyone had died.'

'Evidently not,' he said and laughed again, making her join in. She had to lean on the back of the sofa to steady herself. Faber began to open the letter, got as far as pulling it from the envelope then, quite suddenly, his chuckles subsided into coughs and sobs.

Candida continued to lean against the sofa and waited quietly for him to finish. When he showed no signs of doing so she went to stand by him. He had dropped the letter and was having a kind of fit of grief.

'Stop it, Faber,' she said quietly. 'Do stop.'

'He'd have loved her,' he gasped. 'He'd have been so proud. I'm such a bloody fool.'

Not understanding a word and wondering if she could extricate herself from this profoundly uncomfortable situation before Iras came home from school, she lifted a hand to his shoulder and gave a little squeeze.

'Do stop,' she said. 'I'm sure it's all right really.'

But her touch seemed to act as a trigger and, seized by a fresh spasm, he flung himself on her shoulder and wept all over her new blouse. She stood stoically on, rubbing his back as though to bring up wind, and staring at the sketch of herself over his fireplace. His grasp was strong and his back was broad and firm. His skin was warm, hot even, and the heat of his body drew woody-sweet scents from his skin as though he had just taken a bath.

Then there was a jangle of keys outside and all at once the door was open and Robin was standing there. They stared at each other a moment. She had not seen him since their moonlit jaunt to Blackheath. Tongue-tied, she tried to free herself from what, to all intents and purposes had become an embrace but Faber held her the harder. Robin said nothing. He left his keys in the lock and disappeared towards the pavement. She found her voice at once.

'Faber! Faber you must let me go. Faber!' She shoved him aside. He was still weeping. 'Didn't you hear anything?' she asked, but he had sunk onto the sofa and was scrabbling on the floor for that woman's letter. Candida spoke loudly and clearly. 'That was Robin. He saw us. I think he misunderstood.' Having wrecked her blouse the wretched man finally found a piece of paint-stained rag and blew his nose on it. She couldn't wait. 'Stay here,' she said. 'I'm going after him.'

Robin was running towards the tube station. It was only when she had sprinted several yards in pursuit across the wet grass that she found she had kept the presence of mind to bring her bag with her, and the precious disc.

'Stop,' she shouted. A few people out walking stared at her, amused recognition in their eyes. 'Please stop him someone!' she panted. She was getting a stitch. Someone took a photograph.

40

Robin ran. The sight of them in each other's arms so soon after he'd turned on her shockingly spoilt son was more than he could cope with. Her face was full of explanations and he wanted none. So he ran. Drizzle was making the common slippery and he was in sailing-shoes with no socks so he felt the cold wet sharply.

He had suffered several attacks since the one in Faber's studio, most of them out-of-doors, one of them, nightmarishly, during a concert he went to with Iras. He told Faber none of this; Faber was still in no state to listen. As Robin ran now, with no goal in mind, he felt another coming on. He heard it first in the challenging roar of the lorries, then in the cruel squeak of a playground swing and finally in Candida's cries as she chased him. He stopped and shouted back through what was now quite thick rain.

'Go away!' he cried. 'Stop! Go back!' But the sound of his voice blew back at him and she kept on running. She had taken off her shoes and was running barefoot. Someone seemed to be running after her. Robin turned and ran on. The tube station's booming acoustic made it the worst shelter he could have chosen, but there were no taxis in sight, and a train seemed the only way of losing her and going somewhere else fast. He ran down the corridor to the Southbound platform. It was crowded and the noises down there were so bad that he had to cover his ears. No one seemed to mind greatly —

but they stood away from him, depriving him of anywhere to hide.

'Come on!' he told the train. 'Bloody come on.' He leaned over the platform's edge and saw lights in the tunnel and the driver in his cab. He couldn't hear much, because his hands were over his ears, so he failed to hear her shouting his name, if indeed she did, and he had no warning of her wild approach.

Suddenly she was tugging at his elbow. His hands left his ears and the din sprang to attack him. They swung there, stupidly a moment.

'Don't,' she screamed, her shoes still flapping in her other hand. 'Don't!'

Then she slipped or Robin pushed her and down she went under the oncoming train. The strangest thing was that, just before she dropped away from his grip she hissed, 'I love you.'

It didn't mean much because she was pulling a frightened, urgent sort of face.

The screech of the train's brakes did something to his brain and the attack stopped as though a plug had been pulled. Everyone surged forward around him. Evidently he was less their concern than what they might see on the tracks. The train's doors remained shut as it was only halfway into the station and Robin met a few accusing glances through its windows. He started to pull back, then turned, then took a few quick steps. He came face to face with a very fat, bald man who did a sort of dance in his path and shouted, pointing,

'That's him. I saw him. I'm her driver. He's killed Candida Thackeray and I'm her driver. I saw them running here over the common. She told me to go for a cup of tea but I didn't want to so I saw them and I ran here too.'

Robin punched him. Just the once, but it did the trick and he sank onto the platform looking faintly surprised. It was the rush hour so all the while Robin had been waiting more and more people had been flooding down from the street. His flight was slow therefore, but the force of the crowds that slowed him slowed anyone on his tail too.

He caught a taxi at the traffic lights outside the station entrance. As always, the passing of the attack had left his mind unnaturally clear.

41

Jasper had been cleaned with Andrea's best shampoo and dusted with her special talcum powder. His hair shone and bounced and he smelt delicious but he was avoiding everyone's eye and she doubted he would be allowed to come again. She waited beneath her umbrella up on the pavement to accost his nanny with an explanation and had written a note to be passed on to Candida.

'Are you Andrea Maitland?'

It was another Australian, a marked contrast to her predecessor in both the spectacular auburn of her hair and a kind of light that shone in her eyes. It was either glee or a terrific sense of mission.

'Yes?'

'I'm Tanya. Jasper's new nanny.'

'Hello,' said Andrea and shook her hand, waiting for more.

'Oh yes. Here's my ID.' She held up one of the Brownes' headed postcards with a scribbled note from Jake on it.

'Fine,' Andrea laughed. 'Let's go and find him. I'm afraid he had a bit of a shock today. My son came to help with the art class and he and Jasper had a bit of a row and Jasper got paint all over him.'

'Oh dear,' laughed the girl.

'We've got him quite clean but he's bound to be a bit frightened. It was unforgiveable of Robin – that's my son –

and I feel desperately responsible because I was out of the room at the time. I've written a note for Candida. Could you be sweet and pass it on?'

'Of course.' Jasper was already waiting for them at the bottom of the area steps. 'Hello, little J,' said Tanya.

Jasper said nothing, but merely held up his hand to be clasped by her. Peter came out behind two mothers and children. He was holding a bright yellow model of a church.

'You forgot Willum, Jasper,' he said. Jasper wouldn't take it, so Tanya did and relieved Peter of the awkwardness with cunning exclamations at Jasper's achievement that seemed to be having their effect by the time they were clambering into their jeep.

'Any more?' Andrea asked under her breath.

'Just Rupert,' he muttered back. 'Ah, Grahame.' He held out an arm in welcome to Rupert's father. 'There you are. Rupert's just coming. Filthy day, isn't it?'

Rupert was duly handed over and bid a happy weekend, as were the Señoritas Fernandez, who had done such sterling work with Jasper that a bottle of gin was stuffed into their pannier before they roared off to aerobics on their bike.

Alone with him at last, Andrea told Peter about the unexpected cheque from Marcus and her disappointment at the travel agents.

'Well, let's go away anyway,' he said. 'Just for the weekend.'

'What? Now?'

'Why not? Not the Caribbean, obviously, but somewhere.'

'But we've so much shopping to do tomorrow. I was going to get you to drive me over to the cash-and-carry. I was onto the nut people in Kent and they said they can't get us anything before Thursday . . .'

'Bugger the nut people,' he said, 'and sod the cash-and-carry. Let's go away now. Let's go to Paris.'

'We haven't booked.'

'It's off-season. Let's just go to the airport and write a

cheque to the first company that has anything. We could go
to Dublin. You've always wanted to see Dublin.'

'It's pouring with rain.'

'So?'

She stood a moment, undecided between responsibility and
gross self-indulgence.

'Mmm?'

She caught his eye, smiled and they began a noisy race
upstairs to do their packing.

In the hall they came face to face with Robin who had just
come in.

'Hi, Dob,' said Peter, out of breath and sheepish. 'I mean,
Robin.'

'Robin, darling, we just had this wild idea to run away
somewhere for the weekend. Will you come?' Peter pinched
her hand behind her back. She pinched back. Robin was
looking anxiously over their heads. She wished he would
meet her eye. 'We thought Paris perhaps,' she went on, 'or
Dublin. Anywhere we can get a ticket to. We've just had a
little windfall. We'll treat you.'

'Oh, piss off will you, children,' he said after a moment and
pushed past them onto the stairs. Brevity stayed in the hall
and retreated beneath a chair.

'Hey!' Peter shouted after him.

'No,' she said quietly, pulling him back.

They heard him run into his room and tug his chest
of drawers open. There was a terrible sound of breaking
glass.

'That's his mirror,' she said.

'Thirteen years bad luck,' Peter muttered.

'Don't be pathetic,' she heard herself cluck. 'And don't just
stand there waiting,' she said. 'Go and see what's happening.
He could have cut himself.' She snorted impatiently, 'Oh,
I'll go.'

'No. Wait,' he hissed, tugging her back off the stairs. Robin
came rushing down again with a bag.

'Robin!' she called, breaking away to chase him to the front door.

'Just piss off to Paris,' he called back. There was a taxi waiting for him. He jumped in and was carried off into the rain.

'Peter?' She turned to him for help. 'Peter, he's gone again! He had a bag. Can't we go after him?'

'It's too late. We won't know which way he went. Maybe he's just gone for the weekend. He must have friends we don't know about. Maybe some friends of Faber's . . . Oh, look, don't cry.'

'I can't help it,' she wailed.

'Well, shut the door at least.'

'Why should I shut the bloody door?' she wailed on, pulling it wider. She ran onto the top step and yelled into the rain, 'I'm crying! I'm crying for my poor mad boy!'

She felt his arm warm round her shoulders and allowed herself to be led through the hall to the kitchen. He went to shut the door then came back in and poured them each a whisky.

'Drink this,' he said.

She did as she was told, knocking it back. She remembered to cough so he wouldn't know how often she helped herself to the bottle. She noticed the glass in his hand.

'Peter, you're drinking!'

'Of course I'm bloody drinking,' he said then poured them each another. She drank her second glass in fast sips.

'What shall we do now?' she asked. 'We can't go to Paris now.'

'We could go upstairs and change.'

'Mmm.'

'Let's go up and change, then.'

'Yes. Do let's.'

They were just leaving the room when there was a knock at the back door. Andrea ran to open it. It was a very wet Faber and a slightly less soaked Iras. Iras had a mac on.

'Look who it is,' said Andrea.

'I rode on his bicycle basket,' said Iras. 'We went incredibly fast. The rain felt great. Is that you, Peter?'

'Yes.'

'Hello.'

'Hi. Long time no meet.' He ruffled her hair.

'Where's Brevity?' she asked.

'Upstairs, hiding,' he told her.

'Faber come in,' Andrea called. 'You're getting wetter by the second.' Faber stayed put.

'Is Robin here?' he asked.

'He's just gone. Faber, it was awful.'

'I know. How do I get to Whelm?'

'Train from Waterloo to Cloud Regis then a boat. You have to ask at the marina about those. They're pretty irregular.'

'What makes you think he's gone there?' Peter asked.

'Faber knows,' said Iras.

Faber laughed grimly at her.

'Yes,' he said. 'Faber knows.' Andrea had run to find him a coat. She tossed him one Peter used to use in the garden. 'Thanks,' he said, and started down to his bicycle again. 'Oh yes,' he said, coming back. 'If the police or anyone comes, you don't know anything and you haven't seen me. Robin's gone. That's all you know.'

'The police?' gasped Andrea.

'If you hurry you might catch him before he gets on the train,' said Peter. Faber sped away, and Peter shut the back door to keep out the rain.

'You've both been drinking whisky,' said Iras. 'I can smell it on your breaths.'

'We felt we needed it,' said Andrea.

'Could I have some? It's meant to be good for chills.'

'Certainly not. I'll make you some cocoa. Give me your mac and dry yourself on this towel.'

She busied herself with heating milk for Iras's cocoa and

finding something for their supper. Peter went upstairs to watch the news.

'Hey!' he shouted down to them almost at once. 'It's Candida.'

'What's new?' Andrea shouted back.

'Robin and Faber call her Candida Albicans,' said Iras. 'What's thrush?'

'No, she's not reading it,' Peter continued. 'I mean it's about her. Come and see.'

42

As though her mind were wading through deep, dark water, Candida became slowly aware of the smell of dirt and oil close by, then of an immense noise and then, in waves, of intense pain on the back of her head. She opened her mouth a little then shut it because of the dust. She tasted blood.

'So, I'm not dead,' she thought.

Suddenly the noise increased, she had the terrible sensation of something large and black starting to move over her head and all at once she remembered she was lying under a train. She screamed blue murder. The nearby shouts redoubled and the movement overhead stopped.

'I'm not dead,' she added for good measure and was pleased to discover that at least she could talk. Apart from the pain on her head she felt no particular discomfort, but she had often heard how one lost all feeling on the chewing-off of legs or arms during shark attacks. Presumably the principle was not so different concerning tube trains. She tried to picture a future as an intensely popular but utterly reclusive radio personality and, as if in panic, felt her toes wriggling.

'Ms Thackeray, can you hear me?' some idiot shouted.

'Yes,' she said, politely as she could.

'Can you move at all?'

'Not much. I don't think I've broken anything.'

Where's my bag? Christ, where's my bag? she thought, and felt wildly about her. Her fingers made contact with familiar battered suede and tugged it nearer. 'And my hands work too,' she thought. 'Praise be.'

'Right-ho,' the idiot went on. 'The thing is, the train's emergency brake has jammed at the back so we couldn't reverse it and get to you straight away.'

'How long have I been here?'

'Fifteen minutes or so. But someone's climbed into the tunnel and uncoupled the rest of the carriages from the front one so we can drive it forward and set you free.'

'Can't I just crawl out?'

'That's the trouble. You fell just on the wrong side of a concrete support. If you feel in front of you you should find a sort of wall.'

Candida felt and found.

'Ah,' she said, thinking of rats and catching a preliminary whiff of hysteria. 'So what do I do?'

'Just get as low as you can and don't move an inch. You were very lucky to miss the conductor rail.'

'Where is it?' she asked, panicking slightly.

'To your left. The opposite side from the platform you fell off. Just stay put and we'll help you climb out in a second. OK?'

'Fine.' Her voice shook involuntarily.

'Just tell us when you're ready.'

'Now seems as good a time as any.'

'Pardon?'

'Ready.'

'Here goes then. Let's get this show on the road.'

Idiot, she thought. Star for a Day.

The darkness overhead began to shift again. Terrified, Candida shut her eyes tight. Then, over the noise of the train, she just made out the whirring of automatic cameras winding on their film.

Viewing figures, she thought, to distract her thoughts from pain. A Sunday supplement profile. She clutched the bag tighter to her. The train rolled clear and several fools jumped down to help her. She opened her eyes and saw a big crowd pressing up against a yellow Police cordon and no less than three television cameras trained on her. She pictured the studio boss's face, then herself treading on it. Leaning gracefully on someone's arm then heavily when she found that both her legs had gone to sleep, she allowed herself to be helped upright and borne to safety on an assortment of strong male hands. Her skirt rode up. She let it rise. A doctor jumped forward and started examining the back of her head.

'Who was he?' shouted someone.

'Did he push you or did you push him?'

'What was the story you were after in Clapham, Ms Thackeray?'

'It was a suicide attempt,' someone else shouted. 'We have witnesses. Who was he, Ms Thackeray? Why did he want to die?'

'Poor Dob,' she sighed. Then she saw her blood on a cloth that someone had dabbed to the back of her head and felt her long legs give way. As they lifted her onto a stretcher and bore her to a waiting ambulance she felt someone take her hand and heard Jake say,

'Candida. Thank God you're all right!'

A chorus followed.

'Quick. It's the husband.'

'What does he do?'

'Did you know the man, Mr Thackeray?'

'He's called Browne, idiot.'

She squeezed the hand back and flattened her tongue on the roof of her mouth to make her chin look firmer.

'On millions of family screens across the country,' she told herself. 'Candida Thackeray comes back from the dead. Bless you, Robin. Bless you.'

When Jake climbed into the ambulance beside her for the last photo-call before tomorrow morning, he would find a peaceful smile on her perfect, dusty lips.

43

Luck of some sort enabled Robin to catch the last boat that was sailing to Whelm that evening. It was the fisherman who brought the post across in the mornings, the one who had ferried him to shore a few weeks ago.

'I've got their new boiler,' he said. 'Didn't get here till half an hour ago. If you help me carry it up there, I'll take you over for nothing.'

'Done,' said Robin.

'Come back, have you?' the fisherman asked, 'Seen the error of your ways?'

Robin said nothing, so the fisherman left him alone, started the engine and sent them chugging through the darkness.

The boiler was about the size of a family fridge and just as heavy. The rain had turned the island paths to slippery mud and the fisherman was old and tired. They had to stop every twenty shuffles to set the boiler down and let him find his breath. A grizzle-haired monk Robin didn't know, a visitor perhaps, opened the gate to them. Unsmiling, he paid the fisherman and sent him away then hoisted his half of the boiler with unexpected strength and they carried it through to the kitchen. The place was silent and Robin realized that compline was over and all the rest were in bed.

'So you've come back,' the monk said.

'Yes. Do you know who I am?'

'I've heard enough idle talk to guess.'

'I need to talk to Jonathan.'

'You can't. The Abbot's asleep, they're all asleep. Anyway, he's sick.'

'It's important.'

'It'll have to wait. Have you eaten?'

'Yes,' Robin said. He hadn't but frustration at having arrived so late left him no appetite for anything but sleep. He was wet and shivering.

'Your old room's still empty. You'll find sheets in the linen room.' The monk sat at the kitchen table, opened a large, foreign-looking book and in seconds was absorbed in it.

Robin found his way to his old room without turning on a single light. The linen room was just across the corridor. The hot water pipes that ran through it were cold as the grave. He wondered how long they had been without a boiler. He took a couple of blankets and a bare pillow, flung himself with them onto his damp mattress and lost himself in blank exhaustion.

'Robin, wake up.'

His shoulder was being rubbed through the blanket. He was one acute ache.

'Robin!'

More rubbing. The ache grew worse as the smell of the damp mattress and the abrasive rumple of slept-in clothes reminded him that he was far from Faber's. He clutched the blankets closer for warmth and sat up. It was Luke. He was smiling.

'I was coming out of the linen store and I saw you lying here,' he said. 'What a surprise!'

'I've come back, Luke,' said Robin.

'I gathered that. Why?'

'I want to join. I want to be a novice.'

'I can't believe that for a moment.'

'Nor can I, really. But it's what I want. I can't be anywhere else. Not now. Luke!' Robin saw Luke's new habit. 'You've gone all the way. They've sworn you in.'

'Last week,' Luke said, proudly. 'I thought it was time I took the plunge. It was partly Jonathan falling sick, too. I've been sitting in his room a lot, reading to him and talking with him. It helped me make up my mind.'

He was so happy, sitting on Robin's bed. He looked so complete, healthy. Smug?

'Damn you,' Robin said. 'Damn you all.'

'Don't say that.'

'Help me, then.'

'I'll try. What's happened?'

'What time is it?'

'I'm not sure. About six, I think. Maybe later. It'll be light properly soon.'

Robin sat up completely and swung his legs round so that he was sitting with his back against the wall. He shivered at the touch of cold paintwork on his neck and tugged the blankets around him like a shawl.

'I've killed someone,' he said.

'Who?' Luke stopped looking smug.

'That's irrelevant. But I've gone and killed them. I pushed them under a train. Or they fell because I was trying to stop them. I'm not sure now.' Luke hugged him. Robin pushed him off. 'It was Candida.'

'Your friend who'd just had the baby?'

'Yes,' Robin snapped, mimicking him. 'My friend who'd just had a bloody baby. I was having an attack and she misunderstood and ran after me. I think she thought I was going to kill myself or something daft. She grabbed me and I pushed her away or she pushed me. I don't know. And then she sort of slipped down through my arms and went under the train.'

'Are you sure she was killed?'

'Of course she was killed. She went under a train, you silly prick.'

'That's terrible.'

'Anyway. I wasn't going to hang around to find out. I came straight here.'

'I'm glad you did.'

Luke's quietness and sympathy enraged Robin, and reminded him why he had come here. He grabbed him by the silly neck and began to throttle him.

'Damn you,' Robin said. 'Damn you and damn Jonathan and damn you all with your apples and beeswax and damn those fat, sick, peculiar women on the island next door. You should never have let me go. It's all your fault. You should never have let me go. You should have kept me here. Locked me up. Forced me to be a monk. I would have been if you'd forced me. I'd have sworn to anything. I didn't want to leave. I wasn't ready. But you were all so bloody sympathetic and undemanding and you went and let me go and now she's gone and fallen under a train.'

He released Luke's neck, throwing him back against the wall. Luke's cowl flopped upwards as he went so he didn't crack his skull, but Robin could see that the violence had woken him up. Luke wasn't smiling now and he was frightened too. Robin could tell because he didn't even rub his neck, which must have been hurting him.

'Listen,' Luke said.

'No,' Robin went on. 'You always made me listen. You all pretended to listen to what I was saying and none of you ever lectured me or preached at me but you did it around me, over my head, behind my back. You thought that that way it wouldn't count and that you wouldn't be to blame if anything went wrong. All those phoney ideas about love and sacrifice and stillness and sympathy and contemplation. It's too passive to be anything but phoney. It may make sense here but out there it's just sex, money, achievement and influence. Nothing else counts. Nothing else works. Love and sacrifice don't work out there. Love is for babies and children. Love for adults is something you're expected to grow out of and be cynical about. Things won't last here, either. Look at you,' he shouted, angry because he wasn't talking logically and Luke always had quiet logic at his command. 'Your abbot falls sick, the boiler breaks down and the whole place tumbles down around you. You'll turn into sharks too, overnight.'

'What?'

'Sharks. It's a turn of phrase.' Robin stood and stumbled, sleep-lame, to the window. A thin dawn had broken. The postboat was arriving. 'Candida should have pushed me,' he said quietly.

'Look,' Luke insisted. Robin turned and saw that Luke had stood. He was furious, cheeks white, green eyes black. Robin had never seen him like that before. Perhaps it was something to do with becoming a monk. The new black cassock dignified him. Robin was frightened and his exhaustion swept back. If Luke hit him he would crumple. Then, perhaps, he would leave him alone. 'Look,' Luke repeated. 'That's an evil thing to say. Candida loved you. She was trying to show you that.'

('I love you,' she had hissed. Her face was all wrong with fear but the words remained.)

Robin thought he felt the first cold touches of an attack, or was this feeling fear?

'Your mother and father loved you and still do. Candida's husband. The weak man with the fancy job . . .'

'Jake.'

'Yes. Jake. Jake loved you, in his way. He found it impossible and tried to ignore it but he loved you. Jonathan here loves you, even though he's probably dying. If I ran up there now and told him you were here he would smile. That's love. That artist you were introduced to at the baptism.'

'Faber Washington.'

'Yes. Him. He would love you. I could tell. That's why I felt safe leaving you there as I did. All this love makes your life worthwhile. Not just for your pleasure, though that will come, but because a life lived wholly is an occasion for love.'

'Occasion for love. Where did you steal that quaint . . .'

'Shut up!' Luke spat. 'It's an occasion for love. And for what it's worth, I love you too.'

Robin remembered the wind in apple trees, the rustle of paper, the scent of new fruit.

'You don't love me,' he jeered. 'You just fancy my unecclesiastical body.'

Now Luke did punch him. In the stomach. Winded, Robin doubled up and tottered about gasping like a stranded fish. Luke led him to the bed and let him collapse on the edge of it. There were sounds of other men rising. Taps were turned on, lavatories flushed. Doors shut and opened. Mumbled early morning greetings. Luke shut the door and came to stand by Robin.

'Sorry,' he said.

'That's OK.'

'You made me promise to explain everything once,' he said. 'Remember?' Robin nodded, watching his sockless, sandalled feet beneath his habit. He never used to punish himself like that. 'And I said that if you'd wait, I'd show you. Well, you're too stupid to be shown, or too obstinate, or too bound up in your own useless attractions and dislikes. Robin, I came here for exactly the same reason as you – innocence and a tendency to love too much without trying to understand. Very dull really. A very common complaint. I met her at technical college. She was training to be an engineer like me. She wasn't beautiful or anything, but she was blonde and witty – and not many people were, there, I can tell you – and she gave me time. And time and time. I worshipped her. We went to the cinema. We drove miles to look at bridges. We sat together in lectures about the history of rivetting. And I never laid a finger on her so, after a month or so and quite understandably, she went off with the first bloke who did, who just happened to be my best friend.

'So, no, Robin. It's a very nice body, but I don't fancy it.'

They stayed there for about three minutes, Robin sitting, Luke standing and, Robin supposed, staring down at him waiting for an answer. He didn't give him one. Robin found himself stupid, cross and wordless.

Then a commotion of some sort started at the far end of the corridor. A man was protesting and others were trying to shout him down. It came nearer. Luke sighed impatiently and tugged open the door.

'Where is he? I have to speak to him!'

'In here,' Luke said. 'Go on, it's all right. You can let him through.'

Robin looked up to see what was going on. Luke moved back into the corridor gesturing towards him with his arm. Faber ran into the doorway and stood there staring at him wildly. He was clutching a tabloid.

'Look,' he said, but Robin was looking at his face. 'No,' Faber said crossly, 'Look here. Look.' He held the paper up and banged its front page with the back of one hand.

'CANDIDA LIVES!!' it said.

44

The farce with the train and the 'TV personality' had been explained and laughed over then Luke had steered the monks away to their morning business and Faber found himself alone with Robin. Robin reached towards him for a kiss but Faber pushed him away.

'How could you?' Faber asked. '*Why* did you just run off like that? You didn't think that Candida and I . . . ?'

'Of course not. Not really. But I'd just hit her son and . . .'

Faber broke in. 'She came to talk about Iras's novel. She didn't know about Marcus and then Marcus's secretary suddenly came in with a letter from the solicitors and, well, I dissolved on her. Poor Candida. Oh yes.' Faber sighed. 'All of a sudden we're rich. Very, very. Marcus left us everything – me and Iras, that is.' He drifted to stare out of the window. He drummed his fingers on the cold radiator. 'Why did you come here? If something was wrong you could have stayed and told me. Oh, but of course, I forgot: you'd killed Candida. Sorry. I'm burbling. I'm very, very tired. And I'm cold. Why isn't the radiator on? Does that make it more holy? I spent the night on a bench in the bloody harbour waiting for a boat. Sorry. Well, say *something*!'

Robin had been sitting on the bed all this while. Now he stood and held out an arm towards the open door.

'There's something you should see,' he said.

They walked in silence along a blank white corridor down

a broad spiral staircase and out into a courtyard. Faber had been in such a rush when he arrived that he had barely looked at the strange building around him. Whelm resembled a nineteenth-century monomaniac's idea of a French château. The pointed roofs and pinnacled turrets were in poor repair. The cream paintwork was streaked with green. The fine blue-grey slates had been replaced here and there with cheap green alternatives. The place stirred uneasy memories of Faber's strange schooldays. Robin led him out of the courtyard to a large outbuilding. A barn, perhaps, or a stable.

'In here,' he said, opening a door.

It was as large as a barn, with high beams and great, barred doors but instead of hay bales there were apples and pears everywhere on trays in old wooden shelves that rose at least fifteen feet high. There were long ladders fixed to rails which ran along the lines of shelving.

'Apples,' said Robin, sliding one of the ladders towards him. He jumped onto it and slid away from Faber. The air was heavy with apple. 'They call it the Fruit Library because of these things,' he said. 'Have one.' He tossed Faber an apple. The tissue paper slid away in Faber's grasp. The fruit's skin shone red-green in the dim light from the half-open door.

'There must be more here than they can possibly eat in a year,' Faber said.

'Oh yes. Some go to the girls on Corry in a swop for honey and wax, otherwise the surplus is sold in the market at Cloud Regis. They make cider too, and chutney. I found some of the chutney in a grand delicatessen in Chelsea so it's not as amateur as it looks. I very nearly died in here,' he went on. 'I should have, really.' Faber replaced the apple and caught up with him.

'How come?' he asked.

'When I first arrived, eight years ago.' Robin came down from the ladder and took Faber by the shoulders. 'Faber, listen. I'm not well. I have attacks.'

'You're better. You said so. The breakdown's finished. Anyone can see that.'

'No. I still have attacks. It's like . . . They're like panic attacks. Paranoia. I don't know. I read up on them a bit in London. I even went to some doctors. I think I might be schizophrenic. It could get worse.'

Faber locked his hands over Robin's arms.

'You should have told me,' he said.

'Would it have made any difference, then?'

'Of course not. But you should have told me.'

'How could I? You had enough on your plate and I . . . I thought it had gone away.'

'What brings them on? These attacks.'

'Nothing in particular. Stress, perhaps. I don't know. Faber, it's not fair on you. It's not fair on Iras either.'

'You running away isn't fair. We love you, Robin.'

'I hadn't had one when I got here first. Not badly. Not since the mild ones when I was younger. I was just running. I just wanted to get right away from everybody.'

'What happens when one comes on?'

'Noises all go wrong. It's as though everything's hostile.' Robin's voice rose. 'That sounds nothing, but I can tell you . . .'

'Ssh. I know.' Faber held him. Robin kept talking.

'I arrived in the evening – at dusk. I only knew about the place from a theology tutor I'd talked to a bit – he'd spent time here – so I didn't know my way around. An attack started as I came off the boat and was walking up here. The seagulls sounded like . . . just horrible. You can't imagine.'

'I think I can.'

'You can't, Faber. You couldn't possibly.' Robin broke away and snatched up a pear. He handled it absently as he talked. 'Anyway, I just ran and all I could think of was getting indoors. This was the first door I found unlocked so I ran in here and slammed it shut behind me. People came and shouted outside – they'd seen me racing around like a rabbit and come to help. But their voices made it worse so I bolted the door. Then I tried to climb to get away. It was dark and I didn't see the ladder. No one was sure what happened but Luke – that's the one who was with me when you –'

'Yes, Robin. We've already met.'

'Of course you have. He said that when they unpadlocked one of the other doors and got in I was buried under about a ton or more of fruit and timber. This lot had collapsed. See? Here, where the wood's newer than the rest. I was bruised a lot, I'd bust an arm and I was out cold for a day or more. It's a wonder I didn't suffocate. Apparently I only came round in order to go into a kind of, what's the word, catalepsy? Catatonia?'

'Don't ask me.'

Robin drop-kicked the pear to the far side of the room.

'I have no memories until five or six years later,' he said.

'Christ!'

'Quite.' Faber went after Robin and held him close. 'You don't want me,' Robin mumbled. 'I don't work properly. I malfunction.'

'You function fine.'

'Hardly.'

Faber rocked him gently against a ladder.

'Fine enough,' he said. 'We'll cope. When you have an attack, I'll hold you like this and I'll take all the sound away. We'll find a specialist. I'm rich now, remember? We're rich. Rich people get better . . .'

'I don't want to be rich,' Robin cut in.

'Think of all those bus rides! Unlimited bus rides! Once a week you can change the life of the beggar of your choice.'

'Don't be flippant, it ill becomes you. Will you still paint?'

'Stupid! Of course I will and you'll still have to get a job and Iras will still have to go to school. Come home, Robin.' Robin still felt hard and resisting in his grasp. Faber breathed in the rich apple smell and wondered if he had ever felt such desolation. 'Please,' he said. 'Please, please come home. If you don't, I'll . . .' Faber faltered. Robin pulled back and looked at him.

'You'll what?'

45

Candida kicked off her shoes then unzipped her dress, slipped it neatly onto a hanger, and sat at her dressing-table. Tanya, the new nanny, would be taking a heap of clothes to the dry cleaners tomorrow. Tanya was a blessing. More than that, she was a Good Person. She was firm in her kindness, even to the point of measuring out advice to Candida several times a day, which in anyone else – the ghastly Samantha, for instance – would have irritated her employer beyond measure. In Tanya however, Candida found it an awesome quality. Tanya told her to stay in more and entertain less. If the phone rang while Candida was reading Jasper a story or cuddling Perdita, Tanya told her to stay put then told whoever it was that Candida was unavailable. When Candida finished her brief stay in hospital, Tanya told her (as Jake had tried to do) that it was out of the question for her to return to work without at least one day's rest at home. In some dim, neglected corner of her spirit, Candida had discovered a slightly lazy liking for being told what to do. She didn't want Tanya to go the way of the others and she was treating her well. She was sure the Lady Canberra agency had no inkling that Tanya was a fervent follower of an extreme Right-wing Christian organization called 'Families First', but Candida had no intention of letting the agency or Jake or anybody know.

'If I were you, I wouldn't tell Jake about the little incident with the young man at Jasper's school,' Tanya had said. 'He'd only worry and insist on Jasper being moved. Jasper will be far happier staying where he is. Change isn't good for them at that age.'

So Candida had told Jake nothing. A quick chat with Peter Maitland had made it clear that that particular problem was thoroughly out of the way. The other evening Tanya had seen the pills in Candida's bag. She had told her to hand them over for examination then, pleasantly and calmly, handed them back and stood over Candida as she flushed them, one by costly one, down the waste disposal unit. The elder Maitlands were coming to a supper in a few days' time; Tanya had been asked to join the party.

'Mummy!' Jasper ran in without knocking. Candida registered the fault but said nothing. Tanya had said he was too young to learn and that formality would make him more nervous than he had already become.

'Hello, poppet.'

'You're home!'

'Yes.' She bent down and swung him up onto her lap for a kiss. He sat there and played with her hand mirror. 'Hello, Tanya. Good walk?'

'Lovely, thank you. We met Mrs Maitland with her little dog.'

'She's called Brevity,' said Jasper, examining his nose closely in the mirror. 'When can we have a dog, Mummy?'

'Whenever we like, Jasper. When would you like one?'

'But you always said no before!'

'Well, silly Samantha didn't like dogs. She said they made her sneeze. But Tanya says she'd enjoy it.'

'Would she?' Jasper threw a questioning glance at his new nanny.

'It would stop me missing our ones at home,' said Tanya.

'When, then?' he asked Candida.

'Wait and see,' she said, tapping his nose.

'It can't be for my birthday because I've already found the Cacharel jersey you said you'd give me if Perdita got chrissed.'

'Christened,' Tanya corrected him.

'Yes, that,' he said. 'Well?'

'Wait and see.' Candida said again and smiled.

He looked sceptical.

'I think it's time for my tea,' he told Tanya, who laughed and led him away.

Candida held her hand mirror so that it reflected the back of her head into the main looking-glass before her. After the bandages had been removed, there had still been bad bruising and an ugly line of five stitches on her scalp. Her hairdresser had cunningly teased her hair to mask it all. Turning her head slightly, to catch the light, Candida lifted his handiwork with her free hand, and inspected the damage. The bruise had almost gone. A nurse was calling at the studio tomorrow morning to take out the stitches.

She heard Jake's car pull up outside. Since her wild cover-up attempt and its awkward results the other night they had not tried to make love. At first she had thought they were sulking with each other. Now she understood that they were manoeuvring with extreme delicacy, like two unwrapped burns victims in a confined space. The unfamiliarity of the sensation was such that she had misinterpreted it. Under Tanya's benign rule, they had recently found themselves with a 'quiet night in' and had spent it listening to records and reading on either side of the fire. The extraordinary peace of the evening and the sudden sense of kinship with her husband had been almost frightening. In the days after their fight, she had thought she would never forgive his deceitfulness, but the pique her vanity had received in finding she had been Jake's second choice was shamefully soothed by the secret consideration that Jake, *her* Jake, had been Robin's first one.

'Anybody home?' Jake called in the hall. She heard Jasper call out to him and then both their voices in the kitchen. Quickly, she patted her hair back into place, dabbed on some scent and pulled on a woollen dress Jake had bought her once, that she had never worn enough. He met her in the hall.

'Hi,' she said.

'Hello.' He took her hand and gave it a gentle squeeze. The gesture felt more intimate than any brief kiss.

'I've got you a present,' he said. 'Well. I've got *us* a present.'

'Where?'

'In here,' he said, smiling, enjoying his mystery. She followed him into the sitting-room. She could see nothing at first then he switched on a light. She looked around her and gave a gasp of genuine surprise. In place of the sea-green abstract that usually hung over the mantelpiece there was a new painting. 'I bought it days ago but it's only just come back from the framer's,' he told her.

She recognized its elements as swiftly as if it had been a photograph. Robin. Iras Washington and part of Faber's studio. The colours were beautiful. Faber's paintings were usually cold as though he were shining too harsh a light on his subjects, but this one glowed. The frame was smooth lime-bleached wood like driftwood.

'Is it by who I think it is?' she asked.

'Yes, but he hasn't signed it, which might affect the value. Do you like it?'

'Yes. Well. The colours are wonderful. "Like" is hardly the word, though. In the circumstances.'

'But it's good,' he said. 'Isn't it?'

'Very,' she reassured him. 'I'm surprised he wanted to sell it.'

'He didn't.'

'Ah.'

She walked up to it. Robin seemed to be teaching Iras how to read. The sun played in their hair.

'We can't possibly hang it in here,' she said.

'Why ever not?' I'm sure Faber wouldn't mind.'

'Jake, just think a little. People will come to this room.

Not just Faber and Robin, other people. This is our painting. Look. I've got the perfect place. I'll show you.' She lifted it off the mantelpiece and carried it upstairs. He followed her into their bedroom. 'See?' she said, leaning it on the mantelpiece in there. 'If we hang it here, the sunlight in the picture's going the same way as the sunlight in the room. It'll be the last thing we see at night and the first thing we see when we wake up.'

'Oh yes.'

She was glad he agreed to join in the lie.

'Jake, it is special. It must have cost the earth. Thank you.' She kissed him. He smelt of car leather and offices and tension; smells she liked. She kissed him again. He kissed her back urgently. Whenever he did that now she would think he was trying to prove some point about his manhood. It was a strain they would learn to live with. Like the painting.

He pulled back, looking over her shoulder at the colourful canvas and her childhood friend. Perdita was crying and they heard Tanya's quick, light footfall on the staircase.

'What's that bit?' he asked.

'Which.'

'There.' He pulled away altogether and pointed. 'The orange thing in the shadow on the table.'

'Oh, that,' she said, reaching out to squeeze his hand in sympathy. 'Orange peel. Don't you remember? Robin's peeled an orange to make a perfect F. Faber may not have signed it, but he's there.'

46

Andrea was watching television. She was so excited she could hardly sit down. She kept leaning forward to adjust her books and newspapers that were on the table between her and the screen.

'Come on,' she said. 'It's nearly time.'

'Coming,' Peter called from below. What was he doing? There was a report on school meals going on. A clock in one corner of the screen said it was a quarter to nine. Faber had said that they'd be on by then.

'Quickly,' she shouted. 'You'll miss it.'

The report finished but unexpectedly, Candida announced Cartoon Time and the screen was taken up with the antics of violent mice. Perhaps there was some hitch in the studio. Iras was bound to be nervous, poor dear. Peter started to sing *Happy Birthday to You* on the stairs.

'Oh, hell,' Andrea thought. 'I'm fifty. I don't want to be fifty.'

He appeared in the doorway with a beatific grin on his face and something behind his back.

'You'd thought I'd forgotten, hadn't you?'

'No,' she protested, laughing.

'Yes, you did. You sat there being pert and polite all through breakfast because I hadn't said anything.'

'No, I didn't.'

'And you wondered where all the mail had gone.' He

brought one hand from behind his back to reveal a fat clutch of thick envelopes, which he tossed onto the table before her.

'Well . . . I . . .'

'Happy birthday, darling.'

He brought out the other hand and dropped a large cardboard carton in her lap.

'What is it?' she asked. 'Oh, what *is* it?' She tore off the sellotape, half guessing, and opened the box. There were layers of tissue paper and some wonderful black silk. She gasped, took the silk and lifted it, standing as she did so. The box fell, the paper slid away, and she found herself holding a perfect black dress. Not too long, not too short, and simplicity itself. She held it against herself to feel its sensuous slipperiness.

'Like it?' he asked.

'Peter, it's perfect.' She kissed him. He tried to kiss her back. 'Don't crumple it,' she said.

'Silk doesn't crumple.'

'Nor it does,' she said and let him kiss her.

'Aren't they on yet?' he asked.

'No. There's some delay. It'll be after the news now, I expect. Darling, thank you for this. Can I wear it tonight?'

'Of course. That's the whole idea. You said you'd always wanted the sort of thing you'd only wear once a year.'

'I did and this is it exactly.' Her mother had worn one just like it. It was too small, she could see that at a glance. He found it as hard as she did to accept the relaxation in her measurements. Andrea was fifty. Worse still, she was in her fifty-first year.

'And that's not all.'

'Not another present.'

'Sort of. Wait there.'

'Not a cake?'

'That's for later. Wait there.'

She waited on the landing, keeping half an eye on the cartoon. He had run up to their bedroom.

She heard a preparatory note or two on his clarinet then he launched into the slow movement of the Mozart quintet. He used to play it to her when they were first married. She had been so proud and had asked him, in ignorance, why he couldn't play it with an orchestra somewhere. Still clutching the dress she walked slowly upstairs. The music's sinuous melancholy drawing her on. She sat on the stairs outside their room, leaning her head against the banisters to listen.

I'm fifty, she thought, and he can play this again. He'll join another orchestra soon. He'll get bored. I'll get old and grey. I'll find another choir. I'll enrol myself for evening classes. My nectarine breasts will sag into unrecognizable overripeness. Why is it all so cruel and unrelenting?

Unwatched downstairs, Candida Thackeray was introducing Iras Washington and her father, the rising painter, to the breakfasting nation.

'Iras's first novel, called – simply – *Touch*, has just found a sympathetic publisher with Brian Delaney of Pharos Company, who's with us too this morning,' Candida explained. 'Brian, perhaps you'd like to tell us first what makes *Touch* so special.'

'Well,' said Brian. 'Quite apart from Iras's extreme youth and the fact that she's precocious by the standards of her age-group, let alone by those of blind children, she tells an extraordinary story. Given that everyone demands a pigeon-hole nowadays, I suppose one would have to call it a piece of science fiction but it ends up being more than that. To simplify things grossly, it's about a young girl who is taken away from her rather blandly happy family by friendly aliens who want her to visit their planet to teach them Latin so they can decipher a copy of the Aeneid they've stolen from an astronaut. Their sun had been blotted out by a nuclear winter and over the years they've evolved a new environment beneath the ground and a new way of life. They've managed without light so long that the planet is effectively blind and run entirely by voice and touch. This is what Iras does so well, she succeeds in conveying everything so vividly that by the end of the book one no longer notices the absence of visual imagery. When the girl returns to earth she has an accident. A blow to her head deprives her of sight and, to the scandalized dismay of her family, she welcomes what they see as a disability as a privilege. *Touch* is quite simply very funny, moving and, well, proud.'

'And I'm sure Iras is thrilled to have found such a committed publisher,' Candida cut in. 'How does it feel to be getting published so soon, Iras? Iras?'

The camera cut across to show Iras who was responding in fluent sign language.

'She has several deaf friends at school,' Faber explained.

'Ah,' said Candida. 'How nice.' She was evidently discomforted at the loss of sound and at being unable to know where she could interrupt. 'And, er, Iras,' she ventured to cut in at last, 'perhaps you'd like to tell our studio audience how long you've been writing.'

Iras turned politely to the studio audience and went on to tell them how long she'd been writing. She told them in sign language. There were chuckles, perhaps from the cameramen, perhaps from the audience, then laughter. Things broke down. Candida announced a break for advertisements but the advertisements evidently weren't ready yet and the cameras merely showed the audience standing up to stretch its legs and Candida trying in vain to control them. A few pictures flashed up with distorted sound then died and across the nation the viewers were handed back to the studio. Faber had beckoned Robin out of the audience and, holding Iras by one hand, was hugging him with his free arm.

At last the latest in a much discussed line of advertisements for *Capital* took over the airspace. Just before it did however, several million schoolchildren dawdling over their cereal, their fathers fretting over their unironed shirts and their mothers calmly buttering toast, were treated to a lingering close-up of a mixed-race, single-sex kiss.

Patrick Gale

The Cat Sanctuary

Judith and Deborah are sisters driven apart by traumatic events in their childhood, but thrown back together again when Deborah's diplomat husband is accidentally assassinated. Judith's lover, Joanna, the instigator of this awkward reunion, finds that as the sisters' murky past is raked up, so too is her own, and the three women become embroiled in a tangle of passion and recrimination.

'He writes about difficult emotions with delicacy, perception and a rare ferocious charm.'   *Guardian*

'Powerful and moving novel in which the darkness is often lightened by the author's deft touches of comedy.'
Sunday Independent

'Gale is a charmingly idiosyncratic writer who could not write a cliché if he tried. Spiced with mischievous irony, this engrossing story contains some interesting aperçus on the process of novel writing.'   *Daily Telegraph*

'A book with claws.'   *The Times*

'Like Gale's previous novels, it's an elegantly menacing, enjoyable read that starts as it means to go on – dynamically. It's a deep and moving book; highly recommended.'
New Woman

'Gale's writing is marvellously entertaining, and there is a compelling sense of biting deep into the core of the bitter truth.'   *Cosmopolitan*

ISBN: 0 586 09061 4

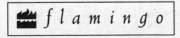 *flamingo*

Patrick Gale

Dangerous Pleasures

Curious childhood loyalties, long-hidden memories, newly discovered joys, startling loyalties, dislocated relationships, overwhelming, thrilling passions.

In prose which is always vivid and fresh, Patrick Gale explores the subtle boundaries that shift between the fantastic and the shockingly real. With characteristic insight and wit and with consummate ease, he draws the reader into lives both familiar and strange, revealing a world that shines with possibilities in a collection that will never fail to delight.

'The prose sizzles with acidic observation.'

Independent on Sunday

'The stories deal with revelation, with what people can become given the right set of circumstances and with the danger that comes with change. Sparky stuff.'

Sunday Express

'Patrick Gale has long been a master of short fiction. Wit and wisdom, metaphor and moment constantly combine to delight.'

The Times

'He excels at capturing emotion and while his sexuality and vivid imagination throw up unusual situations, he deals poignantly with universal themes of love, loss and embarrassment.'

Daily Telegraph

ISBN: 0 586 09146 7

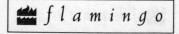

Patrick Gale

The Facts of Life

Edward Pepper, a successful composer, surveys his grand-children as they come to terms with the harsher facts of modern life. As a young man, Edward was exiled from his native Germany by the war. Struck down with TB, he is left to languish in an isolation hospital. But then he falls in love with his doctor, Sally Banks, and his world is transformed. They set up home in a bizarre dodecahedral folly, The Roundel – a potent place, which grows in significance as it bears witness to their family's tragedies and joys. The years pass, and Edward watches from this sanctuary as both his grandchildren, Jamie and Alison, fall prey to the charms of Sam, an enigmatic builder, and have to come to terms with some of the tougher facts of life.

'A rural English blockbuster. It is impossible to put *The Facts of Life* down. It is beautifully done.'   *Daily Telegraph*

'Wonderfully vivid, this novel is peopled with characters who compel you to care.'   *She*

'A wonderfully readable family saga. Fifties movie stars, waspish dons and wise old women make up the supporting cast in a novel that is as straightforward as it is otherworldly – like reading Iris Murdoch without the puzzles.'   *Independent*

'Imbued with a generosity of spirit towards all its characters. A memorable achievement.'   *The Times*

ISBN: 0 00 654768 0

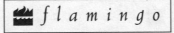

Patrick Gale

Ease

A novel about downsizing from a life of ease and upgrading to one of sleaze.

Many people would kill to be Domina Tey. She's one of life's successes: an award-winning playwright living in a beautiful house with an equally celebrated writer. A lucky woman. And she knows and appreciates it. But she isn't happy. Life is too easy. It's becoming stultifying, negating her creative force.

Domina decides upon a spell of sleazy living to give both her work and her soul a spring-clean – and elopes with her typewriter in search of just a hint of degradation. She finds it in Bayswater. Safe in bedsit land, she immediately sets about getting to know her neighbour, a candidate for the priesthood half her age.

'Patrick Gale writes with the understated fluency that is the hallmark of contemporary British fiction, and with the irony that usually accompanies it. Like William Boyd and Martin Amis, he skilfully blends the light and the dark, moving unobtrusively from comedy to drama without losing narrative momentum or integrity.'   Book World, US

ISBN: 0 586 09147 5

flamingo